This book is a work of fiction organizations, places, and in the products of the Author's i̶m̶a̶g̶i̶n̶a̶.̶.̶.̶ Any resemblance of actual persons living or dead, events or locales is entirely coincidentally....

Published by: Key to Life Publishing
                  Amazon

Book Cover Concepts: Ace Capone & Tea Capone
Book Cover: Kevin Carr
Editor in Chiefs: Ace Capone, Tea Capone, Angie Davis
Editor: Sydney Branch
Consulting: Ace Capone, Sydia Bagley & Charles Ford

ISBN-13:
978-1475087307
ISBN-10:
1475087306

Library of Congress Cataloging-in-Publication Data

FIRST PRINTING
Printed in The United States of America

Key to Life Publishing
P. O. Box 266
Warren, Michigan 48090
Email: *keytolifepub@hotmail.com*
Facebook: *GO HARD A.T. Capone*
Twitter: *1acecapone*

Ace vividly pens a graphic tale that only could be told through the eyes of a person who has lived it. This is an excellent read and well crafted. 5 stars!
- NY Times Best-selling Author JaQuavis Coleman

I feel like Ace was on his way to being to Philly what Birdman, Master P, P Diddy, J Prince & other moguls were to their cities. He's a huge inspiration in the way I build my brand, with this classic book & more to come. His legacy lives on - Free Ace Capone!
  - Tone Trump

The book is riveting. I couldn't put it down. It reads like a movie and should be one. Ace Capone has created a true jaw dropper.
-GoldenGirl "The Black Barbee" Author of Sex and Celebrities and Radio and TV Show Host.

Go Hard- The Takedown of Ace Capone demands ten stars plus one hundred more...Wow, this guy can really write. A true urban book to die for. So bold and informative, I could not put it down....I loved it! I can't wait for the sequel.
- Nathan Welch, Author of A Killer'z Ambition

This book is Belly, Scarface and Menace to Society all in one
-C-Murda from Court Street (NWK)

THIS BOOK IS AS REAL AS THEY COME!
ONLY A MAN THAT'S BEEN THROUGH THE STRUGGLES OF LIFE CANPUT IT DOWN LIKE THIS. A 5 STAR CLASSIC!
  - JIMMY DASAINT- BESTSELLING AUTHOR OF BLACK SCARFACE

Capone is indeed one of the best storytellers known to man. His ability to captivate his readers through words and cultivate their cravings and desires for more is enamoring to say the least. This masterpiece is one of the greatest purities to come out of the concreted jungle and trenches of the ghetto.

-Sydia Bagley (author / poet)

Unjustly tried, Ace Capone was destined to be the next great record mogul in the city of Philadelphia. He, being well-deserving of a new trial, is the author of this book that is a vivid picture of his life and unfair federal justice system. Free Ace Capone. A father, a businessman, and the Author of an intriguing novel.

-Thomas Overton, Author of (Murder with a Deadly Weapon, Infidelity, Keys to the Franchise)

Dedication:

"To all the Go Getters in the hoods, and ghettos all across America, who never lay down and always make a way out of no way. We remain strong through hardship, poverty, and illness at our most troublesome times… "This book was not written to glorify the game. It was written to reveal the aftermath of what happens as a result of being a key player in it. Although the book is solely for entertainment purposes for the readers, the overall lesson is to learn from our mistakes and to lead those that are misguided."

Ace Capone

♪It's a Hardknock Life!!! ♪ (Jay-Z)

♪This for my hood niggas…For my rich niggas…Got a 100 on the head of a snitch nigga♪ (Ricky Ross)

♪Go to the grave for I be a bitch nigga…Ya betta behave ya dealin with some rich niggas…Born in the ghetto now I'm worldwide… ♪ (RickyRoss/feat. Jay-Z)

In Memory Of:

R.I.P – Arnold **"Tee-wee"** Waters (Darby)
R.I.P – Joe **"Stink"** Smith (Baltimore)
R.I.P – Ted Baukman (Southwest Philly)
R.I.P – Nino bro. **"Keon"** (Southwest Philly)
R.I.P – **"Randy"** (from Chester)
R.I.P – **"Brother"** (West Philly – from down the bottom)
R.I.P – Kyle Kemp (Darby/Paschall Projects)
R.I.P – Lou **"Pop Pop"** Johnson (Southwest & West Philly – down the bottom)
R.I.P – Lee **"Pop Pop Lee"** Gordon (West Virginia)
R.I.P – Trayvon Martin (Sanford, Florida)

ACE'S APOLOGY TO THE STREETS

I sincerely apologize to anyone I may have hurt or mislead in the past. I will never try to justify my wrong actions; I will only briefly explain that my actions were simply due to misguidance. To those I have hurt, I hope that you can find it in your hearts to forgive me. I remind you that if God can forgive us all - who are we not to forgive each other? And to those I have mislead (friends, family, youth, etc)I call you all to enjoin what is right (good) and to forbid what is wrong (bad), and I encourage not to indulge in any form of criminal activity.

Respectfully,
Ace Capone

The real Ace Capone is serving a life plus 55 yrs. sentence at U.S.P Big Sandy, P.O Box 2068, Inez, KY 41224. He is currently awaiting his appeal process.

More about "Key to Life Publishing": Key to life publishing will continue to bring you stories that our fans can enjoy and relate to. We aim to promote strong messages within each story; therefore, each story we bring you will represent true to life situations from which we all can truly learn a lot. God Willing! Our motive is to deter people from criminal activity, and we do so by sharing stories with both beginnings and endings we can take from.

Everything in life happens for a reason, and our overall goal is to help make people aware, so we can break the negative cycle (misguidance / blind following) often create. Please follow us and look out for other good books in stores now and more to come in the near future.

In stores now:

"Go Hard" (The Takedown of Ace Capone) by A.T. Capone
"The Hoodrat Chronicles" (Converting to Ratism) by Tea Capone...

Coming soon:

"Go Harder" (Capone's Cocaine Gang) by A.T. Capone

<u>Acknowledgements</u>

First and foremost I want to thank Allah. All praise is due to Allah, for He is the best of all planners, Most Merciful, Oft-forgiving. Secondly, I want to thank my lovely wife Teasha Coles – for encouraging me to complete this story. Allah has truly blessed me with a Muslimah with all the characteristics that I look for in a woman. You are the first woman I actually fell completely in love with for all the right reasons, and that alone – along with Allah's guidance are the very reasons you're the first woman I officially married. Masha-Allah(By God's Will). "I love you Baby!" "May Allah reward you for your faithfulness, loyalty, non-stop support and love to me as a good wife." Ameen!

I want to give a special shout out to Crystal Perkins (my Consultant) on this project, and a very special shout to Angie "Mrs. Pepper" Davis (my Assistant) who made the difference with this project. Mrs. Pepper, you worked as hard as me on this project (you put just as much time/love in it as me) and I got mad love for you for that. We have future projects ahead of us so there's a lot more work to do, but I'm very proud and extremely blessed to have you a part of 'Team Ace' for longevity. Insha-Allah "May Allah reward you both with many blessings." Ameen!

It was times I stalled and actually considered giving up on this project, and I want to thank Allah for surrounding me with the right people in my corner, who inspired me and gave me motivation during the roughest time of my life. Through this hardship Allah allowed me a moment of time to reflect on the true purpose of life (which is to solely worship Allah, alone without partners...implementing Islam). Throughout my hardship I have realized I had to work on myself (my faith), and as I got myself together I was able to identify all my negative ways, fake friends and the love I have for my true family and friends. I want to thank my mom for being there for my two youngest children (Naseem & Sajae) at such a crucial time for me. I also thank you for forgiving me for my old foolish and misguided ways in the past. Despite all that has happened, I sincerely pray that our relationship as mother and son truly grows stronger from here on out – we are family. "I love you mom!"

I want to thank my children's mothers (Levette, Kris and Rain) for simply raising my children. To my children Raina, Toya, Zakeira, Alton, Nyrah, Nyile, Naseem, Sajae (Daddy's Babygirl), and Caloni (Princess Capone): Daddy loves all of you more than you have to the ability to know. Alhumdu-illah (All praise to God).

Now let me get to some friends - Shout outs to my man Braheem "Brody" Edwards for still being a real homie throughout my bid. I'm gonna always have love for you pimp. Real Talk! Big Shout out to the entire C.B.G (Capone's Book Gang): Tea Capone, Nino "Dot" Brown, Charles Ford also known as, Bone, Kareem Evens also known as Lil Man, Jalil, Nathan Welch, also known as Big Nate, Sydia Bagley and Jihad also known as, Grady... my official all-star lineup of book writers at this time - - all of you are extremely talented writers that I commend. Each one of you have a special gift from Allah and now that I'm in the book game; we are gonna keep it coming like mixtapes...Insha-Allah we seriously about to take this book game to another level. Real talk! Point Blank! Flat Out!

Big Shout out to Golden Girl – I'm gonna always have lots of love for you, and as long as I got something going on (which will be always) you gonna be involved. Real talk! Shout out to my cousin Raheem and his wife Tara, Lavena Johnson, Monique "Babygirl" Pullins, Amanda Young, Mia Pullins, Mom Pullins, my brothers Amin, Mitchell, Michael, and to my two favorite ladies, Mrs Dolores "Nana" Johnson and Mrs. Pauline Coles (my grandmothers). I love and respect you both more than you have the ability to understand for raising me as if I were your own son, and being the women Allah created you to be. Point Blank!

Big Sandy Shout outs to: Ibraheem, Habeeb, Wasi, also known as, Shorty Lo, Basheer, Ghazzi, YaYa, Omar (from Trenton), Aziz, Yusef, Hassan East, Has, Sabir, Ahmed Judge, Dawud, Sydiq and the entire Muslim community. (Philly car) Travis, Flamer, Wayne, Jus Blaze, Syfullah, Boxing Bob. (New Jersey) Terrence, Mega, Reckless, Drop, Zariff, Puerto Rican Boobie. (Detroit) Jay "7 Mile", Bam, D-Bo, Whitey. (Carolina) Fatboy. (Barbershop) Sleepy, Pee-Wee, Shea, Chef. (DC) String Bean, London, Mo, Jamal, Hakeem, Nook, and Six. (NY) Rob, Danny, Touch. (A-1) Pimp, K.D., Shorty, Jalon (Missouri), and everybody else who was on my unit when I was on A-1 and C-3, (Ohio) Weazy and Khalil. (B-1) J-dog, 2G, Green Eyes, ATL, Abdullah, Jezzo, Basil, TomTom, Yougin, Cee (Court St. Newark), Jalil, Ein, Mr. Rice, Skull, E.P., Rubin, Naeem, and the whole Challenge program.

Special shout outs to my co-defendants who kept it 100: Tim Gotti, Jay "Jihad", Thais, Asya, Nino, Jamar, R.C., Dirt Bike Hov, Mac, Randall "Ran" Austin, Hak, Dante and Hammer. My prayers go out to you continuously. Always remember that victory is for the believers because we hear and obey! We couldn't duck Allah, but Insha-Allah we learned from our situation and became better people following this life changing experience decreed. I love you all for the sake of Allah, and for your courage along side me in court. You deserve your respect throughout this life – now let's earn our way into the next life, seeking Paradise (by implementing Islam).

Final Shout outs to: Shabazz of "As Is Magazine", Jaquavis Coleman of "Cash Money Content", Tone Trump, Russell of "Trap Magazine", Philly Freeway, Cuzin E, Philly Swain, Mrs. Baker, Muffin, Jackie, Tammie, Cris Moore, Tia, Malika, Alicia Watkins, Chanel, Shaft, my cuz Haron, Forty "40" from Coatesville, Saleem from Newark (MDC Brooklyn), Chris Chizer (Texas), CW (BMF), Cuzin Chris, Watley, Beanie Sigel, Oschino, Peedie Crack, Daytona, Bugsy, Caution, Minute, Philly Swain, Snake "Young Eza", Mike "Millions", Jerv, Uncle O, Mikey Dredd (The Hot Boyz), Cosmic Kev, Q Deezy, Pooch Man, Charlie Mack, Daryl Shuler, Saudia Shuler, Marty Shuler, Donnie Dudat, Muhammad (Palmers Club), Jamal (Superstars Barbershop), Barry, Raby, Tanya (Center of Attractions), and Rosa from Camden...Listen "I am Ace Capone". I can keep on going and going with the shout outs. I know way too many people so please forgive me if I forgot to name you specifically. With that said, **Big shout outs to each and every one of my friends on Facebook** and **"EVERYBODY"** who got love for me in the streets. If I forgot to mention you, just email or write me to remind me. It's simply been a long time since I've heard from you. Ya Dig? But I still got love for you too. Real Talk!

Now for the movement everyone has been waiting for, so sit back, relax, enjoy your flight, or just get comfortable because I'm getting ready to take you on a journey, introducing the entire world to the City of Brotherly love (Philadelphia) from an official gangsta's perspective. It's about time the world recognizes the mean streets of Southwest Philly! Ya Dig? Yall know I always do it for TV, with that said, here's some motivational music because you will enjoy this book like it's a movie!

"Welcome to the hood" D.J. Khalid featuring Rick Ross, Plies, Lil Wayne

PROLOGUE

On a cool rainy day, in November --- November 11, 2007 to be exact; Chris Warner, a handsome high-paid defense attorney exited his 2008 Lincoln Towncar, wearing a dark blue suit under his tan Burberry trench coat. As he walked toward his office, he noticed a lot of people in line at the newsstand. It wasn't unusual to see a crowd at the newsstand in downtown Center City, Philadelphia, but to see and hear people cursing, pushing, bumping, and shoving each other while reading at the stand; piqued the middle age lawyer's curiosity.

Eager to see what all the fuss was about, Chris Warner made his way through the sea of people and grabbed a copy of the latest *Philadelphia Inquirer.* Soon as his eyes scanned the front cover, Chris Warner's face grew a deathly pale as if he'd seen a ghost. The ghost being his newest and most high profile client --- **Ace Capone,** in which a lot of negative press revolved.

This is not good...This is not good at all, he thought, watching his client's face on the front page of an eight page exclusive article that read: **THE TAKEDOWN OF ACE CAPONE... A STORY OF GUNS, DRUGS AND RAP!!!**

*　　　　　　*　　　　　　*

Later that day, Chris listened to the ABC's 6:00 evening news, only to hear more negative press about his client. That's when he realized just how full his hands were going to be in the upcoming trial of Ace's life. Chris was no stranger to the camera. He was used to media attention from representing other Mafia style clients, most notably Joey Merlino. Only this time, his young black client who went by the name of Ace Capone had broken a Philadelphia record by selling over 800,000 copies of the Philadelphia Inquirer in a single day.

Who says Crime Don't Pay?

The *Philadelphia Inquirer's* usual quota for selling newspapers was normally anywhere between 200,000 to 400,000 on a daily basis, and that was dependable on the news coverage. When all the hype hit the streets that the Infamous Ace Capone was on the front cover of an eight- page article (in a 2 day / 2 part story), newspaper sales immediately skyrocketed. All of Philadelphia's Tri-State area and surrounding suburbs wanted to read about the crime, wealth, and status of the well respected rap mogul, drug king-pin, gangster: Alton *"Ace Capone"* Coles.

Stuck in a deep trance, Chris Warner thought, *"We should have never lost that pre-trial motion to suppress the wiretap evidence. Judge Carter was totally wrong for not making the government reveal the five cooperating sources that gave up information towards the initial wiretap affidavit. The law doesn't cover the re-dacted information on wiretap affidavits. My client has the right to face all of his accusers, but Judge Carter didn't wiggle out of that issue good enough, when he denied that motion. Out of all the motions in Ace's favor we should have at least won that one ....We start trial next month and with all this negative media attention surrounding the case, **how the hell can I possibly win this damn trial???"** That questions along with a few other questions haunted Ace Capone's attorney as he began reading another in depth article on his infamous client...

CHAPTER 1
(CAPONE'S COCAINE GANG)

It was a cold morning on March 4, 2008 in the city of brotherly love. The bluish, gray cloudy sky was giving off signs of rain, but that didn't stop many people or the numerous news reporters from standing outside of the federal courthouse; which held one of the biggest cases in the history of Philadelphia today. Every radio station and television news broadcast system was in tune with the conspiracy case that the government labeled the **C.C.G (Capone's Cocaine Gang).**

News stands all over the city and surrounding counties doubled their numbers in sales, due to the very anticipated high profile case. Law enforcement had to push people back as the numbers grew continuously around Philadelphia's federal court building, and court wasn't in session yet, so everyone waited impatiently…

        *   *   *

Hours earlier Alton Coles, who is better known as Ace Capone, was in his cell washing his face and brushing his teeth to prepare for court. Ace was detained at F.D.C Philadelphia; indicted on **848 C.C.E** (Continuing Criminal Enterprise) for heading a **$25 million dollar** cocaine conspiracy.

"Mr. Coles you have twenty more minutes before we leave for court," Officer Smith announced politely, walking pass Ace's cell door. The correctional officer told the same thing to three other inmates who were scheduled for court that morning as well. With that said, Ace hurried along with his grooming. Within minutes he walked outside of his cell headed towards the phone. On his way, he saw other inmates watching the news, which took coverage in front of the court building. Ace picked up the phone, paying the news coverage no mind; he already knew what all the hype was about. After he dialed the numbers on the phone, he placed it to his ear. Nikky, one of his three main girls, picked up after the third ring and quickly accepted his call.

"Hey baby," Nikky uttered sleepily, yet cheerfully through the phone. She was home on bail as one of his 22 co-defendants. Nikky faced a lengthy jail sentence. She was charged in the drug conspiracy itself, but even in their current situation, the sound of his voice still brought joy to her heart.

"For some reason I feel like today is the day we just might get a verdict Babygirl, so make sure you pray and make dua's to Allah for all of us." Ace replied calmly – trying to suppress her hidden worries, as he looked at the wall noticing the time was now 6:30 a.m. "It's time for **salat** (prayer) so get up, pray and get yourself together for court. I aint gonna talk long because my minutes are low; I just called to say I love you. "

"Alright Baby, I love you too." Nikky replied.

Ace hung up and headed towards the common area where the TV's held everybody else's attention. One of the other inmates informed Ace about his ongoing fame that the media built up day after day over the last few months. Ace didn't reply. You could read no feelings in his eyes, or see any movement. He just stared blankly at the TV screen.

This is Charles Vernon for Channel 6 News. I'm here at the federal courthouse in Center City awaiting the court hearing for Philadelphia's crime boss Alton "Ace Capone" Coles. It's been 12 days now, and the jury is still in deliberation. This does not look good for the government's prosecution. Court is scheduled to start session at 8:00 a.m. But as I stated before, this is an extremely bad sign for the prosecutor, because normally a jury who deliberates this long is confused. Which can more than likely lead to a hung jury or a not guilty verdict. We will have more news coverage on this extremely complex case as the day continues. This is Charles Vernon, live at the federal courthouse in Center City, back to you Jim.

*　　　　　　*　　　　　　*

"Alright guys, Court and sanitation recall! Let's go!" The correctional officer yelled out, cutting the TV's off from the officer's bubble.

It took Ace 40 minutes to walk the underground tunnel from F.D.C shackled in a green jumper to the courthouse building across the street. Ace had been waiting for over 3 years now for this day. Ace stared off into a deep thought as he, Jihad, and Tim sat in the marshal cage.
They needed to get out of the ugly green jumpers to put on their street cloths and await the judge clerk's next instructions.

"Damn! I wonder what the hell is taking them so long pimp?" Jihad asked Ace.

"I don't know. But I pray it's all good for us. What you think, Gotti?" Ace replied tiredly.

"Only Allah (God) knows what's going on in there, I'm tired of racking my brain about it. I just want to get this whole trial over with. I know we're a done deal. I wish they would hurry up and bang us, that way we can just get back on appeal. Lovette knows they fucked up in the beginning – with the raids, and the wiretap order was foogazey." Gotti replies with frustration.

"Man, fuck is you talking about! What you mean they can just bang us? I'll take a hung jury over a guilty verdict any day, Pimp. They can just bang us? You talking crazy as shit! Real talk." Ace snapped with sarcasm apparent in his tone.

"If we get a hung jury, that means we gonna have to go through this shit all over again. If they do bang us, at least we can move forward to the appeal process, and get rhythm at that stage without all the media attention." Jihad said confused and frustrated, trying to reason with himself to possibly agree with Gotti.

"Man dig this here, both you niggas bugged the fuck out. I will go through a three-month trial again, before I even think about waiting for an appeal. An appeal can take anywhere from two to five more years, and it ain't no damn guarantee we gone win at that stage either. These muthafuckas trying to take my life, and at least 20-30 years of y'all lives as well."

Little did Gotti or Jihad know, Ace was more than frustrated; he was extremely pissed off. Ace realized during the trial that his own co-defendants had already gone against him. They even somewhat unconsciously blamed him for being indicted.

Chris Warner privately told Ace the first day of trial that it was just he and Ace against everybody. Chris had been through big conspiracy cases many times before, so he knew the character and conduct of his legal peers from previous experiences.

In most cases, they simply didn't prepare for trial properly. Unbeknowest to their clients, the attorneys were to make it seem as if their clients were innocent by indirectly throwing the boss under the bus. And Gotti's lawyer, Jack McMahoon was the worst of them all. His defense strategy for Gotti consisted of indirectly and/or blatantly blaming everything on Ace Capone at the right time. He knew the government and the media gunned directly at Ace, so Jack McMahoon figured he'd create a shadow of protection for his client. Little did he know – Jack only helped the government's case and Gotti Baldwin (Ace's supposed to be man) did absolutely nothing the whole trial to stop his lawyer's deadly plan of attack.

Ace, on the other hand, actually controlled his lawyer the whole trial by having him help with everyone else's defense, as he defended him. Ace's love and loyalty to his squad wouldn't dare allow him to sit back and let his lawyer say anything to hurt any of his co-defendants.

Jihad's lawyer, Wayne Powl, had only threw one back shot towards Ace during the cross examination of Jihad's own expert witness. Ace's so-called fiancé, Iesha's lawyer, on the other hand, made him seem like a low down dirty Chicago pimp, in hopes of getting her a not guilty verdict. Iesha's lawyer and her parents played their parts in pushing her far away from Ace right before the trial. They advised her that it was best to stop all contact with Ace since she was now caught up in the government's web. Iesha's parents felt although Ace was good to her, now that he was in so much trouble with the Feds, interacting with him was no longer in her best interest.

Iesha really loved Ace, so she wouldn't snitch him out for nothing in the world. She rode with him all the way up until trial, and then fell way back, allowing others to dictate how she should carry her relationship. Although that bothered Ace a great deal, it didn't prevent him from keeping it gangsta. Prior to the trial, Ace wrote Iesha's lawyer a detailed letter encouraging her lawyer to do anything he felt he had to do in order to get her off. Even if it was prejudicial towards him, Ace simply wanted Iesha to win. Iesha was the only other defendant besides Ace who actually took the stand in their defense. Despite all the harmful comments her lawyer made about Ace during her defense, when she took the stand Iesha surprisingly somewhat defended Ace.

Ace sat back and paid close attention to everybody during trial. His very life was on the line, so every time the lawyers joked along with the judge or government, Ace became furious because there was absolutely no comedy in fighting for a man's life; especially when it's his life! Ace caught his own co-defendants laughing at times during the testimony of some of the rats. Most of the rats directed their testimony towards Ace, so they were overdosing with lies that sounded foolish at times, trying way too hard to get their 5k1 motion. Ace felt like even though the rats sounded like unbelievable jackasses at times, there's nothing funny when your life is on the line and testimony is loaded, cocked, and aimed at you. **Point blank!**

"Alright guys, they are ready for you." The old chubby marshal replied.

*   *   *

Five minutes later, Ace, Jihad and Gotti entered the courtroom through a little door near the judge's stand. As Ace looked into the crowded courtroom, he knew it was time for the verdict. Although twelve days of deliberation seemed to look in favor of the defense, when Ace looked at the faces of Nikky and Iesha, he saw and sensed their fear for the outcome. The courtroom was packed like sardines - with law enforcement, politicians, family, friends and nosey pedestrians. This case was so complex that no electronic devices, cameras or camera phones were allowed in the courtroom. Some of the media personnel had to stand to take notes because there were absolutely no seats left to sit in the extremely loud and crowded courtroom.

Order! Order, Order in the courtroom!" Judge Carter, a middle aged white man, with snow-white hair shouted, sporting his black robe, while he banged his gavel.

The jury now entered the room, and there were 20 of them in total, 12 jurors and 8 alternates. On the initial 12 there was only one Black middle age women, two Chinese and the rest were Caucasians.

"Has the jury reached a verdict?" The judge asked.

"Yes, we have Your Honor." The heavy set white forewoman replied, as she stood fixing her glasses.

"Alright, let's have it." The judge said, as the bailiff went to retrieve the 50-page verdict slip slowly and passed it to the judge.

Iesha slowly looked at Ace with a caring, yet worried expression. She thought back to the note Ace had passed her and Nikky when the jury sent out notes to the judge with questions about the jury instructions. Ace's note read: *It looks good for y'all. I don't even care about me, at this point; I just want y'all two out of this shit. Real Talk!*

Nikky looked at Ace with a look of concern as well. Ace smiled at her and said, **"Fear Allah."** Everyone was nervous, mentally drained and left in suspense. Nikky and Iesha's friends and family members thought for sure the girls had won, because the government did not prove their case against either of the girls, and as far as they were concerned the girls were innocent as hell. However, as far as the government was concerned, the girls were guilty by association for simply being in a relationship with Ace. Truth be told, the feds had only indicted the girls to force them to flip on Ace. The government had offered both Iesha and Nikky cooperation deals numerous times to testify against Ace, but the two girls were in love with a boss playa and reluctantly the two girls turned them down.

The prosecutor, Rich Lovette, along with Agent Nikko realized that Ace really loved the girls, so they figured by indicting the girls; Ace would more than likely cooperate to save them and his own ass. Their textbook scheme didn't work though – cause Ace kept it "G". Ace could never rat to get out and become a whore for the government, as most niggas often do. Most of the evidence they gathered against Ace was all circumstantial. Truth be told, the government was a bit concerned about taking Ace to trial, because they knew Ace's financial status and street credibility would make it a bit difficult for them to win at trial. Ace could definitely afford the best legal team money could buy. Not to mention the fact they understood in most high profile cases, the witnesses are usually intimidated to testify against a man so well respected, rich and powerful – cause they would be known as rats, cooperating witnesses, worldwide.

Ace's hands were actually clean. He hadn't been caught with or around drugs, so the government had their hands full. The prosecution had to paint a picture of Ace being a kingpin in order to win their case, and the best evidence they had against him was his money and the mysterious wiretap. Ace never reported 100 percent of his legal income, and that alone gave the government an advantage. They also had the deadly wiretap evidence, but they didn't have anyone on the actual phone conversations cooperating with them to testify against him in trial. However, they were able to use over 3,000 very incriminating phone conversations at trial to mislead the jury. *Whatever happened to being able to face your accuser? I guess that went out the window with the electric slide.*

"Will the jury please read the verdict as to count 1, 848 Continuing Criminal Enterprise conspiracy as it relates to Alton Coles?" The judge requested firmly.

As the forewoman stood up to read the verdict, the courtroom was so quiet; you could hear a pin drop.

"We the jury, find the defendant guilty!"

Ace's whole body went numb. Everything in the courtroom seemed blurry to him, as he kept hearing the word **GUILTY, GUILTY, GUILTY,** repeatedly. It was as if he were dreaming, while he sat awake, and he only snapped out of his zone state when he heard the guilty verdicts for both Nikky and Iesha. The sound of Nikky's voice as she softly sobbed "Uh-uh-uh," is what Ace could hear. However, Ace couldn't bear to look Nikky or Iesha in the face without shedding a tear; not after hearing their guilty verdicts, so he didn't look in their direction in order to hold his composure like a true boss is supposed to.

In the midst of everything Ace noticed something strange. One of the jurors, a young white woman in her late 20s suddenly burst out into tears, as if she knew the guilty verdict shouldn't have been. The young white juror cried as if Ace and the girls were a part of her own family. Ace tapped his lawyer, bringing the emotion of the juror to Chris's attention. Chris, also noticed two other alternate jurors shaking their heads in disbelief regarding the verdict.

The jury was actually picked on December 18, 2007, and it was now March 8, 2008. The jury only took breaks a couple of days during the trial for holidays like Christmas, New Years, and Martin Luther King, Jr. Day. Ace and his lawyer believed that someone forced the few jurors that were trying to hold out on Ace's behalf to change their minds and go with the conviction.

The marshals immediately cuffed Ace along with his co-defendants, and then escorted them back over to the Federal Detention Center where they were to be held until sentencing. Today was a sad day for Ace and his co-defendants. But, based on a very valuable discrepancy that happened during the trial, Ace silently vowed to get a new trial on his appeal…

Meanwhile, outside the courtroom, every radio and television broadcast station within the tri-state area conducted live coverage….

"This is Charles Vernon reporting live outside the federal courthouse, where the jury has just disclosed a **Guilty Verdict** for *drug kingpin, rap mogul* Alton "Ace Capone" Coles. Prosecutors provided evidence to the jury that proved Ace Capone had been the mastermind behind a drug enterprise from 1998-2005. Investigators say that Coles put more than 2 billion dollars worth of cocaine on the streets of Philadelphia, New Jersey, Baltimore and surrounding areas over a 7-year period.

Prosecutor, Rick Lovett proved that Coles himself is worth millions, and **conservatively** quoted an **1800 kilo estimate of 25 million dollars** in the actual indictment for the drug conspiracy. Coles faces **Life plus 55 years**. Gotti Baldwin, Coles' under-boss faces **30 years to Life**, James Morvis faces 10-20 years in federal prison; Iesha Richards is one of Coles' girlfriends, who purchased a half-million dollar home with Coles, faces **5-10 years** on one count of money laundering. Out of all the women in this case, Nikky Pullet, another one of Coles' girlfriends, faces **10-20 years** on a more serious charge for playing a role in the actual drug conspiracy. And last but not least, Tish Tompson, the girlfriend of Jihad Morvis, faces up to **5 years** for perjury. This has been a 3-month long trial on a case investigators say took 7 years to build, and an additional two and a half years to actually prepare for trial (to convict Ace and his gang). I'm standing right here with Prosecutor Rich Lovett. How do you feel about the win Rich?"

"It's very fortunate that we got this violent crew off the street. They are responsible for over 22 shootings and 7 murders that we at least know of. The system does work, and today we send a message to other drug crews because we won!"

"I see. Thanks for your time Rich." Charles Vernon replied, while rushing away trying to get another interview after quickly noticing Ace's defense lawyer exiting the crowded courthouse.

"Chris, what happened in there? For a while it seemed as though the defense team was winning."

"Well, it's a devastating loss – a complete miscarriage of justice. However, we did establish a lot of good appeal issues during the trial that I believe we will win in our favor." Chris replied confidently, yet sincerely recognizing his client's strongest point for a new trial on appeal.

"Thanks Chris. Well, you heard it here first folks – we will keep you posted on all updates concerning this extremely complex case. This has been Charles Vernon reporting live at the federal courthouse in Center City, for Channel 6 Action News."

CHAPTER 2
(BACK INTO TIME)

In the summer of 1998, Ace and a dime piece chic were making their own music on a bed inside suite 223 at the Taj Mahal in Atlantic City, NJ. Ace had the sexy 5-foot-7 young project chic's legs wrapped around his waist as he slid deeper and deeper up in her pussy. She gyrated her hips pushing her pussy back on his long hard dick as they fucked faster and faster. Their bodies glistened with sweat while they got busy on the bed like two porn stars.

"Oh shit Yes…Yesss Daddy, Yessss…Damn --- you fucking the shit out of this pussy!" Erica moaned out in a light whisper, contracting her pussy muscles to clench down tightly on the invading love muscle that seemed to stretch her sugary walls with each long, pounding stroke.

"Yeahhh! You like dis dick don't chu?" Ace groaned as he continued pounding her pussy out like tomorrow would never come.

"YESSSS! Oh My God Yessss! I love this big, juicy dick! Fuck me daddy…Fuck me hard…Yesssss right there…Mmmmmm shit, I'm about to cum Ace!" She shrieked out loudly, fucking him back faster and faster to meet his pulverizing thrusts.

The king size bed couldn't take the carnal activity happening as it broke down and began squeaking louder and louder. *Squeak! Squeak! Squeak*! Was the only sound being heard, along with the moaning and groaning they did during the intense fuckfest.

"Yesss! Right there daddy! Right theeeerreeee…Oh My God! I'm about to cum, I'm cummmmmin, I'm Cummmmiiinnnggg!" Erica yelled out in ecstasy, biting down on her bottom lip, letting the feeling of his jabbing ram-rod take her to another world.

"That's a good girl…cum for me Ma, cum hard", Ace demanded aggressively while sawing in and out of her gushing, wet pussy with a steady rhythm.

"It's here Ace…Mmmmm Shit…It's here Daddy…I'm cuummming…I'm Cummmiinng…ph God Yesss! Damn you good". She yelped, tossing her ass back like a champ.

"Tell me where you want me to nut, in ya face or in ya pussy?" Ace asked.

"Mmmmm, in my pussy Daddy. Please leave it in, and don't pull it out this time. I wanna feel that shit shooting up inside of me." Erica begged.

"Nah, flip over and swallow dis dick!" Ace directed her as she eased off the dick.

Erica quickly got up on all fours, grabbed his dick and started sucking it sloppily as she jerked on it continuously. Ace exploded with a crazy burst of warm semen all over her face and mouth, as Erica rubbed her face and tongue all over his spurting dick. A few splotches of fresh, warm semen hit her breasts during the excitement, causing her to quiver a little. Erica slowly slid his dick back into her mouth, and sucked him dry until he started shaking and pushing her head away from him.

"Damn girl…get up off me!" Ace replied jokingly, exhausted and unable to take anymore of the pleasure at that time.

Erica blew his mind every time she did that shit. Ace knew her head game was truly a work of art, which is another reason why he didn't dismiss her like most of the chics he met; fucked once and never called back for seconds.

"Damn that milkshake was good," Erica joked as they both sat up and started laughing.

"I know one thing – I be testing ya ass and you gonna stop tryna get pregnant by me. You ain't slick and my ass ain't dumb!" Ace checked her matter factly after the laughter died down.

Erica had been trying and wanting to get pregnant by Ace every since he had been hitting it raw. Being the baddest, sexiest chic from out the projects that Ace took a liking to, Erica thought her red-bone, thick, curvy shape, flat stomach, and ass like *Buffy the Body* would keep Ace from seeing what she was trying to do. But Ace was hip to all the games women played when trying to hook a baller of his caliber. Something about Erica drew Ace to her constantly. Part of it was all the tattoos she had covering her sexy, light skinned body; along with the fact that she kept it ghetto as hell, always representing and riding hard for her dude.

"You heard what I said girl?" Ace asked sternly from within the bathroom.

"Yeah, I hear you. Dang!" She replied softly, sucking her teeth as she heard the water running in the shower. "What you doing?" She asked, in an attempt to ignore him by changing the subject.

"You know what I'm doing. I'm taking a shower!" He called out. "And don't try to ignore me. Ima crack ya fuckin' head about that baby shit! Real Talk!"

Before Erica could respond, Ace's cell phone started ringing. She stared at it for a second, wondering who was calling him. Then she called out to let him know he had an incoming call.

"Ace, one of ya phones is ringin – want me to answer it?"

"Woman, you know better!" He said, while emerging from the bathroom. They both laughed at his remark, as he walked over to answer his phone.

"Hello?"

"Yo," the voice replied, as Ace instantly recognized that one of his barbers and childhood friend, Duece was calling him.

"What number you calling from pimp?" Ace asked.

"Some chic's crib." Duece answered in a nonchalant tone. "What's up?"

"Listen, Young Bull Tee-Wee is dead." Duece informed him.

"WHAT!" Ace blurted out; caught off guard. "What happened? Matter- of –fact, don't even tell me. Just meet me at Erica's crib."

"Aight, how long?" Duece asked.

"One hour."

"Aight, one." Deuce replied as he ended the call.

Ace had a look of concern plastered all over his face that Erica quickly picked up on. She could tell that there was a serious problem.

"Damn Ace, you said we were going to stay until Sunday, which ain't till tomorrow." She pouted, sucking her teeth after overhearing the meeting he just set up at her house.

"Girl, get your ass dressed. We gotta go!"

"Aight dang, so who got locked the hell up or killed?"

"What made you ask that?" Ace replied, giving her a funny look.

"Cause ya ass just won like 30,000 thousand dollars between playing craps and blackjack last night. You only took a break for grub and a quickie, now we're leaving? So I know it's gotta be some type of emergency." She stated matter of factly.

Ace looked at her and asked, "You think you know me, huh?"

"I know I do, cause you my heart." She smiled.

"Then hurry up and get ya ass dressed so we can go, cause my young bull checked out."

"Who?" Erica asked puzzled.

"Tee-Wee."

"What happened?" she asked, sounding nosey.

"I don't know yet, but let's go and you driving cause I'm tired as hell. You better not ding my damn rims." He told her, as he passed her the keys while they both continued to get dressed.

Minutes later, they left the hotel and jumped into Ace's '98 silver Benz wagon (E420) with the 21inch chrome rims on it, by Carlson. The luxury wagon had the chrome muffler and some black leather seats with Ace cards engraved in the headrests. The crazy ass Kenwood stereo system let people know Ace was coming from a mile away whenever he chose to quake his sounds up to capacity. The sporty wagon also had TVs, and numerous speakers placed throughout the entire car.

Standing 5-foot-9 and weighing in at 267 pounds, Ace was considered to be a fatboy by most. In fact, many people called him **Fatboy** because of his stocky, chubby frame, yet most of the ladies in the city still considered him sexy chocolate.

Ace repped hard for the big guys, although it wasn't in his genes to be big. Once he started making a lot of money, along with going out to wine and dine various women he met, Ace just blew up gaining weight out of nowhere. He had so many women feeding him and pampering him that it didn't make any sense. Plus the only exercise he actually got on a regular basis was the act of sex itself.

Ace loved to spoil his women and they spoiled him back. He didn't even have to wash his own ass much, because his women did it for him. They dressed him and even put deodorant under his arms for him. Whenever Ace dressed, he stayed fly like a true Dapper Don, only wearing the best clothes, furs, jewelry, sneakers and shoes that money could buy.

14

Ace had huge walk-in closets at every house he owned, which were fully stocked with high-end clothes. He was getting plenty of money and all the pussy a man could ever dream of, from the prettiest women. Some trophy women wouldn't get caught dead with a fat boy, but Ace Capone wasn't your average fat boy. His slanted eyes, wavy hair and well groomed beard only enhanced his dark complexion that complimented his pearly white teeth. Ace had all the features to be arrogant and cocky as hell, yet he was kind and humble. A solid, good, intelligent man with swag and money is every woman's dream catch of a man. Ace was a caring provider, and a woman's sweetheart, who had a devilish, yet cute smile, which sometimes made him appear to be arrogant.

Ace's cell phone rang, invading his thoughts. He answered it on the second ring.

"What's up?"

"Yo Ace, I'm pulling up now." Duece informed him.

"I'm on my way out now." Ace replied before ending the call to head out of Erica's house.

Ace had two barber shops: One in Chester, PA and the other one down in the heart of West Philly, right there on Holly Street. Soon as Ace heard Duece's car pull up, he opened the front door to exit the house and approached the car.

"Damn Pimp, so what happened to Tee-Wee?" Ace asked while leaning on the car as Duece looked up at him from the driver seat through the opened window.

"Man, I don't know what the fuck happened." Duece said. "All I know is he was zoomed out of his mind. I think that nigga was poppin pills and snorting heroin and shit, cause all of a sudden he just turned blue like he wasn't breathing, so we put him inside the bathtub because his body was hot."

"Who the fuck is we?" Ace grilled him.

"It was me, Pone and some smoker we had with us inside the hotel room out in Lancaster."

"Aight, so what the fuck happened?" Ace snapped, anger evident in his tone.

Unbeknowest to Duece, Ace was already highly upset with him –
which is why he stopped allowing Tee-Wee and Duece to hang
around him as much anymore. They both had bad drug habits,
yet they wanted to be drug dealers too, and that didn't sit well
with him. Reason being, Ace didn't do drugs at all, primarily
because his father was a crack head. And after years of seeing his
father strung out on drugs, Ace took that as a learning tool and
made a mental note to never use any type of narcotic, especially
the kind that his father was strung out on because he never
wanted to be anything like his father.

Ace knew a true hustler didn't get high off his own supply
or anyone else's supply for all that matter. As Duece continued to
explain what happened, Ace learned that Duece and Pone had
panicked after Tee-Wee passed out and stopped breathing.

"Yo, we wanted to drop him off at the hospital and keep
going, but we didn't wanna draw no heat on our ride. We even
thought about leaving him at the telly, (motel),but we needed the
room. It was already paid for, and we needed a place to sleep
since we were outta town hustlin."

"So what did yall do with Tee-Wee?" Ace asked, still
confused.

"We just pushed the nigga out da car while we was on the
highway by some trees and shit."

"WHAT!" Ace bellowed. "What the fuck you do that
for?" Is that how yall niggas would have done had it been me?"
Ace retorted with rage, making Duece a little nervous.

"Man yall need to tell his family, so they can bury him
properly. That was some fucked up and disrespectful shit you
niggas did. That's our fucking young bull and you treated him
like a enemy with that stunt." Ace snapped. "Man go tell his
fucking family where he at!"

Without another word, Ace turned around as he shook his
head in disbelief and walked off, never having any ideas that his
demands to Duece would come back to bite him in the ass much
sooner than later…

     *   *   *

On the corner of 59th and Cedar Avenue, Kim, a 5-foot-2 pregnant woman who is one of Ace's girlfriends, walked to the corner store to re-up on supplies after running out of paper cups to dip her water-ice in. Ace had bought the water ice, candy stand for her and placed it in front of her grandmother's house. As Kim went to the store, a short fat man ran up the steps, into her grandmother's house. The chubby intruder quickly rummaged through the kitchen cabinets hoping to find drugs, but was only able to steal the water-ice money, and kick her cat 'Spot" on his way out.

Ada, Kim's grandmother, who slept in the living room because she was sick and elderly, had seen the bandit as he left getting away with his heist. When Kim returned, Ms. Ada told her what had happened and Kim immediately rushed to her phone to call her man.

"Yo." Ace answered his phone.

"Ace! Ace, somebody just robbed us!" Kim said, in a frantic tone, causing Ace to grip his phone tightly in anger.

"What!" Ace yelled. "Somebody did what?" He asked in disbelief as his blood boiled.

"Somebody robbed us Ace!" Kim repeated in an angry tone. "Ace whoever did the shit had to be watching me with they grimey ass."

"How you know that?"

"Cause as soon as I went to the store they went inside the house right after that. They must've thought Ada ain't recognize shit cause she's old and sick, but my grandmother know who the fuck comes in and out of her house."

Ace listened as she ranted about the robbery. He remained silent, trying to keep his anger from boiling over. Ace felt like somebody was disrespecting him by robbing his girl, and whenever Ace Capone felt disrespected it usually turned out ugly for the perpetrator.

"Ada told me she saw who the robber was too." Kim said, invading his thoughts. "She said he came over here with you once before."

"What?" Ace said, tuning in to what she was saying. "Who? Matter of fact, I'm on my way there right now." he said and quickly ended the call.

Ace drove like Mario Andretti, racing over to Kim's grandmother's house. When he arrived, Ada described the intruder to a tee.

"Aight Ada, thanks you did good." Ace said, getting a good feeling of whom she was talking about because he didn't bring anybody to that house, which made the process of elimination very easy.

Coincidently, about nine weeks ago, Moe saw Ace chilling on Kim's front porch as he was driving by, so he pulled over to talk to him. Moe grew up around Ace cause he was from Paschall Projects. Moe had a bad habit of smoking laced blunts: *Crack mixed with weed, a combination to make your eyes bleed.* He had just got out of jail when he saw Ace. He had that stocky, short, chubby frame of one who had just got out of prison with a daily workout regimen. Put more frankly in ghetto terminology, **Moe had that fight back glow!**

When Ada told Ace the robber was short, chubby with a stocky build, he knew the description fit Moe's grimey ass to a tee.

That nigga got to be strong on that shit again to do something so petty and stupid, not to mention negatively detrimental to his health. He only walked off with 30 dollars in quarters. Now, I know his ass not trying to die over no damn 30 dollars? Ace thought, making a mental note to deal with Moe later.

      *   *   **

MEANWHILE, out in Darby, PA - Detective Ricardo Gaffney responds to a missing person's report of a man named Jermond Walters, a.k.a. **Tee-Wee.**

"All I know is that he left here in a car with two other boys that he knew and I haven't seen him since." Tee-Wee's mother said, after telling the officer everything else she knew that could be helpful towards the investigation. Mrs. Marcy was extremely upset after they informed her that there's a strong possibility that her son might be dead; a message that no mother wants to receive about her child, no matter the age..

"So tell me who actually gave you the message that your son died Ma'am?" Detective Gaffney asked, as he scribbled notes in his yellow pad.

"His friends – Deuce, Stevie and Mike." she said, sobbing.

Detective Gaffney jotted down the names that were too familiar to him from prior police arrest. Now that they were suspected of foul play, Detective Gaffney wanted to nail their asses to the cross, simply because he hated who they were related to.

"Okay Ma'am, are you referring to the Coles family?"

"Yes." Mrs. Marcy replied, not recognizing what the implication fully meant.

"And Deuce that works for Ace correct?" Detective Gaffney asked, hoping she added all the pieces to his puzzle.

"Yes!" Mrs. Marcy blurted out as she started crying uncontrollably, yet again. "Oh my God, Tee-Wee! Why! Why! Oh God, where is my baby?"

Unfazed by her emotions, Detective Gaffney reached in his pocket and gave her some napkins he got while eating at McDonalds. He felt somewhat bad behind her loss, but he was happy that he potentially had something to finally pin on Ace Capone and a few of his family members.

"Ma'am we clearly understand the pain you're feeling right now, but I need to ask you just a few more questions okay?"

Mrs. Marcy agreed with a simple nod of the head.

"Did Tee-Wee owe Ace Capone any money?"

"I don't know. Why you ask that?" She asked in return, now completely puzzled.

"Ma'am, I know this might be difficult for you to register, but I need your full cooperation." Detective Gaffney added. "I need you to help me, so I can locate your son, and I need to know if Tee-Wee sold drugs for Ace?"

"No-No-No! Not that I know of." Mrs. Marcy yelled out in defense, now completely agitated.

"Ma'am, please understand this is only a procedure to make things go faster. I'm sorry, but this guy Ace Capone is very dangerous. He's a mafia style guy who will not hesitate to kill over his drug money. So if your son is hooked up with Ace in anyway, then there's a strong possibility that not only is he dead, but he may have been murdered by his so-called friends." Detective Gaffney replied, pouring it on thick.

Hearing the detective's painful words caused Mrs. Marcy to gaze off at the flowers Michael Coles sent, offering his condolences to her and her family before the police even found a body to confirm the death. With Detective Gaffney's input on things, Mrs. Marcy was now confused and had Ace in her mind as a suspect concerning the odd disappearance of her son. At that point, she felt compelled to make some kind of statement about Ace based on her suspicions.

"Ace did shoot at my son about two years ago. My other son told me that Ace shot at his brother over some money that he owed, but Ace said he was only trying to scare him by shooting in Tee-Wee's direction. Ace claimed that he had no intentions on hurting him"

Check Mate! I finally got something that can stick to your ass, Detective Gaffney thought while quickly jotting down and adding his own yeast on the information that she had just given him.

"Ma'am did your son ever pay Ace that money?"

"Um, I don't know. I really don't know." She replied sadly, as she unconsciously wondered off mentally.

*   *   *

Moe and L.T., a lesbian street hustler, were counting the money they had just stolen from a bank in Yeadon, PA. They normally robbed banks with notes and got away with 3,000 to 5,000 dollars at a time. Moe would be the one who went inside the bank while L.T. drove the getaway car, because Moe had been wildin out after he got hooked on drugs again. He now graduated to smoking straight up crack all by itself becoming a certified crackhead.

Moe had been doing a lot of dumb shit lately – like robbing all the young bulls out the projects for their packs (drugs), and not to mention the stunt he pulled at Ace's water-ice stand. Moe's little shenanigans were catching up with him and although he didn't see it, he definitely sensed it. Being extra paranoid from the abundance of crack he'd been smoking, Moe kept trying to call Ace to pick his brain about his knowledge of who robbed his water-ice stand. After a few days of non-stop calling, getting no response, Moe got alarmed. He tried Ace one more time and someone answered.

"Yo, Ace what's good fam?"

"Who dis?" Ace asked puzzled.

"It's me – Moe."

Soon as Ace heard the name, he gave Moe nut ass the quick brush off. "Yo listen, I'm in a real important meeting right now – so let me hit you back." Ace said and quickly hung up before Moe could even respond.

Moe looked at the phone in disbelief, and felt at that moment something was wrong. Moe knew Ace was dangerous, so his paranoia started getting the best of him. He started getting the vibe that Ace knew he was the one who ran up in his girlfriend's house, and he personally witnessed some of the violent things Ace was suppose to be responsible for so he started acting nervous. Every time Moe smoked crack, it intensified his paranoia and fear of Ace, which always ruined his high.

Being as though he couldn't enjoy his high anymore, Moe figured if someone else knew about Ace wanting to hurt him over the water-ice stand caper, then maybe Ace would actually back off for a while. Moe's theory was if people actually knew why he got touched, at least it would lead straight back to Ace. Moe knew Ace was getting way too much money to make a dumb mistake over something small, especially for a crack head like him.

*   *   *

When Donnie pulled up on Ace and told him everything Moe said and done, Ace just gave Donnie a devious smile because he saw straight through Moe's crack head intentions. Moe didn't realize that it was now personal to Ace. His soon- to-be baby momma and family was violated, and that was a definite no-no in Ace's book. Moe's action was one of the lowest signs of disrespect which had to be dealt with accordingly, in due time in Ace's eyes.

"Man, fuck that nut ass nigga! I know what he did and he gonna pay for it ultimately. I don't give a fuck if he tells the whole muthafuckin hood, I'ma get that muthafuckin' crack head ass nigga!" Ace snapped, more so out of anger than anything else.

"Man, you got that nigga shook." Donnie said. "That nigga scared to death; I think you should just leave that nigga alone, he ain't even worth it. Matter of fact, that nigga ain't even Moe no more, he's a straight up junkie."

Ace smiled in an evil manner and said, **"WORD!"** Which was his way of saying, *yeah right, I'm not tryna hear none of that shit!*

When Donnie left Ace, he called Moe to tell him about his conversation with Ace and explained the response and attitude Ace had towards the whole situation. Donnie simply advised Moe to stay as far away from the hood as possible to avoid Ace's wrath until things blew over.

"Hopefully Ace will let the nut ass shit you did go, simply cause we all damn near grew up together."

"I know, that's why I thought you could talk to the nigga for me." Moe said, still shaking in his boots.

"I tried, but he just said word!" Donnie replied, before he ended the call with Moe.

Moe actually knew Ace's nonchalant attitude all too well, so he knew trouble was headed his way soon. Moe felt that shit in his bones because he knew he fucked up by violating a real ass nigga who doesn't hesitate to make an example out of anyone who violates.

Moe started scheming as he remembered that Ace had an old active warrant for drugs in New Jersey for over seven years now, under his alias Lamar Johnson. With that in mind, Moe decided to play his trump card to give himself some safe time, without having to look over his shoulder constantly.

After calling information, Moe got the number he was looking for and made the call quicker than Peyton Manning called an audible in the Super Bowl.

"Hello, Fugitive Task Force?" An operator answered in a cordial tone.

"Yeah, I got some information on the whereabouts of someone who has a drug warrant out of New Jersey." Moe advised.

"Is that so, where would this fugitive be living right now Sir?" The operator asked.

"He's currently staying out in South West Philly at, …" said Moe.

CHAPTER 3
(ALPHABET BOYS)

Bringing in the 1999 New Year right, Ace walked around his house getting ready to go out and celebrate his birthday like he does every January. However, while putting on his jewels and fitted cap, Ace received a disturbing phone call from Rain, his children's mother and long time girlfriend.

Rain is Ace's sweetheart; he could never get enough of her 5-foot-8, 144 pound, caramel brown, curvy frame. Rain always kept her nails and hair done. She loved rocking that Halle Berry pixie styled haircut, which still made her look sexy as hell, even after giving birth to Ace's two kids, Nyrah and Naail.

"Yo, say that again." Ace said, slightly disturbed about the information that she had given him.

"I said the Feds just came to the house looking for you. They were asking all these questions about you, and tried to search the house, but I wouldn't let them…I can't even believe I'm about to say this, but for the first time ever, I'm actually glad you didn't stay here last night."

Ace knew Rain had his best interest at heart, and she has always been his *Rider Chick*. Rain even went to jail before as Ace's co-defendant, and held her grounds without giving it a second thought. The incident happened in the winter of 1996 while Ace and Rain were checking into a fantasy room at the Father Nest Inn somewhere in New Jersey.

*A racist redneck cop had decided to pull them over in a parking lot because Ace was simply **DWB: "Driving with bling on".** The middle aged white officer saw a young black man wearing a lot of jewelry and driving a sleek looking rental car, when he had automatically put in his mind that Ace was up to no good; straight racial profiling! After pulling them over, the cop immediately made them get out the car to start searching the vehicle.*

"Bingo, now whaddaya have here?" The redneck cop stated in a sarcastic tone while holding up a few baggies of crack.

Ace looked dumbfounded. At first Ace thought the cop had planted the drugs, until later he found out that his cousin Jerv put it in the ashtray and forgot all about it. Ace tried to eat the case so they would let Rain go, but the prosecutor on the case in that county wasn't having it. They held the charges over Rain as well. However, they agreed on giving her probation for a few years, only after Ace plead out to do four years of jail time in New Jersey State Prison.

"Word!" Ace smirked after his lawyer at the time informed him that he was allowed to remain out on bail, until after Christmas and the New Year's holiday season to start his bid. Of course, Ace never turned himself in. His motto was: **I pay up when they catch up!**

Earlier that day before calling Ace and giving him the news about the Feds, Rain went to the porch to grab the mail. Soon as Rain reached the mailbox, she noticed a dark blue suburban parked outside of her home. Her antennas immediately went up as she opened her mailbox, and when she pulled the mail out, several white men emerged from the truck and walked straight up to her. Ace had schooled Rain over the years since she'd been with him, and that's why her mind instantly thought --- *That's the police!*

"Excuse me Ma'am…Ma'am. We're here to take Alton Coles off the streets!" The agent said, as he flashed his gold badge; his colleagues did the same, not fazing or scaring Rain one bit.

"So, why are you telling me?" She snapped.

"Because he lives here with you, doesn't he?"

"Look, Ace left me and my kids months ago. He don'tstay here no more and I haven't seen or heard from him since he left. His no good ass has two kids by me, and he hasn't even seen his kids since he left us." Rain said, giving the federal agents a lot of bullshit. Rain was good at being deceptive.

"Ma'am, do you think we can take a look around the house for a second?" One of the agents asked, figuring that she was lying. He was going off that fact that the tip he received three months ago about Ace staying at this very address in South West Philly had to be true. After being in bureau for a few years, the agent saw first hand how many loyal women protected, lied and even went to jail for their criminal spouses, all in the name of love and loyalty. He just wanted to make sure that the woman standing before him wasn't another one of the so-called *down to ride or die for her man type.*

Catching on quickly to the agent's question, Rain knew they only wanted to see if there were any signs of Ace's clothes freshly lingering around the house.

"Ain't no need to search my house. I done told you that Ace don't live here nomore, nor does he sleep here anymore, so it's no use in searching my damn house! What y'all need to do is go find his other bitch, come back and let me know where he's at, so I can pay his ass a visit too."

"Shit, I got a chicken bone to pick with him my damn self, huh!" Rain ranted, pouring it on thick and coming off very believable.

The agents looked at Rain funny, because she seemed very convincing to them. One agent pulled out his business card out and gave it to her, figuring that she hated Ace enough to actually assist them in arresting him. *A woman scorned is very dangerous and knows no bounds*, the agent thought to himself with a smile as Rain took the card from him.

"Just give us a call if he shows up or calls you okay?" The agent said, while back pedaling to the truck.

"I sure will." Rain lied as the federal agents jumped back in their truck and drove off. After making sure they were gone, Rain bolted back in the house to call Ace immediately. As soon as he answered the phone, she gave Ace every single detail of the incident as it happened.

"Damn…you did good Rain." Ace told her.

"So what you gonna do now?" Rain asked.

"Look, I can't come back to the house now. At least not until I find out what the fuck is going on. Ya dig? It ain't like we renting that house; we paying a mortgage, so we can't just up and leave at the drop of a dime. I mean the kids have their friends, school and a decent place to live. Plus I don't wanna just up and move y'all, cause then them Feds gonna know you bullshitted them. Right now they in the dark. Ya dig?" Ace explained.

"I understand, but I'm gonna miss my Teddy bear," she whined.

Listen, you already know I got plenty of places to lay my head at during times like this. So whenever you need to see me to get some money or sex, I got chu…all you got to do is call me and we'll meet at your mom's crib. We'll make that thang happen just like in the old days." Ace said, matter of factly, but in a joking manner.

"Boy you crazy!" She replied, as they both laughed. "For real tho Al, you know I love you so I'm always with you no matter what, but can you please be careful?" Rain said, sincerely.

"I will be very careful. I love you too." Ace replied.

After leaving Ace's house and heading back to the field office, one agent mentioned the fact that he'd been hearing Ace's name a lot lately.

"So what you wanna do?" His partner asked, already knowing the answer.

"I think we should start an investigation up on this guy and see what turns up on him. You saw it for yourself. We go to the guy's house to bring him in on a petty fugitive warrant, and that shit looks like the inside of a Hollywood actor's house. That nigga's bitch looks rather intelligent, she probably even has a job, but I doubt she makes enough money to live like that. Nope, something's not right and I suspect our guy is doing way more illegal activity than what he's wanted for."

According to the agents, serving fugitive warrants and bringing in the perps was decent money on the side. If a person had an out of state warrant, then the fugitive task force could be sent out to get them anywhere cause they are actually the Feds. After witnessing Ace's immaculate home, one of the agents saw it as a potential bust for him and another stepping stone to his success in the Federal Bureau of Investigations.

*   *   *

Back on the other side of Philly, Ace was mad as hell that he had to cancel his birthday party this year, but he knew he had made the right decision. He simply couldn't take a chance of going out and celebrate to get pinched on a humbug. He trained himself not to make any stupid or careless moves, plus he needed and wanted to find out which federal agency actually came looking for him and more importantly – why?

After cancelling all of his party plans, Ace called up his good friend and lawyer, Scott Griffith, who answered on the third ring. "Attorney Scott Griffith speaking."

"Yeah, Scott it's me Ace."

"Hey, what's up Ace? How are you?"

"Not too good. I need to know who is Special Agent Michael Nikko and why is he looking for me?"

"Hmmm, let me have his name again?" Scott said as he pulled out a notepad and an expensive pen to write with.

"It's Special Agent Michael Nikko." Ace replied as he read the card.

"Uh, huh I know Mike…Let me give him a call and see what I can get out of him, and then I will get back with you immediately. In the meantime, you do me a favor and stay out of sight until I find out exactly what's going on – alright!" Attorney Griffith said.

"Yeah, yeah I hear you." Ace said and exchanged a few more words with him before ending the call.

If it ain't one thing, it's another, was all Ace could think about – wondering why the Feds were on his back all of a sudden…

CHAPTER 4
(Gotti - Trust)

GOTTI WAS ON HIS WAY TO THE BARBER SHOP in Southwest Philly on 70th and Elmwood Street called *Center of Attraction*. His barber and long time friend, Barry, is considered by many the sharpest barber in Southwest Philly. He is also one of the sharpest barbers to come out of the Tri-State area all together. Standing 5-foot-5, Gotti had a chubby brown skin frame, but he hid it well by wearing the best clothes money could buy. Gotti had a closet full of expensive clothes that could probably fill an entire house between him and his girlfriend Tiffany.

Tiffany possessed a sexual chocolate 5-foot- 6 130 pound frame that had all the curves a woman could want. Being a street diva and Gotti being a street hustler, they complimented each other well. Gotti spoiled Tiffany to death. He bought her clothes, jewelry and always kept her hair and nails done. They looked great together and shared a son name Boo-Boo.

As Gotti and Tiffany entered the barbershop together, all the men's eyes zoomed in on Tiffany's shapely hips. Today her perfectly shaped ass suffocated in the tightest pair of Versace for attention. She also had on a fitted Versace shirt, revealing most of her flat stomach and some bad ass Louis Vuitton platform sandals with a matching Louis Vuitton bag – that put the finishing touch to her outfit.

Noticing all the gawking eyes, Gotti never allowed other men lusting looks over his woman to bother him. Truth of the matter was, Gotti didn't care who stared at his woman. He made her fly, so he didn't mind if she flaunted it and others looked at her. She was his to keep, and he knew in his heart that nobody but him could get that pussy from Tiffany.

"Yo who's car you driving?" Gotti asked Barry while getting his haircut.

Ace would let Barry drive his cars, bikes, and trucks whenever Barry wanted to because he knew that Barry was a responsible youngbull. Although Barry owned the barbershop, people often mistakenly thought that Ace owned the shop, because he hung out there alot and they knew he owned two other shops himself.

"Damn Youngbull, it's like that? You can't tell me whose car you driving?" Gotti asked again, invading his thoughts.

"It's my man Ace's car." Barry answered.

Gotti glanced out the window, taking in the triple black Acura Legend Coupe LS with 18-inch Carlson chrome rims. The breathtaking vehicle had a crazy ass system by Alpine and just seeing the car shining under the gleaming sun made Gotti want it.

"Damn! That thang looks good as shit!" "Do he wanna sell it?" Gotti asked.

"I'm not sure. I'll ask him cause that nigga do got all kinds of toys." Barry replied and then said, "Listen, y'all two need to hook up anyway cause both of y'all remind me of each other. I'm sure Ace could look out for you on the weight side of things or whatever you're getting. Plus I already told him about you. He'll front you whatever you buy from him. I know you will come up if you fuck with him," Barry whispered to Gotti.

As the noise level rose up in the shop, Gotti told Barry that he wanted to get nine ounces right now.

"Let me call'em and see whats up?" Barry replied.

"You do that and call me when you ready for me to pick it up." Gotti said.

With that said, Gotti and his girl, Tiffany left the shop with all eyes glued to Tiffany's beautiful shapely behind. Once outside, Gotti took another look at Ace's Acura Legend before he and Tiffany jumped in his Infinity J-30 and drove off…

    *   *   *

TWO HOURS LATER, Barry saw Ace and told him what Gotti wanted. Barry informed Ace that Gotti was the person he'd been telling him about.

"I want chu' to meet the nigga yourself and look out for him. He's a good nigga." Barry said, convincingly.

"Aight, tell'em to come on." Ace told him.

When Gotti arrived, Ace realized that Gotti wasn't a complete stranger after all. They had seen each other in traffic and actually did business once or twice. Ace just didn't know that Gotti was buying it through his uncle sometimes. Ace took a liking to Gotti because he was quiet, and had a laid back kind of demeanor.

Ace ended up giving Gotti nine ounces and fronted him nine more.

"Welcome to the team." Ace said with a smile, giving Gotti some dap.

"Good looking out fam." Gotti replied, while shaking Ace's hand.

Ace was fair with Gotti from jump street. He would give Gotti good numbers on the half of kilo of fish scale cocaine at 10,500 dollars. Gotti had only wanted 9 ounces for 5,800 dollars, but he had an extra couple of thousand on him so he gave Ace 8,500 dollars, which left him with a 2, 000 dollar debt he owed Ace.

After their first official business meeting, Ace and Gotti got off to a good start and began getting plenty of money together. Ace knew Gotti was a good dude because he would pay off all of the debts that he owed to Ace right off the top. He would usually have it the next day. Gaining more and more of Ace's trust, Gotti eventually got rewarded by getting the whole kilo from Ace. Ace gave Gotti his first kilo and the two became good friends as time went on.

Gotti hustled on 55th Street, right off Woodland Avenue, between Woodland and Greenway Avenue; a block that was around the corner from Ace's grandmother's house. The whole neighborhood called her Nana.

Gotti wore glasses, looking like a smart, school nerd that most bullies loved to pick on. Some people would sleep on Gotti, thinking shit was sweet just because of the glasses. Howver, make no mistake about it, Gotti was far from a chump. In fact, he could be very dangerous at times...

One night, two guys dressed in all black rode pass the bar on 55th and Woodland and saw Gotti get in his car. One of them noticed who Gotti was because he'd seen him with Ace a few weeks ago. The two *stick up kids* watched Gotti while they smoked a laced blunt full of weed and crack. As soon as Gotti pulled off, they did the same and followed Gotti home.

Once Gotti got home, he got out of the car and walked up the steps. Thinking Gotti was sweet, the two stick up kids jumped out of their car and tried to get a quick come up on Gotti's money and jewelry.

"Ay Gotti!" One of the men called out, as they approached him.

Gotti looked their way and his street senses kicked in automatically. Feeling a weird vibe, Gotti began backing up.

"Don't move nigga!" One of them ordered, pulling out his gun.

In that split second, Gotti dove straight through his front window like a stunt man, thwarting any attempts of a robbery. Already high, the two would be robbers got nervous from the noise of shattering glass and took off running.

Getting to his feet quickly, Gotti ran to his stash spot and grabbed one of his special toys: A semi automatic mac-11, with an extended clip. Ready for whatever, Gotti bolted back out of the house. He didn't see the two guys, so he got in his car and drove down the block looking for them.

When he stopped at the red light on 52nd and Greenway, Gotti noticed a car turning the corner and spotted the same two guys who had just tried to rob him. He rolled down the window and as soon as they rode past him, Gotti let the mac-11 sing its own deadly tune.

Boc! Boc! Boc! Boc! Boc! Boc! Boc! Boc! Boc! Boc! Boc! Boc! Boc! Was all you could hear being fired from the mac-11 as Gotti tore their car into pieces.

Sccccurrr! Were the sounds of the stick up boys' car tires screeching as they got away from the onslaught of hissing missiles that tried to take their heads off. They got away, but lost a few windows and hub caps in the process. Also, they gained about twelve bullet holes in the body of the car too, but even after taking the heavy gunfire, surprisingly nobody got hit.

The following day, Gotti went to re-up on his supply of drugs and told Ace about his previous night's encounter.

When Gotti pulled up, Ace noticed a hole in Gotti's driver side mirror and said, "Damn, what happened to the mirror pimp?"

"Man, I shot my own shit last night tryna tear these two niggas ass up!" They both laughed.

Then Ace asked, "So, what happened pimp?"
Gotti explained the whole ordeal from start to finish. After Gotti described the two guys to him, Ace wore a puzzled look on his face.

"Describe dem two niggas again. They sound familiar. What kind of car was they driving?" Ace asked.

"One of them was short, like my height, kinda built like he's in shape. They were driving a blue Corsica, and that piece of shit looked like it was crashed on one side. Why, you saw them before or something?" Gotti asked.

"I don't know why, but that car sounds so familiar pimp!" Ace repeated, while wearing a blank stare…

CHAPTER 5
7-ELEVEN (CLOSE CALL)

As Gotti and Ace were handling business, Ace told Chuck to stop at the store to grab a few items for him. Chuck was a dark skinned short brother who stood 5-foot-7 and weighing roughly 170 pounds. Chuck had a head full of waves and no beard.

Pulling into the 7-Eleven around the corner from Ace's spot, Chuck jumped out his ride and rushed inside the store. As he entered the store, there were several customers there along with a slew of off duty and on duty cops. The on duty cops were chilling on their lunch breaks. Most of them were plain-clothes narcotics officers. Chuck grabbed a few items and went to the register to pay for his things.

"Dat will be 18 dollars sir." The Arab clerk said in a heavy accent, while placing Chuck's items in the bag.

"Man, yall getting too much money up in here…18 dollars for three boxes of sandwich bags, a bag of ice and some baking soda, that's crazy, but it's a hustle!" Chuck said, in a mocking tone.

"Yes, but you have zee jumbo baking soda, zee jumbo cost more money and we sell zee best ice, thank you very much." The clerk responded. "You good Osama! You'sa funny motherfucker!" Chuck said, as he laughed at the man's funny accent, and jumped inside his grey LS400 Lexus, never having a clue that the plain- clothes cops were watching his every move.

Detective Riddick, a 38-year-old black cop, was the neighborhood drug dealer's worst nightmare. If Riddick was out to get you or if you just happened to cross his path, and he thought you were up to no good then he would plot to get you one way or another.

"Say partner, did you just see the guy who just bought everything associated with drug paraphernalia?" Riddick asked.

"Yeah, I saw his dumb ass and if he didn't get in that Lexus, I still would have pegged him for someone who was about to go cook up some crack." Riddick's partner replied.

"That stupid nigga lucky that we're off the clock, cause I'd follow him and bust his natural black ass!" Riddick said, as they both laughed.

Chuck pulled up at Ace's dope spot right around the corner from 7-Eleven and honked his horn. Ace was taking a shit, so he looked out the upstairs bathroom window, and he saw that it was Chuck.

"Nigga chill the fuck out with that horn. "You drawing!" Ace shouted.

It was a peaceful neighborhood, mixed with both white and black people. The neighbors never noticed all the traffic Ace had coming in and out of the house serving playas from Chester, Delaware, Pittsburgh, West Chester, New Jersey, Baltimore and other surrounding areas. Only people from Philly that came to this spot were Gotti, Chuck and Uncle Hak, who were all part of his immediate team.

Gotti was pulling out of the garage in his Infinity Coupe when Chuck drove up to the house.

"Hurry up Blacky!" Chuck yelled out to Ace.

Meanwhile, Detective Riddick was sitting at the light on 70th and Dicks when he looked up and saw the same Lexus that had just left the 7-Eleven five minutes ago. Seeing the same black male who drove the car now talking to someone in a house window, Detective Riddick's curiosity got the best of him. He wanted to see what was going on.

When Riddick saw a familiar car pulling out of the garage of the same house, he knew something fishy was going on.

"Well looky here, it's Gotti Baldwin, off duty or not we may have a nice bust on our hands being that those two guys are together. After what we just saw at the store with the perp in the Lexus, we may have just hit a lick!" Riddick said with excitement.

With that said, Detective Riddick's partner began tailing Gotti Baldwin's car and called for back up to secure the house where the other perp was standing, talking to Ace.

Ace was wiping his ass when he heard a strange voice yell, "Get the fuck on the ground now chump!"

When Ace first looked out the window, he thought some niggas were robbing Chuck because the men had on glasses, plain clothes and fitted hats. As Ace went for his gun to help Chuck, he suddenly heard the strange black man say, "This area is secured. The perp was talking to someone on the second floor on the west side of the location."

Oh shit, it's the police! Ace thought and immediately went to get his dope so he could get rid of it.

Outside, Chuck was shitting in his drawers, saying, "I don't live here. I was just visiting a friend. I got a license and I work at the juvenile detention center." Chuck started straight up bitching…

Back in the house, Ace ran downstairs and made sure that all the doors were locked. After shutting all the shades on the windows, Ace quickly sprung into action and began flushing two kilos of raw, uncut fish scale cocaine….

Around the corner, Gotti suddenly noticed the Narcs on his back and mentally prepared himself to take them on high-speed chase if they tried to pull him over. Seconds later the cops hit the disco lights, in attempt to pull him over. Once Gotti saw those flashing lights, he mashed his foot on the gas pedal, pushing his car like a driver in a Nascar race. Gotti hit a few corners and made a few illegal turns, losing them shortly; just enough so he could get out the car to run.

As he ran up a small street, Gotti noticed a lady carrying some grocery bags from her trunk. He had the cops beat at least a few blocks and was trying to hide instead of continuing to run. Looking at an opportunity in his face, Gotti dove right into the lady's trunk and showed her a big ass stack of money.

"Please shut your trunk and let me hide in here until the cops leave, or drive me outta here. It's about 3000 dollars or more here," he said waiving the money at her. "You can have all dis shit. It's yours, please just help me!" "I'm cool everybody knows me!" Gotti pleaded.

The lady knew exactly who Gotti was and knew he was part of Ace's crew. She wasn't into the streets, but she respected the fact that Ace and his squad ran the neighborhood peacefully. Truth be told, she needed that money for so many damn reasons, so she quickly agreed to assist him. She immediately shut the trunk with Gotti inside, jumped back in her car and calmly drove off. Detective Riddick and his partner were looking high and low for Gotti, having no idea that he escaped their pursuit. The only evidence they possessed was Gotti's car, because he jumped out and left it, but it was clean.

Chuck tried to explain so many different stories just so they would let his monkey ass go it was pathetic. The only thing that stopped the narc, which by now had transformed into a full pledged team, from gaining entry was two of the prettiest, meanest pit pulls you ever seen in Ace's back yard. The narcs plotted on entering through an opened basement window, while neighbors watched in awe.

They had no warrant to break into the property, nor enough evidence or probable cause to produce an affidavit to get one, but they tried anyway. They waited and schemed on getting inside the house one way or another – legally or illegally they wanted in.

Tattoo, an all black male pit with white spots on his chest and around his eyes, and Hanna, an all white female pit protected the house. Ace had fighting pit bulls in other locations, but Tattoo and Hanna were his people eaters! These two dogs would go crazy to bite and shake a motherfucka to death. Unless you were Ace, Rain or the kids, they would readily attack without warning.

After having no luck in finding Gotti Baldwin, Detective Riddick and his partner returned to the scene of the property on 70th Street where the narcs already had the house surrounded. Riddick approached the detectives who were interrogating Chuck.

"What's up with this perp?" Riddick asked, staring down at Chuck.

The detective explained everything Chuck had said which Riddick automatically took as a pack of lies. Riddick already knew a perp would say anything just to get away.

"Well, we been here for over an hour now watching everything," Riddick said, looking at Chuck. "And soon as the warrant arrives, we going up in that house, so if your boy is smart, he'd start flushing."

"What do you mean we?" You just got here." Chuck replied.

"Oh, I was here and if I would've caught your little friend, Gotti Baldwin, we'd be having one big happy reunion right now!" Riddick said sarcastically…

MEANWHILE INSIDE THE HOUSE, Ace was still washing his hands because they looked like he stuck them in a pot of cake batter, from flushing and breaking up all the coke, so it could go down the toilet easier.

Peering out the window, Ace noticed a K-9 dog specialist unit pulling up at the house. The specialist tried to trick the dogs to go in their cages, so they could gain easy entry inside the trap house.

Although nervous, Ace didn't panic. He simply played it smooth and called Rain. She answered on the second ring, sounding sexy as ever.

"Hello?" Rain said.

"Yo, listen, I may be getting ready to go to jail!" Ace said while trying to keep calm.

"What! What's going on Al?" Rain asked in a frantic tone, worried and concerned.

"Nothing I can't handle." He said quickly, peeping out the window to see what the cops were doing. "But listen, when they come in here and get me Imma go ahead and rock with my alias jawn, Lamar Johnson." Ace said.

"Say no more, I got chu. I love you." Rain told him and ended the call.

Rain was his ride or die and mother to his kids, she definitely knew the drill. More importantly, she stayed on point for times like now. She knew to go along with Ace's story if the cops called her phone. Rain knew to give them a bogus story along the lines of her meeting Lamar at a bar the night before. When she woke up to go to work, she saw that she was late and rushed out the house, leaving him there. She would stick to that story until the very end. Rain, being a master of deception, would pour it on thick by acting concerned and asking the cops was anything wrong, what happened, and is her house fine? Then she would put the icing on the cake by telling them that she was on her way home.

Their charade worked every time because Ace carried a fake I.D. with the name Lamar Johnson on it, but this time things were different. Ace was a little concerned, knowing that the Lamar Johnson I.D. had an active fugitive warrant on his head.

Ace thought quickly and decided to drop the I.D. down the heat vent and put his safe deposit key in the fish tank that was filled with Piranhas. Ace reluctantly placed the keys underneath a small light- house that sat inside the fish tank, and then he ran inside Rain's bedroom.

Once inside the bedroom, Ace turned on the air conditioner and TV, and then set a bottle of allergy pills on top of the dresser.

Outside, the cops were using a piece of meat that no canine could resist. After they lured the pitbulls in their cages and secured them, they quickly rushed the yard and climbed through the basement window.

Ace heard the cops soon as they entered the house, yelling and screaming, "POLICE! WE KNOW YOU IN HERE! SO COME ON OUT AND NOBODY WILL GET HURT!"

Finally, they reached upstairs and banged on the bedroom door where Ace was now butt ass naked, acting like he was asleep.

"COME ON OUT WITH YOUR HANDS UP!" Ace heard a cop yelling, as they banged on the door with their guns drawn.

"Yo, what's going on?" Ace said in a fake groggy tone like he'd just woke up.

"IF YOU DON'T COME OUT OF THERE SLOWLY WITH YOUR HANDS UP, IT'S GOING TO BE A TRAGEDY UP IN HERE!" An angry cop yelled.

"Man, I'm scared and half sleep. You can come in. I'm not moving!" Ace called out in his fake me out, innocent, schoolboy tone.

When the cops bum rushed the bedroom, they roughed Ace up a little bit while restraining him. One cop had the decency to slide some jeans on Ace and led him out the bedroom.

"Why you ain't open up the door?" One cop asked.

"I was out cold. I got allergies so I took six of dem jawms and was in a coma. I didn't know what the fuck was going on until y'all said y'all was the police."

"Is this your house?" The cop asked.

"Naw, I'm Lamar Williams and this house belongs to this chick name Rain I met last night. I think she's at work right now, but here go her number." Ace said and gave them Rain's phone number so they could confirm his story.

Although Ace's story seemed real and corroborated with everything that Rain told them, Sergeant Arnold was no dummy. He suspected something fishy with the guy they had in custody, as one of his officers suddenly called him down to the kitchen.

"Look here Sarge, I think they just got finished cooking some crack in here." The officer pointed out, showing Sgt. Arnold the warm Pyrex pot sitting on the stove.

"See there Sarge, it's crack residue all around the edges."

Sgt. Arnold smiled. He suddenly thought he had the answer and walked into the living room where Ace was being held. Sgt. Arnold was a *G.I. Joe* looking mothafucka.

"I'm going to say this to you one time and one time only…" Sgt. Arnold gave Ace a stern, evil look, trying to instill fear in him. "If I find out that you a bad guy who sells crack to kids and shit, I'll be back. And if I do come back, that pretty black Mercedes Benz and the hot rod in the garage is mine!" He threatened, glancing around the living room, taking a quick inventory of all the stylish furniture, the huge fish tank and the flat screen TV before continuing.

"I'm taking the TV, the fish tank and all the fancy furniture with me too, and I'll personally put those ferocious dogs to sleep myself. Do you understand me Mr. Williams?"

I'm sorry officer, but you definitely got the wrong idea about me. Like I told you before, I don't live here." Ace lied with a straight face. Before Sgt. Arnold could respond, Ace put emphasis on his fake name: Lamar Williams. He also gave them his son's social security number and birth date. He only changed the year of birth to fit his own alias. The clutch time alias came back clean a few moments later, and the cops left the property without giving him any more hassle.

"Damn that was a close ass call!" Ace mumbled to himself as he watched the cops drive away from his house…

CHAPTER 6
Repercussion (revenge)

A few weeks passed and Ace was just getting back to normal. He couldn't go home to Rain and the kids because of the fugitive task force, and now he had to switch up on one of his best stash houses due to the close call encounter with the narcs. However, the decision to switch up couldn't have came at a better time, because he was getting too comfortable at the original stash house anyway.

Ace pulled up and parked in front of Erica's house across the street from Paschall Projects. As he got out of the car heading towards her house, he did a double look up the street where he thought he noticed someone run off. His thoughts quickly emerged *"I have to calm the hell down"* once he saw that no one was there. When he approached, Erica was sitting on the steps in front of her house. He could tell something was bothering her.

"What's up sexy? Why you looking all mad?" Ace asked.

"Cause I wanted this smoker to wash my car, so I asked Corey to move his damn car out my parking spot, but he keep ignoring me." Erica replied irritated.

"Where dat nigga at?" Ace asked, hating to see one of his chics sporting disappointment on her face.

"He right up there." Erica replied as she pointed up the street.

"Corey, move your damn car!" Erica yelled out once again.

Corey was dark skinned and stood 6-foot with a medium muscular build. He would have kept ignoring her as he did earlier, had Ace not been there.

"My bad." Corey said to Ace as he finally went to move his car.

Ace stared at the four-door Corsica and suddenly noticed that it was riddled with bullets and smashed on one side. Corey rolled down the window to kick it with Ace.

"When you gonna let me eat wit cha?" Corey asked Ace.

"When you hungry enough to eat and have good table manners!" Ace replied nonchalantly.

41

Corey just shook his head and laughed as he drove off.

"That nigga must be getting high too, now that he hanging with that crack head ass Moe." Erica laughed to herself as Ace was putting two and two together. *"Damn, I'm betting it was Moe and Corey who tried to stick Gotti up"* Ace had thought to himself. It all started to add up now. Stick-ups were Corey's twist. Which is the very reason Ace didn't holla at him on the money side of things. When Ace pulled up he could have sworn he saw someone swiftly slide off. Erica just confirmed that Moe and Corey had been hanging together tough, so it probably was Moe that Ace saw quickly disappear into the projects. *"Man, they got me fucked up. I'm a kill both of them nut ass niggas."* Ace thought to himself.

"Ace! Ace!" Erica yelled breaking his chain of thought.

"Damn! You lunchin. What the hell were you just thinking about? I had asked you can we do it real quick?" Erica said with a freaky smile. Ace ignored her as he used his cell phone to make a call.

RING! RING! RING!

"Yo! What up pimp, where you at?" Ace asked of Gotti.

"Umm, I'm driving down Greenway Avenue, why what's up?" Gotti asked.

"I knew I had seen that Corsica before. I need you to meet me as soon as it gets dark. We got a date with them two bitches who tried to fuck you, now I'm trying to get some of dat pussy. Ya dig?" Ace retorted. Gotti knew exactly what Ace was talking about and responded, "Say no more!"

They hung up and Ace told Erica he would be back, but quickly noticed she was now standing in the doorway half naked pulling his dick out of his jeans. He couldn't resist her once she got on her knees and began sucking, moaning, and slurping on his dick while caressing his balls, as she slowly continued to bob her head back and forth like a steady heartbeat. Erica knew exactly how Ace liked it. She slowly deep throated as much of his dick that she could, as she moaned with saliva dripping out both sides of her mouth.

"Shitttt!" Ace moaned in extreme pleasure, as Erica used her thick wet saliva as a lubricant to slowly jerk his dick off with both hands while she seductively sucked it at the same time.

Erica knew how to get Ace rocks off. The slurping sound along with her sexual facial expressions she made as she gave him some bomb ass head always turned him on even more. His dick began to rise to maximum peek. The head of his dick swelled up to the size of a peach, and the long, thick dick shaft now reached a whopping ten inches in length. But no matter how good any woman sucked Ace's dick, he couldn't cum from just getting head alone. Head was simply good foreplay for him. Although some head was very enjoyable, Ace needed to feel some warm, wet friction that only the pussy could produce before he could bust a nut.

"Yeaahhh ma! Suck this dick and play with ya pussy. I want that pussy hot, wet and ready for daddy." Ace moaned out in a take-charge tone of voice as he held the back of her head. Ace figured he had a few hours by night fall before him and Gotti were to meet up, so he shut the door and concentrated on the bomb ass head he was receiving and the good pussy he was about to hit...

      *   *   *

It was starting to get dark around 9:10 p.m. Gotti and Ace met up at one of Gotti's spots. Both of them dressed in all black Dickie sets, ready to put in work.

"Man, I'm a put this whole mothfuckin clip in Moe's lil fat ass! That nigga must have been smoking crack to try me like that." Gotti retorted.

"Yeah, that nut ass nigga way out of his league, with dat want to be gangsta take boy shit. He not even built like that. Plus, he went to the point of no return at both our spots, so he gotta go!" Ace replied nonchalantly.

Ace and Gotti drove out Paschall Projects in a gray Ford Taurus and parked on the back street near the horse stables right outside the projects. Ace knew exactly where to find Corey and went right to the location he saw him earlier that day. Ace didn't see Corey or Moe right away so he stayed in the cut for about twenty minutes. Corey finally came out of his cousin's speak easy inside the projects.

Ace looked over at Gotti then gave him the confirmation: there was one of the guys that tried to rob him. Soon as Corey got to his car, he saw two men dressed in black quickly appear out of nowhere like thieves in the night. Corey noticed the cold familiar dark faces, and within a blink of an eye his stomach had turned to knots. Everything seemed to be in slow motion to him as he panicked and screamed out, "Nooooo, I would have never disrespected you like that. I didn't know he was ya folks A." **Boc! Boc! Boc! Boc! Boc! Boc! Chop! Chop! Chop! Chop! Boc!** He never even got the chance to finish his pathetic plea as the two black 40-caliber handguns rang out their deadly tunes....

       *   *   *

Twenty minutes later, Erica called Ace to tell him somebody had killed Corey. She was describing it while the cops were still all over the crime scene. When Ace asked who did it, she told him that according to the cops nobody saw anything at all. Ace smiled to himself on the other end of the phone, as he told Erica it probably was those Jamaican cats, whom killed him – cause Corey had robbed them not too long ago.

Ace knew whenever he did have to put a murder game down; he'd always go ahead and spread some false rumors about the situation. This time was no different, better yet perfect. He knew Erica's big gossiping, ghetto ass mouth would be the first one to actually start spreading the rumor he just planted thinking it was truth to it. After Ace hung up with Erica, he told Gotti she explained how Moe was snapping out acting a fool crying all over Corey's dead body.

"Man that nigga Moe lucky that fuckin helicopter out there, cause I'd use this same gun to go kill his nut ass tonight too." Ace said violently.

"Shit we can go back out there later on tonight and get his ass too if you want. That nigga will probably be around there all night slipping or chasing that glass dick." Gotti said humorously, yet serious as a heart attack.

"Nah, he gets a pass tonight. It's way too hot and risky out there right now for that. Shit, it should have been Moe's ass tonight anyway. But we gone get his ass real soon." Ace assured.

       *   *   *

The next day, Moe was still high from smoking crack all night. He had been up panicking and stressing over Corey's death. He realized he ran out of money and was desperate for more crack, so he decided to do a quick lick. He wrote a small note on a piece of paper and headed to a small bank in Yeadon in attempt to rob the teller for the money in the drawer.

Moe had been robbing banks from time to time, and he would get away with anywhere between 3,000 to 5,000 dollars at a time. Although some of the threatening notes had been misspelled *"Theres ah bomb in dis bag. So give me da money and yah drawers. Don't be herow or else!"* Moe's dumb ass didn't look convincing enough to blow something up to any bank teller. The robbery attempt today would have turned out differently if Corey were not dead. Moe's work was sloppy and it didn't help that he was up all night high off crack, mourning the death of his partner in crime. Mo-Mo knew deep down inside his heart that Ace was somehow behind Corey's vicious killing – he was extremely nervous now, because he knew sooner or later Ace was gone get his ass too if he didn't get the hell out of dodge asap.

Today, when he entered the bank his whole demeanor made him look suspicious. Moe didn't even notice the two fully uniformed officers waiting to cash a check from inside their police cruiser in the drive thru line of the bank. Once he handed the teller the note, she panicked and quickly pushed the silent alarm. Moe didn't even realize that she had pushed the alarm; he simply just got nervous when he saw the two cops cashing their checks at the drive thru window.

Moe ran for the door, but was tackled to the ground by the bank's manager who happened to be an athletic built white man in his mid 40s. The cops came in the bank to assist the manager and arrested Moe. This particular bank happened to be federally insured, so Moe was up shit creek without a paddle. He was taken into custody and transported to the William Green Federal building on 2nd and Arch…

*   *

*

45

Meanwhile, in a cornfield off the side of a road somewhere in Maryland, missing persons and the Lancaster county sheriff's were conducting an accidental death investigation. The body of a young, black male was discovered dead. The unidentified white drug informant took the investigators straight to the body of a young man he knew only as Teewee.

It had been three months now since Jermond Walters – aka- Teewee had been reported missing. The hot, muggy weather throughout the summer months, along with the help of some wild animals and insects had caused the body of the young unidentifiable male to be listed as a John Doe.

Although the clothes and sneakers the dead carcass had on fit the description Teewee was last seen in, there was absolutely no way to positively identify the body. The crows, flies, mosquitos, worms, mice and other field animals ate at his eyes, ears and mouth. Different body parts were swollen because of all the blood that shifted to one side of the body, and the scorching summer sun burned the darkened dead skin to a light crisp.

As the sheriff held his nose to block the foul stench from the body that permeated the air, he noticed something strange. There appeared to be a few ink pen-sized holes in the shirt of the John Doe. Although the cooperating source had taken the investigating authorities to the unfortunate gravesite, the young sheriff didn't know if he could fully believe the source's story.

As a missing person agent was snapping a series of photos the Lancaster County sheriff thought to himself, *'I don't know if this guy really overdosed yet, but if this poor kid was actually violently murdered, whoever is responsible needs to be brought to justice. So, until lab reports confirm the body through dental records, and rule the death an accident, this case is going to stay active as a possible homicide'...*

   *   *   *

Once Moe was federally processed, his high began to wear off. He asked the two agents who had taken over his booking process was there anything he could do to help himself. The agent, a white man in his early 40s, responded to his question; he told Moe that it depended on what kind of information he had to tell them in order to determine a cooperation deal. Because of all the surveillance they had in evidence, they were planning to charge Moe not only for this one bank, but also for a string of other unsolved bank robberies.

The agent had bluffed Moe, cause all they really had on him was one bank robbery. The Feds know exactly how to scare cowards like Moe. The FBI could smell a coward a mile away faster than a dog can smell a bitch in heat. It didn't matter to Moe anyway because he knew it wasn't safe for him on the streets anymore. He was afraid of Ace more than he was afraid of the Feds.

Moe had a flashback and thought to himself about the time before he started getting high off crack when he went along with Ace on a shooting. Gary John had made the grave mistake of robbing Ace at gunpoint and leaving him alive afterwards.

For some strange reason Gary must have never learned an important respectful rule for all hood niggas across the globe. **Wolves take from sheep; they don't take from other wolves!**

It was pouring down raining on this particular night and Ace had been laying in the dark between some bushes for at least 25 minutes. Gary's car was parked across the street from the house whose yard Ace was hiding in. A black male and female were running towards their car, in an attempt to hurry up and get out of the rain. Moe was slouched down inside the get away car when he noticed that Ace patiently assumed the position to act out this deadly event. Moe saw the park lights flash on Gary's car, showing someone was close enough to the car by disarming the alarm and unlocking the doors by remote.

As Gary hopped in the car, he never even had a chance to think about starting it. Ace had run up to the vehicle militant style and shot Gary through the car windows, while Moe shot from across the street through the opposite side of the car's door. A hailstorm of bullets hit Gary in his face, chest, and stomach as the female screamed in fear of her life. She refused to even look up at the assailants, praying they would at least spare her. Her prayer was answered; Ace spared her simply because she was innocent. She had nothing to do with the personal beef Ace had with Gary. Although Gary survived the deadly attack, he had stayed in a coma for two long months and now lived off one lung, no peripheral vision and a defecation bag. Luckily he lived through the violent shooting, but the fear he will have for sitting in a car with intent on warming it up will haunt him for the rest of his life.

Moe remembered that incident point for point, and he knew the only reason Gary was still alive was because the tech nine Ace had used jammed up after five or six shots. So, Moe knew exactly how dangerous Ace was and what he was capable of doing. Moe made a quick choice, and then looked at the agents.

"I got some information on a drug dealer from around my way. His name is Ace Capone. I know about several shootings, murders, and other people who are a part of his drug organization." Mo-Mo said with a shaken voice.

The agents glanced at each other in disbelief, as if they had just hit a jackpot or won the lottery.

"If you help us get Capone, you will go home scot-free." The one agent replied, matter of factly.

CHAPTER 7
Crazy Baby Momma

Kim was talking on the phone with her best friend, Niema, thanking her for giving her some good advice to help her snag a big time drug dealer.

"Girl! That shit worklike a charm. You was right Niema. After I went to the doctor and had my walls scrapped, I got pregnant like the next month. All I had to do was keep him horny. After he bust a nut or two with the condom on, I waited and woke him up by sucking his big dick in the middle of the night for another round." Kim said.

"No you didn't?" Niema gasped in a joking manner.

"Gurl What! Once he woke up and realized that it wasn't any more condoms, he just went up in me raw. I'm not fuckin nobody but him anyway, plus I told him I couldn't get pregnant that easy. I'm glad that I am now because he be punishing my little ass. My coochie be sore as hell from all that sex. Child, I had to get used to the size, okay." Kim said in a playful, laughing mood, which caused Niema to laugh as well.

"Shiiiiid, bitch you all the way in now cause you pregnant and now that nigga belongs to you." Niema told her.

"Yeah, he mines now and I will kill a bitch before I lose him to her, real talk." Kim added.

Kim, also known as Cooch, was as ghetto as they came, but sexy as hell. Ace used to only stash drugs at her grandmother's house at first, but Kim started to bag up his drugs and sell some of his work whenever he wasn't around then give him the money whenever he showed up.

Seeing that he had a little rider chick on his hands, Ace began flirting with Kim. One thing led to another and before they both knew it they were having sex more often than they realized. Whenever Ace showed up to get some of his work, best to believe Kim didn't let him leave without getting some dick.

Spending more time around Kim and her one-year-old daughter Shakiera, Ace thought by the way she treated her child, keeping her well groomed and in all the latest fashions for girls that she was a decent mother.

Kim's baby father was in prison serving 30-to-life for murder. He was a *youngbull* and Ace figured maybe Kim was trying to ride with him until she informed Ace that she didn't fuck with her baby father anymore. Meaning, no mail, no phone calls and no visits. Kim was your average ghetto chick who had gradually fallen in love with Ace. Although he didn't see it at first, Kim tried hard to make him see it.

Kim would wash Ace up every time he spent the night. She would even put on his deodorant, lotion him down, and clothe him. She tried desperately to win Ace's heart. That's part of the reasons why she'd cut off all ties with her other male friends. She knew Ace wouldn't fuck her raw unless he was the only man hitting it, and she knew he would never take her serious unless she won his heart.

Once Kim told Ace that she was pregnant, he tried to convince her to get an abortion because he didn't want any other kids on Lorraine.

"No Ace, No, I'm not killing my baby for nobody, not you, not nobody at all!" Kim screamed. She faked an attitude one day while he was talking to her about having the abortion. Little did he know she planned the whole pregnancy from jump street; from the moment she first laid her eyes on him at her grandmother's house.

Ace asked her if she was positively sure the baby was his. Kim cried behind his doubt and told him that she would take a lie detector test to prove she hadn't fucked any other man since they started having sex. Her tears were convincing, but Ace made a mental note that one day he may see to it that she did take a lie detector test and a DNA test just to be 98 percent sure. Ace sat Kim down and explained some sensitive things to her. After that, Kim was more than willing to come to terms of the agreement and her position of being his girl number two.

Kim had to respect the fact that he was with Rain first, and promised to keep the pregnancy a secret until he felt comfortable enough to tell Rain himself. Ace respected Rain's feelings and didn't want her to hear it from the streets first.

Ace eventually remodeled Kim's grandmother's entire house, including the baby's bedroom. His soon to be son's room that Kim was expecting to give birth to looked like something out of a rich and famous housing décor magazine. Ace paid for the house to be painted, had new kitchen and bathroom appliances installed, and he put new wall-to-wall carpeting throughout the entire house. He also bought brand new furniture for the entire house. He let Kim pick out new bedroom sets, a new 62 inch flat screen TV, and he even brought her a brand new 1998 Acura TL.

Far as Kim was concerned, she was wifey number two, not just his girl. She had never experienced this new lifestyle in her whole life. This was her dream come true and it would only get better. As time went on, Ace eventually told her to start looking for a new house. He was getting too much money now, and felt that it was time for her to move out her grandmother's house. Ace assured her that her grandmother was more than welcome to move with them. He also let it be known that her daughter, Shakiera would be treated as if she was Ace's own daughter. He offered to adopt Shakiera, but as far as he was concerned, Shakiera was his daughter now. Ace took a liking to Kim even more after an incident where the cops and the Feds tried to get a search warrant to get inside her grandmother's house.

One night, Ace was getting out of his car and noticed four guys dressed in black walking towards him. He heard one of them say his name in a low tone. Ace was already suspicious and alert, because he was in the middle of some beef with some other niggas he was going to touch for disrespecting him.

Ace didn't recognize it was four guys from around Kim's hood. They were walking around with a smoker named Ron, trailing behind them. It was Ron who had actually called out Ace's name to see if he needed any handy work done, but Ron wasn't aware that Ace had pulled out his .44 magnum cautiously, ready for whatever.

Suddenly, a black tow truck drove by and stopped. The driver, a fat white man, saw Ace's weapon drawn and yelled, "ATF, put the gun down!"

Out of reflex, Ace mistakenly pulled the trigger with the gun already pointed at the ground.

BOOM! Were the sounds erupting after the powerful handgun exploded, forcing the fat agent to jump for cover, which gave Ace enough time to make a dash for it through an alley way. Dogs were barking and drawing vicious tips on his escape route. Ace climbed over Kim's grandmother's gate, into her back yard. Looking around frantically for an escape, Ace tapped on the basement door, he hid under the porch where one of the dogs was.

When nobody answered the door, Ace called Kim from his cell phone and told her to come open the basement door. She had the basement door open for him in a matter of seconds.

Once inside the house, Ace found out everything after Kim informed him about what the neighbors said they saw. The only problem now was the cops were all over the place trying to obtain a search warrant to enter the house.

The Agent who saw Ace with the gun said, "The black male who fired the weapon ran inside one of those three homes. I think he ran inside that house." The agent pointed out Kim grandmother's house, as the cops sat in the patrol car waiting the approval of a search warrant.

Ace had a couple of kilos and a bullet proof vest inside the safe he had kept in Kim's room, scared that the cops would get the search warrant to find the drugs, Kim put the vest and two kilos underneath her coat and walked right outside past the cops. She placed them next door inside her neighbor, Ms. Wilson's house. Kim figured the cops wouldn't bother her until they got a warrant to search her grandmother's house. Ace realized right then that Kim had to love the shit out of him to take a chance like that.

The cops never received their search warrant because there was not enough probable cause evidence to search the house, because the ATF agent wasn't 100 percent sure which house Ace had actually ran into. After a few frustrating hours of waiting, hoping Ace would come out of hiding, the Federal Agent and local cops left the area.

*   *   *

After making it out of that sticky situation, Ace decided that he would take Kim out of the street life and keep drugs away from her since she was his Ride or Die Chick!

Kim took the chance of getting arrested and caught red-handed with enough drugs to put her behind prison bars for 10 to 20 years, just to save him from that very same fate. So, Ace wanted to make Kim happy and secure for the rest of her life.

After having sex with Kim that night, Ace drifted off to sleep, feeling comfortable with the woman lying beside him. Kim stared at Ace possessively, thinking, *this dick is too damn good and his money is too damn long to have somebody come along and take it away from me. Ain't nobody taking my man away from me. I will kill a bitch first!*

With that in mind, Kim grabbed Ace's cell phone and started jotting down all the female names and numbers he had stored inside. She had every intention on calling each and every female in due time to let her know who she was.

Soon as Ace left the following morning, Kim called Adrina's number. The first female phone number that showed up on Ace's phone screen. Adrina answered on the third ring.

"Hello?" Adrina answered still half asleep.

"Hello, can I speak to Adrina?" Kim asked

"This is she." Adrina answered

"Adrina, this is Ace's fiancée! Did he tell you that he has a girl and a baby on the way?" Kim asked with an attitude.

"Who the hell is this?" Adrina asked with an attitude.

"I'm not going to repeat myself. I'm just asking you woman to woman, if you could leave my man alone and not become a home wrecker." Kim said in a nasty tone right before hanging up on her.

Without giving it a second thought, Kim called every female number Ace had programmed in his phone and gave them the same spill. Unbeknownst to Kim, some of those females were actually Ace's family members.

The only thing Kim respected was that she couldn't call Rain with her bullshit. That was violation; Ace specifically told her to never commit under any circumstances. Kim knew if she crossed that line, she'd lose Ace forever, which was something that she never wanted to happen.

So Kim's motto was: ***All other Bitches besides Rain must go!*** She wasn't about to share her knight in shining armor to risk someone else plotting and trapping him like she was doing herself…

CHAPTER 8
Stink (Brother on the run)

At the end of 1999 on New Year's Eve heading into the year 2000, Ace and Stink was preparing for the party of the century later on that night. Stink was Ace's cousin from Baltimore. Stink had been living in Philly with Ace for about a year now. Stink had caught a body, murder case, back in Baltimore and was on the run for a heroin indictment. Once Stink made bail, he heard that his cousin Ace was the go to man and made the smooth transition from Baltimore to Philly.

Ace was more than happy to accommodate Stink's request for a place to lay low until the heat died down back in Baltimore concerning him. Ace knew Stink was a soldier, plus on top of that he was family. How could he refuse him?

Ace also knew that Stink would have his back, and together they had the force and power of two lions. They would confront any beef head on and kill anyone who got in their way.

Soon as Stink touched down in Philly. Ace supplied him a drug set. He fronted Stink all the cocaine he wanted to get his spot up and running. He taught Stink how to cook up, stretch his coke and keep all the smokers coming back for more product. While getting his grind on, Ace introduced Stink to everybody who could help him advance in the game. From there, Stink took off, adapting quickly, showing that he too was a natural born hustler. Stink came up fast in the game. The only difference now was he sold cocaine instead of heroin, and in Philly, Stink had respect because he was Ace's cousin; not because of the rep he grounded back in Baltimore.

Several months later, Ace, Gotti and Stink had plans to attend a party that was hosted by the Golden Girl from Power 99 FM radio station.

"Yo, you gon' crush em' tonight in dat coat you got made Yo." Stink said. "I might not even go."

"Why not?" Ace asked.

"Cause yo, you and Gotti got on minks and shit. Yall niggas flossin too hard. I'm not tryna spend no money like that for just one night. I ain't built like that yet yo, so I ain't even gon front."

"Nigga you just tight as shit wit that paper, that's all to it."
Ace joked, causing them both to laugh. "You can wear one of my
other coats or buy one, matter of fact. I got a black mink you can
buy for something small, but you gotta go out tonight. Nigga
tonight, we celebrating something special."

"Aight pimp, I'll be there, but first lets go get dat mink."
Stink said, as they both smiled and agreed to meet later that
evening...

*   *   *

Ace and Kim were home getting dressed, as Ace
stepped in the bathroom to view himself in the mirror. He
noticed Kim was already dressed.

"Damn girl, you looking sexy as hell. I wouldn't believe
you just had my son five months ago if I didn't see it for myself."

Kim smiled at his compliment. She had on a short, white
leather skirt, some white alligator calf high boots and a matching
white leather strapped backless shirt. To top it off, Ace had
brought Kim a white Norwegian fox coat to go with her outfit.

The owner and stylist of Rodeo Kidz on South Street
made Ace and Kim's entire outfits for the special event. Ace
wore some white dress pants, a white tight fitting Versace V-neck
shirt, and a pair of bone white Mauri big block gators with a
matching belt. Ace also got himself a stunning white, three-
fourth-- length mink jacket made with a belt and shoulder straps.
He sported a white mink cool cap to match.

Entering the event, Ace and Kim looked smashing
together, crushing the whole party as best dressed for the night.
All three couples looked good tonight and wore some type of
animal as a coat.

Gotti and Tiffany were together along with Stink and
Charlie, who all came with Ace and Kim.

Golden Girl was looking stunning tonight in her pink and
white attire as she introduced Mary J. Blige to the stage.

"Aight ladies and gentlemen! I'm the Golden Girl, your
host for tonight. And I want to bring to the stage one of my
favorite female artist and personal good friend, Miss Mary J.
Blige!"

The crowd applauded as the lights went dim, as Mary J. Blige walked out on stage and started the night off singing one of her old a smash hits: "Real Love." The crowd went wild as they sang along.

"Ay, Yo, so what's the big occasion that you wanted us all here together tonight with our women Yo?" Stink asked Ace, who was smiling and snapping his fingers to Mary J. Blige's melodic voice.

"Cause I'm excelling pimp!" Ace replied with a smile. "A lot of good things happening and we livin'! This New Year gon' bring us a lot of fortune." Ace continued. "2000, gon' be our year and we gonna blow up! That means better prices for yall, and I can do that now cause it's better for me as well."

"Cheers to that pimp!" Gotti said, raising his chilled bottle of Dom Perignon champagne in the air.

"I also will like to share my trust and new fortune with my family. I just brought some land with a new house in Jersey, but I want to see my bothers move their families out the hood soon as well." Ace revealed and then raised his champagne glass.

They all put up a toast and then Stink gave a quick comment. "To our success and congrats to my cousin Ace! He don't want to say it but we all know the nigga's a millionaire!"

Everyone at the round table cracked up with laughter and finished drinking their champagne. It was true that a lot of niggas be fronting or acting like they got it, but Ace made his first million and has been growing stronger since the end of 1999.

This young hood nigga reached the impossible and became a self-made millionaire off cocaine. Ace smiled at the thought as Kim hugged and kissed him while the whole club counted down to the New Year.

Ten…Nine…Eight…Seven…Six…Five…Four…Three… Two…One… HAPPY NEW YEAR!!! Everybody yelled in unison, while Ace Capone just took it all in thinking, *Damn I love being me!*

*   *   *

Ace had already bought Kim a three-bedroom house
with a finished basement, front yard, back yard, with a garage
attached in Northeast Philly. However, he decided to give that
house to his mom, since he had brought some land in New Jersey
to build another house from scratch for him, Kim and the kids.

Kim was now his kid's mother, so Ace wanted her and the
kids out of the hood for good. Ace designed the house himself,
alongside his contractors, Yusuf and Reggie. Ace had out done
himself with the walk-in bathroom in his master bedroom. You
could walk down a hallway that had mirror sliding doors on both
sides leading to the bathroom. The bathroom had a walk-in
shower like one similar to luxury hotels, only classier with marble
inside the shower from the floor to the ceiling. It also had jet
sprays everywhere, so that water would hit you from all angles
once you got inside.

There was also a huge Jacuzzi style tub separate from the
shower enclosed in marble. The master bedroom was on the first
floor, and even had its own door to go outside on a patio. The
kitchen had a stainless steel island, a double door stainless steel
refrigerator, marble floors, and granite counter tops. The fine
home had 'timberland colored' hard wood floors that ran through
the entire house, except in the bedroom, all the bedrooms had
thick black Italian carpet. The ceilings in the master bedroom,
kitchen and living room had recess lighting.

The dining room lighting was provided by wall scorches,
and was occupied by an antique table set that could sit eight
people to eat comfortably. Ace had the table shipped directly
from Italy. The basement had ceramic tile on the floor –
furnished with pinball machines, a movie room and a red cedar
closet with a built-in freezer to store both Kim and Ace's slew of
fur coats over the off season.

The four-bedroom house was fabulous inside and out.
Ace had landscapers come in and design two acres of his land to
resemble Hawaii. He paid to have palm trees installed and added
a half basketball court alongside the tear drop shaped driveway
that led to their beautiful home which sat on top of a hill.

Ace had ten acres of wooded land that surrounded his
house, so he installed kennels for the champion pit bulls he
specialized in breeding solely for fighting.

One of the dogs, Kemo, a Cane Corso, was trained to guard Ace's family and his house without barking or growling. The dog was a vicious attack dog. Kemo would maim and kill anyone who wasn't a part of Ace's household. Ace didn't use Kemo to fight; Kemo was simply a watchdog.

Eight of the kennels were five by five cages built side by side to each other, then there was one big eight by eight cage for his 185 pound Cane Corso, Kemo.

Kemo was a man-eater and a beautiful one. He resembled a male lion without a mane, with his light brown eyes, cropped ears, and short cut tail. Although Ace had this exquisite, rare show quality, champion bloodline dog to guard his house, he still paid to have a top of the line security system installed. The security system gave Ace the ability to view the entire property from inside and out. There were cameras to view the outside, and monitors built into his bedroom walls. Some houses were just houses, but Ace Capone's house was a home - an impenetrable fort! A spectacular home that could have easily been given a time slot on an episode of MTV's "Cribs"...

CHAPTER 9
Motherly love (My son is big-time)

Shirley Coles, now a middle aged churchwoman, still had stubborn and selfish ways. She seemed envious towards the women in her oldest son's life for one reason. Unlike some of the women in Ace's life, Shirley had worked hard, honest jobs all of her life. She didn't have the help of any of her kids' fathers to help her raise her four boys, so she felt as though the girls had it way too easy - unconsciously showing envy towards them. Ace felt like his mother had no right to be envious of his women – because unlike her – his kids' mothers took on their responsibilities as mothers. Shirley abandoned him along with his three brothers at very young ages, and kicked them out at the young tender ages of 12, 11, 9, and 4 years old.

After informing her family that she was putting her kids in foster care, they were all forced to split up and cared for by different family members. Ace and Mykal went to Paschall Projects with their father. Mitchell and Amin had to go with two different family members because their real fathers were both incarcerated.

Although Ace and Mykal's father was on crack, he was not a crack-head junky. In his eyes he was different from a crack-head because he didn't rob or steal to get a fix. He was a functional crack user who worked an everyday nine to five job and got high after the bills were paid.

The results from Ace's childhood were simple; the streets raised him. Ace had to fend for him and his brothers. He took on the responsibilities of a man and personally made sure none of his brothers ever got involved in the street game. Throughout their rough childhood, Ace always acted as if he were their father. If anyone would attempt to pick a fight with any of his younger brothers, he would rush to their defense. Big, small, old, or young it didn't matter to him. Win, lose or draw, by nature, Ace had no picks when it came down to his family, always willing to die protecting them.

They grew up poor, but Ace loved his mom and dad. Only after his mom abandoned them is when he unconsciously buried a deep grudge in his heart with a bit of hatred specifically towards her.

His dad was addicted to drugs and barely able to take care of himself, but he did attempt to take care of his sons when Shirley dropped them off on his doorsteps. Ace felt that his mother had no valid excuse, because all her kids knew was her as a parent and she wasn't on drugs. Children don't ask to be born into this world; even wild animals will care for their young until they are of age where it's strong and smart enough to care for themselves. So, since animals don't even leave their young defenseless- Ace always held painful, bitter thoughts of his own mother, cause no matter how hard the struggle is, or how uncomfortable its conditions actually are, he often wondered *how a woman could actually be that cruel and heartless to her own children?*

Ace is all grown up now, so he put the past behind him. He tried to somewhat keep the ties with his mother open. Ace loved his mother and did what any son who loves their mother would do once they became successful. Not only did he put her in a house, he also brought her two cars to drive or simply park in her driveway. Shirley was first treated to a black **Saab 9000** with tan leather seats, then Ace brought her a brand new sport edition 1999 black on black buggy eye **Mercedes Benz E300**. The relationship between Ace and his mother was fair, until a certain incident occurred that happened between Shirley and Kim.

Kim had a bad habit of putting Ace's family members in the middle of their personal arguments. Although every couple had their ups and downs, Ace preferred his household issues to be kept in the house. Little did Kim know, none of Ace's family ever cared too much for her, anyway, they only tolerated her because of his kids. Shirley would always purposely give Kim bad advice when Kim told her about her problems with Ace. Kim would constantly complain of his cheating ways, and explain the fights they would have whenever she did confront him about his infidelity. Kim didn't know how to talk calmly with respect, so her ghetto ways and poor demeanor always allowed her to lose control, or hit him. On a few different occasions, never closing his fist, Ace regretfully put his hands on Kim. Most females will never fully understand that the tongue alone can cut a man deeper than a sword at times, and to actually throw the first blow during a heated argument was simply ludacris. At times like this, Ace would leave Kim for two to three weeks at a time. He was sick of the fussing and fighting altogether. Kim would call his mother hoping she would talk Ace into coming home. However, envious of how easy the women in her son's life had it, Shirley would only tell Kim if it's so bad, she should just take the kids and simply leave him. Shirley didn't care to see Kim with her son in an exclusive relationship anyway.

After a while Kim finally caught on to Shirley's scheme, and one day Ace and his mother had an argument over something Kim went back and told him. *Ace had gotten locked up out of state and needed three signatures along with the 100,000 dollars he needed for bail, because he got caught using an alias to avoid other warrants he had in different states. When Shirley was asked to sign over her house as part of the bail, she caught an instant attitude. Shirley felt like she didn't commit a crime so why would she sign over her house, car or anything else for that matter. Kim ran to his aid to sign for her man and was mad at the comment Shirley made, but she only let Ace know for two reasons. One, she wanted him to fall out with his mother. Shirley had more access to his money in various bank accounts than her. Two, she wanted to gain more trust in her man, hoping that he would actually allow her more access to his money.*

Ace was very upset because he was the one who brought everything for his mom. Even if he were bailing out with intentions on skipping bail, he would buy her a new house to replace it. However, Shirley knew full well that he turned himself in to finally put an end to the case, so Ace couldn't understand why she stunted on him when he provided it all for her. The day Ace got out of jail he confronted his mom about the comment. During the heated debate Shirley directed all her anger towards the culprit who started the problem. She was so furious; she lost her sound train of thought, and picked up a bat and charged towards Kim with vengeance. Kim was seven months pregnant at the time, so Ace had grabbed his mother, holding her back to keep her from physically attacking Kim. Kim's ghetto instincts kicked in and she threw a cheap shot, punching Shirley in the face a few times while Ace was trying to hold his mom back. Ace became furious as he somehow subdued the two violent angry women from fighting each other.

Ace cussed Kim out so bad afterwards he considered kicking her ass himself and leaving her for actually swinging on his mother. It didn't matter if his mom went after Kim first he thought he had control of the situation. The fact remained that Shirley was his mother. Kim figured it would take a while, but she would do whatever she had to do in order to get back on his good side. However, the relationship Ace had built with his mother would never be the same. Once again it was severely damaged....

Shirley received a call from her cousin Daphine back in Baltimore, Maryland. "Hey Shirley, how's Stink doing up there in Philly?"

"He's fine I guess, but you know I should tell you. I really don't think that it's in Stink's best interest to stay for good." Shirley replied.

"Why did you say that?" Daphine asked, somewhat puzzled and confused.

"I just don't think that it's wise or safe for him to be too involved with my son. Ace is into more than just owning barbershops, day care centers and racehorses. He lives a very lavish and dangerous lifestyle. I pray he doesn't get locked up or hurt out in them streets, but the fact remains that my son is *bigtime!*" Shirley replied.

Daphine paid Shirley no mind; Daphine knew Shirley still held hurtful feelings inside behind the fact that her own mother took in her kids after she abandoned them. After raising her own 13 kids, Pauline Coles was 60 years old when she took in Ace and his brothers. Shirley's mother didn't even have the means or health to raise them herself, but her heart wouldn't allow her to see them kids be raised by a drug addict father.

Truth be told, the whole family was upset with the stunt Shirley pulled by leaving those kids. Then for her to sit back and watch her own mother struggle with her kids, while she lived life chasing behind a man was down right heartless and disrespectful. Times were hard for everyone, but not hard enough to give up your kids, yet alone to someone who was barely making it financially on their own.

Daphine was a down to earth mother. She understood the street game. She was a hip mom who understood her son often made poor choices, but she respected and accepted the fact that he was his own man. Plus, Daphine preferred to see her son on the run, rather than in jail any day of the week. She knew Ace and Stink were in the game; they didn't hide it from her cause she was once in the game herself. She actually supported their decision to be in the game without passing judgment on them. She even went as far as giving Stink advice about the game when he needed it, cause she wanted the best for her son.

"Alright Shirley, they both adults now. We both know grown men gone do what they want to do, so all we can really do is pray for them. God-willing they will be fine." Daphine replied.

"Okey-dokey, you take it easy Daphine. When I see Stink I will tell him you called."

When Shirley hung up the phone she stared at a recent picture of her oldest son. In the photo Ace was holding and hugging his son, and kissing his daughter on the cheek. They were all smiles while standing next to his brand new "cat eye" **S500 Mercedes Benz**. Shirley shook her head in sadness as she sipped on her cup of tea, cause no one else may have known it, but God knew – and deep down inside Shirley truly regretted the day she completely gave up on raising her own children.

CHAPTER 10
Out with Miami, In with Texas (The Connect)

It may have been cold and dreary back in Philly, but soon as Ace exited the airplane from flight number127 at Miami International Airport on a early afternoon in March, he felt the 80 degree weather slap him dead in the face. Ace was in Miami on business. Being the boss he was; Ace always loved mixing a little pleasure with business at times.

Walking over to the baggage claim to get his luggage, Ace noticed the young white driver named Paul.

"What ya driving today?" Ace asked him

"The Hummer, Mr. Ace," He said, pointing towards the vehicle.

"Don't start callin me that Mr. Ace shit! It's just plain ole' Ace pimp!"

"Yes Sir. I ma-mean okay Ace pimp!" Paul stuttered

"No! No! Not Ace pimp. Just plain Ace, pimp."

"That's what I said Ace pimp." Paul smiled and Ace just shook his head.

Paul liked Ace because he was down to earth, never bourgeois and always tipped well. Paul may only have been a chauffeur, but Ace made him feel like a friend. Ace picked up the phone and noticed that he had twelve messages. He started dialing Rudy's number first.

Ace met Rudy through Lump; a friend of Ace's who was now doing a five-year federal bid in FCI Sckulkill for two kilos of cocaine he got caught with during a routine traffic stop. Lump was dealing with Rudy's niece, Maria who was his girlfriend.

Maria, a sexy senorita that stood about 5-foot-6 and135 pounds, with all the desirable curves a man could ask for. She had long, black curly hair with thick eye-brows to match. Maria was simply beautiful and down for the cause. Her brother Mondo was Lumps connect. He would give Lump 30 kilos at a time on consignment, and Lump would run through the drugs in a week tops.

Once Lump got locked up, Mondo had Maria introduced him to Ace, mainly because Lump still owed a tab before he got arrested. Mondo figured that Ace was a true enough hustler to replace Lump while he was down, so Ace and Mondo worked out the kinks to get Lumps debt paid off – to begin a good business relationship amongst themselves.

"Yo, after I do this shit, I need some better numbers pimp." Ace said

"Whatddaya mean my friend?" Mondo asked, testing Ace. He already figured that Ace would ask for something for paying off Lump's debt.

"That work, that's what. I'ma give you an extra 20,000 dollars on each and every flip until the 120,000 dollar tab that Lump owes you disappears, but chu' gotta' work with me pimp…For real, for real that tab that Lump has ain't even mine. But as a show of good faith of us working together I'm willing to sacrifice if you are."

"You drive a hard bargain, but I like that…It tells me that you're a good businessman, and I would love to work with you…Come, let's talk about giving you some better prices." Mondo said before leading Ace into his luxurious home.

After Ace got his deal with Mondo, he started laying his hustle down. Behind the scenes, Ace had a secret admirer: Maria started to be infatuated with Ace, after seeing him each time he came by to give her money to put on Lump's books. Maria liked Ace a lot. She thought he was attractive and heard rumors about his sex game. Maria was lonely and horny, which only enhanced her lustful thoughts – plus she saw firsthand how well Ace took care of his women.

As time went on Maria and Ace became friends, and made a deal to secretly sex each other on occasion until Lump hit the streets again. Although she was still Lump's broad, Maria wanted to give Ace the pussy bad, and one day Ace simply couldn't reject her sexual seduction any longer. They became somewhat of an item, and by sleeping with Maria, Ace eventually stumbled onto a major connect. **The real connect**. Maria decided to cut out her brother Mondo, and she introduced Ace to her uncle Rudy. She felt that her uncle could give Ace the good numbers he was looking for, which Mondo couldn't provide after Ace turned it up in six months. Another reason why Marie introduced Ace to her uncle was because she loved the ground that Ace walked on. But, Ace prevented himself from loving her, by setting boundaries on his mind and heart.

Ace knew they both were out of pocket for sneaking around and fucking each other behind Lump's back. To Ace, Maria was a decent person, but a freak with a strong craving for niggas gettin' money. Ace knew they were violating, but the perks were great – so he chose to stick around to enjoy the good rice, beans, and learn a little Spanish in the process, from a beautiful chick, while sexing her down real good and disrespectful.

One time, Ace fucked Maria in the ass and then made her suck his dick soon as he pulled it out of her gaping asshole. Ace felt like she deserved it, because she was a dirty bitch for cheating on her man, so he put it in his mind to treat and fuck her like one. He purposely caused her to have multiple orgasms just to blow her mind, cause he knew he would break her little heart in the long run. Ace had plans of stringing her along to stay hooked up with Mondo, because he thought Maria's oldest brother, Mondo was the man, until he found out otherwise.

When she introduced him to her uncle, Ace discovered that Maria's uncle Rudy was the real boss. He was the man for real! After a while Ace got tired of dealing with Rudy because of the hassles he got. They looked at Ace like family due to his dealing with Maria, and treated Ace and Maria as if they were a real couple. This bothered Ace cause he knew Lump would be home one day soon. Rudy was a rich Mexican cat who was into all kinds of business ventures. He owned a toy store that rented out all kinds of flashy cars, from Porsches to Benzes, Roll Royces, Bentleys, Lamborghinis, etc. You name it; Rudy had it to rent. Rudy also owned a hanger with a jet to accommodate it.

Rudy sat in his office looking at the fly Latino Miami Heat cheerleader on her knees, trying to suck her way to his heart. He palmed her head as it bobbed up and down on his boner. Just when her bomb oral skills had him going, the phone rang.

"Que Pasa?" Rudy answered, humping upward, trying to shove all his length down her throat.

"Whats up pimp?" Ace asked

"Ace, where are you my friend?" Rudy asked as the cheerleader began sucking faster and faster causing his dick to spasm and twitch in her hot mouth.

"I'm here. Paul just picked me up from the airport. I like this hummer too. What you want for it?"

"For you my nephew, just take it!" He groaned, releasing a gush of warm semen down her throat, while she nursed on his spewing love rod.

"It even drives under water and provides oxygen for thirty minutes." Rudy said, patting the cheerleader on the butt as she got up and left his office. She stood at the door and held her thumb and pinkie to her ear, signaling him to give her a call.

Rudy just nodded and went back to his conversation with Ace as she left his office and closed the door.

"Rudy, you're a mad car scientist, real talk. But on a serious note, where am I going?" Ace asked. "You know I have to be back by tomorrow."

"I'm having you brought to my store located inside the Ball Harbor Mall. Come and we will talk then. You will be here for a least two days and I will tell my niece to relax." Rudy chuckled.

"I'll be there pimp, peace." Ace said and ended the call. Soon as he hung up, Ace began thinking a lot about spending two days in Miami with Rudy. He was tired of the bullshit and the extra shit that came with the bullshit.

Rudy liked for Ace to come to Miami to go over things then send anywhere from 100 to 175 kilos at a time on the highway inside two or three luxury sport cars that were placed on a trailer bed. Rudy would then Fed-ex the keys to the Lamborghini or Porsche to New Jersey where Ace would pick the keys up to the car. It was smart in a way because Rudy knew if the cops pulled the tractor-trailer over, they'd be amazed looking at 1,000,000 dollars worth of exotic cars on a trailer with no keys and afraid to damage the cars.

The driver would never be nervous because he didn't know anything anyway. He would deliver the cars to a garage in Delaware where the cars would be serviced and cleaned, meaning, they would be cleared of the kilos by Ace.

Ace would also have to load the cars back with two to three million dollars at a time and relocate all the kilos to New Jersey between 4:30 and 6:30 in the morning. Ace thought to himself then called Mike Millions, his man from down the bottom; one of the most dangerous sections of West Philly. Mike Millions had a youngbull named "C" who had hooked them up with a line in Texas – with good numbers too. Since Ace was frustrated, he figured it was time for him to look for another consistent connect to deal with.

"Whats up pimp?" Ace said

"Hey roady." Mike replied.

"Listen, call Jerv and Calvin. We gone take that trip to Texas in like two or three days when I get back in town." Ace said.

"Aight roady, I'm a call Africa now and tell him to book the flights." Mike paused, "Aye roady?"

"What up pimp?" "Wheerre!" "Da shit!" They both laughed before Ace hung up the phone.

68

Ace has been faithfully dealing with Rudy for two years now, and only made a couple of moves with the Texas cats during a drought. Ace knew the Texas cats were strong from the *Scorpion* stamp on their product. Rudy would sometimes take a month off from hustling not giving a fuck about all the guys depending on him to eat, which Ace hated with a passion. It's never a drought; you just have to know where to get it. Rudy was super caked up and had a lot of different businesses, so he could afford to take a month off and not have to worry about nothing. Ace was caked up too, but he was also a pure hustler at heart, so he didn't like his customers going anywhere else besides him to get their work. Point blank! Mix that motivation with greed, ego, power and the heart of a lion; you'd get a dangerous nigga like Ace Capone every time coming out of that mixing pot.

"Hey Paul, tell Rudy we'll meet him later." Ace said. "Yo pimp, spin around and take me to the Black Gold. I need to see my Miami mommy Marcella, with her sexy ass."

"Ain't that a strip club Mr. Ace? I meeean Ace pimp!" Paul stuttered.

"Absolutely!" They both smiled, as Paul made a detour and headed towards the infamous strip club.

The Black Gold looked like a movie theater that had five to six stages. It also had a movie screen that played porn while at least 100 of Miami's sexiest strippers entertained both men and women for the night. Everyone who was somebody in the industry went to the Black Gold.

Juvenile, Lil Wayne and Baby from Cash Money Records were inside the club tonight as patrons. While the strippers danced and got their lap dances on, niggas would literally throw thousands and thousands of dollars on the stage, making it rain on those bitches.

Ace sat in the corner with Marcella, one of his favorite female friends in Miami. Marcella was from the Bahamas. Ace called her his Bahama Mommy. She stood 5-foot-6 weighing 135 pounds. She was a natural beauty, 100 percent of pure sweetness with medium sized breast that resembled a pair of coconuts.

Gazing at Marcella while she gave him a lap dance, Ace thought, *what a shame. This chick is beautiful enough to be somebody's wife. Even when I wear a rubber, she has some bomb ass wet pussy! But I have to remember she's a hoe and a fine ass hoe at that.*

His thoughts were broken when he noticed all the nut ass niggas throwing thousands away, making it rain on a bitch! Ace's motto was **MONEY OVER BITCHES**! He risked his life for his money, so he'd be damned if he ever make it rain on a bitch!

No stripper or chick can get thousands outta me like that. I'd tip 'em a few hundred maybe...but that's about it! He thought already knowing that the only women who was honored to get spoiled from his riches were the women he lived with, and who had been involved with him in a complete relationship! ***Real Rap!***

CHAPTER 11
(High Speed Chase)

Jerv is Ace's cousin, and Tab is one of his close friends. They are both a part of Ace's squad.

"Aye Jerv, it been dry for like three weeks now. I'm a need you to get a **nina ross**, nine ounces of coke, from somebody, cause the big homie out of town. What's up with dat?" Tab asked impatiently.

"Yea, he out trying to make a move so this shit don't happen no more. I can call that nigga Jamaican Peter for you. His shit ain't ain't scales like ours, but his price is right and it will get you through the drought. Ya dig? Shiiiit! I just brought a half of brick myself. It should hold me over until pimp gets back. He should be back any day now, you know that nigga don't be telling nobody exactly when he gonna touch down. But I know it should be soon because the only time he travels out of town without one of his chics, is when it's about bidness. Ya dig?" Jerv retorted.

"Shit. How you know he ain't take a chic?"

"Man you know that nigga only take Rain or crazy ass Kim when he goes out of town. My girl just seen Rain at the market with the kids, and Kim crazy ass keep calling my phone looking for him, while she listen to the background." Jerv replied, as they both laughed at the comment.

"Yea, you right. Any other bitch lucky to get a meal out that nigga, chic better have some good top or some tight pussy if it ain't one of them. That's real talk."

"Pimp only got love for three women that I know of and that's Keisha, Rain and Kim."

"Keisha and Rain got his kids, and Kim has a baby on the way. He suppose to love'em."

"Man fuck what you talking bout. I hate my babymom!" Jerv replied, as they both laughed.

"Aye, Mike and Watley over at Ball Busters pool hall. Lets swing pass there and get some of that sweet money while you call that Jamaican nigga for me."

"Alright, but I'm telling you pimp should be ready any minute. That nina should hold you over, and he gone be mad if he find out we scored off somebody else. Ya dig?"

"That's why I'm only getting nina ross. I'm a bag up some boulders just to keep my crib running."

*   *   *

Back at the pool hall…Mike Millions and Watley were playing eight ball when Jerv and Tab walked in.

"What's up roady? I was just about to call you. I just talked to Ace. We going down to Texas soon as he gets back in town. He said you going too, so be ready." Mike said to Jerv as they shook hands.

"Man, I thought the boat was going to be in once he got back." Jerv replied, instantly frustrated because he missed enough money as it was already. He was expecting Ace to front him his kilos any day now, so he could get right back to work.

"I'm sure he got something. He ain't say we wasn't going to be in."

"Well, why I gotta go? Shit, I ain't stacked up with paper like yall niggas. I need some coke, so I can go ahead and get that money." Jerv replied, hungrily.

"We gonna have something. I think he just trying to make another move so we don't have to go without when it's a so-called drought no more. You feel me?" Mike retorted.

Tab suddenly realized that he just moved too fast. "Damn! I knew I should have waited on pimp, instead of buying this bullshit ass coke from Jamaican Peter!" They all busted out laughing behind his comment. After a few games of pool, Tab asked Jerv to take him back to his crack spot so he could hurry up and get rid of the coke he copped off Jamaican Peter.

As Jerv pulled onto 59th and Cedar Ave, driving towards 60th Street, a cop car hit their lights in an attempt to pull them over.

"Fuck! I think the cops is trying to pull us over." Jerv screamed, over the loud music. He pulled over slowly in Ace's triple black **2000 Yukon Denali**. The husky truck had an 18,000 dollar sound system by Pioneer, fully quaked with Rockford Fausgate speakers and amps. It was completely tricked out and equipped with the latest technology, having three 7-inch flat screen TVs, a DVD player, and a Sony playstation.

The cops heard and felt the bass blocks away, before they even actually saw it was coming from the black SUV driving pass them. Jerv was blasting *"Philly, Philly, Philly Where I Am From"* by Eve featuring Beanie Sigel as the cops pulled him over.

"Damn! You think they gone draw on us? Should I just get out and run?" Tab asked, nervously with his eyes wide open like a deer caught in headlights.

"Man, if they draw, that shit yours right?" Jerv retorted.

"Fuck dat. I might as well get out and run." Tab replied, in a matter of fact tone.

"Nah, hold up! I'm a bounce on em' once he get out and walks close to the truck. Then, when I cut a couple corners where they can't see us, just throw that shit out the window." Jerv replied, as he carefully watched the cops every move.

The rookie cop exited the driver side of the police car. He proceeded to walk towards the driver's side door of the Yukon, in an attempt to ask for license and registration. He had followed them and ran the plates in after he heard the music banging loudly. When he ran the plates, the information came back to a Hakiem Johnson with a Southwest Philly address.

As the young white cop got closer to the vehicle, Jerv suddenly sped off with all the torque, power the 2000 Denali had to offer. The truck was out in no time. After a few blocks, Jerv made a couple of turns and had the cops beat by at least three blocks. He could hear other patrol car sirens closing in getting closer to them, but he didn't see any cops in their path.

Jerv yelled, "Tab throw that shit!"

"No, no, no! Yo got'em beat man. I can't take no losses. Pull over and let me out." Tab replied, anxiously waiting for the speeding truck to slow down enough for the perfect moment to jump out.

"Alright, take my gun with you!" Jerv demanded.

Jerv turned the next corner onto 56th and Catherine Street to slow down briefly enough for Tab to get out. The police sirens were getting closer and closer, and Jerv pulled off a little too quickly, running over Tab's foot.

"FUUUUUUUUUCKKKK!" Tab yelled out in extreme pain as he hopped away amazingly unnoticed. The cops had sped right pass him only paying attention to the speeding black SUV. Speeding away nervously, Jerv made one or two bad turns before he suddenly lost control of the vehicle.

"**Scccccuuuurh**" is all he heard as he violently crashed into the number 11 trolley on 54th and Woodland Avenue. Luckily it was off duty, so the trolley driver was the only one on the trolley car. With his gun drawn, a rookie cop walked towards the truck, which had now resembled a crushed can of beer. The officer could hear Jerv screaming in pain and agony.

"Aaaaaaaghhhhhh shhhhhhit! My leg – I broke my fucking leg!"

Jerv had snapped his right leg in half, between the knee and ankle. As the ambulance and back up officers arrived at the scene, one of the officers in plain clothes recognized Ace's truck right away. Officer Mac McKenzy, a veteran police detective, who is head of the narcotics unit at the 18th district, specialized in guns and drug operations.

Detective McKenzy lit up a cigarette as he pulled out his cell phone to make a call. **Ring! Ring! Ring!**

"Yo, what it do pimp?" Ace replied, as he answered the phone.

"Yeah Ace, I'm fine but somebody just engaged in a high speed chase and crashed your truck into a trolley, which right now seems to be the least of your problems. We also found at least a half of brick of powder cocaine under the driver's seat." Detective McKenzy replied in a low tone, as he stepped into a secluded area to assure his conversation was private.

"What?!" Don't tell me, that fat fucking cousin of mines right?" Ace replied in a calm, yet frustrated tone.

"I think the perps name is Jervis Pringle. At least that's what his I.D. says."

"Alright, I'm in Miami. So I'm gonna have one of my girls to come bail that nigga out. You know I got it covered, so can you make this go away for him or what?" Ace asked.

"Let me see what I can do. When are you coming back in town?"

"I should be back next week, but I'm gonna have Kim come bail him right out. I will call my lawyer Scott Griffith to go and represent him in court."

"Alright Ace. Call me when you get back so we can talk. I was just telling you not too long ago that your friends are bringing you unnecessary heat. Every time they do something careless, your name is the one my supervisors pay close attention to when mentioned. I need to introduce you to a good friend of mine. I can't keep covering up certain cases this way. I can cover the district cops, but your name has become hot as a firecracker. Due to continuous mishaps like this, you gone need some advice and protection from the Feds. The way my superiors ask questions, I wouldn't be surprised if the Feds weren't already interested in you. Especially when your boys get arrested with large amounts of drugs like this, even if your lawyer beats the case, they still may be on yall. You feel me?" Detective McKenzy replied, matter factly.

Detective McKenzy was from the hard streets of West Philly, so he understood the struggles of the young black man. He didn't try to be a top cop; he only worked for the check and did enough to be recognized. At times, he would take money or drugs from certain thugs, letting them go without being arrested. *His motto was simple – when he needed a few extra bucks: Make a choice. You can go to jail for this now - pay a bail and legal fees to beat it. In which there's no guarantee you could win, so you may still do some serious time. Or you could give it to him and go about your merry way. Needless to say, all of the dope boys quickly walked away with the attitude of – **that shit don't belong to me, it's yours!**"*

Although Detective McKenzy had a lot of respect in the hood, he had been looking out for Ace for a long time now, and even gave Ace whatever drugs he took from dudes. Ace looks out for him too, putting plenty of money in his pockets each time. As odd as it may seem, they were actually good friends.

"Alright, I got you covered pimp. Set that meeting up with your friend for me sometime soon as I get back. One!" Ace replied as he hung up the phone.

CHAPTER 12
IESHA (Love at first sight)

It was a nice day when Ace and Jeff pulled up to *Club Flow* to book a date for a going away party for Jerv. Ace's long time friend and lawyer Scott Griffith convinced Jerv that the best thing to do was plead guilty before the Feds picked up the case and it becomes a conspiracy.

Jerv took a plea deal for three years for the high-speed chase and the half of kilo of cocaine he got arrested for. The Judge allowed Jerv to remain on bail – and gave him two months to turn himself in to do the time.

Ace planned on letting Jerv go out in style. As they pulled to the nightclub, small lines of people were outside, trying to get inside. There was a small, black film festival going on inside the club. All heads automatically turned when Ace parked his baby powder blue Bentley right in front of the club. His Bentley had 23-inch deep-dish rims on it with the chrome buttons, made by Asanti, earning the rep as the hottest Bentley in the city of Philadelphia. The only other ballers who had Bentleys in Philly at the time were Allen Iverson, Beanie Sigel and Bernard Hopkins. They were all either basketball players, rappers or boxers. Ace came from a different class: ***The School of Hard Knocks!*** He made his money the fast way; the dopeman way. He learned other tricks of the trade in business management to clean up his dirty money, so he didn't have to be a rapper or baller to buy what he liked.

Today Ace stepped out of the Bentley with a green Boston Celtics jersey on, a fitted cap, a pair of Rocawear long shorts and a pair of green K-Swiss sneakers with the white stripes. Everyone always paid attention to a big guy, so Ace was drawing all types of glares and stares from the people hanging outside the club. Ace's platinum chain was iced out with a huge Ace Card medallion hanging from it that was iced out too. The bangle bracelet he wore resembled Wonder Woman's - only it was fully iced out with 60 karats of beautifully crafted VS-1 quality diamonds. The watch he wore was by Luminor that had a customized diamond bezel on it as well.

His pinky finger had a huge platinum ring covering it with a 2-karat stone in it that made bitches mouths water. Ace's jewelry made street niggas throw hateful glares, or cause them to tuck their jewelry in whenever he came around. They did that to save themselves from being embarrassed by the flossin' Boss.

Jeff is a laid back pretty boy. Chicks would give him the pussy on his good looks alone. But by hanging with Ace from time to time, Jeff got even more looks from countless bitches who was chasing behind Ace and his Bentley.

Iesha and Juleen opened the club door and everyone in line started heading inside the club, to take their seats. The two girls were interning at the club to help Mrs. Jackson for her film festivals' sign up list and movie screening today.

Iesha is a young beautiful 20-year-old woman. She dark skinned, 5-foot-7, weighing roughly 150 pounds, thick in all the right places with big breast and a nice round fat ass to match. Iesha's body is firm and tight with no waist. She has a very seductive look to her, due to her bushy, thick, dark eyebrows, which complimented her thick, black shoulder length hair. Upholding her good girl look, cause she's very well mannered.

Juleen walked over to Iesha and said, "Damn Girl! Did you see those two guys over there?"

"Yeah I saw them. Who are they?" Iesha inquired, sneaking a glance over in Ace and Jeff's direction.

"I don't know, but go see who they are Iesha." Juleen whispered.

"NO!" Iesha hissed through clenching teeth. "You go Juleen, I'm scared!" She belted, causing them to erupt with laughter.

"Iesha, you need to stop girl." Juleen sucked her teeth. "Now you the one who said that you wanted a dark skinned brotha' with a beard. Well here's your chance, cause look at who just walked in looking cute like a teddy bear. You need to stop trippin', go get what you want and stop talkin' about it...Shoo' couldn't be me. If I see something I want, I go and get it!"

"Juleen, I don't go approaching men. That ain't my style." Iesha replied.

"Girl, you're trippin!" Juleen sucked her teeth and passed her some tickets. "Girl, just take these tickets over to him and sell him some tickets to our play. While you're at it, get in where you fit in and sell him that beautiful smile you got." Juleen told her with a sneaky edge in her tone. "And if that fails, which I'm sure it won't, you have the perfect ass to get his attention, now go on!"

Iesha looked at Juleen and smiled, knowing that she did have a perfectly shaped round ass and a pair of breast that sat up to salute you. "You're silly."

"And you're single, now get!" Juleen urges, giving Iesha the confidence to go over and approach Ace.

"Um, excuse me…Are you here for the festival?" Iesha asked, looking directly into Ace's eyes.

"No Ma." He said, taking in her beauty. "I'm here to see the club's owner."

Iesha was pleased that Ace had a prismatic smile. She had endured all the name calling in high school – when she wore braces, which made her appreciate men with straight white teeth like Ace's. She also loved a man that smelled good and Ace smelled excellent to her! She recognized that scent of *Versace Black.*

"Are you wearing Versace Black?" Iesha asked him.

"Yeah, how you know?"

"It's my favorite," She said smiling and looking away to keep him from seeing her blush.

"Um, I can direct you to his office if you want, but before I do, can I interest you in buying some tickets to our play?" She asked, batting her bedroom eyes at him.

"Are you in it?" Ace blurted without thought, because he was so into what he saw in Iesha.

Ace was attracted to casual dressed women with class, women that didn't show any cleavage or legs, leaving more to the imagination. Iesha fit the bill perfectly. She wore a long Sunday school dress and sweater, but Ace could tell that she had a nice body underneath her garments.

I can definitely do that and do you, Ace thought while waiting for her answer.

"I am in it," Iesha said. "It's actually tomorrow night at my school." She thought it was cute that he took interest, wanting to know whether she was in the play.

"What about your friend over there?" Jeff butted in, referring to Juleen.

"Yes, she's in it too." Iesha said.

"Good." Jeff said. "That's real good," Jeff casually winked at Iesha and started heading over in Juleen's direction. "I better go talk to her and find out more about this play." Jeff called over his shoulder, leaving Iesha and Ace alone.

My nigga's too smooth with his shit, Ace thought while sizing Iesha up, imagining all the freaky things he wanted to do with her in the bedroom.

"So, what school you go to Ma?"

"Temple," she said. "My name is Iesha." She said, extending her hand to greet him properly.

"Ace." He said, as he shook her hand noticing her soft French manicured touch. *Damn, her hands are soft. I have to get this young jawn*, Ace thought to himself before continuing the conversation.

"So you a college girl huh?"

"Yes, I'm studying communications. I have plans of going into TV, news or radio once I graduate."

"Okay, well I guess I will support the cause, Gimme ten tickets." He said with a smile, unconsciously still holding her hand.

She finally pulled her hand away from his soft grip and said, "But you don't even know how much they are."

"It doesn't matter." Ace said with a smile while looking deep into her eyes. He didn't bother telling her that money was no object. "How much are they?" He asked, figuring that she wanted him to know.

"They're ten dollars, but I only have five on me right now."

"Well that means that we have to meet again so I can get the rest of my tickets." He said with a smile.

Ace was a modest man that didn't normally flirt with women, but something about Iesha made him go out on a limb. To support his desire to see her again, Ace gave her a 100-dollar bill all the while thinking, *Damn, I'm loving her eyebrows!*

"Okay, well I need your number so I can get these tickets to you."

"No problem Ma, anything for you." He slipped that in there with a devilish smile as they exchanged phone numbers, promising to meet again.

*   *   *

Today, Ace had absolutely no desire to argue with Kim, his pregnant baby mother. When he pulled up in front of her grandmother's crib on 59th and Cedar Avenue in West Philly, Ace had every intention of telling her that; especially since she was on the front porch, arms crossed over her breast, ready for war!

"Look at her pimp. Out there pregnant with my seed and ready to show off." Ace told Jeff. Jeff gave Ace a, *what you expect* look as Ace continued talking.

"I'm telling you pimp, I'ma find me someone classy and nice to replace this ghetto ass crazy baby mama of mines. She's the only headache outta all of them." Ace said, with an attitude.

Jeff laughed and said, "yeah, but you love her though! She loves the ground you walk on and she moves without hesitation."

"Yeah, she definitely moves and I love her, but why did I have to knock her crazy, jealous ass up! STUPID ME!" Ace shouted.

"Ace, Kim will kill you dead before she let you leave her!" Jeff said while he and Ace began laughing.

"Man, don't say that shit! Cause that nut is well capable of it, but I ain't even gone go into detail about that." Ace commented. "If that chocolate, pretty Iesha pass all my test, she might be the one pimp."

"Damn, how you know that already?" Jeff asked.

"I can just tell pimp. I can just tell." Ace said, slipping into a vision of Iesha. Ace couldn't wait to see her again.

The pounding on his window, snapped him back to reality quickly as he looked up and saw Kim knocking on his Bentley window with more force than allowable.

Standing at 5-foot-2, Kim was sexy, but ghetto as hell. Thanks to her half Indian and Black genes, her beautiful complexion was just a few shades darker than light skin. Kim has the curves and body a model would have to work out on a daily basis to get. Genetically, she maintained her sexy figure after giving birth to their first son, Naseem. Now in her third pregnancy, Kim still had the look and grain of hair some women would die for. However, Kim would only rock a fly ass ghetto weave, never allowing her natural beauty to appear.

Jumping out of his car, Ace got up in her face.

"Have you lost your fucking mind?" He shouted, sending a few particles of flying saliva in her face.

"NO NIGGA!" Kim shouted back, raising her tone higher than his. "You lost your fucking mind for not calling me back. Evidently, you were with one of them bitches that's probably why it took ya ass so long to call me the fuck back!" Kim screamed with attitude.

"I'm so fucking tired of your mouth and your bullshit Kim! You should be mindful of that. Ya' nut ass so busy going through my cell phone and calling chicks back that you think I'm fucking. Your simple ass done called my cousins Janeen and Jennel thinking they was chicks that I was fucking, wit' cha' dumb ass! You's a simple ass bitch! Stay the fuck outta' my phone, Point blank! Damn!" Ace barked angrily as his cell phone rang.

He checked the caller ID and ignored the call. Just as Kim got ready to slam Ace with a few choice words of her own, Ace's ringing cell phone changed her direction.

"Why you ain't answer your phone? I bet that was one of them bitches you fucking. I'm tired of the bullshit Ace!" She screamed at him.

"Good!" Ace replied, staring at her with venom in his eyes. "I had enough of your bullshit myself!" He shouted.

"And what the fuck is that supposed to mean Mr. Alton Coles?" Kim retorted.

"That means I'm sick of your complaining! I'm sick of you letting your girlfriends tell you lies and rumors about me. Anything they say you believe it- just like when you believed I took pictures in a fucking packed club with some bitch! And you go through my phone looking for bitches that don't even exist!"

"They exist... Ph, they exist, I just ain't caught cha' ass yet!" She snapped, causing Ace to shake his head.

Ace had started getting major money, and just like most successful young men he began to stunt harder. Ace knew he was at fault for Kim to be on top of every little move. But, despite him doing him, Ace had some respect for Kim cause he loved her. However, that didn't stop him from being irritated whenever she accused him of doing shit he had not even done. Kim stayed with the wrong info based off lies, and the shit he really did do, he got away with it.

"Look, we can't get along anymore anyway, so before you make me hate you, why don't you let me buy you another house for you and the kids and we can be done. I only want to keep the house we have cause of my dog kennels. I need that land that we have. You just take everything out of your name and put it into my aunt's name so we can be done." Ace said calmly.

"Oh, you done thought about kicking me to the curb huh?" Kim said sadly.

As her eyes watered up, Kim stepped closed to Ace with a calm sneer on her face. Ace stepped closer, bringing them face-to-face.

"Pretty much." He said sarcastically. "Look, it just ain't gon' work between us."

"Well hear this Ace, OVER MY DEAD BODY! I will never take any piece of property you got out of my name! EVER! You won't leave me! Now, Point blank that!" Kim shouted confidently as she walked towards her 2002 745 BMW.

Before hopping into the driver's seat, Kim had one last thing to tell her man. "OH, I DON'T PLAN ON DYING ANYTIME SOON!" Kim shouted angrily before slamming the door and pulling off.

Bitch, you'd be gone in 30 seconds if I wanted you to be dead. Ace thought while hopping back into his Bentley.

Pulling off like a Nascar driver, Ace told Jeff, "I told you don't be saying certain shit. That witch is crazy. I told her I was done with her and that fool told me. "OVER MY DEAD BODY!" Ace mimicked Kim' angry screams causing him and Jeff to burst into laughter as Ace sped down 59th Street, heading towards Cobbscreek Parkway....

    *   *   *

Iesha had left Ace a message on his voicemail while relaxing across her bed in a yellow lace panty and bra set. She almost unconsciously left the description of the sexy attire she was wearing on his voicemail. Iesha was disappointed that Ace hadn't answered his phone or returned her call.

Despite meeting him hours earlier, Iesha wanted to hear his romantic voice, a voice that turned her on. There's something about him that she adored and for some reason she saw him as her potential man. While laying in the bed thinking about Ace, Iesha never had a clue that the feelings were ever so mutual on Ace's behalf.

This was an unusual emotion for Iesha, because she had only experienced feelings with one guy. When she reached the age of 19, Iesha lost her virginity to her college sweetheart. He eventually broke her heart after getting the pussy from her. Iesha had caught him in bed having sex with another girl who lived in his dormitory.

Iesha was raised to be a faithful and dedicated woman, having watched her mother do it quite eloquently. She was her mother's only child and her father's youngest out of four children. All of them were raised properly and went to prestigious schools. Iesha's brother, Pooh Richards, even made it to the NBA as a prominent basketball star. So, Iesha had all the qualities and background that would assure she pass Ace's test with flying colors.

Why hasn't he called me back? Iesha wondered before picking up the phone to leave Ace another message on his voicemail.

*   *   *

Weeks later, the deck outside of *Chrome Nite Club* was crawling with Philly's finest who came out looking fly, dressed to impress. They were in the building at the ***Can't Stop Won't Stop*** album release party for Chris and Neef.

Ace wasn't able to get Club Flow for the date he wanted for Jerv's going away party so he hooked up with Steve Brody and Daryl Shuler to do it with the album release party for the Young Guns.

Ace had a motto: ***Let's get money and have fun at the same time!***

83

Easing out of his S-500 Mercedes Benz with 22-inch Brabus rims, Ace took a deep breath, smelling the fresh scent of the Delaware River. Ace walked towards the club entrance while glancing across the river at Camden, NJ. Cars were lined up and traffic stood at a standstill up and down the Delaware Ave. Everybody was trying to find parking spots, so they could get up in the ballers event.

No doubt, ready to promote and get money, Ace casually rocked a white t-shirt that read **TAKEDOWN RECORDS** on it with a pair of State Property long jean shorts. Ace's butter Timberlands, all white Phillies fitted hat and his jewelry completed his outfit for the night. Ace and his squad were in the building: Mar, Jeff, Mike Millions, Jerv and many more. They nonchalantly strolled through the club, commanding attention. *"Even Though What We Do Is Wrong"* was thumping through the club's speakers as they went upstairs toward the VIP section off the deck to get some air.

I'm not tryna visit da' morgue, Freeway get it in like ten in da' Morning' Mane and I'ma get it wit' da' chicks while a' yawnin' Mane...Mane...

Yo' let me get em' Free...Hova' never Slackin' Mane...

The crowd went berserk when Jay-Z's voice invaded the club's speakers. Sexy women were spread around the club, trying their best to hook a celebrity or a baller who had the same amount of cash or more.

Liking what they saw, a few females were choosing Ace and his clan just on the fact that Ace and his team were rubbing elbows with Jay-Z, A.I. and Eve.

Stepping through the crowd of true ballers, who came out to party with the best of them, Juleen spotted Ace and Jeff.

"Girl, look." She said, tapping Iesha on the shoulder so she could see Ace.

Iesha had on Seven jeans that hugged her every curve and a pair of black and red Christian Louboutin pumps. She wore a simple black Dolce & Gabanna blouse with cherries on the sleeves, and carried a fabulous matching handbag to top off her outfit. She had maxed out her credit card to purchase her attire for the evening, knowing Ace would be there.

"He's not thinking about me girl." Iesha sighed. "I called him a few times and left messages; none of which were returned and he never answers the phone. He didn't even come to the play." Iesha said sadly.

"Maybe he was busy." Juleen said as she danced to Beanie Sigel's: "*Sigel is the name that they gave me!*"

"He not too busy to return a call Juleen." Iesha said. "Besides, I had his money too."

"Does he look pressed about 50 dollars Iesha?" Juleen said, her tone oozing with sarcasm.

"You think I'm too boring for him Juleen?"

"Girl, shut up! You not boring at all..."Juleen said. "Hello, you're in a club, not a dorm with a geeky study group. Now go over there and talk to him." Juleen urged her in a forceful tone.

"No way! Nope, I approached him first at Flow." Iesha said.

"Good point, but..."

"But my ass!" Iesha blurted, cutting her off. Juleen started brushing Iesha's shoulders and fixing her collar.

"You're looking good and went in debt on your outfit to impress him, now go ahead." Juleen said with a smile before lightly pushing Iesha towards Ace's direction.

Sipping from a bottle of Dom Pergnon Rose', Ace noticed Iesha walking in his direction. All the men in his crew had their eyes on her. Peeping their looks, Ace stepped off and started walking towards her in an effort to meet her halfway. Ace wanted any nigga with predator eyes focusing on her to know that she was rollin' with Capone.

"Hey Ace." Iesha said excitedly and posed in front of him with a lovely smile on her face. She pulled the 5 tickets and 50 dollars from her purse. "Here's you refund since you didn't get the tickets." She said sarcastically.

Ace smiled. He liked her style. "Sweetheart, keep your money. It's yours and I apologize for missing your play. I was tied up on some business." Ace responded, looking her up and down.

Damn, she sexy! Again, she was dressed stunningly but not too revealing! Ace thought.

"That's okay, I understand." Iesha said and stared into his chinky eyes. "I see you're a busy man."

"Yeah, but I will make it up to you by coming to your next play. I'm sure you did a good job on stage. Matter of fact, can I take you to dinner sometime?" He asked. He really wanted to get to know her because he had a few tests for her.

Iesha blushed and replied, "Yes, when?"

"When you free?" Ace asked.

"Um…I'm free tomorrow evening." Iesha told him.

"Then it's a date." Ace said.

"Are you gonna' call me, cause you never returned my calls?"

"Oh! I'm sorry. I never checked my messages until it was too late. Sometimes I don't check them at all. I must have not recognized your number so let me lock it in so your name can come up when you call me." He told her before typing on the cell phone keypad. After he programmed her number into his phone, Ace showed the screen to Iesha.

"Wifey?" Iesha said smiling after reading the name that he programmed her number under.

Despite her chocolate complexion, Iesha was turning red from blushing so hard. She secretly hoped that she would be his wifey one-day….

Radio Jock, *Golden Girl* was on stage getting the crowd's attention.

Ace told Iesha, "Look, I gotta go do my thing. I'ma get at you tomorrow night and take you somewhere nice."

"Okay Ace." Iesha replied, as he pulled her into his arms for a tight, warm hug.

"I'm your host, Golden Girl and I want to shout out my man's Ace Capone, Steve Brody and Daryl Shuler for throwing this crazy ass party."

The crowd went nuts, screaming and hollering "TAKEDOWN! TAKEDOWN! TAKEDOWN!"

"You're a rapper?" Iesha asked Ace.

"No, I just own Takedown Records."

"Alright!" Golden Girl said. "Without further delay here's my boys coming to the stage to perform their smash hit, 'Can't Stop, Won't Stop!' Chris and Lil' Neefy!"

Two months later, Ace finally had Iesha where he wanted her: On his sofa kissing her passionately. She moaned as he unbuttoned her shirt. Their hands slowly wandered over each other's bodies. Ace couldn't help but notice that she had passed many of his tests during the two months they spent together hanging out.

Ace and Iesha had experienced dinners and movies together. What impressed Ace most was Iesha's approach to treating him. On their second date, Iesha had treated Ace to a spa on her. To top that, she treated him to Six Flags Great Adventure the following week. She had won him over without even throwing her goodies on him.

When Iesha told Ace all about the nightmares she experienced seeing her ex-boyfriend having sex with another woman, Ace felt her pain. She convinced Ace that she hadn't had sex with anyone since that painful day. That was eight months ago. With that in mind, Ace reached into her panties and gently rubbed her clitoris. All she had to do was prove to be tight and this young pretty woman would be his…

"Mmmmm, ssss…" Iesha moaned with her eyes closed as Ace looked at the ecstasy plastered all over her face.

She looked so good turned on as he nibbled on her neck and ear. He knew that she wasn't sexually experienced, but he planned to take her to a place she hadn't imagined.

Ace pulled her to her feet and led her to his bedroom. Once in the bedroom, Ace started kissing her slowly while removing her clothes. Her nakedness was a perfect work of art that should have been bronzed and put on display at the art museum.

Ace worked his way out of his clothes, and then laid Iesha down on his bed. Ace then climbed on top of her. They kissed and slow grinded on one another as Iesha let her hands roam along Ace's body until she had her hands full with his throbbing love muscle. Feeling the thickness, length and full hardness of his boner, Iesha became nervous, anxious and wet all at the same time.

"Ummmm, please be gentle with me Ace." Iesha whispered as he rubbed his throbbing dick up and down her wet slit, making contact with her budding clitoris.

"You want it sweetheart?" He asked in a throaty whisper as his dick spasm sporadically a few times against her slippery opening.

"Mmmmmm, yes boo! I want it, please be gentle with me." She moaned as he slowly slid deep inside her tight, wet love tunnel with one long stroke.

Her wet pussy fit just right around his penetrating love pole: A perfect combination that convinced Ace that he was keeping Iesha in his life forever.

"Ohhhh… Ssssshhhhiiieett." Ace groaned as he entered a special place, feeling her pussy contracting with each thrust to accept his thick girth.

Iesha had her eyes shut with ecstasy. "OMIGAWD!" She cried out after feeling his dick stretching her sugary walls. She grabbed Ace's back tightly and pulled him on top of her.

"YESSS ACE! YESSSSS!" She shrieked as he continued to slowly grind in and out of her tight wet pussy.

Performing different strokes from circle eights to straight penetration, Ace kept his slow and hard stroking at a nice and steady rhythm that forced Iesha to bite down on his shoulder blades and cry out in ecstasy.

"Ssssss Ohhh Sshhiieett! You gonna' make me cum Ace!" She huffed while he kept digging harder and deeper.

"Yessss, Oh God Yesssss…Ummmmm, give it to meeeee!" She gasped as he went to work, sawing in and out of her gushing wet pussy. He angled his dick to rub vigorously against her hard clitoris while he burned her little box up, which drove her crazy.

"Ace…Ace… I'm Cuuuummmmmmmiiingg… I'm Cuummmmiinngg Boy!" She panted, feeling her juices releasing all over his stabbing boner.

Soon as Ace felt her first climax, he turned her over onto her stomach and penetrated her from the back: That's right, face down – ass up!

Ace had a sexual program that usually turned all the women out that he fucked. From fucking so many women, Ace became very familiar with various women tender spots. Once he learned that, he just kept hitting different women in those different spots until he had them climbing the walls at night and looking for him with a flashlight in the daytime after the sexual encounter. Tonight Ace planned on hitting all of Iesha's spots in one night and made a mental note to dig for certain spots. He stayed buried deep in the pussy until it clinched and gripped onto his dick while he jammed it inside slow, hard, fast, slow and deep to enhance her orgasm.

Iesha's pussy had to adjust to his huge dick before he went at it like a machine, causing her to climax harder this time.

"OOHHH SSHHHITT! YESSS BABY, YESSSSS!" Iesha screamed out in total passion as she climaxed again all over his slamming pole.

Ace was almost there too, but before he released inside her, Ace asked, "You on the pill?"

"No, Baby… No, you… umm shit… you have to pull it out puhhleeaassseee!" She gasped with her face and body in a world of pleasure, which caused her to bite down on her bottom lip.

"Damn, ya' pussy good!" Ace groaned, extracting his glistening boner and exploding all over Iesha's plump chocolate ass cheeks. So much hot semen spewed from his dick that he could have filled up a coffee cup.

Iesha's chocolate beautiful back view was now glazed with his nut - her pink pussy still opened wide, dripping wet. As she slowly turned over to face him, the look on her face showed that she was head over heels.

Smiling, Iesha kissed him passionately and said, "Thanks."

Ace looked at her puzzled as she continued.

"I've never experienced an orgasm with a man before…" She didn't mention she had by her own hands or her vibrators plenty of the nights.

"Well now you had two." Ace said and kissed her. "C'mon I got another few rounds for you but let's make it more interesting by getting in some water." He smiled; knowing from here on out she was Wifey.

They both felt good after the first round of lovemaking and were thinking the same thing: *This could be love?*

The following morning, Ace dropped Iesha off at her house. Mrs. Marissa, Iesha's mother, watched them from the porch window as they hugged and kissed. Ace walked back to his car and waited for Iesha to go in the house. He pulled off after Iesha walked inside.

Mrs. Marissa thought, *that boy seems very nice, but it's something I sense about him. Iesha said that he's involved in the music and club business. But I don't know...I just don't know? He's doing something else. I just can't put my finger on it...*

With that in mind, Mrs. Marissa went to meet her daughter with intentions on making Iesha some breakfast. She also wanted to interrogate Iesha on the sly about the new guy she was dating...

CHAPTER 13
"Deal gone bad" (Miami to Texas)

It was damp and wet outside from the drizzling rain on a Sunday morning when the house phone ring. **RING! RING! RING!** "Hello." Kim answered

"Good morning, can I speak to Ace?" The male voice with a Spanish accent on the other end requested.

"He's sleeping right now, can I take a message?" Kim replied.

"Tell him its Rudy. It's rather important, I'm sure he'll get up."

"Hold on!" Kim replied with a slight attitude in her voice. She knew whenever it was one of those types of calls; Ace would most likely be leaving out the house. Afterwards Kim walked into the bedroom and nudged Ace on his side, "Ace get up! Somebody named Rudy on the phone. He claims it's rather important." Kim replied mockingly.

"Rudy!!" Ace said groggily as he looked up sleepily to grab the cordless phone from her.

"Yea, hello!" Ace asked with concern.

"My friend, I have been calling you all night on both phones. I figured I would catch you at home since you didn't answer any of the cell phones." Rudy said while laughing at his own comment.

Ace didn't find Rudy's comment amusing at all considering he was awakening out of his sleep for the call. Everyone in Ace's squad knew that when he didn't answer any of his five different cellphones, he was probably home with Kim. That's the only time he would leave all his phones inside the secret compartment in his car. He only did that so Kim couldn't go through his phones harassing people trying to chase away, or find out about females.

"Oh, you got jokes huh?" Ace said sarcastically. "What's going on that had you call my house so early anyway?"

"I need you to come down and see me right away my friend. I need to see you tonight. It's very, very important." Rudy replied seriously.

"Damn Rudy! What you mean tonight? You are killing me. I done promised this damn girl I was gone stay in the house for a few days. Now she gone have a pissy fit and I'm a have to hear her nut ass mouth."

"My friend, do what you must do, but I need you here ASAP." Rudy replied.

"Alright. Let me go so I can have her look on the computer to find me a last minute flight." Ace said.

"Don't bother my friend, I'm sending the jet. Be at the private airport in N.E. Philly at 7:00 p.m. My pilot, Benjamin, will be there to pick you up. Paul will be at the hanger to drive you from there." Rudy explained.

"Man, send me some entertainment. You know I hate jets worse than commercial flights."

"No, my friend. I need you to have all your energy, so no candy girls for this flight." Rudy sternly replied.

Ace began to think to himself, *"No candy girls! I need to have all my energy? What the hell is Rudy up to?"*

"Alright, I'll see you later." Ace replied as he hung up the phone.

Kim was standing there the whole time gritting her teeth, and giving Ace the stare of a cold serial killer. Ace said nothing to her, as he got up to get dressed to head to the airport. A gift and a curse; Ace's loyalty was one of his best characteristics. He was 100 percent loyal to those he dealt closely with in the business. As he showered he had over a million and one thoughts as to what Rudy could possible want so awkwardly. Usually when Rudy sent the jet, he would also send along with it a few of Miami's sexiest women on board at Ace's service. Ace and a few of his home boys would have at least four to five flawless females to give them massages, and other hospitalities, which always lead to sexual favors throughout the duration of the flight. For Rudy to send the jet for this trip was strangely different, cause it wasn't even All- Star weekend or Superbowl Sunday. Ace couldn't pinpoint what Rudy actually wanted with him in such short notice.

*   *   *

As the jet landed in Miami, it pulled into the private hanger owned by Rudy. Plus, Ace began to look around for Paul, who was always on time, but strangely there was no sign of him today.

Ace noticed when Benjamin, an older white man, in his late fifties open the hatch to the jet's door. The old man quickly grabbed his chest, and slowly collapsed as if he was having a sudden heart attack. Ace rushed to his aid to see if he was all right. When he removed Benjamin's hands from his chest area where the pain seemed to be coming from, he realized there were several blood stained holes in the pilot's shirt.

"What da fuck?" Ace whispered harshly, to himself as he ducked for cover.

He thought to himself, „A sniper? Fuck! I knew this was some bullshit!' Danger was present and someone was out in the hanger with a silencer on his or her gun ready to take out whoever was in the path.

'Why would somebody kill the pilot?' Ace questioned himself as his heart raced with thoughts. Suddenly he heard a familiar voice say, "Relax. I apologize for the inconvenient surprise my friend." Rudy replied calmly as he slowly approached the inside of the jet.

"Rudy! What the fuck?" Ace shouted in confusion. "What the fuck is going on?" Ace continued angrily without really letting Rudy get a single word in.

"I am very sorry for putting you in the middle of that situation without any knowledge of it. That piece of shit has been stealing from me for years and didn't expect me to figure it out. So, he will be a casualty of war, cause I don't want anyone to know that you are here in Miami. No one besides me needs to know that you are here, because I have a very important job for you that will benefit the both of us."

"Nobody but you needs to know that I'm here? What do you need me for? And what are you gone to do with that body just laying over there dead?" Ace asked, concerned and anxious to hear the response.

Don't worry my friend. I have a special clean up guy that works at my funeral home. I use him for things like this and he will clean this mess up in no time." Rudy replied with an evil sinister grin on his face. Ace made a mental note, 'This taco eating muthafucka is no longer to be trusted.' The little trust he did have for Rudy was thrown out the window like an old eight track. Just like the dead pilot lying before him, Ace had no idea what he was really in store for. However, Ace knew Rudy was unpredictably dangerous, and he wouldn't allow himself to be caught slippin' in the future like Benjamin had just done. Ace would stay fully alert now and ready for whatever.

Later that night Rudy had explained everything to Ace. But, Ace never expected that he would actually be down in Miami on some extreme assassin shit.

"So let me get this straight. You want me to fly out the Bahamas tonight and kill a person I absolutely know nothing about. Why me?" Ace asked in a frustrated tone of voice.

"Simply because I know that I can trust you, and I know that you will never speak of this again. My friend, I need you to understand that the person I want you to kill is indeed a very powerful man. So, I can't just entrust anyone to take out someone of this man's stature." Rudy said, as he drifted out in thought, while looking out the window of his condo. He continued to explain, "If I could do it myself I would, but I need someone I can definitely trust on this job. The situation is very complicated. There is only so much you even need to know, but I can assure you that once this man is eliminated, we will eat very well for the rest of our lives."

"And you're sure that no one besides you knows that I'm here?" Ace asked, still leery.

"Absolutely no one besides me." Rudy replied convincingly.

*   *   *

As Ace rode in the helicopter to the Bahamas, the short flight from Miami seemed like it lasted forever as he daydreamed away. The Bahamas is actually only a twenty-minute ride from Miami by chopper. Ace was used to going there on Rudy's helicopter, but normally it was for pleasure trips. Not business trips. Ace snapped out of his daze and glanced over at Juan, a Mexican pilot, assassin who rode with Ace as back up. Ace looked over at the two sexy twin .45 caliber Smith & Wesson handguns that came equipped with silencers, which was only two of the extreme firepower Rudy had supplied them with for the job.

The plan was to kill the target, head back to Miami, and clean up all traces of evidence that could possibly lead to Rudy or Ace. It was dark, quiet, hot and muggy as the helicopter landed on the semi rough tropical ocean water close to the shore. The floating chopper now docked like a boat on a small private pier. Juan knew where the target was located. He also knew how to escape quickly after the hit was executed. As they approached the small luxurious cottage on the beautiful island, Ace quickly noted the two huge Preso-Canary dogs guarding the cottage. He also saw there were at least three men armed with assault rifles playing cards on the porch. Ace used the binoculars to scan the area and spotted the target alongside a female in their bedroom lying comfortably asleep. Juan immediately wanted to take the guards out first, and Ace now understood why he was actually needed so badly. Ace knew how to kill and get away with it quietly. It took more than street instincts and balls for this particular job. It also took patience and brains, in which Juan had neither one of those qualities. Ace knew the dogs would most likely bark fiercely if the guards got shot first, which would inadvertently alert the target who was probably armed with a gun as well.

To keep the job easier and cleaner he decided to take the dogs out first. Ace was there to be the mastermind on the deadly assassination operation. So, he told Juan to wait as they lay in a dark spot on the sandy beach. Both dogs cropped ears stood tall when they finally walked with suspicion over in their direction. The dogs were alert of some kind of presence, but before the dogs could get close enough to ruin their cover, four muffled shots went off almost simultaneously. **„PHHH, PHHH, PHHH, PHHH.'** It sounded as if someone threw four darts at them, but the dogs didn't even whimper.

Ace gave Juan a signal that the dogs were down. Juan may not have been a leader, but a good soldier he was. He was crafty too. Exercising his killing expertise, Juan quickly crawled like a snake to the front porch where he quietly let the three guards have a feast of bullets. The army assault rifle Rudy provided had a muffler. It was a venomous piece of artillery, which took 50 rounds of .45-caliber ammo. The three-armed men never even saw it coming. There was no chance for survival once Juan began spraying them; all center mass for quick executing purposes....

As Ace walked into the bedroom of the cottage, he found the target and his female companion still lying asleep. He suddenly sensed danger. Even though the target looked to be sleep, Ace dumped five bullets into his helpless body. **„PHHH, PHHH, PHHHH, PHHH.'**

The target was a middle aged, clean, shaved, well - groomed Mexican man. Ace hesitated to shoot the woman, who was now awake looking directly into his eyes. For some strange reason he froze stiff, and stared awkwardly at the beautiful peculiar woman.

"I know who sent you. He was the only person that knew we would be here until morning. I never trusted Rudy. His evil greed just put you in grave danger."

Ace couldn't help but listen to her. Something inside of him told him to stop and listen. Ace was good at evaluating people; sometimes by looking and simply listening to them speak. Her eyes said alot, plus Ace sensed treachery to Rudy's secret assassination plot, from the very beginning.

Suddenly Ace heard a door shut. A young innocent Mexican boy nervously appeared. The young boy came out of hiding looked in fear after just witnessing a murder, and now the very same gun was pointed at his older sister. Ace put his finger to his lips, signaling the little boy to remain quiet and stand still. Desperately trying to create a diversion for her little brother, the beautiful Mexican woman spoke out loud.

"You killed Carlos Martinez! Do you have any clue what you've gotten yourself into?" She questioned.

Before she could say another word, Juan quickly put six deadly shots in her face, neck and torso, killing her almost instantly. The sound of a door quickly closing is all Ace heard. When he scanned the room the young boy was nowhere to be found. Ace thought to himself *"Fuck!"*

Ace and Juan briefly searched for the boy, but the boy was no longer in sight. Ace may have remained calm, but he knew they had to get back to the helicopter as quick as possible….

*   *   *

Ace and Juan landed in Miami a short time later. As soon as they landed the helicopter Ace turned towards Juan. *PHHH, PHHH. PHHH!* Ace had put three fatal shots into the back of Juan's head as he was shutting down the choppers propellers.

*   *   *

Rudy was in his lavish three-bedroom condo in Ft. Lauderdale where Ace arrived afterwards.

"Good job my friend. I greatly appreciate you. This will benefit us both in a great way, you shall soon see. And to show a token of my gratitude there are 300 kilos waiting for you at the usual spot. I actually doubled it up like you previously had been asking me to." Rudy said as he smiled devilishly behind the thoughts of his new found plans of fortune.

Ace thought about the three million dollar drug debt he still owed Rudy for the previous load. He was still upset that Rudy even got him involved, specifically without any kind of details. Ace couldn't prevent himself from making an evil sinister thought *„I should just burn this taco eating muthafucka for everything.'*

"So you telling me that there are 300 kilos already waiting on me in Delaware?" Ace asked curiously.

"The product is there right now as we speak my friend." Rudy replied matter factly.

"Rudy, my bad if I come off disrespectful, but I just got to be sure that nobody knows I was a part of what just went down. I'm sure you understand where I'm coming from. So I have to ask you again. Are you sure no one knows that I'm here in Miami?" Ace asked respectfully for reassurance.

"I understand. And I assure you absolutely no one knows you're here my friend." Rudy replied convincingly.

Rudy walked over to the bar area to pour Ace a drink, hoping that it would take the edge off his trustworthy associate. Rudy wanted to have a celebration drink to their up and coming future success. Ace smiled devilishly as he pulled out the same two .45 caliber guns he had just killed Carlos and Juan with. Rudy looked up suddenly realizing that he was now on the wrong end of a gun and in front of a deadly, venomous man.

"Ace! Que Pasa? I thought we were friends." Rudy replied in a sudden state of fear and shock.

"Shut ya fuckin mouth. You are a vicious snake. Not only have you put my life in jeopardy, you have successfully put my family lives in harms way as well. I just unknowingly killed Carlos Martinez, who happens to be a very dangerous man who's well respected worldwide, and even politically connected. You didn't tell me shit cause you knew that I knew of Carlos for being one of the biggest drug lords on the east coast. But you didn't even have the decency to let me know who I was killing so I could decide whether or not I wanted in or not." Ace replied with rage.

Rudy had told Ace a pack of lies. He never told Ace the targets name; he only stated that the target was a political figure that was somehow interfering with their drug trafficking business.

"You are a piece of shit Rudy; the worst kind too. So, I'm gonna' have to kill you before I allow you to bring me down with you." Ace said disappointingly, while still pointing the gun at Rudy.

"Carlos people will probably figure out it was you. And I'm assuming they gone torture your nut ass until you tell them everyone who was involved. Ya coward ass would probably give me up before they even apply some real pressure to your snake ass." Ace spat angrily.

"No, no, no Ace. I would never do that. My plan is brilliant. My alibi will check out and no one will ever suspect that I had anything to do with it. No one will even notice that Benjamin or Juan is missing. They are both ashes as we speak. Now that Carlos is out of the picture, my friend, I will be the number one go to guy on the east coast, which means I can give you better numbers now. Somewhere in the single digits; like 8,000 dollar a kilo for you my good friend. Nobody else in the states will have ability to give you that number." Rudy pleaded desperately.

This all sounded so good to Ace; a part of him didn't actually want to kill Rudy. But the problem was simple. Ace knew he fucked up when that little Mexican boy got away. So no matter how well versed Rudy's alibi was; Carlos was a boss and member of a well-connected and powerful Mexican cartel. They simply weren't to be fucked with, and only Ace knew that the little boy heard his sister implicate Rudy for his treachery before Juan viciously killed her.

Ace knew it would only be a matter of time before the cartel catches up to Rudy. So Rudy had to die and die fast. For all he knew, the Mexican cartel could already be on the way. Ace wasn't taking a chance like that to risk his family's life or his life for Rudy's sake.

"Sorry pimp, it was all good while it lasted." **PHHH, PHHH, PHHH, PHHHH, PHHH, PHHH, PHHH, PHHH, PHHHH! PHHHH!** Ace dumped countless shots into Rudy's head and torso...

    *   *   *

     Ace was at Miami International Airport to catch the first flight back home, this time to New York instead of Philadelphia. He had to retrieve the actual keys to the luxury cars waiting for him back in Delaware. The very thought of 300 free kilos hidden inside those exotic automobiles actually caused Ace to have a mental moment to himself. *"I had intentions on dealing with the Texas line anyway. Fuck it, I'll adjust. I still got plenty of work left, and I got 300 more birds with no tab. Not to mention the 3 million dollars cash money that I had for Rudy, and taco pimp won't need any of that! Real talk!"* Ace smirked unconsciously to himself as he boarded the plane...

CHAPTER 14
(Signs & Warnings)

As Ace was putting his key in the door of his apartment, he noticed the same silver Q-45 following him from the club. It seemed as though he had seen the same car earlier that day, but the windows were tinted so dark he couldn't see the driver. Ace street instincts kicked into high gear as he pulled his already cocked and loaded, always ready to do damage .40-caliber glock.

The silver car pulled up suspiciously as the driver side window rolled down, and a familiar voice called out.

"Damn Roady. I been trying to get at you for like four blocks now." The familiar male voice said.

Ace smiled with relief as he put the gun back on his waist. He walked towards the car after recognizing the voice of the person in the car. All of a sudden things seemed to move in slow motion to him as he saw sparks flashing in his direction coming from the car. He suddenly froze, while feeling excruciating pain throughout his body after hearing a series of deadly shots. **BOC, BOC, BOC, BOC, BOC, BOC, BOC, BOC!**

Ace quickly jumped up from his sleep grabbing his chest repeatedly, sweating rapidly from head to toe. As he began to regain consciousness he thought to himself, '*Damn, just another nut ass dream.*' Iesha woke up immediately, instantly frightened at the bizarre intrusion of her peaceful sleep.

"What's wrong boo, you alright? Is it another nightmare?" Iesha asked extremely concerned.

"Yea, boo. I'm cool though." Ace replied as his speeding heart rate began slowing back down to normal.

It's been eight months now since Ace and Iesha have been dating. Although he never officially told her they were exclusive, comfortability, attraction and attachment let them both know she was in fact his woman. They had been spending a lot of time together. She even had her own set of keys to the penthouse he had on Lincoln Drive. Before they even had sex Ace sat Iesha down and openly explained his situation and relationship status with his baby mom Kim, because he was interested in seeing where the relationship him and Iesha had was going. Ace wasn't going to allow Kim to ruin their relationship, as she had done so frequently in the past with other women.

Iesha understood her position. She respected Ace for being openly honest with her about it, leaving the decision up to her on whether or not she wanted to deal with the circumstances of sharing a man. Ace's feelings for Kim decreased, but they did share kids together so he cared for her a certain way. Ace had a big heart. He had love for Kim, but hated her ghetto and ignorant ways. Kim had a nasty attitude that derived from jealousy and poor people skills she had become accustomed to growing up. Kim's mother was a crack head. Her father was a drug dealer who despised her mother for stealing and using crack, so Kim's father didn't want anything to do with her or his daughter by her.

It's always worse in that type of environment when a woman or mother is on crack, because it direcly affects the home in a negative way. Ace and Kim were both products of their environment. Kim was a female who came up rough like Ace, both of them born in circumstances that didn't offer them a decent chance at life. Ace understood this, so he sympathized with Kim, which is one of the very reasons why he dealt with all of her shortcomings.

Ace was no fool, but he made a foolish decision in accumulating some of his assets over the years. He now had over 2 million dollars in properties and cars in Kim's name alone. Being a street nigga who hustled hard to get his, Ace had no intentions on losing any of it due to a bad break up. He risked his life to gain his success, so Iesha would simply have to deal with the Kim factor if she wanted to be a part of his life. Like any other woman, she didn't like it, but she accepted it. Ace made her happy and secure. Sharing a man may be a hard pill to swallow, but as far as she's concerned Ace was well worth it. Iesha appreciated that he was being honest, caring and upfront about it. She loved him for many reasons, and hoped to bare children for him as well.

Iesha wrapped her arms around Ace in a loving manner as she kissed him on his cheeks softly. "Do you want to tell me about it this time boo?" She asked sincerely.

"Naaah. You know I'm not supposed to reveal my bad dreams, we only reveal the good ones. Besides, I'm fine." Ace replied as he kissed her on her forehead.

Ace's dream caused him to make a mental note to himself „Trust no one' As a Muslim, he believes that Allah (Almighty God) shows him signs and warnings in his dreams, as well as in other areas within his life at times. His beliefs are the very reason why he has been fortunate all these years. In his dream, Ace felt like someone within his inner circle was actually plotting on him „But whom?' He thought.

"You hungry boo?" Ace asked Iesha, cutting his own thought short.
"Uhhh, it's 4:30 in the morning Ace. I don't even have an appetite." Iesha replied, hoping he wouldn't ask her to get out of bed to cook him something in the wee hours of the morning.

"Well you gonna have one after Mr. Johnson here, snacks on Ms. Muffin." Ace replied in a sneaky, freaky and playful way, as Iesha smiled and laughed out "Ummmm, you so nasty."

"Come here girl - let me snack on my muffin." Ace said seductively as they slid under the covers to begin a round of passionate lovemaking….

    *   *   *

Ace was awakened by the delicious smell of scrambled eggs, beef bacon, cheese grits and pancakes. He walked in the front room of the luxurious penthouse where Iesha greeted him from the kitchen.

"Good morning boo. I was just getting ready to bring you breakfast in bed."

"I'm up now. You can just set it up at the table. What time is it anyway?" Ace inquired.

"It's 10:30 a.m. Why? I was hoping to get another round from Mr. Johnson after you eat." Iesha replied, as she smiled bashfully with a glow on her face.

"Oooooohhh! So that's the only reason I was getting breakfast in bed, huh?" Ace laughed out.

"Yeeaahhh boo! You bad! Michael Jackson Badddd. Uhhh, I'm a need another round of that before you go about your day today." Iesha said in a playful, yet serious tone.

They both smiled playfully as they enjoyed their breakfast. Suddenly, Ace thought back about his dream.

"Aye, I want you to start looking at another apartment for us to stay. My lease here is up in a few months and I really don't want to renew it this time."

"Why boo? I love this place. It has a gym, tennis court, indoor and outdoor pool, plus the security is tight just like you like it." Iesha responded, confused about his awkward request.

"Yeah, but we can get all those amenities and more somewhere else too. It's time for me to switch up. So look for something around 2700 to 3500 dollars a month." Ace instructed.

"Okay, so what area do you actually want me to look into?" Iesha asked.

"King of Prussia, Delaware, New Jersey. It doesn't really matter to me. You can look anywhere as long as it's nice and I can get to the clubs within 30-45 minutes, I'm cool with it. I heard the new luxury apartments down Delaware Avenue right on the pier are nice. But I can't be that close to the clubs. I'd be drawing. It's not discreet enough for me, so look for something in the suburbs outside the city. Ya dig?" Ace retorted.

Ace knew exactly why he wasn't going to renew his lease. His dream was a warning that he was too comfortable with his associates, and now he was going to pay close attention to this sign. Only a few of his so-called friends had been to his penthouse, but after his dream he had last night, that was one too many. Ace only kept a small circle of immediate friends, who were pretty much the same people that watched his status and organization grow to what it is now.

Ace never really chose the game; the game chose him. He was fifteen years old when he was literally smacked in the face with drugs. *It was the fall of 1989, when a Chevy Beretta was getting chased down Greenway Avenue by Philadelphia police. Southwest Philly was something like Vietnam. Paschall Projects was known as one of the roughest neighborhoods in Southwest Philly. The vehicle was fleeing from the police when it turned into the projects, and the passenger threw a bulky brown lunch bag out of the window. The bag hit 15 -year old Ace dead in the face. His two friends Duece and Spank both watched in awe, as Ace looked inside the bag - quickly noticing a ziplock bag full of caps,10 dollar valves of crack, and a .25 caliber handgun. Ace was flabbergasted by the contents of the bag. Ace was a young kid with a lot of potential, but didn't have the proper parental guidance. For that reason Ace did what any natural born hustler would have done. He sold the drugs, and it was on from there. The streets raised him, so as he got older he found his way to various troubles.*

His Nana didn't condone him selling drugs. But once she saw that she had no control over his life, she gave him sincere advice. Ace reminded her of her husband, his grandfather, Lou Johnson, so Nana saw trouble headed Ace's way right through his eyes. She loved her first-born grandchild. She was actually the one who taught him how to save money once she saw that he was carelessly wasting it.

She explained to him that he should always have some available in case he got arrested. If he should ever get arrested, he shouldn't even make it to the county jail. His bail should be paid for at the police district. Nana also advised Ace to put away at least 300 to500 dollars a week just for savings. Hustlers don't get retirement money, so as he got older, wiser and more advanced in the game it went up to 5,000 to 10,000 dollars at which Ace he would put up for personal savings.

Ace, now 29 years old, was sitting on some serious paper. He knew by the signs Allah had been sending him, that because of his wealth and status his life was in grave danger. No one could be trusted now, so he had to move more cautiously to protect him and his family....

As Ace and Iesha ate their breakfast, he thought to himself *„Shit as good as this woman is, I'll probably be buying another home soon instead of leasing an apartment. Plus the sex is great, and she can hook up a mean meal.'*

"And why are you over there smiling, sneaky?" Iesha asked with humor.

"I'm just sitting here thinking about our future together." Ace replied honestly.

"Ahhh boo, so do I get the white picket fence and a cute little dog?" Iesha replied excitedly in her young, schoolgirl voice.

"You'll get all you want and some as long as you keep me happy." Ace replied, while he kissed her neck and cheeks.

"Well now that you got me all horny again, can I see Mr. Johnson real quick before you leave for today?" Iesha asked devilishly, as she leaned over to grab his dick out of his boxers. She began giving him head to raise him to the occasion and accommodate them both for another round of great mind blowing sex.

CHAPTER 15
(Envy – Brother or Hater)

Clippers, scissors and razors were being put to work at Center of Attraction. This barber and beauty salon was always filled with patrons throughout the week. Shampoo girls were constantly flirting with customers making sure their tips were fat. Some of the girls even exchanged numbers, always ready to turn a baller into a trick.

Rabby was in the shop selling cologne and perfume to everyone, as usual. Barry, the shop owner, had rap's emerging face **50 Cent's** *Get Rich or Die Trying* cd on as „Many Men' whispered through the surround sound.

No barbershop would be complete without an argument or debate over any issue. Most issues were of no concern to anyone there. Today's debate would be about which company made the best car. Mercedes, BMW or Lexus? Half of the niggas in the shop didn't even own either of the cars, but a good debate always lasted for hours at a time. The same niggas who argued the loudest, most likely drove a squatter, Crown Victoria, Lumina or Chevy Impala. Truth be told, they were all nice high end cars, so which car is the better buy always boiled down to ones individual taste.

The only thing that could top a good debate was the latest gossip, or a bussing session. Center of Attraction lived up to its name. Outside, there were luxury cars parked up and down Elmwood Avenue. The owners of those cars were inside getting their hair freshly cut and dyed Beijing black. If you were balling, you spent 50-100 dollars for each haircut at least twice a week.

Through the front glass, patrons quickly noticed the new flossy silver **2003 Q45 Infinity**, as it parked directly across the street from the shop; it was now the new center of attraction. It wasn't the most expensive car parked on Elmwood Avenue, but it was new and definitely in a class to be respected. The million-dollar question everyone in the shop wondered was: who is the driver?

"I'm gone see who up in that joint." Shante whispered to Rhonda, another shampoo girl, as she discreetly rushed outside. For reason unknown to any sane woman, Shante loved a nigga with a nice car.

"Giirrlll, you always ready to be on a nigga's dick. It could be a bitch up in there!" Rhonda replied, as she laughed at the sudden fake, sexy switch Shante put on walking towards the door.

"That's fine too Boo-Boo." Shante said as she walked outside with a salacious smile on her face.

The new Q45 was parked on the opposite side of the street. The driver's door opened as a fresh Timberland boot appeared, before the number 13 trolley rode pass blocking the full view of the still unknown driver. Shante stood desperately at the door prepared to hold it open to escort the baller to her shampoo station. After the trolley passed by Shante's thirsty anticipation turned from gold to bronze.

"Girl, it's Tab!" Shante said disappointed.

"Tab! What that nigga doing in a new Q45." Stink said smiling and shocked, as he turned away from watching television. Stink loved to bid off Tab, cause Tab always grinded him up in bussing contests.

"Damn, that joint nice and clean. I'm feeling that silver too." Barry added.

Just as he opened the barbershop door, Tab overheard someone say, "I bet it's Ace's shit."

"I bet it ain't Ace nothing, hater!" Tab shot back sarcastically.

Tab knew they were talking about him. Ace had actually got the car for Tab, but Tab owed him the money for it, so it was still his, not Ace's. That's how they worked things out at times. Ace didn't mind doing favors for his squad cause he wanted all of them to shine. Ace had a lot of love for Tab. He knew his money was good even if it took Tab a while to pay him back. Tab is a 285-pound, dark skinned nigga with good straight and curly hair. Although he was a big kid at heart, he was a brave soldier who would bust his gun quick for Ace. He was one of Ace's closer associates so he received respect simply for that alone.

However, Tab wanted more. He was nothing but a lieutenant with desire to become general, which seemed simply impossible. Tab couldn't manage a team at McDonald's, let alone run a high-level notorious drug organization.

"Oohhh, so that's you, huh?" Stink asked Tab with a dumbass **yeah, right** smirk on his face. Everybody in the shop got quiet to hear Tab's response.

"Man, you niggas are haters. I don't know why yall niggas acting like I'm not getting at that fuckin money. Yeah that's my shit!" Tab retorted, daring anyone to challenge him.

"We ain't saying all that. We just used to you fronting hard in my cousin's shit all the time." Stink said, as he continued on mocking Tab's voice, which sounded like a over excited kid when he talked about Ace.

"Did you see Ace's Bentley? Did you see that new Chinchilla Ace had on last night? Did you see Ace's this, did you see Ace's that?" Stink mocked him sarcastically, as the shop laughed out loud.

Rhonda overheard the joke all the way in the back of the shop, where the beauty salon for woman was when she followed up on Stink's comedy with the girls.

"Did y'all see Ace's big dick?" Rhonda said mocking Tab's kiddy-like voice too.

"Girrll, yes! We was calling that nigga superman, the way he fucking that bitch. Tab showed us a sex tape of him and Ace pulling a train on some Hawaiian looking hoe. Well, Tab wasn't actually fucking." Shante explained with laughter.

"What the fuck was he doing then?" Stink laughed and added, "Now, I just know you didn't sit back and watch him fuck a bitch?"

"Fuck out here nigga. I fucked that bitch too." Tab defended and added, "Matter fact, you wasn't talkin that shit when I dicked ya ass down Rhonda." Tab responded, laughing out loud.

Shante held up her pinky, "No nigga. You were grinding on her, not fucking her. Just like you did me, but thanks for the check boo-boo." The whole shop burst into laughter.

"Let you tell it you, you can buy everything Ace sales you. But you can't change the size of your dick nigga!" Rhonda added while laughing.

"Yall nut ass bitches love to hate. Don't be mad cause a nigga only smutted ya. No nigga in his right mind going to wife any of you bitches. Yall just some convenient last minute, club let out, late night on the way to the telly, McDonald's, Burger King drive thru sneek creep- freak hoes. Broke ass bitches can't even get a decent meal out of a nigga." Tab replied humorously.

"And Stink, I don't know why the fuck ya funny looking ass is over there rapping. You look like Popeye the sailor man's twin brother with braids, after he eats his spinach. You hardly get any pussy. Shit you ain't even fuck Rhonda or Shante, and everybody in the shop done fucked the both of them whores." Tab laughed out loud.

Although Tab did his best not to show it, he secretly vowed he would one day get to Ace's status. Tab didn't even realize that he lacked three of the most important and strongest things you needed to actually gain that level of boss type status. **Money, power and respect**!

As everybody in the shop continued to laugh at his last comment, Tab thought to himself, *'I'm a show these muthafuckas anything Ace can do, I can do better.'*

CHAPTER 16
(Parties/headquarters)
Palmers Social Club

It was 6:30 p.m. this rainy Saturday evening when Ace decided to call it a day. Kim was downstairs in the basement doing laundry as he walked in the house.

"Hey, you scared me. Ya food is in the microwave. You hungry?" Kim asked, startled as she hurried up the stairs. She was shocked to see Ace in the house this early on a club night.

"Yeah, I'm starving." Ace replied as he strangely noticed the quietness in the house. "Where my kids at?"

As Ace walked upstairs looking for the kids, and could hear bath water splashing. Shakiera was blowing bubbles in the tub trying to make **6-month-old** Naseem laugh. Kim quickly ran upstairs towards the bathroom.

"What the hell did I tell you last time?" Ace snapped violently at Kim.

"I only left him for two minutes Ace. Damn! Don't start ya shit." Kim replied as she picked the baby up out of the tub.

"I told you my cousin's daughter died that same way." Ace said angrily as he collared Kim up.

'*Two years earlier Ace's cousin Jeneen had left her baby in the tub alone while she went to answer the phone. Jeneen thought it was safe because the baby was in a bathing chair device. She only talked a couple of minutes too long. When she went back in the bathroom she discovered the baby chair upside down with the baby drowning under water. It's extremely hard for any mother to hold a dead baby. But to feel like the one responsible for your own baby's death is a harder task to deal with altogether. We shouldn't question why God allows certain tragedies to happen, for he does it with His own great wisdom. However, any baby's burial was a hard funeral for anyone to attend.*

"Ace stop!" Kim said angrily.

"I'm a tell you right now. If my son ever dies because of your stupidity and carelessness, you might as well kill your damn self, cause I'm a do it in one of the worst ways humanly imaginable." Ace swore venomously with a sinister still cold look in his eyes.

When he let Kim go, she walked away mumbling something sarcastically under her breath. Out of sudden rage, Ace wasn't thinking when he grabbed the closest thing he could find to throw at her. Kim continued trash talking as it raced through the air at high speed, and she unknowingly turned around towards Ace. 'WHAAPP!' Was the sound of the small bottle of baby lotion that hit her directly in her left eye.

A mother's reaction is simply amazing at times; cause Kim never dropped her baby, even as her face stung with instant pain as she cried. **Four-year-old** Shakeria was still in the bathtub nervous from overhearing the ruckus between her parents. And like any kid her age, she hated to see her parents fight. Plus, Kim was the type of mother who would take out her anger on her kid when she was angry with her man. Shakeria knew the drill all too well, upset about the thought of being stuck at home now with a miserable mother for at least a few days.

Ace didn't intentionally aim the bottle at her face; he was only trying to hit her in the back of her head. Now he regretted actually throwing it at all. He noticed Kim's eye swelling up immediately.

"Now look what you done made me do! You are a headache broad. Maaan, I can't do this shit no more. I'm done!" Ace replied in a frustrated and convincing manner, as he headed towards his closet to pack him a few outfits to leave.

"Please don't leave me Ace. I'm sorry. I won't do it again. Pleeeease don't leave me." Kim cried out desperately, as she dropped to her knees hugging and holding on to his legs.

"Come on Kim. I'm done. I told you last time we had a fight, the next time you hit me or cause me to put hands on you, I'm through! I can't deal with no hardheaded, slick talking, trash can mouth chic. I just can't."

Whether it was the look in his eyes or the sound of his voice, at that very moment she realized he was really fed up with her so she regrettably let him leave as he asked her to.

**Five hours later, at 12:15 a.m., the Palmer Club was
filled with people** from Philly, New Jersey, Delaware and the
whole tri-state area. Palmers was one of the club venues that Ace
hosted weekly parties at. All Takedown entertainment events
attracted celebrity guests each and every week. Sports celebs like
Allen Iverson, Donovan McNabb – rappers like Freeway and
Beanie Sigel would come out each week to party at most of Ace's
star studded events.

Tammy stood sexy at 5-foot -3 weighing 125 pounds. She
was a beautiful hood version of Rocsi from B.E.T's *106 and
Park*. Tammy worked at the door at the club for Ace collecting
money from the patrons to enter the party. Amin, Cuzin Chris,
Jeff, Mar, Boz, Ray and Bilal, also known as,Twin Towers all
played their parts as usual to run the club successfully and
smoothly each and every weekend.

The rain had stopped, but it was still kind of damp
outside. That didn't stop the people of Philadelphia from
partying at one of the hottest club spots the city had to offer. The
line was wrapped around the corner when Ace finally pulled up.
He was stunting hard, as usual, in his triple black 2002 Cadillac
Escalade truck, sitting on 24-inch rims. Even when Ace came to
the club by himself, he would unconsciously attract an entourage
before even entering the venue.

Niggas would try to walk in the club with him to avoid
having to wait in line. Bitches would try to walk in with him to
avoid having to pay to get in the club altogether. If you were very
popular – real bosses and playas – you didn't have to pay to get in
the club. It was like they had an invisible black card on site to get
in any club. All smart club owners and promoters knew any
baller getting money attracted more patrons, and spent money
crazily, poppin bottle after bottle all night long at the bar, so to
change them to get in was insane. You have to treat them like the
stars they are, and capatilze off the money made from their
presence alone.

Porn stars Menage and Pebbles were in line as they noticed Ace's truck pull up. They partied with him in the past and were considered friends of his. Menage is famous for her 7-inch long tongue. Pebbles is known in the porn industry for having one of the best, wettest deep throat blow jobs, and also known for taking the biggest dicks, double penetration style by two different male studs.

Ace saw them both in line as he parked in his reserved spot directly in front of the club. He had a sudden mental moment as he remembered the time he saw Menage practically fuck a bitch with her 7-inch tongue. Ace thought he knew how to eat pussy the best, until he witnessed Menage cause this chic to have multiple explosive orgasms. The chic nutted so strong that it was ridiculous. Afterwards, Menage turned around and sucked his man's dick, literally wrapping her 7-inch tongue around the shaft of his dick and pulling it back into her mouth. *'She's a fuckin beast'* Ace thought.

He also thought about the first time he fucked Pebbles fine sexy ass. Before she sucked his dick, she told him, *"You might wanna put a towel under you to protect ya' bed, cause you finna get wet!"* Ace had grabbed himself and simply shook his head at the wonderful thoughts, as he turned off the ignition to the sporty truck.

"Hey Ace! That's my fuckin brotha right der!" Menage said out loud in a half drunken state, as Pebbles secretly smiled finger-waving hi to him.

"They with me." Ace told the bouncers as he walked pass the crowded line, headed straight to the front door of the club.

Menage was feeling good, so she starting showing off as the bouncers let them through. She made the bouncers let in a few other people out of spite, since she no longer had to wait in line.

"Uhhh, let me see here? Ohhh, she's extra chocolate and pretty. She with us too." Menage replied flirtatiously as she pointed to a tall, slim dark skinned woman with long silky wavy hair. She knew exactly how Ace liked them. Slim in the waist, pretty in the face. He was especially sweet on pretty, dark skinned women…

Ace and Mar were on the first floor of the club shooting pool, when a sexy caramel brown skinned girl casually walked over to them.

"Excuse me. Hey, Ace. My name is Chanel. I'm sorry if I interrupted your game. But my girlfriend absolutely loves you. She goes to all your events simply to see you. She really, really likes you and she acting all scared to come over here with me so she can meet you. I told her you were cool. So, can you please walk over there with me so she can actually meet you?" Chanel said playfully.

"If you wasn't so cute, I'd tell you no." Ace replied jokingly, as she took his hand to lead the way.

Now why couldn't she be the one trying to holla? Watch it be an ugly ass girlfriend waiting over there to meet me. I'm giving her a quick hug and I'm gone.' Ace thought to himself.

As he got closer he couldn't believe his eyes. One of the most beautiful women Allah created stood in front of him, and his appreciation; she was extra chocolate, dark skinned.

"Ace, this is Nikky. Nikky I would like you to finally meet the infamous Ace Capone." Chanel replied excitingly. Shortly after a brief conversation they both agreed to get together for a dinner date later on that week. Nikky smiled and blushed as they exchanged phone numbers.

At 3:30 a.m. the music went silent. The party was over, so Ace went into the back office to count his money and to pay his staff for the night. Looking like a younger darker version of Halle Berry, a homer-lover-friend of his named Toot waited outside in Ace's truck behind the dark tinted windows.

*   *   *

Two hours later, at 5:30 a.m. that early Sunday morning, Toots 5-foot-1,122 pound curvaceous, sexy, petite chocolate frame was glistening wet from their sweat. Ace had pinned one of her legs down, while the other one rested on his shoulder as he slowly continuously punished her pleasurably.

"Ooooohhhh Shhhiiiittt! Mmmmmmmpphhh." Toot gasped out loud, as she tightened her face now looking like she was Chinese.

Ace knew her small sexy frame couldn't take too much dick, but he would bottom out her tight little pussy purposely every four to five strokes anyway. Toot's pussy was so tight he had to spread her legs wide just to penetrate her comfortably with his fat dick. The pussy was so good he already came once inside of her, and he was still working hard on another explosive nut.

"Ohhh God!" Toot hollered, as he stroked her wet, slightly bald, pussy. It seemed as if his dick was in her stomach, but the pain mixed with pleasure felt absolutely, wonderful to her. She slowly licked and sucked on his nipples as she came once again. Toot felt Ace's dick getting harder as he plunged deeper and deeper at a steady rhythm. She felt his dick jerking and throbbing inside her tight warm gushy tunnel. She knew what he liked when he came, so she desperately tried to take the entire thick, long black dick he was giving her.

"Shhhiiiittt!" Ace whispered in a yelp, as he gripped the pillow beneath her head tightly, focusing on the wonderful sensation he was about to receive. He started fucking her deep, strong and steady like he was digging for gold to finally release his own hot load of creamy love gunk.

"Mmmmmph!" Toot moaned and cried out in ecstasy, yet relieved he was finally finished.

"Damn! That was good. You alright?" Ace asked tiredly, as he rolled from off top of her, dripping with sweat still breathing heavily.

"Yeah I think so." She lied in a light whisper. Toot had three powerful orgasms during the intense sexual encounter, so her pussy was now sore and sloppy. All she wanted to do was take a long, hot bath. She secretly hoped Ace didn't want to go another round as usual. Little did she know he had already cum twice…

Toot and Ace were sound asleep at 10:30 a.m. when the house phone in his apartment rang for the hundredth time. *'Don't nobody be calling here. Must be telemarketers or someone trying to sale something.'* Ace thought to himself as he woke up out of a comfortable sleep.

"Come on sweetheart. We got to go." Ace shook Toot, waking her up so they could leave.

Twenty minutes later as they walked to the truck, Ace and Toot were suddenly startled. Both of their eyes opened wide like two deer caught in headlights, as they heard the engine roaring from a four door 2000 Chevy Malibu quickly running down on them. SCCCUUUURRRRRHHHHHH! The tires screeched as the car came to a sudden stop directly in front of them. Kim jumped out of the car explosively, wearing a headscarf, sweatpants over her pajamas, and sporting a fresh, now bluish-black eye.

Ace almost simultaneously pissed and shitted in his pants. At first he thought it was homicide detectives running up on him. But now, for some reason even though it was only Kim he didn't feel any better.

"You know what, I'm a just ask you woman to woman. Did yall just have sex?" Kim asked.

Deep down inside Kim knew the answer already, she just didn't want to believe it, and so she had to hear it for herself. Ace was still in shock so nothing registered fast enough. Kim was acting way too calm and iffy for him. He thought to himself, *'Toot if you tell this crazy nut we fucking, she gonna messa round and kill us both.'*

It must have been the mad,crazy,deranged, yet calm look in Kim's eyes that scared Toot;causing her to simply tell the truth.

"Yeah." Toot said as she shook her head in a state of fear.

"Did he tell you he had a fiancée?" Kim replied as she slowly held up her one and one half karat diamond ring.

This was all strange to Ace because normally Kim would have been fighting all over a bitch. Kim saw that Toot was pretty and passive, so Kim wanted to say all she could to scare Toot and keep her away from Ace in the future.

"He ain't any good. Look what he did to my eye last night. I have his son and he still kicks my ass." Kim said.

Ace saw Kim breaking down. He never saw her act this way, so he was nervous of what could happen next. He knew full well that Kim was legally licensed to carry a firearm. He was the one that actually instructed her to get it when she worked at one of his hair salons. It was also broad daylight outside and Ace had his gun on him through all the commotion. He knew he needed to defuse the situation before it got out of control and the cops really came due to all the drama. He gently and slowly walked over to Kim.

"Aye listen. Boo, I'm sorry. I am truly sorry. I thought I could leave you, but you are crazier than me. She means absolutely nothing to me. It was a frustration fuck. I only love you. We have a family together and I am coming home." Ace said sincerely as he softly held Kim by her face.

"I need you to go home. I don't like you out here looking crazy like this. Just let me take this girl home, and Allah is my witness, you will never have to worry about me seeing her ever again." Ace said, knowing he found the right words to calm Kim down, as he made Toot get in the truck to take her home.

Kim shook her head yes as she cried. She was very hurt, but she didn't want to risk losing him forever. She knew the fight they had early yesterday evening was almost the straw that broke the camel's back. She thought she had lost him, which is why she switched cars with her sister, Mooky, to spy on him. What Kim just witnessed truly crushed her, today she was attempting to be that submissive, obedient woman she didn't know how to be, but realized Ace wanted her to be.

Although it took everything inside of her to act out of her character, she hurtfully did exactly what he said at that moment and simply went home.

*   *   *

Ace was dropping Toot off at her house. He couldn't believe she shook her head yes, telling Kim they just had sex. Ace figured even though he still smelled like sex he could of semi-lied to Kim and got himself out of the jam. He was highly upset with Toot for fessing up to their dealings. Ace didn't even talk to Toot about the bizarre confrontation during the ride to her house. *'Damn! She got some bomb ass pussy too, but I won't ever hit that again. Point blank! I done messed around and swore to Allah about it. How da fuck did Kim even find my damn apartment?'* Ace curiously thought to himself as he pulled off.

CHAPTER 17
Streets are watching (stick-up boys and narcs)

Somewhere in Tiawanna, Mexico an older man name Roberto Gonzalez was smoking a cigar, grieving over the loss of his son. Things had seemed strangely suspicious to him after receiving the news about his good friend Carlos Martinez's assassination. Then three short days later Roberto finds out that his own son has been brutally killed as well.

Miami homicide detectives ruled it a cat burglary turned homicide. They came up with this conclusion because Rudy's penthouse was ransacked, and everything of value was missing from the lovely apartment. They figured that Rudy came home surprising the robbers, who were probably gang members and was murdered.

A heavy muscular man named Po-Po stood at 6-foot-4, weighing 350 pounds, spoke to console his grieving long time crime boss.

"Senior, I know it won't make it any easier for you to handle, but we will find Rudy's murderers. I got a few close business associates looking into it as we speak." Po-Po said.

"I'm sure you do my friend. I just miss my son. We never had the perfect father and son relationship, but we did very good business together and I loved my boy." Roberto replied mournfully.

"I know senior, I know. Which reminds me, I'm tracking down all of his customers for you, so we can keep things in proper order. I learned that his main client who sold most of his ye-yo, is a young, black guy out of Philadelphia, PA named Ace Capone. From what I hear, Ace still has a good and steady flow of business even after Rudy's death. Which leads me to believe that he either owes money or he's quickly dealing with someone else." Po-Po said, with concern.

"Then you need to fix that immediately! Matter of fact, if my memory serves me correctly you should call my sister's daughter, Maria. Ace is her boyfriend. I saw his potential some time ago, but Rudy got to him before me. Get Ace to me ASAP!" Roberto demanded sternly.

120

"Senior! I don't mean any disrespect, but are you sure you want to meet and deal with this guy personally? I hear he's too flashy. Maybe you prefer me to deal with him for you instead?" Po-Po eagerly suggested.

"No-no, my trusty friend. I will deal with him myself. Ace needs no middleman. Even if he is a little too flashy we can mold him into a more discreet businessman. Rudy told me personally himself that Ace is trustworthy, loyal and reliable. Associates like that are hard to find. The bottom line is I can trust this guy with large amounts of money, and he is capable of making fast turnovers. Someone has to replace Rudy, and I believe that someone is Ace." Roberto replied convincingly.

*   *   *

It had been two months since Rudy's death, and Ace had to re-up twice with a line out of Texas. This was a headache for Ace cause a middleman was involved. Ace now realized that even though Rudy's way to transport the drugs seem like a hassle, it truly had him spoiled. Rudy got it to him without problems and on consignment – which was more convenient. Ace had to spend cash money with this new Texas connect, so he would only buy 50 kilos at a time. That would have to hold him over until he mastered a plan to get a larger load of cocaine back to the Philadelphia area. Getting the coke was easy. Getting it back to Philly **safely** was the hard part....

Back in Philly, business was sweet as usual for Ace and his team. All the hair salons, barbershops, bars, clubs, and even the jails had Ace Capone's name in their mouth. Ace whole team was the talk of the town. Chics either wanted them or gossiped about them because they were getting crazy money. Niggas either gossiped or hated on them because they wasn't them, but really wanted to get down with the flamboyant drug gang, quickly remembering that famous *saying 'if you can't beat'em, join em.'*

Ace and the C.C.G was like Kobe Bryant and the L.A. Lakers, they simply couldn't be beat right now. The streets crowned them champions because Ace Capone's cocaine gang was winning by a landslide.

*   *   *

Everything seemed good, but Ace was tired of dealing with the Texas line through Cee.

"Listen pimp, you my man and all. But you in my way, you blocking better business for us, and you don't even realize it. I'm a make sure you eat. But I got to start dealing with them gwalla gwalla's myself. Ya dig?" Ace said calmly to Cee.

"I'm cool with that." Cee replied nonchalantly.

Truth be told, Cee wasn't really cool with it but, he knew he had little choice in the matter. Cee knew that whether or not he directly connected Ace to the line or not, Ace would eventually find a way around him. The Texas connect had already inquired about dealing with Ace directly anyhow. They knew from the streets that Ace was the go to man in the Philadelphia tri-state area, and wanted to propose a weekly deal with Ace. They even told Cee they would pay him to officially introduce them to Ace.

"I will set it up for you to talk with them whenever you ready." Cee told Ace, quickly realizing he would now get paid for the meeting on both ends.

"Pimp, you need to set that up ASAP!" Ace replied.

Ace's cell phone was ringing, as he looked he noticed Maria's name on his caller ID. He started to let it go to his voice mail, but thought to himself *'Man, I ain't hit this pretty pussy in like a month of Sundays',* as he answered the phone.

"Hello."

"Hiiii Papi!" Maria replied happily, thankful that he actually picked up.

"Hey Ma. You miss me?"

"Of course I miss you Papi. I want to see you," Maria said in her spoiled, childish, lips poked out voice.

"Alright sweetheart, I'll be over there tonight." Ace replied.

"Baby, are you really coming over? I miss you Papi. Besides, my uncle called me and says he really wants to meet you." Maria replied, concerned if he was really going to come see her.

"Your uncle?" Ace asked surprisingly. He knew Rudy was dead and he never dealt with any other family members of hers besides her brother Mondo.

"Your uncle who?" Ace asked suspiciously.

"My uncle Roberto. He's really my great uncle. He's uncle Rudy's father, Papi." Maria responded.

Ace got nervous almost instantly. His mind wandered all kinds of ways *„did the young Mexican boy notice my face? Did I leave a trail back to me? What da fuck did I miss?'* He thought to himself.

"Alright ma, I'll be there. I need a drink so I may be a little tipsy. But I will be there; I want to put a workout on my little Spanish kitty kat." Ace said, realizing that he had to keep calm.

"Ya bath water will be ready. Call when you close Popitto. Love ya, bye-bye." Maria replied happily, as she smooched him a kiss over the phone.

Ace never responded back to her last comment. He looked out for her, but he only allowed himself to love his main girls. Ace cared for Maria a lot so he would never lie to her about something as serious as loving her. Maria assumed that Ace really loved her. She just thought he was too macho to admit it.

Ace decided to have a few drinks at the **Goldcoast**, a neighborhood bar *down the bottom,* in West Philly, on Lancaster Avenue. He was lost in thoughts as he remembered Rudy's last words while he was pleading for his life. *„I can give you better numbers Ace, in the single digits my friend. $8,000 dollars a kilo!'*

As Rudy's voice echoed in his drunken state of mind, Ace came back to reality after repeatedly hearing the female bartender's voice.

"You alright baby? You were in outer space. You got me a little worried." Blondie said as she softly touched his forehead with the back of her hand to check his temperature.

Blondie is a super *baadd bitch* and one of Ace's favorite sex partners. Blondie stood 5'8" at 145 pounds, and had the body of a Greek Goddess. She had the perfect boob job, that Ace had nicknamed the twin towers. Ace also had two bodyguards at the club who were actually called the **Twin Towers**. Ray stood 6'7", weighing in at 370 pounds, and Bilal was 6'5" weighing in at 350 pounds. Needless to say, Ace's favorite Twin Towers belonged to Blondie.

Blondie is a lesbian, but she liked dick on occasion too. Ace only appreciated seeing her naked cause her body was flawless. Blondie had tattoos that covered 65 percent of her caramel brown skinned body, which enhanced her intoxicating sex appeal. Her short, blonde boy cut hairstyle had natural waves, that gave her a distinct look and made her every man's fantasy.

"I'm good sweetheart!" Ace replied sourly.

"You know I can make you feel better Daddy. If you feeling frisky I can bring some company along with us tonight, just tell me what flavor you want? Spanish, White, Korean, you name it; you got it. You know I love watching you punish em' while I make em' take that big dick all crazy!" Blonde said, with a seductive smile, as she had a sudden flashback of one of their crazy erotic threesome episodes.

"Naaaah, unfortunately I'ma have to pass on that tonight sexy, but I do want you to get at this new chick I got in line. I want to see ya sexy ass eat some of that pussy. Ya dig?" Ace said, matter factly.

"Anything and anyway you want it Daddy. Just let me know who and when." Blondie replied.

"I will let you know soon and you gonna' love this chic. You know she's a dime if I bring her, just like when you bring em'." Ace said with a smirk, as he thought about how good that moment is gonna be and added, "Matter of fact, I think I'm a hook that up next Saturday after my horse race. Hopefully your red light won't be on, so don't make any plans."

Ace got up and paid for his drinks. He tipped Blondie something husky as always, and attempted to leave when Blondie tried to make him change his mind.

"Awwww man! Now I got to be jealous all night because someone else about to get the Henny dick. I want it Daddy." Blondie pouted with disappointment in her face and voice.

"Come on Blondie. You can't get me with that cute sympathy expression tonight sweetheart. I got go home tonight sexy, but you know what to do when I'm not available. Just go a few rounds pleasing yourself while you think of me, or enhance the fun by popping in one of our good ole sex tapes." Ace replied, as he smiled and kissed her forehead goodbye....

As Ace left the bar, D-Rock and Tone were driving down the street in a tinted out Chevy Lumina. When they circled the block for the fourth time, Tone quickly noticed the unexpected.

"Shit! There he is right there!" Tone said with excitement and surprise.

"Damn! I didn't know you was talking about Ace." D-Rock replied shockingly.

"Yeah, I know him as Al. I'm so used to calling him Al, I forgot they call him Ace too."

"Damn Tone this gonna be a risky robbery if we go through with it."

"Nah, it will be easy. Remember I know where his babymom live. I can find out when they ain't home then all you got to do is creep up in his crib. I know he got some kind of money there, maybe even some work too." Tone said matter factly.

"Maybe money, but I doubt that he got some dope up in there. What makes you think that?" D-Rock asked curious about Tones analogy.

"My girl and his babymom are sisters. One day my girl seen Al and one of his homies go in the bedroom, and they didn't come back out for a long time. She said they had to be counting a lot of money cause she overheard them using a money machine. His man was trying to holla at my girl, so I want to get that nigga too. Anyway, one night she said she seen a big ass duffel bag full of money in her sister's room after Al left. She heard him tell Rain to make sure no one goes in the bedroom. Rain's whole family was over there that day, so my girl went in his room to be nosey.

D-Rock listened to Tone talk as he cautiously drove past Ace watching him get into his car.

"Alright. I have you, but, you gonna have to be more involved for us to get away with this properly. We gotta catch that nigga slipping." D-Rock said sternly with a cool look in his early eyes.

"It will be sweeter if I let you know the next time Rain is over my house – and Al drops his cars off at the carwash. That way if the kids at my house with Sandra, you can do a simple, quick, clean cat burglary. No one will know who did it."

Tone was pressed and desperate. He washed cars at Butter's carwash for a living, and money was always tight for him. Ace would look out for him if he asked, but pride and envy was in Tone's filthy heart. All Tone and Sandra's problems evolved around finances. Bills were overdue, creditors constantly called, and the kids always needed something. Times were tight for them, and they lived check to check each and every week. The only breather they received was around income tax time, and even then the check was gone before they could spend it.

D-Rock, on the other hand, had many concerns. He knew going at Ace was dangerous, but as usual, greed always overruled and tampered with a man's intelligence.

"Alright, we gone get that nigga, but it got to be kept completely quiet and carefully thought out. So start by telling me every little thing you actually know about Ace?"

"Man, I can show you where Rain live at and where Iesha, another one of his kids mother live at. Shit I can even show you where that nigga's mom live at!" Tone replied confidently.

D- Rock drove as he listened, *„who would believe square as Tone could be so valuable? Shit, I'm fresh out of jail. This is the come up I been looking for'* he thought to himself....

*   *   *

Maria had planned to get her freak on, but after washing Ace up in the tub and rubbing him down with lotion, he fell fast asleep. Maria always thought that Ace looked like an innocent schoolboy while he was asleep. Due to all the ripping and running he normally did, she decided to simply let him get some much-needed rest. Maria understood how hard Ace worked when he was in the streets.

Usually Ace slept with one eye open like CBS. Not tonight, he was exhausted. His half drunken state, combined with extra comfort, caused him to pass out; sleeping peacefully. Maria admired Ace, as she gently kissed him on his lips and lay down beside him until she fell asleep.

Due to the hangover from last night, Ace woke up the next day with a headache. The loud noise from Spanish kids laughing and playing didn't make it any better.

"I said keep it down damn it, Papi is resting!" Maria screamed as she closed their bedroom door.

126

"Damn Ma! What time is it?" Ace asked, as he held his face between his hands.

"It's 1:30 in the afternoon Papi. You feel any better?"

"Nah. I need an aspirin or something. I feel like shit."

"Awe, Mommy will make you feel better. Then you can make me all better." Maria said sincerely, yet playfully – and serious as a heart attack. Ace smiled at her indirect sex remark as he checked his cell phone for missed calls. Suddenly he remembered something he had on his mind.

"Aye Ma, what's this about your uncle you were saying yesterday?" Ace asked cautiously, but concerned.

"Oh yeah Papi. He is in town and he wants to meet you. He won't tell me, but I think he wants to pick up where you and uncle Rudy left off."

"What you mean where we left off? What he thinks I owe Rudy some money or something?" Ace retorted defensively.

"No Papi. Relax! He probably just wants to do business with you. That's all, I think. My uncle Roberto is *the man who supply, who supply you, who supply you.*" Maria replied as she mocked one of Beanie Sigel's verses.

Ace sat there puzzled. He wondered why he didn't allow himself to love Maria like he loved Rain, Kim and Iesha. Maria was truly a major asset to him, not a liability like the other girls. Ace only blocked his feelings for her because she used to be with Lump. Ace knew he was out of pocket for even fucking his man's girlfriend, especially now that she done abandoned Lump altogether behind the fact that she fell in love with Ace. Ace came back to reality as he heard Maria talking to him.

"He wants us to meet him today at my mother's house. He actually came in town a couple of days ago."

'He never said exactly why?" Ace asked, somewhat concerned, as he figured it was most likely safe cause her mom's house had to be off limits for war.

"No, he didn't say exactly why, but he did tell me specifically not to let Mondo know he was in town. That's why I think he wants to do business with you. Rudy is gone and uncle Roberto won't do business with Mondo like that. My brother knows my uncle is the man." Maria replied convincingly.

Ace wanted to smile. He was thinking recklessly for nothing. He knew he couldn't run from it, so he had to face any suspicions because his family wouldn't be safe if he didn't. He still felt a bit uneasy due to his conscious of what he did to Rudy, but everything Maria analyzed to him made perfect sense, so he relaxed.

"So what time we supposed to be there?"

"6:00 this evening for dinner. Mama's cooking." Maria said with excitement.

Ace rubbed his stomach and licked his lips as he thought about Mama Gonzalez's delicious cooking. She had a special chicken, rice, and beans dish that was coated with melted cheddar cheese and honey, poured over crisp nachos. *Taste so good you want to smack ya mama!*

"Alright, that means I got a few hours to work up a bigger appetite. So bring your sexy taco eating ass over here Ma!" Ace said playfully as he grabbed Maria by her waist, putting his hands in her panties gently rubbing his fingers through her neatly trimmed landing strip.

"UMMMM, P-A-P-I! The kids are downstairs playing." Maria whispered seductively, concerned, but craving for his loving so badly. She knew she desperately wanted to make way too much noise during their sex, as usual.

"The door is shut right?" Ace asked sneakily as he continued to seduce her while fingering her wet pussy.

"Ooohhhh, yessss Papi!" Maria whispered in pleasure.

"Alright then, just keep it down." Ace said, devilishly.

Ace's sneaky intentions were to force her to be quiet while causing her to silently scream out in ecstasy. Maria had on one of his throwback jerseys with nothing but panties on underneath. Ace began passionately kissing on her neck, as he laid her down onto the bed. As he slid his jersey off Maria's body, he noticed how erect her tootsie roll sized nipples were immediately noticing how hot and horny she was. He squeezed both of her breasts together and put both of her nipples in his warm, wet mouth, at the same time. Ace worked his tongue like a porn star, and Maria couldn't take it any longer. Ace could tell the way she grinded her wet pussy against his stomach that she was ready for penetration.

"Papi plleeeaase! Put it in!" Maria begged softly as Ace slowly placed the head of his throbbing hard dick in her wet pussy. "Yesss!" Maria whispered in pure pleasure as Ace gently entered her warm, wet love nest with one slow, long, hard stroke, letting his dick sit deep within her pussy.

Maria gripped the bedrails with her hands and squinted her eyes shut as Ace passionately fucked her. It's been a couple of months since he last hit her pussy, so he knew it wouldn't be long before Maria came, because he felt her walls pulsating for her orgasm. Ace sat up and opened her legs spread eagle. Her luscious wet view was something beautiful. He slowly inserted two fingers into her bitter sweetness, and passionately made love to her pussy with his tongue.

"Ummmmmm Poppitto! Yesssss! Maria whispered out in a sexual bliss, as she bit down on her bottom lip, enjoying the erotic tension rapidly building up, as she prepared to explode. The wonderful wet succulent sounds from him eating her pussy so good caused her to squirm, fighting the urge to run. **"Mmmmmmmmmpphhhhhhhh"**Ace could hear her whimpering in pure enjoyment, as she simultaneously tried to be quiet, while he took her to a place no other man could ever bring her to…

*   *   *

Ace, Maria and her kids arrived at her mother's house around 6:30 p.m. After they ate, Maria and Mama Gonzalez were cleaning up the kitchen, while Ace and Uncle Roberto were in the den chatting.

"So, I want to be clear about all this. You want to supply me with 500 kilos a week at 10,000 dollars a kilo. But if I can get rid of more than that, the number gets even better for me?" Ace repeated, making sure he understood the proposal Roberto had just told him.

"Si, my friend. But to get a better price on each kilo, you are gonna need access to a plane. I can actually handle the plane connections because I have plans for you, but we will make that happen in due time. For now, I suggest we stick to the 500 kilo deal so we can get started." Roberto replied earnestly.

"If you don't mind me asking, what plans do you actually have for me?" Ace asked curiously.

"Eventually I want you to also deal state to state with some of the other customers Rudy left behind. I trust your knowledge and judgment. I believe that you can handle my business affairs as well as Rudy did, if not better." Roberto replied matter factly as he added.

"You should look into getting a place in Florida, and in Texas as well. You will be doing a lot more traveling for business purposes now. Maybe get you a nice beach house in Ft. Lauderdale, and few acres of farmland in Texas for close to nothing. I could help with that as well if you need me to. I have a few close associates highly involved in the real estate business." Roberto explained.

Ace listened while hiding his anxiousness. Everything Roberto told him sounded too good to be true. He knew he was about to **takedown** the game for real, as he finally shook his head yes, officially accepting the offer.

"I'm all in. Just tell me when do we get started."

"Very good my friend, very good. Here's an address to a farm in New Jersey. You need to be there tomorrow at 4:30 a.m. sharp! There will be two commercial tractor-trailer sized dump trucks waiting for you. Each truck is carrying a ton of gravel. The product will be in the bed of the truck underneath all the gravel. The farm is safe and I trust you know how to move safely from there?" Roberto retorted. Ace simply nodded his head yes with a smile.

"Another thing Ace - If you owed Rudy any money it's yours. That was you and his business. I could request the debt because it belongs to me, but I ask you one personal request in return." Roberto said in a very calm, yet stern manner.

"And what might that be?" Ace asked with a puzzled look on his face.

"Find out who murdered my only son!" Roberto replied angrily.

Ace saw a look of pain and rage through the old man's eyes. Roberto was laid back, wise, rich and powerful, which made him very dangerous. Ace kept calm, knowing that dead men don't talk. He realized that no one had a clue who had actually killed Rudy.

"I miss Rudy too. He was family to me - a good man and a great business associate. I sincerely send my condolences to you and the family, and I hope you consider me family as well. I will keep my ear to the streets to find out what happened, and when we do find out something, rest assure, you can count on me for sweet deadly revenge!"

'So, I've heard my friend, so I've heard." Roberto explained as they both stood to shake hands.

"El postre esta listo" Maria yelled, in Spanish, to Ace and Robert so they could come have dessert.

   *   *   *

The next day everything ran smoothly when Ace unloaded 500 kilos of good quality white fishscale cocaine. Roberto separately sent a cell phone *via mail* for the load. He would only talk to Ace on this particular phone, and in the future every load would contain a different phone to serve the same purpose. The phone would only be used once the load was picked up, and whenever Ace was ready with the money for a new load to come.

   *   *   *

Off to the races...

Ace and Rachael was at Charlestown Racetrack located in Charlestown, West Virginia waiting to see Ace's thoroughbred **Strike Adduce** race his one and three-fourth mile race. The winner's purse was 57,000 dollars for this specific race, and Duce's odds were only 3-1 today. That was a big difference from the first time Ace and his grandfather Pop-Pop Lee raced the fine thoroughbred. Strike Adduce's odds were 33-1 the first time he stepped his hoofs on Charlestown Racetrack's soil. No one had heard of the young horse yet, not to mention his new owner Ace, who was new to the sport altogether. Duce was actually bred from a **Kentucky Derby Winner** who won over 3 million dollars in purses alone, and was bred to a Philly that won over 600,000 dollars in purses. These two outstanding horses go by the name **"Strike the Gold"** (the sire) and **"Adduce"** (the mare). Duce is chestnut brown with a white stripe down his face. He wore bright green and white colors for his race today. Strike Adduce is an absolutely, beautiful strong looking horse, and one of the best-bred horses on Charlestown's track.

Rachel was highly impressed. She could only imagine how this young, black, hood rich nigga got into owning and racing thoroughbred horses. Rachel is a business owner herself. She owned her own hair salon in Southwest Philly, directly next door to the barbershop **Center of Attractions.** Rachael is a straight up dime piece. She is of Latin native decent, and stood at 5-foot-3 weighing135 pounds, withholding the look of a sexy Puerto Rican belly dancer. Her extremely long, black, silky hair only complimented her natural beauty. She could have easily made the cover of *Curves Magazine* and no man would get tired of jerking off to her spread.

The racetrack environment was cluttered with all sorts of people tonight. Everyday people, mobsters, the rich and famous, and even high government officials were sitting anxiously, waiting to watch the race. Professional horse racing is a spectacular sport that attracted many people from everywhere. This is where the opposites meet for one common purpose, with one common understanding **TO WIN**. Girlfriends and married women alike, pranced around in their expensive jewelry and enticing clothes while playing their positions as trophies to their men.

People of the audience were placing their bets to receive their tickets. In horse racing, you can place bets all kinds of ways. You didn't have to bet one specific place the horse would come in. You could actually bet a horse to come in first, second or third place. There's also a huge payoff if you place the **Trifecta** and won. This is where you play it like a lottery mixing the numbers around to the horses so that it comes out in the order you put it. Put more frankly, gambling is extremely unlimited when it comes to horse racing.

Ace was sitting beside Rachael as Pop-Pop Lee glanced up at the status board. The big colorful board lit up brightly, displaying the odds to the race. The three of them just left from Duce's stall where Ace had pepped talked the young Mexican jockey. They were now on the bleachers anxiously awaiting the race. Ace secretly knew the injection of non-detectable drug his grandfather just shot into Strike Adduce's neck merely 30 minutes ago, could possibly allow his horse the extra stamina and strength to win this race….

Riiiinnnnnng-a-ling-a-ling! Was the sound of the bells as the announcer screamed "**And they're off!**"

As the horses took off, Strike Adduce was behind by six horses, it was 12 horses in the race altogether. Tonight Strike Adduce wore the number 9, and the horses were already a half of a mile into the race.

"Come on number 9. Let's go!" Rachel shouted with excitement. She had no idea that she would be this much into the race. "Rove it Duce." She added quickly noticing him picking up momentum as he passed two horses turning on the inside lane.

Strike Adduce was kicking up massive dust gaining on three other horses before passing them in a violent rage. The horses were on the last stretch but the one horse ahead of number 9 was still looking good.

"Duce, move your ass!" Rachael screamed out in the unexpected passion she was now lost in. Her outburst made Ace look at her in disbelief and shock, which caused him to smile.

It was like Strike Adduce had heard Rachael's demand as he quickly began gaining on the leading horses. They were now running neck to neck with only yards to go. Within a second Duce took the lead. Rachael screamed with excitement "**Ahhhh Baby Duce is winning!**"

Strike Adduce finished explosively in first place leaving all the other horses behind to eat his dust. Ace clapped with a proud look on his face while Rachael continued to scream with joy. She had never been to a horse race before, let alone with someone who actually owned the winning horse.

Rachel was even more excited about the money she won. After watching Ace place a 10,000 dollars bet on his own horse, she placed a 500 dollar bet of her own for Duce to come in **1st, 2nd or 3rd place**. Pop-Lee, Ace and Rachael walked towards the winners circle to meet up with Duce. All of them including the jockey, trainers, and even the stall guy who fed Duce everyday had posed for the winning photo. Ace smiled as he called Blondie to tell her about his win.

"What's up B? Guess who won again?" Ace retorted rapidly then added. "Remember the person I spoke highly of that night at the bar? Hold on, she right here. She wants to meet you. Here sexy, say hello." Ace said as he handed Rachel the phone.

"Hello." Blondie said in a sexy voice.

"Hi Blondie. I heard such wonderful and interesting things about you. I can't wait to meet you." Rachael said flirtatiously.

As they conversed, Ace thought to himself „*Bull you stay winning'* as he stared at the tattoo on his left forearm which read, **Winner Takes All,** surrounded by a horseshoe covered in money, co-signing a myth some of Ace's closest friends always said 'that he has a lucky horseshoe stuck in his ass.

CHAPTER 18
(Crooked cops)

It was a quiet, slow day in Paschall projects because of the shootout last night. A few of the younger neighborhood guys got into it with a guy from Bartram Village. However, just like your average ghetto shoot-outs, no one who did the actual shooting got shot. Unfortunately, an innocent child or pedestrian normally gets fatally wounded behind the senseless shootings, but this particular time no one got hurt. The only thing that got shot up pretty badly, this time was a 99' Pontiac Bonneville. This was the only information Detective Reese could get out of the people from the neighborhood. As Detective Reese searched the riddled Bonneville he noticed a valid P.A. license sitting between the seats. He picked it up and read the name Charlie Hemm on it...

Detective Reese had been on the force for fifteen years now, and due to his continuous good police work, integrity and dedication, he was promoted to detective five years ago. Detective Reese learned that the Bonneville was registered to a Gwen Walters of 5808 S. Cecil Street, in Philadelphia, PA. To further his investigation, he decided to visit the address on the license. He ran the name Charlie Hemm in through the police data bank. When the information came back he learned that Charles is a convicted felon for the sale of narcotics. *,, Maybe the shooting was over drug turf? Or maybe it could have been a gang dispute? Whatever it is, I hope to get to the bottom of it before someone gets hurt or killed'* he thought to himself as he headed over to the Cecil Street address.

    *   *   *

Pooh had just got done whipping **nine ounces of cocaine into twelve ounces of crack** when his cell phone rang for what urkingly seemed like the 100th time.

"Hello. Yeah nigga, I'm on my way. Damn! I'll be there in like ten minutes" Pooh said arrogantly and impatiently to his crack head runner, as he quickly hung up the phone.

As Pooh left out the house, he suddenly realized that he didn't have his license. This was second nature to him because he never drove without his license when he was riding dirty. Pooh was so in a hurry that he never noticed the plain clothes cops parked across the street, who had been sitting there over the last five minutes now.

"Charlie Hemm! We need to speak with you sir." The detective said, very casually as he walked up.

Soon as Pooh heard his government name called he got extremely nervous. He began to act a bit fidgety as one of the officers quickly noticed a bulge in his waistline.

"Freeze! Put your hands where I can see them. Don't move!" Detective Reese yelled in a hostile manner.

The twelve ounces of crack and a gun, which had the serial numbers scraped off, should have been more than enough reason for Pooh to run for his natural black life. But his nervousness caused him to simply freeze, Pooh had bitched up out of fear and shock so he was taken directly into custody with ease. Before Detective Reese even read him his rights, Pooh had offered to cooperate fully if it could help his charges disappear…

*   *

*

Officer Mykal Coles was on break at the 12th district, drinking coffee and eating donuts when Detective Reese walked in the busy police station. Detective Reese pulled officer Mykal to a private area so he could give him the details on the new C-I (confidential informant).

"Man you had to see this piece of scum. I got to give him credit though. He's not a dummy. He knew he was facing a very long jail sentence if he didn't cooperate." Detective Reese replied humorously and added.

"Pooh tried to open up a new crack house from Paschall, but the neighborhood guys gave him trouble because he wasn't from those projects, so he simply wasn't welcomed to get money on their grounds. That's what led to the shootout last night. Shit, he's even willing to let us wire him up for sound to set up various connects that he constantly or seldom buys his drugs from." Detective Reese replied seriously.

"Un-fucking-believable! These guys never surprise me. They turn on each other in a half of a second and they call themselves gangsters? Shit! We the mothafuckin gangstas! We honor the code of silence with pride, trust and integrity. When a cop gets arrested we go to trial. Our partners don't rat us out. If we go down, we go down together!" Officer Mykal replied as he asked. "So who are some of his connects?"

"Two losers name Tab and Hak. Our new C-I ordered a half a brick,18 ounces, of cocaine from them. They are about to meet him at Tamika's Lounge, on 58th and Elmwood Avenue, to serve him. When they get there we gonna take them down right there. Nothing too complicated, just a normal buy and sell drug sting. Plus, we can pocket some good ole tax free cash." Detective Reese whispered.

Officer Mykal fell into a deep trance *'Tab, Hak, Tamika's Lounge. Oh shit! I got to call my brother.'* He had thought to himself as he quickly responded.

"Aye man. We can't bust those guys, they part of Ace's crew!"

"Ace's crew? Shit, our C-I never mentioned anything about Ace." Detective Reese replied surprisingly.

"Yeah but Tab and Hak are two of his top guys. I know them personally. Tamika's Lounge is the bar they all hang out at. If I'm not mistaken, Ace is hitting Tameka. We can anonymously give her the heads up." Mykal said as he searched the police data bank to retrieve the phone number to Tamika's Lounge.

"Fuck! We got to tip her off quickly. I already sent a team over there, waiting to do the bust. We only got 2 hours before the deal goes down."

"Alright. That means we got time to throw in a lil monkey wrench to fix this." Mykal replied.

"You need to tell big bro to go ahead and put us on his payroll. That way this type of shit won't be happening. We could be providing him with confidential information to help him clean up or stay away from untrustworthy associates who are cooperating." Detective Reese suggested.

"He may very well go for that. It actually sounds like something he may be interested in, so I'm a run it past him and let you know. Right now let's fix this situation."

Philly's finest were all up in Tamika's Lounge. They were searching for drugs, Tab and Hak. Thanks to the anonymous call Tamika got 2 hours ago; there were no drugs there to be found. When the cops left the bar Tamika picked up her cell phone to call Ace. *„To leave a voicemessage press 1. Beep'*

"Hey Babe, it's Meek. We need to talk. It's important so come by tonight." Tamika replied nervously.

Tamika is a cougar, who at 40 years old, still remains as sexy as the original Foxy Brown (Pam Grier) herself. Back in her day Tamika was one of the baddest, top-notch chics in southwest, and to this day still she had no problem pulling herself a sugar daddy. Whether he was old or young she attracted any man's lust. Tamika owned the small bar located on the ground level of a property her parents owned. It started getting slow so her parents considered closing it down. Instead, they had allowed Tamika to take it over. Business was gradually picking up; cause Ace and his squad started hanging out there so she could make decent money. Customers came from all over just to hang out in the same place with Ace and his squad.

Tamika had a lot of respect for Ace. Even though he was younger than her, she admired his ability to control and run both an illegal street operation and several legitimate businesses. Not to mention the mere fact that he would blow her old ass back out from time to time. Tamika is from the old school, so she respected the game and appreciated a man who played it correctly.

Ace had unconsciously made her bar a hang out spot for ballers. It also became the go to spot for known dealers to meet up or score their drugs in weight from Ace. Ace made plenty of money in her establishment so he made sure she got a piece of the profit too. Ace motto was: **If everybody eats, everybody is happy!**

Detective Reese entered the small interrogation room, to inform C-I #151 that the attempted drug sting was infact a failure.

"Well Charlie, the deal was unsuccessful. Now I'm gonna to keep my word and release you because you tried. But, you will have conditions! You are now my personal source of street information, and if you ever hide or give me bullshit, I will make sure you do every bit of the next 30 years of your life in prison. Are we clear?"

Pooh shook his head yes, in a state of fear as he looked and listened to the rest of Detective Reese's demands.

"In three days you are to report to me and me only! I want more info on Tab, Hak and whoever else is involved with these guys. Understand?" Detective Reese retorted as he opened the door for Pooh to leave.

Pooh tried swallowing hard because of the big lump in his throat. However, since he was now free to go he had a sense of relief as he exited the door. Detective Reese watched Pooh from behind as he left. *„You low down dirty rat scum. I won't have any remorse seeing you exterminated. You're a waste of time and oxygen, and I'm sure we will get a pretty penny handing over your snitch ass.'* He thought to himself as he sipped out of his cup of Dunkin Doughnuts freshly brewed coffee.

CHAPTER 19
"Mr. Williams" (Diplomatic Gangstas)

As Ace listened to the details about the possibilities of paying the cops for info on rats and drug dealing protection with his brother Mykal, Ace had a look of great concern - simply because they were cops. Truth be told, Ace barely trusted his brother because he was with the boys in blue.

"Man, I don't know pimp? It sounds good but I hate to fuck with the police. Especially crooked ones. Them muh'fuckaz can pull anything on us and get away with it because they got badges." Ace pointed out.

" I hear you bro, but it's for your good. I think you'll be better off with it than without. Shit almost got fucked up for you the other day- know what I mean? Plus you my big bro. I gots ya' back just like I had that day." Mykal replied.

"Maybe you're right. If I do decide to fuck with it they got to deal with Mac and only Mac or you. I never want to deal with any of them besides you." Ace said sternly.

"That shouldn't be a problem. So when do I have my peers meet with Mac?" Mykal asked curiously.

"I'll have him call you tonight?" Ace said.

As Mykal left, Ace picked up his cell phone to chirp Mac on his *Boost Mobile* phone.

„*Chirp'* "Yo Mac!" *'Chirp'*

"I needs to see you right away." Ace replied. *'Chirp'*

"Uhh, I'm on my way then. Where you at?" Mac asked. *'Chirp'*

"Meet me at TGI Fridays on Cityline Avenue." Ace replied while holding the chirp button.

"Alright. That works out perfect because I'm with that friend I had told you about that you need to meet. Is that cool?" Mac asked. *'Chirp'*

"Yeah, that'll work. I'll be there in about forty-five minutes." Ace said.

~~~

One hour later, narcotics officer, Mac McKenzie from the 18th District walked into TGI Fridays, alongside a well dressed man who appeared to be in his late 60s. They walked over to Ace's table. Ace was seated with his beautiful date Nikky. Ace and Nikky were having drinks, awaiting their food, when they notice Mac and the older man approaching, as Ace stood.

"Babygirl could you please excuse me for a moment. I need to discuss some things with these fine gentlemen." Ace said, as he smiled and shook both men hands.

The three men walked over towards the bar area to have a seat, and chose a small booth to sit and talk.

"Damn, she's pretty as shit Ace." Mac said.

"You know me pimp. Pretty in the face, slim in the waist." Ace replied nonchalantly.

"She may be special so don't lust pimp." Ace added in a serious tone.

Mac laughed and replied, "No doubt. I see you're still a sucka for pretty chocolate women!"

"Anyway, this is Mr. Williams, my old friend and a former Federal prosecutor." Mac said and added. "He's cool and I thought you two should meet. He's the one I been informing you about who can help us keep the Feds off your ass. Like I told you before Ace, I can handle the regular cops, but you need federal protection and this here is your guy." Mac said in one breath.

Ace shook Mr. Williams' hand and looked into his eyes. Mr. William spoke. "Hi Ace I've heard a lot about you. I think I can be a consultant to you to keep things in perspective."

"Can you explain how this will work and what's it going to cost me?" Ace replied calmly. The sarcasm was evident in his tone. Ace was interested, but concerned.

Ace had to make sure that he wasn't getting shook down for money from the powers to be. Mr. Williams was clean cut - wearing an expensive suit by Armani and shoes by Mauri, so Ace peeped Mr. Williams was in style from head to toe. A look that definitely meant he was about his money. Ace respected his taste – he only questioned Mr. William's style. Can this old nigga be trusted? That was the million-dollar question. Which is why Ace felt a little suspicious. Ace looked for signs of a crook or a respectable businessman. Mr. Williams spoke, "Let me start by saying this son, the biggest crooks ain't criminals. The biggest crooks are politicians, judges and lawyers. Those are just a few of the people of power. Payoffs are not the right answers to solving criminal matters. Favors are, one hand always washes the other. Sometimes it's just the person turning his head the other way for the other party to gain higher status and wealth. It's all business son, It's all business! If there's no crime, there's no punishment. That means no fines, no criminal judges, no criminal lawyers or prosecutors needed. The list goes on from jails to simply buying food to feed prisoners. It's all business. Are we still on the same page?"

Ace nodded his head in agreement. As Ace listened, he thought, *"I'm feeling this old head. He's knowledgeable and smooth.* Ace sensed maybe he could do some business with Mr. Williams.

Moments later, Ace looked at his watch, and quickly excused himself for a moment. He remembered that Nikky was still waiting on him to join her for dinner. As Ace walked over to the table, he smiled.

"I'm sorry Baby Girl. This meeting gonna' take me about another thirty to forty five minutes, and I can't have you sitting here alone while you wait on me. That's simply not proper for me to do. You mind if we change plans a bit by you taking my car to go buy some DVD movies for us to watch, and I will meet you at your place in about two hours tops?"

Nikky really liked Ace alot. She secretly had a crush on him for about a year and a half now, so she didn't mind the change of plans at all. As long as she was spending time with her Ace, she was fine. She never drove a Bently Arnage before, and she quickly accepted his offer so she could go show off to her girlfriends.

Ace handed her $500 so she could pick up some movies and snacks for them. He gently placed his hands on the small of her back and kissed her on the cheek before she left. Ace walked back over to the small booth where Mac and Mrs. Williams sat. Wanting to finish up the meeting, Ace sat down, cleared his throat and said, "Now where were we…?"

After listening to an hour of Mr. Williams' explaining things to him, Ace realized that he would gain a lot more than just a Federal lookout. Mr. Williams promised Ace diplomatic services and more. Now whenever Ace goes out of the country on a trip, he would get diplomatic services from the time he landed on foreign soil. A diplomatic driver in a Lincoln town car would be waiting for him, and Mac would now become Ace's personal full time bodyguard with the abilities to board commercial planes with his gun. Mac's resume was impressive – he wasn't just a detective for the Philadelphia police, he was an ex-marine and a part time air marshal for U.S. Airways. With all these perks Ace's gansta persona and reputation would now gain diplomatic status.

With all the contacts Mr. Williams had to offer him, Ace thought to himself, *NOW THAT"S GANGSTA FOR REAL!*

All these perks would come a lot less than Ace had imagined it would. Mr. Williams was fair, very crafty and smart. He gave Ace no specific price. He simply would put together a contract between him and Ace's company, where Mr. Williams would consult on all safety issues at the club. Mr. Williams would prepare Ace's security to properly deal with certain altercations involving patrons. Ace would give Mr. Williams how much money he thought it was worth according to the hours he put in each week, based on the contract. Only Ace and Mac would know the quality of information and protection Mr. Williams really provided for him. Ace intended to be fair with Mr. Williams for all his contacts and abilities. Ace also informed Mac of the payroll situation with the local narcotic unit, which would cost him weekly as well.

Ace quickly figured out a way to make everyone comfortable and content with the new arrangement. He would have Uncle Hak collect money from everyone of higher status in Ace's organization. Hak would do it to pay off a couple Narcs a total of $5,000 a month. In return, Ace's crew would be given a pass to hustle freely on their strips. Plus they'd get information on all raids before they happened. Ace would also get information on who was snitching, and all Ace had to do on his end of his deal was make sure they kept the gun violence down. By doing that, the local narcs would actually guarantee Ace's crew a pass to sell all the drugs they could. Ace smiled, thinking to himself, *Things couldn't get any sweeter!*

Mac and Mr. William offered Ace a ride after the meeting. Ace declined, saying "Nah, that ain't a good look – Plus Amin on his way to pick me up. Matter of fact, there he goes right there. You gentlemen have a nice evening, I've got to get going." Ace stood, shaking both men hands before he left to go finish his date…

CHAPTER 20
"Nikky" (Beauty & Baby girl)

Ace used his key card for the first time. Nikky had given it to him a few weeks ago. Entering her 5th floor apartment, Ace noticed the aroma of vanilla scent. He immediately spotted the flickering of candles. The windows were open allowing a comfortable cozy spring breeze to enter the apartment. It was nice and quiet, so Ace could hear bath water slowly moving around. Nikky softly bathed herself; Ace crept slowly inside the apartment, locking the door behind him. The bathroom door was slightly cracked open so Ace knocked softly.

"Can I come in Beauty?" Ace asked.

"Yes." She replied in her schoolgirl voice.

Nikky was a 22-year-old chocolate beauty. She's 5'7" and weighs roughly 147 pounds. Dark skinned, tall and slim, Nikky possessed a pair of long beautiful sexy legs. Nikky also had the prettiest, silkiest long black hair ever known to man. Because of her slanted eyes and complexion, Nikky was often mistaken as Dominican or some type of mixed breed. But make no mistakes about it; Nikky's a full-blooded African American beauty. The sexy gap between her two front teeth gave her an astonishing look, and at her young tender age, Nikky was the youngest of all his paramours, which is why Ace nicknamed her "Baby girl".

Ace stood there watching Nikky as she bathed, smiling to himself, as he admired her captivating beauty.

"Are you just going to stand there and watch me or are you going to join me?" Nikky asked in a sneaky seductive tone.

"Oh, I'm getting in!" Ace replied, as he climbed in the tub with his clothes and shoes still on.

Nikky laughed loudly. "Uh Unnnh Baby! You Crazy! She said.

She sat up and mounted Ace. "What you don't want to take off your clothes?" She kissed him before he could respond.

As she passionately kissed him on the lips and down his neck, Ace said. "Ummm, of course I do, but I was so anxious to get next your sexy naked body I forgot."

"Ummm." She moaned as she continued to seduce him.

"Now I see I have to send you shopping for clothes or else I'll be stuck here with ya' sexy ass until my clothes dry. It ain't like I got a wardrobe here." Ace said, in a whispering tone, completely aroused by her seduction.

"Well, we need to adjust that and start you a wardrobe here, don't you agree?" Nikky replied before she passionately kissed him.

She started to remove his wet clothes.

"Damn, we making a mess Baby girl. The floors is soaking wet." Ace said.

"Not as wet as me." Nikky replied softly.

"Oh yeah?" Ace asked, getting even more anxious.

"OHHHH YEEEAAH!" Nikky replied, as she stood up over top of him, dripping wet with soapy water all over her beautiful dark skinned,sexy body.

Ace stood and picked her up. She wrapped her legs around his back as he climbed out of the tub and carried her into the bedroom. Still soaking wet, Ace placed Nikky down softly on the bed and proceeded to make love to her...

*   *   *

After a few months went pass, Ace felt as though he could somewhat trust Nikky. He didn't involve her in too much of his business, but kept her around alot. Nikky had no kids, and she loved to be in Ace's presence no matter what he was doing. She knew about his relationship status with Iesha and Kim, and she respected it for what it was. What made Ace like Nikky even more was the fact that she was a Muslim just like him, so Ace thought he may have plans for her in his life once he got himself settled properly. He honestly wanted and didn't mind having Nikky around – unlike most girls.

Dante, had only been out of jail for 2 weeks, and was right back in the dope game before he even seen his probation officer for his first urine test. Dante tried not to get in the game, but after he saw all the cars, jewelry and pretty women Ace and Gotti had, he couldn't control his desires.

Chirp: "Yo Ace." Dante said into the phone.

Chirp: "Yeah, what's up pimp?" Ace replied.

Chirp: "Where you at cause the Virginia bulls is coming and my Pittsburgh homies on the way too. I need to get with you." Dante told him.

Chirp: "I'm at Babygirl's crib. I need you to meet a few people too, so come on." Ace said.

Chirp: "You need me to bring something?" Dante asked.

Chirp: "Yeah, stop at the spot. I left fitty' of 'em there. Bring all of them pimp." Ace responded.

Chirp: "Damn, my day pretty much gon' be spent with you huh?" Dante replied with laughter.

Chirp: "Yeah pimp. Some players called today so don't make any plans." Ace said before ending the call.

Ace rolled over to kiss Nikky on the forehead, and he told her, "Don't you make no plans either, cause after I'm done making a few moves, I'ma need you to count that money."

"Baaaby! My thumbs still hurt from counting all that money last night." She whined.

"Use the money machine. How you think my fingers feel if yours hurt?" Ace replied, sarcastically. "Oh yeah, we going to Vegas for a few days. I feel like gambling heavy and we doing some shopping so don't even pack us any clothes. Cosmetics and underwear is all we need." Ace told her.

"Vegas!" Nikky screamed out excitedly. She had never been to Las Vegas before.

"Alright, are you hungry?" She asked.

"Yeah." Ace replied.

"I'ma make us something to eat while you in the shower."

Nikky walked into the kitchen, thinking, '*I never seen anybody make so much money in my life. I'm kinda' scared, but I love him so much. He does make me feel protected and comfortable, so I will be alright. I just hope he keeps me in his life.*'

Ace was in the shower washing up. ***"Casino's have plenty of cameras. I can actually use this as good alibi. So while I'm in Las Vegas the boys can do some extra cleaning, extermination*** he thought to himself as he grinned with a sinister smile before yelling out. "Aye Babygirl!"

"Yeeeahh" Nikky replied loudly, from in the kitchen cooking breakfast.

"Aye, I tell you what Beauty, I love you and me!" Ace yelled playfully and devilishly, at the thought of his next scheme. "Aawwww, I love you too baby!"

CHAPTER 21
Extermination (Rid of Rats)

Once Mac put Detective Reese and a few other narcotic officers on payroll, things went smoother for Ace and the crew. The payroll also included Ace getting a list of names for the narcotics unit's confidential sources. Only a few names were recognizable as rats that were somehow involved with someone in his circle. They had only copped their coke off some of the lower level guys in the crew. Local nobody rats who would give the cops nothing of value, besides rumors and gossip with little or no truth to it – basic street rap.

Ace gave Ran and Boz specific instructions on killing two snitches, while he was out of town. There was a catch to these particular assassinations – cause two different rats had to be dealt with in two different areas. Once Ace noticed these two particular names, he wanted them both disposed of immediately. Ace hadn't actually dealt with either of these guys himself personally within the last few years. However, he knew the Feds could go as far back as 5 – 10 years if they wanted to build a conspiracy case. So Ace was not about to risk his freedom for a couple potential witnesses to be used against him. Ace was always a realist knowing one day he would become part of a federal investigation. He had a motto that he shared with all the women in his life (Rain, Kim and Iesha), which was – if they were to date either a doctor or lawyer in the early part of his career they would be involved with an extremely busy man. They had to willingly deal with the distance and quality of time if he strived to excel in his medical or legal field. That's where sacrifice comes into a relationship. A relationship with a man who seeks success and wealth can really be distant at times. This fact even applies to a regular man who registers in the army, navy, air force or marines, and serves our country.

The point being, Ace was living his life successfully now and his women were enjoying the fruits of his labor. Ace is in the **dope-game** and is now able to afford the same things a doctor or lawyer could. In the event the Feds did get him one day, the girls should be willing to stick out their relationship with him for whatever amount of time he received, and if he had to do five to ten years in jail one day for getting money now, actually risking his life and federal time. Ace figures it might as well be worth it, and he would be a millionaire when and if the Feds finally did get him. He explained to the women in his life that if they didn't have the **love, strength, dedication and faithfulness** to do a bid with him, then they were simply involved with the wrong type of man. Point Blank!

Ace knew Mr. Williams had his back on the federal end of things, but he also knew the less people he had to potentially cooperate against him meant the less chance he had of being convicted. With that being said, two necessary hits were established – which meant there were two rats labeled as dead men walking.

*   *   *

Randolph, also known as, Iran is 25 years old, standing 5'10" weighing in at 200 pounds. Ran is a gun ready and willing to kill anything moving at Ace's command. Iran was a good hustler and soldier, who loved Ace because he made it possible for him to get money. Iran drove and brought his own luxury cars, and he was a big factor of the well-respected crew. Ace paid Ran $2,000 - $3,000 on a weekly basis for him to simply serve weight to some of Ace's customers, but Iran also had his own clientele as well. Ace would front him whatever he needed, so Iran was getting plenty of money, not to mention Iran would even re-rock cocaine, turn 1 kilo into a brick and a half, to serve his own customers.

Basil, known as Boz on the streets, is a 6'3", 240 pound,38-year-old muscle bound maniac. His great physical health and prison bid caused him to look a lot younger than he was. Boz did time for a homicide when he was 19 years old, and got out of the pen looking like **D-Bo** (from Ice Cube's "Friday") when he was 30 years of age. Ace had been looking out for Boz every since he'd been home. Because of his muscular size and violent reputation, Boz's job came easy. He didn't even have to sale drugs. Ace had Boz do what he did best, which was to simply be the muscle. Boz dealt with any beef the crew got into. Other than that, Boz got his money two other ways.

First: Anybody that owed Ace money and ducked him or took too long paying the bill had to deal with Boz. Ace was getting way too much money, as he wouldn't allow a petty $3,000 - $5,000 debt affect him. He would simply pull up on a nigga and introduce them to Boz. Ace would let a slow petty nigga know that he didn't owe him anymore; he owed the money to Boz. Boz was hungry and more aggressive, showing no mercy when he hunted a nigga down, and if a nigga didn't have his money on the date and time, they were supposed to have that money - then a nigga faced the strong possibility of getting shot. However, he was most definitely getting his ass kicked and taxed.

Second: Boz was a take boy, strong arm robber, and would take money from a chump by extortion, or simply do it „**D-Bo'** style and take their shit on demand…

Boz and Forty waited patiently, parked on 58th and Elmoowd Avenue. They were in a dark green Chevy Lumina with tinted windows. The front window on the Lumina even had tint, so Pooh didn't notice there were any occupants in the car as he walked by. Once Pooh got close enough Boz slowly exited the passenger seat of the Chevy Lumina.

Pooh was startled by Boz's presence, but tried to remain calm. It was daytime and sunny outside so Pooh figured he was in no danger. Pooh continued to walk to his truck, that was parked directly behind the suspiciously smoked out Chevy Lumina. Boz had a brown paper lunch bag in one hand and a cell phone to his ear as he smiled and laughed. He was actually pretending to be talking with someone on the phone when he spoke to Pooh.

"What's up Roady! You happen to have the time?"

Pooh looked at his watch with relief before he replied, "Uhhh, its 3:30." When Pooh looked back up from checking the time on his watch, all he noticed was what appeared to be quick flashes of fire similar to someone striking a match. Only the flashes made a loud **Boc! Boc!** Noise, quickly popping out of the bottom of the brown bag that Boz had his hand in. **Boc! Boc! Boc! Boc! Boc!**

Pooh's heart suddenly began to beat fast as he felt an intense burning sensation in his neck, chest and face.

As Pooh collapsed against the door of his truck, his heart started beating slower. The extreme pain he felt was overwhelmed by shock, as he slipped into a state of comfort his body began to feel numb and he drifted off into the after-life…

There were a few people that noticed the green car speeding away, but all the attention was on the car fleeing the scene, as Boz jogged away out of sight completely unnoticed and got on a motorcycle that was already parked, waiting on him several blocks away….

    *   *   *   *

Iran and Tab were at the Green Tree Apartments in Claymont, Delaware. "Damn Tab! You sure this nut ass nigga is even here? We been here all damn day and this nigga's car is in the same spot we seen it in two fuckin days ago." Iran said impatiently.

Tab was already irked at Iran, so he responded arrogantly.

"Yeah nigga! We are in the right spot. Damn! But you drawing anyway by using this van man."

"Huh? Oh yeah, I know but I couldn't use mines cause I put them rims back on it." Iran stuttered.

"Nigga you could've' just got a rental car or even a Johnny (stolen car) for what we about to do." Tab replied, as he went on to say, "This is one of the company cars, we going too hard. You were only supposed to pick it up from the shop and take it to the office. Not drive it for the day, especially not this day. You drawing." Tab replied sarcastically.

Tab was upset with Iran for a few different reasons. **One:** Iran was a hothead, so he didn't use his brains. **Two:** out of all times to be high, Iran was high off syrup and pills. **Three:** They were supposed to be on a mission that needed to get done specifically this weekend, and absolutely no mistakes were a part of Ace's specific instructions.

They didn't catch up with who they were looking for the last couple of nights, so Iran got a little high today, thinking they probably won't catch up with who they were looking for again today. Ace explained that the task was important, and had to be done this weekend, so Tab simply put up with Iran's carelessness. However, Tab figured it would be best if he drove after the job was done even though Iran was the one who had a legal driver's license….

As Ant exited his apartment door he waved to one of his nosey neighbors. Mrs. Jones thought she went unnoticed peeking through her drapes for the 100th time today. '*That nosey ass old lady is funny as hell*' Ant thought to himself as he put on a fake smile while waving at her…

Iran suddenly noticed a guy waving at someone through his side view mirror. He reacted quickly and exited the passenger door of the van. Iran never gave his victim a chance to reach for a weapon or run, as he pointed his 16 shot 9 mm Smith and Wesson to release a hailstorm of gunfire.

Boc! Boc! Boc! Boc! Boc! Boc! Boc! Boc! Boc! Boc!

Ant eyes got big as golf balls as he turned in an attempt to run, but quickly collapsed. His legs went limp like spaghetti and fell from underneath him as he caught three more bullets in his back. His spine had ruptured almost immediately, when Iran walked over semi staggering and stood over top of Ant to finish him off.

"Tell on this ya rat muthafucka!" Iran said aggressively as he gave Ant a wiggy (shot to the head).

Boc! Boc! Boc! Boc! Boc! Boc! Click, Click, Click, Click. Iran had an adrenaline rush in a state of pure rage as he rapidly ran out of bullets, then he ran away and jumped into the white Dodge Caravan that Tab was now driving already running and waiting for him.

*   *   *   *

The police arrived to the scene at Green Tree apartments. No matter how many times it happens, it never seems to amaze the authorities how many people were unwilling to claim that they saw something when it came down to a murder. This time was no different as Ant lay there dead in a pool of blood, curled up in fetal position like a newborn baby.

Officer Cruz started questioning the next-door neighbor, Mrs. Jones. According to Mrs. Jones she didn't actually see any shooting. She only remembered waving hi to Ant as she left her window to go have a cup of tea. Suddenly, she heard a massive amount of shots fired, and dropped to the floor under her kitchen table in fear.

"Did you notice anything else unusual today Mam?" Officer Cruz asked.

"Well, now that you ask, I did notice a white van parked outside for several hours. I'm always looking out my window to check on the neighborhood kids, you know. Anyway, I had seen the white van sitting over there for several hours." Mrs. Jones responded as she pointed out her window to the area where she saw the van parked. "Oh my, it's gone now, but I sware it was right over there."

'Did you notice if there were any occupants in the vehicle Mam?"

"I did notice there was some movement in the van. I think it was maybe two or three people inside of it. I'm not too sure exactly how many it was, but it was definitely more than one person in that van. They were all men. I seen their heavy, long, scraggily beards like the ones those Moooslims wear. I jotted down the license plate, because I was a bit concerned about it. Let me get it for you." Mrs. Jones said, as she searched through the scattered mail and papers on her counter top.

"That would be extremely helpful Ma'am." The young officer replied.

Officer Cruz called in the suspicious van's plate to a dispatcher from the precinct. The response came back across his walkie-talkie three minutes later, "This is dispatch reporting back on license plate number **A** as in Amy, **D** as in David, **J** as in Jack, **4-0-5-5**. The vehicle is registered to a Kim Laphney at 4545 Springfield Avenue, Philadelphia, Pennsylvania.

*   *   *   *

Meanwhile Nikky and Ace were in Las Vegas. They were at Bally's in a princess ballroom suite located on the entire 22nd floor. Shopping bags were spread all across the floor and on the furniture throughout the suite, from every high-end store on the strip in Vegas. Ace had showed Nikky a magnificent time since they first landed. They even attended the fight on Saturday at the **MGM** where Bernard Hopkins lost by decision to Jermaine Taylor in a 12 round bout.

Ace motto was **Ball till you fall**, which was exactly what him and Nikky did. He brought Nikky bags from Gucci, Louis Vuitton, and the Hermes stores. Ace also spoiled her with clothes and jewelry as well. Ace wanted her to have the time of her life, so she would cherish her very first trip to **Sin City**. After sightseeing and shopping all day, they were sitting comfortably in the hot tub located in their room.

"Baby, do you want a massage?" Nikky asked flirtatiously, as she began massaging Ace's neck and chest.

"Yeah, that feels good, but no funny business Ms. Slick ass, Ace responded with humor.

Nikky had to laugh at his comment because he knew what she was up to.

"What you talking about? I just want to rub my baby down. That's all."

"Yeah alright. You think you slick. But you know damn well I ain't running no red light." Ace replied humorously.

Ace didn't like to have sex with any of his women while they were on their period.

'I want to go back to that blackjack table. I'm trying to get in they pockets some more before we leave tomorrow. Ya dig?" Ace retorted as Nikky continued to massage him down in the hot tub.

Buzz, Buzz, Buzz

'Baby, one of your phones is over there vibrating again." Nikky said.

"I'm sure it's probably Kim. She been fucking with me and trying to beef since I got here. I'm not answering it. She'll be all right. She knows I don't answer the phone when I'm at the casino gambling anyway, and I don't feel like hearing her mouth right now. If it's an emergency, she will text me to tell me what's wrong."…..

CHAPTER 22
(Baby mama drama)

Kim was back at her grandmother's house. Once again she was pissed at Ace and wanted to be around the comfort of her grandmother. Kim played a game of spades on the Internet as she was talking to her sister Mookie on the phone.

"Girl, I know his fat ass in Vegas with a bitch!" Kim said agitated and angry.

"You don't know that for sure Kim. He just might be there on business. I got to give Ace some credit, he is about his business." Mookie replied.

"Yeah, he about his business alright. I know my man. Pussy is a part of his day. So if he didn't take me, that means he gonna either get him some pussy there or take some with him."

Although Kim was talking out of anger, the thought of Ace being with another woman turned her stomach. It sickened Kim because she really loved Ace.

"I'm gonna keep calling his ass until he picks up, and I'm a do it just to irk the shit out of him. I know he is up to something! Shit, his cell phone battery will die before I stop calling!"

"Uh, uh! Bitch you crazy as hell." Mookie burst into laughter.

Kim had to actually share a quick laugh herself after her own comment.

"I'm sick of Ace Capone! He gets on my nerves Mookie. Ace is all I want in a man. If only he would just stop cheating on me." Kim replied sadly as she started crying. Her thoughts and memories had built up a lot of emotion, pain and anger within her as she went on to say, "I have been through it all with this nigga. I was around before all the fame and money. I mean he was always getting money, even back when I first met him. But now he getting so much attention, fame and money it's just ridiculous. I even stuck around after he gave me a STD three years ago. He told me some lame ass excuse. Talkin' about he didn't have sex; a stripper bitch had only sucked his dick. That's how he got burnt PLEASE!" Kim said sarcastically as she added.

"Then to top it off, he blames me! Huh! He says if I didn't argue with him so much he would have been home. So I try not to even irk or piss him off anymore, because he will use that as an excuse to disappear for days. Then probably go somewhere to lay up with a bitch. Why he got to hurt me Mookie. **WHY**?" Kim screamed out emotionally as she shredded more tears.

Mookie was lost for words so she just listened as Kim went on and on and on.

"And the sad part is, I love the ground his arrogant ass walks on. But I guess love is supposed to fucking hurt? Huh?"

Mookie didn't answer the rhetorical questions. She simply allowed her sister to vent. She felt that Kim needed to get some of the pain off her chest. Everyone knew Kim could be suicidal at times when she didn't express her pain, cause Kim would let things build up so much at times, she would almost give up on life by trying to overdose on pills and alcohol.

"I am tired of the rumors about him and some bitch living together in Delaware too. But, knowing Ace it's not a rumor. I don't even think he loves me anymore. He takes care of me - **Yes.** We have kids – **Yes.** But do I think the nigga is in love with me – **Fuck No!** We get along fine when he here with the kids, or he out in the yard fucking with those damn dogs. But even then he only stays home maybe once or twice a week. That's the only time we get out of him. The only time I actually get with him alone is when he wants to have sex. I used to always go out of town with him, but he don't even do that anymore. He may take the kids and me to a movie, or we may go out shopping at the market. But that's about it. Shit, I want to go places too." Kim said sadly all in one breath.

"Kim you got three kids now. You can't be following behind Ace like you used to. Not unless it's a family vacation. He does have a lot going on so he busier now than ever before. You should be glad that you got a good man. You don't need or want for anything! Financially, you're secure. Shit, you even on his damn life insurance policy and yall ain't even married." Mookie replied.

"Please! Don't remind me. That's another damn problem Mookie. Why didn't he marry me yet? We been playing house for all these years but he won't tie the knot to make that special commitment. I would feel better then because at least I would know he's mine! I honestly feel like he's going to leave me, but I will kill him dead before I let him do that!" Kim said in an aggressive yet serious tone.

"Kim don't say shit like that! Now you have gone too far. You always either threatening to kill Ace or trying to harm yourself. Who going to raise them kids? It's not cool to think like that." Mookie said, in a stern yet sincere manner.

'Shit, if I can't have him to myself no one will. Point Blank!' Kim seriously thought to herself.

"I gotta go Mookie. Shit! I got a damn headache. I will call you back later." Kim replied with frustration, as she quickly hung up the phone.

Kim hated for anyone to make sense if it seemed like they were defending Ace, but Kim had it all wrong. She just wasn't used to a man of Ace's stature. Instead of realizing that Ace provided safety for her and the kids by moving them out of the hood into a rural area, Kim figured he only moved her far away so she would be out of his way.

Kim's delusional way of thinking was ghetto and pathetic in Ace's eyes. Like any other couple, there were various reasons why Kim and Ace had so many issues. Part of the reason she was so mentally distraught is because Kim is a lazy, miserable and an extremely evil cold-hearted woman. Kim didn't have a clue how she could contribute to their relationship.

She was bored as an everyday stay at home mom and would rather work. Ace didn't want her to work because she only landed underpaying jobs. Every job she landed seemed to pay $200-$400 a week, so it actually cost Ace more money when she did work. By the time you added up the money for gas, babysitter, and toll to get over the bridge each day, it was pointless for her to work. It was better for her to simply stay at home and raise the kids. Ace had even offered to open up some kind of business for her to operate, but Kim didn't know what she was interested in doing besides irking Ace.

Kim decided to take a bath to relax. Deep down inside, she honestly hoped that Ace would come home from Vegas and stay home for a few days. She just wanted him to stay in and make love to her....

It's been 4 hours now since Kim hung up with Mookie, so she decided to dial Ace's number again.

Ring, Ring, Ring

"Yo!" Ace answered the phone tiredly, preparing for Kim to either ask 101 questions or simply bitch at him.

"Yeah, why weren't you answering your phone Ace?" Kim asked in a very soft and calm tone. She had relaxed a bit after venting and taking a nice hot bath.

"Cause man, you trying to beef, and I don't even feel like it today. You trippin for nothing! I'm not even doing shit but gambling. What's wrong?" Ace asked sounding sincere and convincing.

Kim suddenly started feeling bad. „*Maybe he was just gambling'* Kim had briefly thought to herself. She began thinking that she was tripping for no reason. She knew most of the time she never confirmed any proof to her allegations, so she finally considered he possibly wasn't up to any good this time. Kim was quiet as she listened to the background noise of his phone. Kim was so used to doing this that she was unconscious to the fact of what she was doing. Suddenly, she heard a mysterious female voice.

"Ahhhhh! Baby I won! I won!" Nikky screamed excitedly as the bells and sirens continued to ring on the dollar slot machine in the background.

"Who's that?" Kim asked totally puzzled and confused in a brief state of shock.

She got no response, as she looked down at her cell phone to notice the call ended. Kim called right back hoping the call just got dropped because of a bad signal. She was trying to think rational before she got overwhelmed as she tried to suppress her anger, but all she got was Ace's voice mail over and over again. Kim finally snapped in complete rage as she slammed her phone down violently, breaking it into a thousand pieces.

*   *   *

The very next morning there was a hard knock at the door of Kim's grandmother's house on 58th and Cedar Avenue. **'Knock, Knock, Knock!'** Kim got nervous after she looked through the window. She noticed two white men, who looked like cops, dressed in plain clothes.

"Open up Ma'am. It's the police! We have a few questions for Kim Laphney."

"I'm Kim. What's the problem?" Kim asked with concern as she slightly opened the door.

Kim nervously allowed the two Delaware detectives and the one federal agent in the house after they had produced their official badges. They had fully identified the different departments they worked for and began with a series of questions for her.

"Ma'am, do you own a 2000 white Dodge Caravan?" One of the Delaware homicide detectives asked.

"Yes." Kim answered in a frightened and confused manner.

"Ma'am, who drove that vehicle yesterday between 3:00 – 8:00 p.m.?"...

As Kim answered all the questions the officer asked her, Agent Tapia took notice that she didn't appear to be lying. After looking around, evaluating the property, Agent Tapia assumed Kim had been having recent relationship problems. He judged that by the heavy bags she wore under her eyes from being up all night crying, her unkept hair, and the excessive amount of cigarette butts that were in the ashtray.

While Kim conversed with the homicide detectives, Agent Tapia observed the family photos that were hanging up throughout the house. He stared at a specific picture on the wall that showed a heavy set dark skinned man with a beard, together with Kim and two young kids who resembled the man a bit more. *„Old lady Mrs. Jones reported that there were men with beards, two or three of them in a white van'* Agent Tapia had briefly thought to himself. He figured the man in the photo had to be the kids' father.

"Kim is this Ace in the picture? Agent Tapia asked very calmly.

Kim glanced at the picture, which for some reason made her mind wonder back a few months ago. *Kim was snooping around and had found one of Ace's old sex tapes in the trunk of his car. The dates of all the footage proved that the sexcapade took place sometime before they were even together. But the sight of her man having sex with another woman still had her insides boiling.*

Kim seen one of the chics he smashed off the tape at one of Ace's nightclubs a year ago. Kim immediately spotted the chic in the line outside the club with a few other females. Kim was accompanied by her sister Mookie and her girlfriend Niema, walking straight to the front of the club.

At first Kim just passed by the women, then it hit her. Kim took a double take as she turned around to back track her steps quickly approaching the familiar face.

"Are you still fucking my man?" Kim questioned sternly getting straight to the point.

"Excuse me? And who might that be?" The female responded defensively, with much attitude in her short white wrap around skirt and extended weave.

"Ace is my man!"

The girl laughed along with her friends at Kim's comment.

"That's your man, since when? Last time I checked he was everybody's man." The chic responded sarcastically with intention on hurting Kim's feeling, before catching a devastating blow to her face.

That was all Kim needed to hear. Kim's punch sent the chic straight to the ground. Kim started stomping the girl while she was still in her heels. One of the chic's girlfriends tried to jump in but Kim saw her coming and hit her with a vicious two-piece. Kim went back to her intended victim, grabbed the girl by her hair and repeatedly kneed her in the face, causing blood to spill from the girl's mouth and nose.

The bouncers knew Kim was Ace's crazy baby mama, so they handled her with care as they broke up the fight. When the girl got up from the ground, holding her bloody mouth, she yelled at Kim.

"Yeah, you stupid bitch. I'm fucking your man and I'm a keep on fucking him." The chic spat as the bouncers pushed her away from the club.

Kim was heated by that remark and angrily broke away from the bouncers, and stormed into the club looking for Ace....

'I hate that lying ass nigga' Kim thought to herself as she broke out her daydream.

"Kim, I'm gonna ask you again. Is this Ace in this photo? Agent Tapia questioned in a cool and collective tone as he pointed at the male in the picture....

CHAPTER 23
("Plane Crash" (Everything's Fallen Apart)

It's been a few months now since Ace has been doing business with Roberto. The 500 kilos a week had been going lovely, and his whole team was eating heavier. At $10,000 a kilo, Ace was able to wholesale to his heavy weight clientele who bought 10 to 20 kilos at a time. Ace only charged them $17,000 a kilo, but he gave his main crew members the same price, even if they were only getting 1 kilo at a time, Ace would also front them the same amount of coke, on top of what they paid for, spreading the love because he profited a decent amount off each kilo.

Things got even sweeter when Ace hooked up with two cats out of Camden, New Jersey - named Dos and Mark. They were CEOs of **Done Deal Entertainment**, and had a lot of good contacts. Mark got Ace's hands on a private plane to rent, and connected Ace with the security staff at the small airport in Northeast Philly.

Ace paid off the security staff for them to turn their heads to his criminal activity. The large sums of money caused the security to lessen the security procedures at the airport for Kim, which allowed Ace to bring in his product through the small airport twice a month.

Now Ace was paying $8,000 per kilo, bringing in at least 3,000 kilos a month, so Ace made at least $9,000 profit now even when he sold kilos at wholesale price. Only Ace and Roberto knew his prices and how much product he was getting. Ace trusted no one, knowing first-hand: More money, more problems!!!!

At this point, Ace had enough money to stop hustling, but his hustling spirit took control of him - making it very hard to quit. He was addicted to his drug dealing lifestyle just like a crackhead was addicted to crack. Ace knew in his heart that he should stop, but he simply couldn't resist the urge of hustling. Ace also knew that his team wasn't prepared for him to make that transition. They were spendthrifts just like him; the only difference was Ace really had money to blow. His team couldn't affored to retire from the game yet, because they never sacrificed, stacked or saved money like Ace had been doing since he was a teenager. They didn't take the time to invest in real estate, nor did they open their own businesses like Ace did. Ace owned a million dollars in properties alone – that he had been accumulating since he was 26 years old. He didn't even realize that it until his old head, Virg, advised him one day.

"Listen dude, you not even thirty years old and way ahead of the game at your age. You got over a million dollars worth of property and can quit right now."

"I hear you Virg, but the cash keeps coming at me so quickly and so plentiful, it's hard to just turn my back on all that easy money. Ya dig?"

"Just take your time dude. Don't crash and burn while you floating on the highway to riches."

"I hear you Old Head....I hear you."

~~~

On a cold day in January, in Allenwood, PA, a small private plane had crashed in a secluded wooded area off the side of the road. The fire company and the State troopers were now on the scene. State Trooper Richard Webb arrived at the scene first. He reached the crash site right after the Allenwood Fire Department, Rescue Squad got there. One of the firemen waved Trooper Webb to come over.

"Well, won't cha look here? No wonder this plane didn't send out a distress signal as it was going down." The short stubby fireman said, as Trooper Webb walked over to the fireman, attempting to flag away the thick, black smoke that burned his eyes from a distance. Inching closer to the wreckage, he had to take a step back. The fumes were too strong and overwhelming. The flames from the plane were now under control, but the thick awful smoke remained disturbing. The fireman continued to explain his analysis as he showed the trooper a section of the plane that used to be attached to it before the crash landing.

"There must be at least 400 kilos of pure Columbian cocaine spreaded around here that didn't get burned. Only God knows how much actually caught fire and burned away. I assume it was a lot of kilos from the looks of all that smoke. Shit, I'm getting high as we talk Bub' and I haven't had a hit since my brother's bachelor party!" The fireman said in his country voice while chewing tobacco.

Trooper Webb looked around in awe. He walked over to the EMT Unit. "Is this guy gonna make it?" He asked one of the paramedics that worked on the victim.

"I don't know. It looks pretty bad. He has a pulse, but he needs this oxygen to help him breathe because he took in a lot of smoke. He's still unconscious though and his pulse goes lower then resumes to normal so he's fighting for his life." The paramedic responded.

The crash landing was survivable cause it wasn't a nosedive, but the fumes from the fire was deadly.

"I want him handcuffed to his hospital bed and inform me as soon as he gains consciousness." Trooper Webb ordered.

"Hey Webb!" The stubby fireman called out loudly during the busy rescue scene of the wreck.

"Yeah!" Trooper Webb stopped.

"Ah, a few civilians were driving by on the road and said they saw the plane falling before it crashed. They said the damn thing was zigzagging slowly and couldn't gain control before it crashed. I'm thinking it may have just been too much weight on board the small plane. Too much luggage on those types of planes is a freak accident waiting to happen. With all that coke on that plane a shift in the wind current could have easily caused it to lose control. Looks like your smuggler ain't know too much about flying with too much weight huh?" The short fireman said with laughter.

"Where are these witnesses?" Webb replied without finding any of the fireman's jokes amusing.

"They over there." The fireman pointed towards the bystanders on the side of the road. Trooper Webb walked over towards an older looking white woman. The woman had to be in her late 50s. As soon as the women saw Trooper Webb approaching her, she met him quickly.

"Oh dear, is that poor man still alive? I've never seen anything like that in all my life. It's a miracle how the other guy limped away after jumping out of that plane right before it crashed. He didn't even break a bone, he only bruised himself up pretty badly." The woman said, in disbelief, as she recalled the horrifying scene in her mind, while holding her heart as if she was in pain.

Trooper Webb became alert and said, "Ma'am, where's this other fella?"

They took him to the hospital. He got into a car with a nice young couple who voluntarily aided the young man. May God bless their hearts. I'm the one who called 911 from my cell phone. I'm glad my daughter bought it for me for Christmas because I never would have even had a cell phone. I waited here for help to arrive, but it took about 35 to 45 minutes for the first fire truck to get here. Oh my, my nerves are bad! I had to sit here and wonder how many people were injured inside that plane. It was horrible. Is there anybody else in there?' The woman asked, showing genuine concern.

"No Ma'am, no one else is hurt. Now what did this young man look like?" Trooper Webb asked.

"Well, he was tall and slim. He was a young black man. They left for the hospital about an hour ago." She told him. Trooper Webb raced to his car and alerted all nearby hospitals to be on the look out for a young male suffering any injuries that could connect him to being in a plane crash….

~~~~

The following day, the black middle- aged man who was found unconscious at the crash site was identified as an ex Airforce pilot by the name of Tyrone Jackson. He died on the way to the hospital.   He never regained consciousness. Although the small plane crash was survivable, the pilot's cause of death stemmed from being stuck between the plane's control boards. His seat belt was stuck, preventing him from escaping the wreckage. After consuming too much of the poisonous fumes from the plane's fire, the pilot couldn't duck his fate. Burning plastic, metal, cloth, not to mention the hundreds of kilos that also caught fire, which helped unleash the lethal smoke contributed to the pilot's death...

*   *   *

Two months had gone by since the plane's crash. Due to the large quantity of cocaine found on the plane and all the aviation laws that were broken, a team of FBI, DEA and ATF agents took the mysterious plane crash case immediately. The only leads they had to go on were the reports from the eyewitnesses who saw the plane crash.

The name of the deceased ex Air Force pilot, Tyrone Jackson, was their strongest lead. They were also looking into the description of a tall, slim black male, around 30 who had vanished once the young white college couple got him to the hospital's emergency room.

The team of agents followed up on their strongest lead, and went to Tyrone Jackson's last known address to secure more evidence in their ongoing investigation. United States prosecutors, Richard Lovette and Mike Brunshrek were the head honchos on the investigation.

Richard Lovette is a middle-aged prosecutor who gets all the big cases in the Eastern District of Pennsylvania. Mike Brunshrek is a young, aggressive up and coming prosecutor who anxiously looks to make a name for himself.

Richard Lovette continued lecturing his team of agents on the plane crash case. "So, basically the best lead we have is the pilot's information and the things you gathered from his place of residence, correct? So with that being said, I want to start this investigation primarily looking into who is Tyrone Jackson? Who he hangs out with? Who he sleeps with? How many kids he has and so on?" Richard Lovette said sternly.

"I want to know how many pimples are on his ass!" Mike Brunshrek added in a harsh tone with a serious pit bull attitude facial expression.

Brunshrek was upset because as of right now they had maybe the biggest case of the decade in their laps with no leads to who owned the drugs on the small aircraft. Nor did they know from where the drugs even flew in. They ended the meeting as Mike Brunshrek thought to himself, *,, Who did Tyrone Jackson work for?'*...

Agent Mike Nikko and Tony Tapia knocked on the door of the Latisha Jackson. She lived in an apartment complex in Chester, PA. Chester is a small city on the outskirts of Philly. Latisha skeptically answered the door, looking confused.

"Excuse me Ma'am, we'd like to ask you some questions about your uncle Tyrone Jackson." Nikko said as he and Agent Tapia flashed Latisha their badges. Latisha reluctantly let them in.

After fifteen minutes of questioning her about her deceased uncle, Agent Tapia observed several pictures around her apartment.

"So this must be your boyfriend huh?" Tapia asked, holding up one of the pictures.

"Oh no, we're just friends." Latisha replied.

Agent Tapia investigative instincts kicked into high gear as he thought, This guy looks to be around the age of 28 to 30, black, tall and slim.

"So did your boyfriend hang out with your uncle Ty often? Agent Nikko asked.

"Yeah, they were kinda close." Latisha replied. She started getting a little nervous since the questions were now directed towards her boyfriend.

"What's your friend's name? Agent Tapia asked.

"Dee." She replied nervously.

"Does Dee have a whole name?" Tapia grilled her.

"Like I said Sir, we're just friends. I don't even know him like that. I only know him as Dee." Latisha replied in a defensive, but uncertain manner.

Agent Tapia calmly closed his note pad, and tucked his pen back into his shirt pocket.

"Look here Latisha, enough of the crap!" Tapia snapped, scaring her. "I'm not here to play these fucking games with you! I asked you a few different times about your boyfriend. I been doing this shit for too many fucking years to know when I hear somebody fucking lying to me! Your uncle was a major drug trafficker for a major drug dealer, and there was enough cocaine on that fucking plane---"

"Calm down Tony." Nikko cut him off, trying to play the good cop.

"Fuck no! I will not calm down!" Tapia yelled, playing his bad cop role to perfection. "Listen Latisha, there was enough high quality cocaine on the fucking plane to supply the whole fucking city of Philadelphia and your uncle was flying it! I will prosecute every one of your family members from the age 16 to 95. I care less who goes down for that shit! But believe me baby, somebody is going down and it might even be you. I want my perp! I sat here and listened to your fucking lies for over thirty minutes. I also observed your lavishly furnished apartment, with your big screen TV, and other fine items. From the looks of things, I say you're shacking up with a drug dealer who is a suspect in a very serious accidental homicide and drug trafficking crime. Judging by your pictures, the designer clothes, the high-end cars, and your continuous lies, I think Dee is our guy, and if you don't want go down for your deceased uncle flying tons of cocaine across the United States, then I guess you start talking now." Agent Tapia yelled, startling Latisha.

"Young Lady, I suggest you just give him what he wants so…"

"Fuck that!" Tapia blurted, trying to earn best role for bad cop. "Don't sugar coat this shit for her. Either you talk to me young lady, or you are going to prison for a very, very long time. I will tell you this young lady, if I come to find out that you giving me any bullshit, which I know you already have done. I will prosecute your ass by putting you in the middle of a drug conspiracy, and I promise you that you will burn in the flames right alongside your boyfriend, Mr. Dee. Now if you want to continue your young life, and keep your BMW that I noticed parked outside, then you better make a wise decision before I get mad and haul your pretty little ass off to jail."

But I....I told you I don't know—" She stammered only to be cut off by Agent Tapia.

"Bullshit, Mike called in for backup and get me a squad car here to take her ass to jail."

"No wait!" She blurted.

"Time's up honey. I gave you a chance. It appears you want to be on his side instead of ours. You love him that much to spend the next 20 years of your life in prison, so be it!" Tapia said, all in one breath.

"Deeman Fakon is his name, he's from Pascall projects in Southwest Philly!" She blurted, eyes wide open with fear after hearing all of Agent Tapia's threats.

'*Shiiid, that nigga got me involved in his shit. He doesn't give a fuck about me. I'm already on the back burner for his bitch of a baby mom. Why should I protect his ass and go to jail? He just told me to get an abortion 2 weeks ago. So he clearly don't give a fuck about being with me in the long run, and the dick ain't even that good'*, she thought to herself, hoping the Agents would let her off the hook.

Truth be told, Latisha was just looking for any reason to snitch after she thought she could get arrested. Agent Tapia didn't even have to go that far with his threats, Latisha had it made up in her mind that she wasn't going to jail for no nigga, point blank!...

After Latisha informed both Agents about the people that Deeman hung out with and who sold drugs for him, both Agents looked at each other with a look of certainty.

The Agents were not only familiar with the area of Pascall projects, they were also familiar with a few guys Latisha had mentioned who were top dealers on their list for unrelated investigations.

Agent Nikko thought to himself in disbelief, *I should have known this could lead back to the one person we been looking to prosecute for years now. It was always hearsay with no direct evidence to back it up, but I knew that scumbag was a major player! I underestimated his ability and power. I got to go full speed on this now cause with her cooperation and the paper trail we already have on his drug dealings, I should be able to get the proper funds granted to conduct a full investigation on this complex case.* Agent Nikko had other thoughts racing through his mind while Agent Tapia wrote down the information being provided by Latisha.

They ended the statement process and asked for Latisha's final signature. "Here's my card Latisha. You did well. I knew you would and I apologize if I scared you, but it's true. You would have went down right with him." Tapia said.

"So am I cool to stay outta jail now?" She asked, still shaken up a little.

"As long as you continue to give me your complete cooperation, you should be fine." Tapia told her.

"I don't have to testify do I? Cause I don't think I can do that. His friends are bout' they business. They will kill me. " Latisha started crying. Reality had just hit her; she was now a government informant. One day her statement would be exposed to the world. "Don't worry Latisha, we will protect you. We have protective custody and much more when it comes to cases as complex as this one. We will not allow anyone to hurt you, and if you feel any harm coming your way or receive any threats just give me a call immediately." Tapia encouraged.

Latisha continued crying. "I just want to know, right before you do use my statement, so I can get the hell outta' town. I am not cooperating unless his whole squad is locked up! I know you not going to get everybody. Shit being in jail is better than being dead." Latisha explained.

"I understand Latisha. I definitely understand. And as I said, I give you my word, you will be protected, but the choice is still yours when it comes down to it. You may very well have to testify if the case goes to trial or you face a very lengthy federal jail sentence. At this point you have made a very wise decision because I have the power of not even prosecuting you. However, you have to finish out your end of the deal when it comes down to it. Now you relax, go see a movie or something cause it will be some time before I get back to you, but call me if you need me." Agent Tapia said, in a fake friendly tone.

Agent Tapia and Agent Nikko left Latisha's apartment with smiles bigger than the Kool-Aid man himself. Once outside, Agent Nikko stopped by the unmarked car.

"With the plane incident, along with all the other statements we have on Ace from over the years, we should be able to apply for a wiretap."

"Do you really think we'll get it authorized Tone?" Agent Nikko asked.

"I don't know, but Judge Robinson is a good friend of mine." Tapia said.

"Well that works out even better because he hates drug dealers anyway." Nikko smirked. "I heard his daughter is strung out on drugs so, he should definitely be eager to authorize a wiretap warrant on a major Kingpin out of his own area. I'm sure his daughter has smoked, shot up or snorted plenty of Ace Capone's cocaine." Agent Nikko snickered as they climbed into the car....

CHAPTER 24
("We got ya phone tap, what ya gon do sooner or later we'll have your whole crew")

On May 19, 2005, Agent Tony Tapia stood before the court in an attempt to get a wiretap authorization on telephone number 267-784-3964. The phone number belongs to Naseem Coles, also known as, Ace Capone. Agent Tapia had put together an affidavit for the wiretap that stated he had his first hand information gathered from various confidential sources, particularly CS-1, CS-2, CS-3 and CS-4. According to Agent Tapia, all of his sources were deemed reliable by a preponderance of corroborated information and evidence.

A Judge may grant such an order after determining, among other things that normal investigative procedures have been tried and have failed or reasonably appear to be unlikely to succeed if tried or appear to be too dangerous.

Agent Tapia's affidavit was 63 pages long. A brief summary of the affidavit stated that in a 2002 interview, he was present when CS-1, who is not a federal informant prior to this investigation, nor had any prior criminal history, gave an incriminating statement on Coles.

CS-1 stated that he/she observed Coles' drug activity, and that he/she knew of Coles' money laundering methods and his front businesses. CS-1 also states that he/she could identify Coles' associates in Takedown Records, which was one of the premiere front businesses.

In 2004 CS-2 provided information relating to Coles having cops on the payroll, making them his co-conspirators. After the plane crash investigation in January 2004, CS-4 informed Agents about the drug relationship between Ace Capone and Deeman Fakon. The affidavit illustrated that Coles kept all the CSs (Cooperating Sources) at arm's length. None of them were of his confidence. It would be unlikely of persuading Cole's associates to cooperate with the investigators while Coles remains free on the streets. The government seeks to hold Coles without bail once an indictment is granted from the wiretap evidence. Likewise, undercover officers could not be planted in Cole's operation. Reason being, the conspiracy is tightly woven, highly secretive, security conscious and violent. Any traditional techniques such as interviews and grand jury subpoenas continue to carry the risk of discussing the existence of the investigation as to Coles.

Confidential informants could not provide information about locations of bulk cocaine storage that was sufficiently current to be of value. The straw purchases and money laundering activities also impeded traditional surveillance. The parties can only reveal the true nature of transactions conducted by others for Coles and Coles control over the assets through wire interceptions of conversations involved. Search warrants would be ineffective and surveillance efforts would be detected.

The Honorable Edward Robinson, United States District Judge for the Eastern district of Pennsylvania signature had authorized the wiretap on telephone number 267-784-3964 belonging to Alton Coles aka Ace Capone on May 19, 2005.

Agent Mike Nikko looked with concern as Agent Tony Tapia walked out of the empty courtroom with the affidavit signed and authorized.

"All taken care of." Agent Tapia said with a smile, as he handed the documents over to his partner.

"No shit? But I thought the only judge available today would be Robinson? What judge gave us authorization?" Agent Nikko asked in awe.

"Robinson is on vacation, but I talked to him on the phone and he gave me a verbal approval." Tapia informed him.

"Verbal approval? Doesn't he have to sign it Tone?" Nikko asked in disbelief.

"Relax partner, his signature is on there as if he wrote it himself. Only you and me know otherwise. I have been doing this shit for 20 years Mike. My credibility alone is established to a high degree, and Robinson will go to bat for me...so don't worry." Tapia said, shocking Agent Nikko.

"Hey I bet cha' Robinson is doing his sexy little clerk behind his wife's back." Agent Nikko joked.

"I know I would, she's hot!" Agent Tapia added with a devilish smile.

"Let's go over to Dunkin Donuts and celebrate." Agent Tapia said, heading for his car.

"My treat, cause you just hooked the biggest fish in all of Philly." Agent Nikko joked, following his partner to the car....

*   *   *   *

On May 20, 2005 Ace received a phone call. He answered on the third ring.

"Yo!"

"Yeah what's up pimp?" The caller replied.

"Damn pimp, how the fuck you get locked up? What the hell happened?" Ace asked.

"Man, my fuckin' Babymom sister's boyfriend set me up pimp. I'ma get at that nigga!" The caller said in an angry tone.

"Damn, that's crazy Ock! You cool though?" Ace asked.

"Yeah, yeah, I'm good. Thanks for bailing me outta' there. I got you back in a minute. I feel handicapped right now cause they still got my car, my fuckin' keys, my fuckin' cell phone and my fuckin' work ID." The caller complained.

"Why you ain't get any of your shit back?" Ace asked in a puzzled state of mind.

"I'm waiting on my girl now. I just need a ride. I'm trying to hurry up and get there too cause they didn't even find everything. I still got some wizzork' in the trizzunk'," the caller said.

"Damn pimp, you tripping on this joint. I'ma holla back at you, but if I was you I'd get my car before you have more troubles." Ace said and hung up.

Truthfully, Ace was upset because Mar was a good friend of his. Mar worked for Ace at the club, and he was also one of Ace's managers for the record label. He mostly helped out with the entertainment business side of things. Mar just got caught out there moving too fast in the drug game, trying to make a couple dollars without letting anyone know who he was dealing with and that person set him up....

*   *   *   *

"Did we get all of that?" Agent Nikko asked his team of agents who were set up in a rented out home on Hook Rd. in the Southwest Philly airport section. The team posted there for tactical advantages, sting operations and field advantage, while listening in on wiretap interceptions.

"Yes Sir. The caller called from a residential property out of Chester, PA. According to Bell of Pennsylvania phone services, the line belongs to a Jamar Cambell." Agent Charlotte Tablespoon replied.

Agent Charlotte Tablesbpoon is a very nice looking woman. She was thick in all the right places. She stood 5'7" and weighed 157 pounds. She wore her long beautiful red hair in a simple long ponytail, but she was still sexy even in her boyish appearance while at work. Her smile was intoxicatingly beautiful with the most perfect lips. Agent Nikko, although a happily married man, is a man who looked at her on many occasions.

'Man I'd love to feel them lips on the head of my cock. I bet the hair on her cunt is neatly trimmed and red too.' Agent Nikko thought while staring at her.

"Do you want me to run his name in with the local authorities to see where he was arrested?" Agent Tablespoon asked, breaking into Nikko's thoughts.

"Huh?" Nikko replied, coming out of his dreamlike state.

"Are you okay sir? You seem to be daydreaming more than often now?" She replied with genuine concern.

"Yeah, yeah I'm fine. Excuse me... I haven't been getting the proper sleep lately that's all... but yeah, see if any of the surrounding authorities actually arrested Jamar Cambell. It sounded like it just happened recently, if that was in fact him on the phone. It may have been someone else just using his line, but let's go with the leads we have now. We may luck up and get to whatever is in the trunk of that car. I've also detected at least 3 to 4 other phones ringing in the background while Ace was on the intercepted line." Agent Nikko said.

"Yeah, I noticed that too Sir. Ace is pretty crafty, I have to admit." Agent Charlotte Tablespoon replied.

Agent Charlotte Tablespoon admired Ace's power and intelligence. Even though she was out to arrest him, she found herself attracted to him. She was secretly infatuated with Ace's ability to hold down several top-notch female relationships, and successfully lead a team of violent drug traffickers. She also envied the fact that Ace was so successful from the ill-gotten gains that he received.

It's only been 2 days of interception on the wiretap and about 10 months of full surveillance for me on this case, but judging from what I've seen and heard thus far. I wonder just how big and good that dick is Mr. Capone?' she thought with a smile on her face as her panties got wet....

*   *   *

On May 29, 2005, a team of agents overheard very suspicious activity for the first time over the wiretap. They clapped hands triumphantly.

"Alright, let's not get too excited!" Agent Nikko said. "I don't want to blow our cover. This may not even be drug activity, so let's just send in the locals. I don't even want to inform them of our federal investigation. We have to remember that Ace Capone has some of them crooked cocksuckers on his payroll." Nikko said.

"But Mike, we may possibly be able to bust Ace red handed. We definitely need to catch him dirty as possible to make it all stick like glue. Let's not forget about our affidavit." Agent Tapia whispered while, staring at Agent Nikko. Both Agents knew they had a bogus signature on the wiretap.

They simply needed to build a strong case in hopes that Ace would plead out and not go to trial.

Agent Tapia and Nikko expected to find millions in cash, together with hundreds of kilos of cocaine and figured if they caught Ace like that, he'd never go to trial to find out about the false authorization. Plus there would be a strong possibility that he would be forced to cooperate, being that the possibility of winning or getting do-able time would be close to none. That much cocaine caught red handed would turn just about any so called hustler or Gangsta into a **Rat** to duck a **mandatory** life sentence...

    Chirp: "What up pimp?"

    Chirp: Yeah pimp?" Ace asked Hova, one of his players out of Baltimore.

    Chirp: "Pimp, I been waiting on ya man for like two hours. He got me looking crazy out here yo!" Hova said with a down south kind of country accent.

    Chirp: "Alright pimp, but next time you got to call before you come all the way up here. That way I can make sure he around and ready, so you can be in and outta' here in a respectable time. Ya dig?" Ace replied.

    Chirp: "No doubt, no doubt my nigga. I'm at the Rite Aid on 67th and Woodland Avenue. How much longer you gon' be" Hova asked.

    Chirp: "RITE AID!!!!" Ace replied loudly in shock, and added.

    "Nah pimp, you drawing! Come outta' there. Dem Boyz station is right down the street."

    Chirp: "Alright, Ima go to the KFC around the corner then wait there." Hova responded.

    Chirp: "Alright, he should be there in ten minutes." Ace told him before ending the call.

    Dirtbike Hova, Ant and a female were in a 2004 Lexus LS400. Hova had another car following him with another female driving, who was being paid to be the mule to transport his drugs. Hova started his car and cranked up the sound system as he sparked a blunt. He drove to KFC smoking his weed and bobbing his head to Bugsy's street mix tape: *Made Men...*

    Almost simultaneously, the local narcotics unit from the 12th District located on 65th & Woodland Avenue, had received a call from law enforcement. The call alerted them that a potential drug deal could be going down at a KFC in their area.

Narcotic Officer Riddick and his unit quickly headed to Island Avenue. He figured that had to be the correct KFC, because it was the only one closest to their district. It was also the only KFC closest to the Rite Aid they were informed about.

The Narcotics team arrived immediately in two separate unmarked cars, and posted up for survelliance, twenty-five minutes later, a silver 2005 Dodge Magnum pulled into the KFC parking lot.

Narcotics officer Riddick had parked in the Hess gas station located adjacent to the KFC. For several minutes, Riddick watched as a female exited the Dodge Magnum. The woman carried what appeared to be a large object stuffed in her oversized pocketbook. She then walked inside the KFC, as Riddick followed her movements all the way out the other side exit.

The unidentified woman got inside a red Toyota Solara that had Maryland license plates. As she pulled out of the KFC parking lot, a grey Lexus LS 400 with Maryland tags pulled out behind her. Two male subjects who appeared to be smoking weed in the Lexus, were following behind the female inside the moving red Toyota Solara.

The Narcotics team seemed so certain that a drug deal had taken place; they jumped the gun faster than a male virgin getting his first shot of pussy. They simply rushed too fast to take down the two Maryland plated vehicles. The results of their rookie actions allowed Dante, the driver of the Dodge Magnum to get away clean.

As the Lexus LS400 stopped at a red light on Island Avenue and Lindenberg Blvd intersection, Hova prepared to proceed over the small bridge to get on I-95 South, headed back to Baltimore. Glancing up, Hova's eyes got big as a deer caught in headlights when he saw two men dressed in plain clothes with guns drawn, aiming at him.

The gunmen were yelling something, but he couldn't hear what they were saying due to the loud music blaring inside his car. Hova was so high off the purple haze he smoked; he thought he was getting carjacked.

"Oh Shit Yo!" Hova yelled to his partner. "It's going down Yo! It's going down!"

Hova's neck swiveled around just in time to notice all the sirens from several police cruisers converging on the scene, who surrounded the area immediately. Hova quickly noticed two more plain-clothes cops pulling the female mule he had transporting the cocaine out of the red Toyota Solara.

Then everything seemed to move in slow motion when he heard officer Riddick yelling for him to get out of the car.

"GET THE FUCK OUT OF THE CAR NOW! AND KEEP YOUR FUCKING HANDS WHERE I CAN SEE THEM!" Riddick's loud aggressive tone alerted Hova that he was definitely in deep shit.

Due to fright, Hova never even put the Lexus in park. He immediately got out of the car with his hands raised, and the car slowly coasted away and crashed into a parked police cruiser.

"Oh Shit!" Hova mumbled as his high ass got taken down to the ground roughly, and handcuffed immediately. Hova's partner and the female riding in the back seat were also cuffed but placed in separate police cruisers. Frantic and high, Hova's man started yelling, "NOTHING IN THESE TWO CARS BELONG TO ME!" The female passenger remained totally silent, in total shock, as Hova's man continued yelling the same tired song all the way down to the station.....

Agent Charlotte Tablespoon was at the state police impound in Media, PA. She found out that a Jamar Camel was in fact arrested for narcotics; specifically cocaine in Chichester, PA on May 18, 2005, which was a day before the May 19th phone call on the wiretap that was intercepted with a caller on Jamar Camel's home phone line.

The million-dollar question was: Is the guy making the calls the same suspect who was arrested? Or was it someone else using Jamar's name and telephone? Time would tell but the leads were adding up more and more.

As Agent Charlotte Tablespoon searched the trunk of the 1997 Park Avenue, she immediately noticed a pair of fireman boots. Her father was a retired fireman, so she had memories of putting on his fireman outfit and boots. When she pulled Jamar's boots out of the trunk, she noticed that the boots were a bit heavier than normal fireman boots. Once she inspected the boots thoroughly, she found a brown bag stuffed inside the left boot. As she opened the contents inside the bag, Agent Tablespoon stumbled up on what appeared to be at least 9 ounces of pure white fishscale cocaine wrapped in a large plastic zip lock bag.

She called Agent Nikko immediately to notify him about what she found.

"Hello." Agent Nikko answered the phone on the third ring.

"Hey Mike, your suspicions were on point. I found…"

Agent Nikko and Agent Tablespoon talked for over twenty minutes about what she found in the trunk of the car. Their conversation went into other topics like where to go now and what to do next.

"You did good Tablespoon. You did a helluva job." Nikko commended her.

"Call me Charlotte and it was nothing, trust me. A kindergartener could've found that dope."

"Well come on in and give me your report ASAP."

"Will do Sir."

"See you soon." Nikko said before hanging up the phone. He looked at Agent Tony Tapia with a joker like smile.

"Tone, you won't believe what just happened?"

"Are you kidding me - I'd believe a cat could fuck a dog, so what happened?" Tapia asked with a bit of laughter and the least look of concern on his face.

"That was Charlotte. She found 9 ounces in the trunk of the car that belonged to Jamar Camel over at the state impound."

"You shitting me?"

"And it's the same Jamar Camel that was arrested on May 18th during a simple buy and sell sting operation. The ChiChester narcotics unit had an informant call him for four and half ounces of cocaine, which they confiscated along with the firearm he had in his possession during the drug buy." Agent Nikko explained.

"Didn't I tell you once we get the wiretap we was going to be able to really bust into the higher affiliation of this conspiracy?"

"You sure did Partner!" Nikko said, giving Agent Tapia a triumphant high five.

"We are about to bust Ace and his whole crew in due time! A wiretap is definitely a nuclear weapon for law enforcement!" Agent Tapia said with cheer, as he lightly punched Nikko on the shoulder.

"Wait, Wait, that's not the end of it. She also got a hold of the two cell phones Jamar had on his possession at the time of his arrest. She examined the actual phone that the informant called, and it's a Boost mobile phone with direct connect features. She observed the phone number 609-769-8991, which is Ace's home line. The number 267-784-3964 phone number is Ace's cell phone, which we already have tapped, but there's a number 302-555-2233 phone number we're not familiar with as of this moment- all assigned to the same name of the phones memory card." Agent Nikko explained.

"So, whaddaya' mean! You lost me Mike." Tapia said, unable to fully understand that there's phone numbers in Jamar's phone that they didn't recognize. Tapia figured there's going to be maybe two to three hundred numbers they won't be able to recognize.

"So what's the big deal Mike?" Tapia asked.

'Listen Tone, since we gather this Intel' based off the wiretaps on 267-784-3964 cell phone line, and we already know Ace and Kim's home line phone number in New Jersey. That means this 302-555-2233 number has to be a possible drug network phone for Ace, because all numbers are stored under the same alias *FATBOY*. She already traced the line back to a white male by the name of Joe Clark, based out of Maryland. That name seems non-existing and the phone number itself is a Delaware number, not a Maryland phone number."

"So you basically telling me it's a pre-paid phone that belongs to Ace?" Tapia smiled, fully understanding what Nikko had been trying to tell him, and realizing it's most likely one of the various phones they been hearing in the background during the wiretap interceptions.

"Bingo!" Nikko laughed.

"Now we can add that 302 phone number to the affidavit and apply for a roving wiretap to zap that number too."

"But can we wiretap a pre-paid phone?" Nikko asked.

"We the Feds, we can do anything we fucking want. I bet you that's one of the phones with all the meat and potatoes we need to eat his ass alive." Agent Tapia said, with a sinister look on his face, all while thinking, *WE GOT YOUR PHONE TAPPED, WHAT YOU GONE' DO, CAUSE SOONER OR LATER WE'LL HAVE YOUR WHOLE CREW. ALL WE NEED NOW IS THE RIGHT WORD OR TWO TO MAKE IT ALL STICK LIKE GLUE, I GOT YOU!"................

CHAPTER 25
Dog fights (Champion Spade – vs- Mocha)

It's Saturday night and Ace's 2 time winner Spade is scheduled to match against Jihad's pit-bull named Mocha. The match was set for the bitches to come in at 37 pounds, 2:30 a.m. tonight. Virg will be handling Spade in the box since he did the **eight-week keep** on the now two-time winner dog....

"What time is it dude?" Virg asked Ace, as he rubbed Spade down to relax her muscles. Spade looked really good tonight, she was cut up like a bag of dope. Muscles showed up everywhere on the small, wide headed black dog.

"It's 4:30 p.m. She looking strong as shit Virg. We going to crush Jihad or what?" Ace inquired anxiously.

"I don't know dude. I know she's a fucking bulldog, so she gone be there no matter how long the fight goes. They got to kill her to beat us! This bitch is game tested to the fullest. I tell you what though, we gone bring some pain for sure." Virg replied matter factly.

"I'm hip, I'm hip. Shit, last fight she went two and a half hours, so I know she game. I did hear that bitch **Mocha** Jihad bringing is a rough bulldog. I think he chasing us cause we crushed him and his man before. He supposedly had went to Tennessee and paid a lot of money for the dog."

"Yeah, Yeah. Yeah! They all talk that shit and drive all over the world to get dogs. Shit, all we breed is bulldogs. Them niggas are a bunch of gossiping haters, who want to see us lose cause we win more than any of them. Fuck em! He better bring something ruff and game. Spade should bite even harder this match than she did last match. This is the first time I did a steroid keep on her. She gone bite harder, move faster, push and pull harder. I just hope she learns how to get out of a heat cycle quickly, because she may run into one if she comes out too hard, but she got technique, stamina and brains, so she should be fine. She's a smart fighting dog." Virg replied confidently.

"You right, I ain't trippin. I know you the man. Had you been that fat lazy ass Johnny, I'd be a bit concerned." Ace replied humorously cause he never lost a **match** until he used Johnny to work a dog that he brought from Johnny himself.

"Dude, I been told you about fucking with them cats, Johnny, Ivan, Picklehead, and Puerto Rican Sam. All of them are lazy as hell. They deprive the dogs a fair chance cause they don't take care of them properly. Plus they feed'em cheap dog food that's why the dogs teeth be weak, and they lazy during the keep too, that's why they dogs don't come in strong. But they think they got all the sense. Shit, they don't know nothing about dogs, not like I know dogs!" Virg replied arrogantly.

Truth be told, Virg is a good dog-man, but so was Johnny, Ivan and Sam. All good dog-men have different **keep**, workout for dogs, than the next one. Most of them hated on each other's work simply cause they were always in competition with each other.

"I heard Jihad just cracked Mike Vick and them down Virginia last week for $25,000 with a 33 pound bitch."

"Yeah, I heard he won. They gone talk about it forever cause it was **Mike Vick**. Shit, we done beat **DMX, Mark Jackson and Keshawn Johnson**. It doesn't matter if you beat a celebrity. Long as they recognized as real dogman, and not no corner boy backyard rolling match, it's all about the win." Virg retorted sarcastically. Virg was old school and always gave Ace advice from time to time.

"Alright old head, I'm gone down to the club now. Don't forget to call them niggas from the **Firm** (South Philly dog kennel). See if Reesey and them want to buy back that Wolfy pup I brought off them? Plus, I got a 51 pound male I'm trying to take out, so see if they got that weight. If so, go ahead and hook it cause I want you to do the dog anyway." Ace said matter factly, as he pulled his car keys out of his pockets on his way out the door.

"Which dog is it?" Virg asked puzzled.

"Wild Bill." Ace answered.

"Now that's a good, strong, game bulldog dude. You should just breed him all this year, and take him out next year. But it's your dog, so it's your call."

"Why you say it like that?" Ace asked confused.

"I only say that cause you see what happened to Nore when I didn't take your advice, now he dead and we only have a few pups off of him. Wild Bill is bred out the ass. His bloodline is 5 times Gator top and bottom. Plus, don't forget we promised Nino (**Pizzaman**) a few puppies. He would have never sold him to you without that part of the deal, and he only trusted us enough to go with it cause Bill is on our yard." Virg quickly reminded Ace.

"Yeah, I did promise him pups. But shit, I paid $10,000 for that dog. I can't front though, that might pan out to be the best $10,000 I ever spent. I rolled Bill twice since I got him and he killed both dogs in 5-10 minutes flat. He got **mouth**. He go hard too, he chase the same spot every time. He love getting in the chest area, then he actually breaks the dog's chest plate. Shit! If you include the two dogs he killed on Nino's yard in New York, he got bodies right now. That's the reason I bought him in the first place. But he kill shit so fast, I can't even get no time out of him to see how game he really is."

"Well if he anything like his daddy, he's game. He was bred out of **Champion Sammy**. I remember one time Sammy scratched 33 times in one match. Sammy has been producing too. They say he about to make **R.O.M** (register of merit) soon. Wild Bill bites 100 times harder than Sammy, and he bred better than Sammy, so if he anything like his daddy you got something special." Virg replied matter factly.

* * * *

Later that night around 1:30 a.m. cars slowly began to pull onto the grassy field, alongside the graveled driveway of Virg's house in New Jersey. There were license plates from VA, NY, PA, NC, CT and several other states pulling up to witness the highly anticipated match between Ace and Jihad. There was another fight going on between two 45-pound males, while everyone awaited the champion match that was scheduled next. Ace and Nikky had just got done re-counting the $30,000 Ace was betting on Spade, as everyone currently was held captive watching the action packed fight.

The red-nose pit and his opponent (a smoke gray pit) fought relentlessly in their attack. The smoke gray pit-bull was a **bulldog** (aggressive/good dog). He had already broken both of the red-nose pits' front legs. **Latino Ray**, the owner, of the wounded dog was too foolish to stop the fight. The red-nose pit wanted desperately to keep fighting, as it scratched on its belly by pushing with his hind legs. But, a wise dogman would pick up his dog based off that type of gameness alone, realizing the dog won't quit – but doesn't have a fair chance to win. A game dog was more valuable breeding, rather than simply allowing it fight to its death.

Ace quickly noticed this and asked Latino Ray to stop the fight. Ace even offered to pay for his losses if he picked up, cause he knew the red-nose pit was a diamond in the dirt. All the wounded dog needed was the right **keep** and the right handler. Ace wrote this down as another good investment. Latino Ray was acting foolish and arrogant because he knew his dog was going to lose. The dog would end up dying if he continued, but all Ray cared about was the money at this point so he took Ace's offer.

Before Ace bought the dog, Virg wanted to see one more courtesy scratch from the wounded, exhausted dog. Ray took the dog to his corner, and Virg sucked the blood out of the dog's nose so he could breathe better. The severely injured game dog scratched 100 miles per hour across the pit on his belly, again trying to attack his opponent.

They quickly picked up the wounded dog, gave Latino Ray $4500 to cover his loss. Then Virg went right to work like a highly skilled Veterinarian. They intended on doing everything to save the fine animal, as Virg taped up the dog's two front legs and put an I.V. on him to stop the dog from dehydrating. Ace watched in awe *"Now that nigga's a beast! I would neva suck the blood out a dog's nose'* he thought to himself comically while shaking his head. Virg was a top dogman, a breeder second to none, and a credit to the sport …

The main event was 10 minutes away. Nikky watched in amazement as Ace and Virg hung Spade on the scale to officially weigh in. The referee for tonight's main event would be Fat Al from Coatesville, a predominantly black suburb of PA.

"36 ½ pounds, she good weight." The referee yelled out.

After Jihad weighed Mocha they took the dogs over to be washed down. Virg and Jihad took turns carefully washing down each other's dogs with milk. As they completed washing the dogs, they prepared them for battle by getting inside the box with them. Both animals' ears were raised - knowing the box all too well. The two athletic, vicious dogs perked up simultaneously as they both screamed anxiously wanting and trying to fight each other. Spade was practically biting Virg's arms trying to get to her opponent.

"Face your dogs!" The referee announced excitedly, ready to finally see this main event like everyone else. The two dogs stared and growled in response. Both of these dogs had it all: mouth, wrestling ability, indestructibility and gameness. **"R-E-L-E-A-S-E!!!"**

The main event was now in action. Spade's first bite landed on mocha's upper right chest, as she quickly pushed forward charging Mocha into the corner. Once Spade locked her bite, she started shaking Mocha violently. Mocha somehow quickly got herself out of a compromising position, and now Spade switched up and held a lock on her head. Spade pulled and lifted her legs back anticipating her opponent's next target. Spade looked like an airplane, as she simply crafted her style of fight by moving her front legs away from her opponent's mouth.

The beginning of the fight was clearly in Spade's favor, which she took full advantage of. Mocha finally found a lock on Spade's upper left shoulder, but at this point it was useless. Spade was not your average biting dog, she was a pressure biter like her daddy, grand-champion **'Stan da Man'**. Every dog fighter that stepped into the pit dreamed of having one of those crippling, shocking, iron jawed alligators in his hands. Ace somehow luckily had himself a few of them.

Spade was ripping flesh, tissue apart as she shook Mocha's upper chest. Mocha yelled in response to the pain, then Spade went into Mocha's stifles. Spade loved to go to the stifles, trying to break the stronger dog down completely. Mocha was toughing it out, inflicting damage on Spade as well. Both dogs had decent mouth, but Spade was simply too much for Mocha. Spade was more game and she fought a smarter fight (both defense and offense).

Spade defeated Mocha after a 50 minute action-packed, fast-paced match. She slowly broke Mocha down bite after bite, shaking and putting pressure on the much stronger dog. Once she did enough damage to Mocha's stifles, she went back to her chest until the dog turned. When it was Mocha's turn to scratch she simply stood the line and she curred out – not wanting any more punishment from Spade.

Tonight Ace won $45,000 gambling altogether. He had a few side bets outside of the $30,000 in the box, because there was a lot of trash talking during the match. Ace didn't think Mocha was game. It was her first scratch of the night so Jihad betted Ace another $10,000 that his dog would actually scratch. Ace accepted the bet in the heat of the moment and won. Jihad was actually short $500 but definitely good for it so they exchanged phone numbers.

Jay, also known as, **Jihad** was a player out of New Jersey, who also had plenty of money himself. Jay was a low-key country boy, but a self-made millionaire as well. Virg had properly introduced Jihad and Ace because he thought they were the same in a lot of different ways. The bottom line was that they both were about that paper, and they both were trustworthy, so a potential friendship could be beneficial for them both behind the introduction.

Ace had **Takedown Kennels** before he even thought about starting **Takedown Records**. That's where the record label actually got its name....

'**Ace of Spade**' is Spade's full name. She has 3 wins straight now, so she will be better known by many as **Champion Spade**. Ace had plans on breeding her to Champion Sammy as soon as she heals, *"I don't care what they say, ain't no luck to my winnings. I just know how to pick'em!"* He smiled proudly as he thought to himself.

CHAPTER 26
(Love and Marriage)

In February 2005, Ace and Iesha had signed a contract agreement with Ryan's Home to build their new beautiful home. The $537,000 house with the exotic poolside theme, which cost an additional $67,000, would be a great investment for Ace. He decided to move a step forward in his relationship with Iesha, after a confrontation he had with Rain a few months back.

During the heated argument, Rain was crying as she asked Ace why wouldn't he just leave her alone completely. Rain didn't have the strength or heart to leave Ace because she was deeply in love with him. Rain was to the point where she was simply tired of sharing her man, especially with a ghetto bitch like Kim. She felt like she was playing second when she was there first, and the pain and loneliness, she harbored caused a sense of jealousy.

Ace had a lot of love and respect for Rain, and although he didn't agree with her request, he reluctantly granted her wish. Ace was burnt out from all the arguments stemming from his different relationships. Ace cancelled the commitment him and Rain once shared, and moved on, hoping sooner or later she would come back to her senses. Due to the kids, they would simply maintain a sexual relationship, because Rain didn't want to be involved with any other man. The bottom line was he didn't like to see her hurt, and her pain actually caused him to make his decision to end their exclusiveness.

Ace was one of the first homebuyers in the new elegant gated community, which would hold a total of 25 new beautiful homes. Each home will sit on 1 or 2 acre lots, increasing their value anywhere from $900,000 - $1.5 million dollars, which depended on the extremities that each buyer would put into their fine luxury homes as they were built....

On May 9, 2005, after carefully designing the home to a tee, the builders started digging ground to actually put up the house. Based on the concepts/designs that Ace and Iesha both came up with, once their house was completed, it would be simply immaculate..

Iesha requested a greenroom built on the side of the home that will actually be a part of the original structure of the house. The greenroom was fully enclosed by windows all the way around, and had its own A-frame roof, along with a separate heating and central air unit. The oversized exquisite greenroom actually made the basement area bigger causing the home's square footage to be even larger.

Iesha had large cathedral windows installed in the kitchen. The whole back wall in the eat-in section of the kitchen was made so that one could overlook the custom built pool in the backyard while you ate. The poolside theme was a beautifully crafted replica of the Grand Canyons.

Ace designed the basement himself. He made sure they dug it deeper than usual because he wanted a 12-foot ceiling in his finished basement. Ace had thick black carpet installed in the lounge area of the basement. He also built a wrap around bar, similar to the one he had at the club, and fully stocked with liquor. There was a movie theater room, which had a 70-inch remote screen and a high definition digital projector. To accommodate the theater, there was a hot popcorn machine, hot dog grill and several official coming soon movie posters hanging on the walls. The home theater actually resembled a real-live movie theater; only a mini-version of one because his only sat nine people.

Ace and Iesha's home had truly become a dream house. Their custom built mini mansion was built on a gorgeous 2-acre walkout site. It was full brick, and had limestone surrounding in every window. It had a full two -story limestone turret with a unique media room. The custom dark stained maple kitchen was equipped with high quality state of the art appliances, travertine tile, granite everywhere, 8 ft solid doors, Baldwin hardware, Andersen clad windows, recessed lighting, crown rope and mini pendent accent lighting ran throughout the entire home.

The master suite had huge walk-in closets, and an incredible bathroom. There was even a fully finished walkout with a full bathroom and second media area built for the guests. The 5 bedroom, 4.5 bathroom, 3 car garage house was absolutely stunning. Ace purchased the fine home at $604,000 which turned out to be a steal soon as it was built and a very wise investment he stumbled across after Iesha had gotten pregnant.....

2 years ago, Ace had proposed to Iesha on December 25, 2003 (Christmas night). Ace told Iesha he wanted her to finish college first, allowing him time to sort things out properly between him and Kim. Ace actually wanted to break away clean from Kim, but his Nana warned him not to be a fool. She knew from their past problems that Kim was going to be a difficult female to break up with, so Nana advised him that if Iesha really loved him she would be patient and understanding about the entire situation.

Ace had over $1 million of real estate property in Kim's name alone. He also had a few luxury cars amongst other things in her name as well. Ace knew from Kim's childis and ghetto ways that she would attempt to try him, by taking him for bad on everything he owned in her name, out of spite, just to hurt him. Although he could stand the loss, Ace was strictly about money, and didn't see any point or any gain in taking unnecessary losses....

Iesha had already been pregnant by him once before but got an abortion. Basically, because of the Kim factor, amongst other issues, they simply wasn't ready to have a baby at that time. Iesha had gotten pregnant a second time right in the middle of her last semester.

She was supposed to graduate this year so Ace thought it was probably best for her to get another abortion. He figured that it wasn't the proper time for her to have a baby yet, because she had a lot going for herself at the time. Iesha was about to graduate from college, plus she had started working part-time at her first radio job B-101. Although it was only part-time, the job headed her in the right direction, because it was actually in the field she majored in. Iesha wanted to be the next **Wendy Williams** if she pursued in radio, or a news reporter for a prime-time network like CBS/NBC/ABC if she excelled to television.

Those were her dreams so Ace quickly reminded her of her short and long time goals. He assured her that she shouldn't have to feel like a baby was going to a keep them together. Ace loved Iesha and honestly planned on marrying her one-day. Iesha knew Ace was right about her dreams, however she wasn't fully focused on her dreams any more. After witnessing Ace purchase their new home she was living her dream. Now she wanted to seal the deal by finally marrying the man she loved. Iesha didn't want to wait any longer. She felt like they had built the home of their dreams, and had already been engaged for over 3 years now – why not take it to the next step?

One of Ace's excuses to hold off on the marriage was that he wanted to properly introduce her to Islam. Iesha thought he just wanted a Muslim wife so she willingly offered to take her **shahada** (testify to become Muslim) just so they could hurry up and get married.

There was even an occasion where she attempted to rush the marriage along when they were in Las Vegas for a weekend. Iesha asked him could they get married right there in Vegas. Ace thought she was being her playful self, **but Iesha was serious as a heart attack!** Ace wiggled his way out of that one legitimately. He is Muslim so they have to be married by an **Imam** (Muslim preacher) for his marriage to be legal in Allah's (God's) eyes.

Unfortunately, Iesha had eventually gotten the second abortion. Emotionally she took it harder than the first one. Iesha really wanted that baby, but felt Ace began to act funny after she told him she was unsure of her decision. She falsely sensed that he would secretly be upset with her if she actually went through with the pregnancy, which was far from the truth.

Although Ace already had kids, this would have been Iesha's first child. So, Iesha expected more excitement out of him, and when she didn't see any excitement she assumed he really didn't want her to keep it. Iesha secretly got the abortion done without Ace knowing. When she told him she got the abortion Ace was highly upset. He was furious with her, behind the reason she chose to actually get the procedure done. Her excuse for terminating the pregnancy was foolish, and their signals had somehow got crossed.

However, Ace felt horrible for unconsciously making her feel the way she felt. He realized that he might have sent off mixed signals behind all the responsibility he was under lately. Ace explained all the different things he was doing that may have caused him stress. Ace was right in the middle of a film deal with Sony for his record label. They were in the process of preparing to shoot another film called **Menace** (Me-n-Ace) over the summer. He was also in process of buying **8 Street Lounge**, one of the clubs he's been running for over the last two years. Not to mention, the fact that he overstrained himself with his countless construction company projects. Ace was currently fixing up not one, but 3 of his real estate properties he had sitting so that he could rent them out upon completion. He always over-worked himself, which may have caused her to think he was acting funny. After explaining his actions, Ace apologized to Iesha and promised her they would get married next year. He even gave her the okay to use money out of their joint account to go ahead and plan the wedding, hoping to ease her mind.

Ace and Iesha spent a lot of time together since the purchase of the home shopping for furniture. The home was scheduled to be complete sometime in June 2005, which happen to be the same month Iesha would graduate from college, so Ace actually added even more responsibility to himself, but he didn't mind keeping his woman happy....

On June 16, 2005, Ace, Mrs. Marrisa, and a few more of Iesha's family members stood up clapping, as Iesha walked up to receive her college degree at her graduation. A few moments later Temple University's class of 2005 threw their graduation caps high into the air to celebrate a great achievement...

Ace, Iesha, Mrs. Marrisa and the family were on their way to **Hibachi**, Japanese steak house, to celebrate Iesha's graduation over dinner. **Duncan,** the owner of the hibachi, always allowed Ace to hold special parties at the fine restaurant whenever he needed to have an upscale event. Tonight they would simply have a small family get-together/graduation celebration for Ace's fiancé courtesy of Takedown Entertainment....

As Iesha walked to the parking lot where she parked her car she suddenly stood frozen.

"Ohhh my God! My car was parked here. Now it's gone. Somebody done stole my damn car." Iesha said in total disbelief.

"Wait a minute now, are you sure you parked right here Iesha?" Mrs. Marissa replied calmly.

"Yeah I'm sure!" Iesha replied sadly as tears began to well up in her eyes.

Iesha was upset because Ace had just bought her that car. It hadn't even been 6 months since she'd had the fully equipped maroon **2003 Volvo C-70 coupe**. Iesha quickly fell in love with the fine automobile and now it was gone. Iesha quickly thought about her laptop and all the other personal items of value that she always left in the car. Even though she had full coverage insurance certain things simply can't be replaced so Iesha was highly upset.

"Relax Boo. It could have just gotten towed. Are you absolutely sure you parked right here?" Ace said calmly as he pointed towards the empty parking space, quickly pointing out there wasn't any **NO PARKING** signs posted.

"Yessss Boo! I parked right here. I remember seeing that same new Benz truck pulling up to park beside us when I was walking away. When I saw that big red bow wrapped around it, I was like damn somebody got a nice gift for graduation."

"Alright, well I guess we got to report it stolen while yall ride with me." Ace replied.

"Damn! I can't believe this shit! Some asshole done stole my freaking car on my graduation day. This is just great! " Iesha said sarcastically, blatantly showing frustration because she normally don't cuss.

"Ooohhhh My Goodness!" Mrs. Marrisa shouted excitedly in disbelief.

"What now! Iesha replied disgustedly-urked, and unconsciously full of anger.

"Iesha,! Read that!" Her mother said as she pointed to a small sign on the back window of the new silver truck parked beside the space her missing car was once in.

The sign read: **CONGRATULATIONS! I'M YOURS BECAUSE ACE LOVES YOU!!!**

It was an arrow pointing towards the license plate; the same plate that used to be on her now missing Volvo.

"Aaahhhhhh!! Iesha screamed as she jumped up and down in excitement with tears in her eyes. She ran over to hug and kiss Ace, who was smiling joyfully as he shook the keys to her brand new silver truck. Iesha now owned a **2005 430ML Mercedes Benz truck**, loaded with a chrome sport package/chrome 19" AMG factory rims…

*   *   *   *

The next day Iesha and Ace woke up to the smell of breakfast cooking. Mrs. Marrisa was downstairs in the kitchen happily getting her cook on. Iesha still had her room, after dinner they had stayed the night at her mother's house.

"Boo, I need you to take that duffel bag with you when you go home today. I gotta go get the U-Haul truck so Amin, Chris, Cowboy, Boz and my Dad can move everything from the townhouse in Delaware to Jersey for me." Ace said tiredly, as he yawned getting up to get dressed to run his errands for the day.

"Alright, but you know there's another duffel bag under the bed too. It's been there for two weeks now, did you forget? Iesha replied with concern.

"Damn! It's like $400,000 in that damn bag. How did I mess around and forget that?" Ace retorted unconvincingly. Iesha knew he never lunched like that when it came to money unless it was on purpose.

That's cause you doing too much Ace. You left that here, on purpose, now how much is in this one, because I know it ain't no damn clothing in that bag. It's money isn't it?"

"Yeah man, Damn! It's like $670,000 in there. Matter fact, count it for me when you get home." Ace said as he tied his sneakers continuing to get dressed.

"Dang Ace! You got over a million dollars at my mother's house!" Iesha whispered harshly in disbelief as she went on to say, "What if she came in here to clean this room or something? She would have flipped the hell out!"

"Alright, Alright, Alright! I hear you, Damn! Just take it home for me. I got to go see them **gwalla gwallas** (Mexicans) in a minute, and we been doing so much shopping for the house I just left the money close by. I don't leave it all in one spot though; I spread it around between 5-6 spots that way I know it's safe until I get to it. I didn't forget it was here. I just can't leave it all at one spot, that's too risky. Ya dig?"

"Boy, I know you didn't' forget it. I know you too well to even consider that thought. But when are you going to stop Boo! Seriously? I'm scared, and I don't want to lose you!" Iesha replied very sincerely.

"Relax Boo, I'm a cannon remember? Niggas don't want war. The streets respect a nigga cause they know I ain't having it." Ace replied with a cocky demeanor.

"Boo I know you about your business as far as beef is concerned. But, you still human. Somebody you least expect and possibly trust might cross you one day. I'm truly concerned cause even you feel weary about the people in your circle at times. That's why you have those bad dreams you won't tell me about, which actually concerns me even more." Iesha's comments must have hit a nerve, because Ace just stared and listened to her as she went on to ask, "You really not scared to get arrested are you?"

"Alright, now you got to relax, you going overboard now. I'm a stop whenever it gets too hot for me to boogie. Okay?" Ace asked rhetorically expecting her to shake her head yes before he continued. "Once we get situated in the new house, I'm a let Gotti, Jerv, Watley, Hak, Dant and Lump do most of my dealings so stop worrying yourself. Alright?" Ace replied matter factly, hoping the info gave her comfort.

"Boo, that don't make me comfortable, it actually scares me that all of a sudden not one, but four of your closest friends came home from jail around the same time. Matter of fact, all of them damn near came home the same month. Now you know I never say anything, but don't that seem suspect to you?" Iesha asked sincerely.

"Nah man! You trippin! One thing for sure and two things for certain, I ain't gotta worry about none of them niggas I just named crossing me or setting me up! Shit, they know enough already to put me under the jail without setting me up. I could stop hustling cold turkey right here today, but the shit I done did with them already will put me away forever! So why should I even stop now?" Ace said sarcastically.

Iesha leaned up to grab his hands softly, to get his undivided attention. Ace smiled, falsely thinking she wanted to have a quicky. Sometimes after they had a brief disagreement they would engage in a good sex session. But Iesha simply stared at Ace for a brief moment with tears and sincerity in her eyes before she spoke.

"Boo, listen. I'm supposed to be happy right now. I ain't supposed to be feeling the way I am feeling."

"Come on Iesha, what's really wrong with you?" Ace asked puzzled.

"What's wrong is everything seems so right. I'm about to marry the only man I ever knew how to love. I finally graduated from college. I have a salary job at Bank of America, and I work part-time for the radio station, with hopes of pursuing my career in radio. Hell, I even landed my first acting job on a HBO special, not to mention, we are currently working on a baby, and you are finally giving me all that you promised me you would."

"So why the hell are you crying Boo?" Ace asked concerningly as he softly wiped a few tears away from her eyes, while caressing her face.

"Are you cheating on me?" Iesha replied as she started to cry even harder. "I hear things all the time and I'm not naive. I just shut up about it and ignore the gossip. I know my position and I accepted *some* agreements since the beginning of our relationship that I still accept. But new chics aren't part of the deal Ace. I hear you supposed to be involved with some dark-skinned girl, and you took her to the last fight in Vegas. This girl I know whose cousin saw you and thought it was me with you in Vegas. I'm embarrassed. I feel like a nut when someone comes up to compliment me on a dress I supposed to have worn during the fight, when I know damn well I didn't wear no blue dress or even go with you to that specific fight. I don't even bother you with rumors, because I don't ever want to nag or urk you like you say Kim do. I never want to lose the friendship and trust we have, but Ace that shit hurts to hear cause I think there's a lot of truth to it. It **really, really** hurts." Iesha said softly as her voice cracked, Ace felt her pain as he listened to her, watching her try to pull herself together as she went on to add.

"Ace if you gone do that type of activity, then I ask you to please do your dirt more discreetly. Don't play me like that,; disrespecting our relationship and me. At least keep it where I don't hear about it. You know I'm not gone leave you, but if you really love me you will be more conscious of my feelings. Fear and pain mixed with frustration behind the thoughts of you being with another woman is killing me slowly. I hold it in, not saying nothing, but it's unbearable at times."

Ace knew she was in pain, which is why he simply listened to her, allowing her to vent without interrupting or trying to talk himself out of the situation. He felt her sincereness so he didn't even want to lie his way out of it.

"I know you don't care about you getting locked up, cause you willing to take that risk for the money as long as you're successful in the end. But I'm going to end up going down with you, if you ever get locked up, and I don't know how well I can hold up under pressure. I do know that I love you so I'm not going anywhere. I guess I got to die to prove my love for you, cause I love you just that much. Why do you have me so in love with you? Yet, you won't take my advice? You don't even need the money anymore so just stop hustling altogether; that is better for **us**." Iesha said as she cried uncontrollably.

Truth be told, Nikky and Iesha didn't look exactly alike. They were both just pretty dark-skinned women who coincidently shared some of the same features. Iesha's hating ass girlfriends knew damn well it wasn't her in Vegas, but couldn't wait to put some dark clouds and rain on Iesha's sunny lifestyle. They envied her for various reasons, and some of them were just jealous of her relationship. Iesha wore a beautifully custom crafted **5-karat diamond** engagement ring on her finger. She also had the best quality cars; jewelry, pocketbooks and house money could buy, all courtesy of Ace.

They smiled in her face all along they wanted to take her place (backstabbers, backstabbers).

Them hating ass bitches didn't have a man of their own, who was willing to take care of their every need. Most of Iesha's so-called girlfriends unconsciously envied her, and purposely tried to ruin her happiness every chance they could.

Sonya was one of the only friends Iesha had who actually advised her not to even mention any of the gossip to Ace. Sonya's boyfriend Tukky is a grimy ass nigga from down the bottom. Tukky was simply what you call an Ace Capone hater (He didn't even know Ace, but he hated on him because Ace was more popular than him.) Tukky actually told Sonya that he had seen Ace in Vegas with a young chic he used to deal with, knowing Sonya would take the news right back to her childhood girlfriend. Tukky was simply playa hating on Ace, mad about the fact that once Ace started dealing with the chic Nikky he didn't get any more holla from her.

Sonya didn't even tell Iesha about the news until one night, Iesha cried on her shoulder during a tour of their newly built home. Sonya was a smart, crafty street girl who lived around Iesha's grandmother way. Iesha was a silly Catholic School girl who played with Sonya over the summer when she visited her grandmom, so they grew up together as childhood friends.

Her advice to Iesha was simple: When you deal with a nigga like Ace, alot of shit comes with it. But, from what she seen Ace was a good dude. In Sonya eye's Iesha had the ring, the car, the house, and the man! In due time Iesha would have the baby, cause they were currently in process of trying to make that happen. Therefore, she can and should be proudly holding her head high, standing strong by her man....

Ace hugged Iesha tightly as she continued to cry, trying to comfort her while he thought to himself. *Damn! I can't be hurting my boo like this. I gotta tighten up quick. I could move Nikky out of town somewhere in another state? Then maybe all the gossip shit will stop? Roberto said I needed to get a spot in Miami or Texas anyways, so I will have babygirl just look for a spot in either of those places. That's a small price to pay to heal Iesha's heart. It will make Nikky happier too, so I'd kill two birds with one stone. Damn pimp! You got four full plates of responsibility, what did you get yourself into? Real Talk!* Ace quickly snapped out of his thought when Iesha's mom yelled, "Iesha and Ace come on and eat, breakfast is ready.

CHAPTER 27
"Prosecution" (Conspiracy)

August 5, 2005, Prosecutor Rich Lovette is in a meeting along with assistant prosecutor Mike Brunshek and a task force consisting of the FBI, ATF, and the IRS. They were all designated as one to formulate a team built for the investigation of the Coles conspiracy.

"I really think we have enough to take him down right now Rich." Agent Tapia said.

"No. Not just yet Tone. We should wait at least another week to arrest Coles. I believe he is big enough to go after full throttle, so we will cloak the true identity of the full conspiracy by arresting him only on gun charges. For now let's pick up his current state gun charges one at a time, and prosecute him federally on each gun charge. This method will give us some more time to gather more Intel, and possibly gather more witnesses about his money laundering activities. When we arrest Ace we will conduct a raid on 27 houses simultaneously. By raiding him and the members of his crew at the same time, hopefully we'll gather enough evidence to end this case without having to go to trial. My bet is that most of them will cooperate or at least plead out to lesser charges." Mike Brunshrek state confidently.

'I agree with you to a certain degree, but someone always goes to trial. However, don't be so confident that we'll catch Ace Capone with drugs. He's very crafty and I'm willing to bet my life that he'll be clean when we do take him down. I'll be the first to admit that Ace Capone is far from the average drug kingpin. " Rich Lovette stated in a calm matter of fact tone.

"I agree that Ace may not be an idiot, but most drug dealers keep personal use of drugs around all the time, and they definitely keep guns to protect their ill gotten gains. I believe Ace Capone will at least have a few weapons on hand and whole lot of money." Agent Nikko said.

"You're absolutely right Mike, but when during your entire investigation have you ever noticed or suspected Ace of using drugs? He doesn't even smoke marijuana and he rarely drinks liquor for crying out loud. So don't underestimate our opponent. This case is bigger than you guys are visualizing. We will all obtain the status we are looking for to further our careers off this case. Ace has ties to celebrities and thugs all around the globe. I want guys like him and Beanie Sigel, another scum bag, off the streets permanently. Part of the reason we will wait until next week to arrest Coles is because Dwight Grant a/k/a Beanie Sigel, departs from Federal custody on August 9, 2005. Our arrest warrant on Coles for the first gun charge that we adopted is good from today August 5th through August 12th, so there's no rush - we have time to arrest him on the adopted charges. I look to put Sigel's ass directly back into Federal custody for at least money laundering if not drugs too. I know he's mixed up in this organization somehow, which I learned from reliable street sources, and I want to prosecute him to the fullest extent of the law - for getting off on that shooting he beat in the state. Ace has actually crossed over into the legit world of music now, so we have to proceed before he gets too clean/powerful enough for us to be able to touch him the way we want to. He has promoted and established friendships with many celebrities. My guess is, he will utilize those relationships to the best of his abilities once we prosecute him. If so, this will be the biggest trial of the decade, especially if guys like Jay-Z, 50 Cent, Kanye West and many more come to his aid during trial. This is why we must act now, yet still be patient gentlemen. We know from listening to Cole's wiretaps the different rappers he's been talking to on the phone. " Rich Lovette said in a professional and stern tone.

"Yeah, I remember when Ludacris, Slim Thug, and Ann Marie called Ace." Agent Bowman replied excitedly, unconsciously exposing the fact that he is a hip-hop fan.

"That's good, because I intend to go mainstream with this prosecution. I'm talking CNN, ABC, NBC, and CBS, Worlwide news ladies and gentlemen. I also intend on superseding Mr. Ace Capone for the initial drug conspiracy once he's in federal custody sometime early next year. We should be able to hold him without bail on the guns alone."

The Feds knew none of the celebrity artists that Ace dealt with had anything to do with Ace's drug life. However, they did suspect Beanie Sigel of being involved because of the street rumors that Ace is really the street and Beans was behind him, backing Ace with money. That was definitely all lies. Truth be told, Ace is the streets and the money himself! Beans thugged out rap persona caused idiots to say things that were not true. Ace and Beans were just cool, and Ace's Bentley was in Dame Dash's (CEO of Rocafella Records) name. Dame Dash had two partners: Jay-Z and Kareem Biggs (Hoffa). The Federalies hate Hip-Hop simply because rappers say anything they want, and it's message is predominantly for the young black culture. The white youths in middle suburban America love the music also. They support Hip-Hop faithfully, which infuriates a lot of middle-class/Republican American citizens. They hate the fact that young ex-gun toting drug dealers now get rich off talking shit legally. They figure they can go after the music business because they swear that every rapper starts off his career with illegal drug money. Not to mention the fact that some of these guys become not only rich, but also well known, famous idols to some of their very own children.

It's a strange, but true reality that just about every rich successful star loves to live the life of a bad guy. No matter if they play professional sports, sing, rap or act, something about being the bad guy draws them in to want to be the bad guy. A lot of professional rich guys who successfully made it big the legal way wants to live the life of a drug dealer. They are simply infatuated with the lifestyle of the Tony "*Scarface*" Montana and Pablo Escobar's. The silly saying that often times seem true was that *Good guys finish last, and most women love the bad guy!* Even when they have a good guy at home taking care of business, some women still sneak behind the good guy's back with a bad guy who most likely treated them like shit.

The government hoped by taking Ace Capone down, they'd also take down some of the famous celebrities he knew right along with him. Ace was famous enough for his connections alone, but the Feds were relentless. The U.S. government has all the money and power they need to go after anyone, and bring you down hard if they want you. The Feds also have a money-laundering statue that they would apply to your 85-year-old grandmother, so adding this charge to a few different celebrities for media attention was a must for the government. The celebrity ties would just bring more attention to one of the biggest drug conspiracy cases Philly has ever seen.

The Government's first task was to arrest Alton Coles, Ace Capone, the leader and organizer of the drug conspiracy. The plan was to pick him up upon the raid. Then they would hold him in custody by adopting one of his two current gun charges that he had in the state court.

It was a nice cool night back on October 24, 2004 to be exact, and plenty of people showed up to the 8th Street Lounge, one of the many clubs where Ace Capone promoted parties. Daryl Shuler and Ace Capone had presented a birthday party for Steve Brodie that night. The party was jammed packed with people from all areas of the city. North, South, West and Southwest Philly's finest were all in the building. Even people from Delaware, Chester, and Camden showed up to this star-studded event.

*After the party ended, Ace, D.S., and Brodie were leaving with an entourage when Ace noticed Jennifer arguing with some out of town niggas in the parking lot. Jen is one of Bean's ex-girlfriends. She was a dime piece, standing 5'6", weighing 140 pounds. She was light brown skinned with the sexiest and most feminine curves a woman could want. She also possessed a pair of eyes tattooed on the back of her waistline that added more to her unique sex appeal. To put it short, **Jen is a bad Bitch!***

One of the guys she was arguing with took it upon himself to punch out one of the car windows on her Jaguar coupe XJ-8.

"Nut ass Nigga, You'sa Bitch! You only done that shit cause I'ma woman, but you got the right one cause I'll cut chu' the fuck up!" Jen said, going into a rage, cursing and fussing, attempting to challenge the guy even though she was a woman.

Normally Ace didn't get involved with domestic disputes or personal beefs, but seeing how upset Jen was, Ace decided to help because she was cool with him, plus she's a friend of a friend.

"Bitch you better back da fuck up before I beat you da fuck up out here!" Threatened the guy Jen was cursing and fussing at. He aimed his fist at Jen like he wanted to hit her just as Ace walked up.

"Damn Pimp! That's a female ya dig? What chu' in your emotional bag for playa?" Ace asked in a calm yet aggressive tone.

Ace's goons were already alert once he spoke. Soon as Ace finished his statement, all you heard was at least 6 to 9 guns being cocked back. The sounds of the weapons let it be known that the goons holding them were prepared to do some major body damage.

One of the guys Jen was arguing with immediately copped a plea. "Woe, Woe, Woe! Ace let's talk here...I mean we have mutual friends so hold up for a second Brah!" The guy replied in a frantic and scared voice.

Ace was pissed off that the guy even said his name out loud for the whole crowd of spectators to hear it right before a dangerous shootout situation.

That's all the fuck I need is for one of these muthafuckaz to testify that they heard my name right before a homicide took place. I'm already in some bullshit now with fines up to my ass stemming from another shooting that happened back on Christmas of last year, where a few people got shot down Club Flow right after one of my parties that I threw for Cuzin E down on Delaware Avenue. Now this nut ass nigga drawing, Ace thought, looking at the guy with a smirk.

Ace knew he didn't need any more heat. He already had enough headaches, so he decided to defuse the situation. After defusing the drama, Ace made sure Jen got to her car safely before he left....

Ten minutes later, Amin had pulled up in front of Palmer's Social Club for the after party. Ace was in the passenger seat when he noticed a paddy wagon pulling up behind his Bentley.

Mike Millions had alerted Ace that the cops in the paddy wagon were on him. They were staring and pointing at Ace while talking on the walkie-talkie to dispatch.

One of the out of town niggas that Jen was arguing with got on some Sucka' Shit. After getting chumped out of the scary standoff, he felt some kind of way about Ace doing the chumping, so he made an anonymous call to 911.

"Listen, it's four guys in a blue Bentley with guns. They just threatened to kill me." The anonymous caller lied. He even went on to give a full description of what Ace Capone had on: A white baseball fitted cap with a white and blue-stripped button up shirt, and some white S. Carter sneakers.

The cop exited the paddy wagon in the busy nightlife environment and yelled, GET ON THE WALL! YOU'RE UNDER INVESTIGATION!"

There had to be at least 1,000 people outside, between the parking lot and the club. Amin, Mike and Boz got on the wall. They were trapped, and they all had guns on them. Ace had a gun also, but he figured he would lure the cops after him so that the rest of his team could ease off into the sea of people. Ace walked away from the cop, which caused the cop's full attention to shift to Ace.

"HEY YOU, STOP!" The cop yelled as Ace took off running.

Ace could only run far enough to throw the gun away that he had inside his pocket, before the cops quickly swarmed him. About 12 cops beat Ace's ass once one of the cops yelled, 'HE THREW A GUN!" They didn't even realize whom Ace was until after he was in custody. The gun was retrieved, and Ace got arrested. He was immediately escorted over to the Precinct on Benjamin parkway. Ace got out on bail the same night in less than two hours courtesy of Mr. Williams after the club owners had informed him of the problem.

*   *   *   *

Ace had gotten a call from Michelle *"The Source"* Brown on a hot August day.

"What's up?"

"Ace, listen to me baby, I need a huge favor…I'm talking very huge."

"Talk to me." Ace said

"Big head (Beans) is getting out of jail in 2 days. You know he just did 10 months up in the Feds for that gun case." She said. Beanie Sigel had served a one- year sentence on a 922G: being a convicted felon in possession of a gun. His mother-manager Michelle "The Source" Brown decided to call up Ace for a favor. She had partnered up with Ace a lot, on various events throughout the years. She was also a good friend of Ace's and a gambling partner as well.

"Uh-Huh" Ace said, hoping she would just get to the point.

" I need to borrow $15,000. You know I gotcha, just give me a couple weeks. I pawned his jewelry when I lost down Atlantic City and Dame wants to shoot some footage on film of Beans leaving Federal custody. Beans is going to be pissed off with me if I don't have his jewelry.

"What jail he's leaving from?"

"Fairton, New Jersey federal facility. The footage is going to be like some bonus clips to go along with Beans next album release. You know to increase the marketing on the project. I think it's a great idea. Whaddaya' think?"

"Sounds like you got a winner, and of course I gotcha. But you got to come get it."

"Thanks Baby. I'll see you tomorrow ya hear." She said before ending the call....

The following morning, Michelle pulled up in Ace's driveway. When she arrived at Ace and Iesha's newly built home she was simply amazed. Ace came out to greet her.

"Damn Ace! This is really, really nice. I'm talking real nice. When knuckle head Beans see this house he's going to want to move out of his house. He already wants me to move in his house so he can look for another big house, but yours going make him move faster. You know ya'll unconsciously be in competition on that type of shit." Michelle said jokingly.

"Yeah, I'm hip, I like it too, but I only plan on staying here for about three to five years, then I'ma upgrade again and sell this one so I can get an even nicer crib for about $1.5 million."

"Look at chu, saying $1.5 million like it's chump change." She slapped him playfully on the arm as he led her inside the house.

"You know that's small to a giant." Ace playfully bragged. "Last week Yusef had took me to some Old Head's house about 20 minutes away from here and that joint was CRAZY! Old Head had a inside pool in the basement with a full locker room that had showers, lockers, weights, and everything just like a gym. I should've known something was different, because he hit the pimp shit on me when I asked him 'What's behind that door?'

"What he say?" Michelle asked. She loved hearing Ace's stories.

"Some shit like it's the tears and sweat plenty of women put in for him. Some Ole' fly shit!" Ace laughed. "I thought it was a movie room like mines cause it had double doors on it. I should've known something was up when I seen the big ass pipes tho, plus soon as we first walked in there I knew I had smelled chlorine. I gotsta' step my game up!" Ace said with laughter continuing to explain what the Old head's place looked like.

"Old Head even had an elevator in that joint."

"Oh Yeah!" Michelle exclaimed. "What's up with them cars, I know he ain't have no Bentleys in the driveway."

"Old Head had a pearl white Phantom with a driver posted by that joint. Plus he had that new Ferrari Spider joint."

"Yeah, you might have to step up your game baby." Michelle joked.

"Melissa told me Dame gon' look out for the cookout again. I need that Bentley GT Coupe or that all white 62 inch Maybach for me. I ordered them both so who do I get the money to and when do I go to New York to pick them joints up?" Ace asked.

"Boy, you just as bad, as Beans buying all them damn toys!" Michelle said, looking at Ace as she shook her head smiling at him.

Michelle didn't mind Ace splurging. She knew first hand that he could afford it without denting his pockets. But she was also a good friend to Ace despite their age difference. She looked at Ace as if he were a son to her and her family.

"Now Ace I got to be frank with you. I know you don't need or want for nothing cause you're one of the smartest men I know. But answer this for me baby, when are you going to retire?"

"What chu mean?" Ace asked, playing dumb.

"You know what I mean. I mean really, really retire from the game? You a good man Ace, and Iesha is an extraordinary woman, which you know I don't say too often. You know me, I stay chasing all them fat ass little hookers away from you and Beans. But honestly, she's a quality woman and from what I see, she seems to have your back. You need to go on and settle down and enjoy your money now. You can't enjoy it when you constantly chasing it, and the stakes are too high for you to lose at your level baby. God forbid if you get locked up like Beans, cause then I won't know what I'm going to do. That's why I told Fertinottoa Perrry's ass to get that fucking gun charge you still fighting in the state beat ASAP!"

"Preciate it." Ace said with a nod.

"I'm still mad at them no good niggaz of yours, cause one of they asses was supposed to eat that gun charge. You should not have been the one to save the day for they asses. That is like cutting the head off the damn snake! If you cut the snake at the end of the tail it can grow back. But if you cut the head off the snake it will die. Now I know you got to carry guns to protect yourself and your family cause of whom you are, but you damn sure don't have to hustle no more. With that said, you need to really start considering retirement. If not for nothing else, do it for your kids and yourself cause you done what the average nigga can't do. YOU ALREADY WON!!!! Michelle said sincerely as Ace just sat there shaking his head and listening.

While listening to Michelle give him some sincere advice, Ace wondered did she just get done talking to Iesha? Or was it a coincidence that he had heard the word retirement from the game within the same week????????????

CHAPTER 28
(The Raid)

In the wee hours of the morning on August 10, 2005, at 12:30 a.m. Ace and Iesha were in the master bedroom of their beautiful new home asleep. Lil Alton, Nyrah, and Naail, Ace's 3 oldest kids, were downstairs pretending they were camping. The kids had their sleeping bags so they could camp out in the humungous green room. Windows and the wooded land surrounding the home, made it seem as if they were actually outside in the wilderness, enclosed the huge room.

The 2 boys Lil Alton,10, and Naail, 7, were scheming a plot to scare their 9-year-old sister Nyrah.

"Nyrah look it's something or someone outside. Oh shoot, it must be the boogie man!" Lil Alton said as him and Naail snickered quietly.

Nyrah looked with her eyes wide open like deer caught in headlights, before she laughed.

"Shut up!" Nyrah replied playfully, even though she was somewhat frightened by their comment. Suddenly she looked out the window and thought she saw some kind of movement. **"STOP PLAYNG YALL! I'M A TELL DADDY!"**

"Oh snap! We not playing, look right there. What's that?" Naail replied as he pointed at a dark area over towards some bushes and trees, with his eyes opened wide as the sun.

"AHHHHHH, I'm TELLING MY DAAAAADDDY!" Nyrah screamed as she ran upstairs headed to her father's room crying...

Ace was in a deep comfortable dream state snoring away, until Iesha shook him to wake up.

"Boo, wake up. Nyrah is crying, and she wants you."

"Huh? What's wrong Moo?" Ace said groggily as he sat up to focus in on what was going on.

'Dad, Naail and Alton keep saying the boogieman gone get me. I'm scared. I want to sleep with you Dad!" Nyrah cried out nervously.

"Alright, Alright Moo. You can sleep in the bed with me. But, ain't no such things as the boogie man! Okay? If there were a boogieman, daddy would get him before he even thought about getting you. So there's no reason for you to be scared of a boogieman. Okay? Ace replied convincingly enough to a 9 year old who trusted her dad for protection against anyone in the world. Nyrah simply shook her head yes, as Ace kissed his little princess on her forehead...

Thirty minutes later Lil Alton and Naiil didn't even knock as they quickly entered into their father's bedroom.

"Boy, what I tell yall about walking in my room without knocking first?" Ace whispered harshly.

"Sorry Dad, we knew Nyrah was in here so we want to come sleep in here too. There's something out in that yard man." Lil Alton replied nervously, as Naail quickly co-signed his request with a demand. "Yeah man, it's something out in that yard dad. We camping out in here on the floor with you."

As they both laid out their sleeping bags on the floor, Ace simply shook his head at how comical his kids were. He figured his two boys had played around so much trying to scare their sister; they had messed around and scared their own selves. However, Ace thought they were tripping, but the kids really kept hearing and seeing some kind of movement out in that yard...

At 2:45 a.m. everyone was fast asleep when the house phone rang. Iesha finally woke up to answer the phone as she thought too herself '*Who the hell could be calling here at this hour?*'

"Hello, he's sleeping. Who is calling?" Iesha asked sleepily and concerned, then she shook Ace. "Ace! Wake up, somebody wants you on the phone."

"Huh? Who is it?" Ace asked puzzled as he woke up slowly reaching for the phone.

"I don't know who it is, he just said he's a friend and that it's very important that I wake you up, because Clearfield or Clearview St. is about to get raided." Iesha replied puzzled because she never heard of Ace being on or associated with either of those streets, so she didn't fully understand what was going on.

Ace, on the other hand, heart felt like it dropped directly to his stomach. He recognized the street right off the bat! Fear and shock caused him not to focus properly, Ace knew exactly who resided at the Clearfield street address.

"Yo?" Ace replied nervously to the caller as he got up and walked out of his room. Ace walked down the hall into one of the kid's bedroom, away from Iesha so he could talk more privately.

After talking with the mysterious caller for 15 minutes, Ace hung up the phone so he could call his lawyer. It was late so Ace only got his voicemail, and decided to leave a message.

"Aye, Joe, Listen it's Ace. The Feds are getting ready to raid a lot of my spots, so call me back. This time I'm not panicking over no rumors either, it's going down for real! Call me back at my new house number."

Ace couldn't sleep or think straight. His nervousness caused his stomach to turn into knots, and he must have taken a shit at least six different times within the last hour. Ace quickly called a couple of his closest crew members, telling them to **vacuum** (flush/get rid of any cocaine). He didn't explain why because he wasn't sure if the phone were tapped or not, but out of the few people he called only Uncle Hak answered his call to get the crucial message.

The lawyer, Joe Morone finally called back around 5:00 a.m. Joe advised Ace to calm down and instructed him to meet him at his office at 7:00 a.m. Joe would then try to make the necessary calls to see what exactly was going on. Ace felt a little more relaxed after talking to his lawyer. Joe explained to him that most likely the Feds will simply come in to do a search, and if Ace is **clean** he should be fine. Ace knew he was clean, but walked into his study to call Nikky.

Ace had to be discreet about making the call to Nikky, because he didn't want Iesha to know whom he was calling. He didn't want to stir up more concern with her, especially after all the here-say and gossip that had been going around about him and the pretty dark-skinned girl.

RING, RING, RING, RING, RING…There was no answer. Nikky was sound asleep. Ace wasn't himself and Iesha sensed his fear immediately. She tried to be as supportive to her man as she could, so she kept coming in and out of the study trying to encourage him that everything was gonna be alright.

"It's gone be fine Boo. If they do come they should just do a search and leave, cause you don't have anything in here that can cause you trouble." Iesha said confidently.

"Boo, I ain't even got them playing fair, I can't control my fucking nerves for some reason, and that ain't even like me. I hope you right though, but something tell me it's a lot more to this." Ace replied with frustration and concern. His boost phone had been vibrating for the last three minutes. He seen it was Nikky calling him back. "Can you go upstairs to check on the kids for me?" Ace asked Iesha.

As Iesha walked upstairs, he quickly answered his boost chirp.

Chirp: "Damn, Babygirl. You up? I been calling you for the last ten minutes."

Chirp: "Yeah, I was sleeping baby. Why what's wrong? You left your keys or something? You need me to buzz you in?" Nikky asked tiredly because she was still half asleep.

Chirp: "No, No, No! I'm not there, but listen and pay close attention. If you half asleep you need to WAKE DA FUCK UP! REAL TALK!" Ace replied nervously in a low, yet aggressive tone. He had her full attention now, as Nikky quickly noticed the importance and fear in his voice.

Chirp: "I'm up, I'm up! Baby what's wrong? You scaring me." Nikky replied puzzled as she sat up holding her chest to listen in a state of shock.

Chirp" "Listen, don't be scared. Just do exactly what I say right now! Look in the top drawer and grab my black thing that I left over there earlier. You know what I'm talking about?"

Nikky had no clue what he meant as she got up to go see what was black, and in the drawer to know what he was actually talking about.

Chirp: "Yeah, I got it. What you want me to do with it?" Nikky asked now even more scared after realizing exactly what the black thing was.

She had a million and one thoughts, now wondering what the hell he was gonna tell her to do next.

Chirp: "Just get up and go throw it down the trash chute. RIGHT NOW!" Ace demanded loudly, hoping that she got that specific point of urgency.

Chirp: "Baby you scaring me, what's wrong? And is this thing going to go off or something?" Nikky questioned fearfully while her heart raced, as she held the black 9 mm glock lazily in both of her hands.

Chirp: "Nah, don't be scared Babygirl. It's nothing for YOU to worry about. Just put it in a bag and do what I said. Ain't nothing gone go off. Okay?" Ace replied calmly so that he didn't frighten her any more than she already was.

Chirp: "Okay! But stay on the phone with me while I walk out in the hallway to do it. I'm still scared boy. You sure it won't go off?" Nikky asked again for reassurance.

Chirp: "No! It 's not gonna go off Beauty. Make sure you put it in a bag so it won't be just laying around down there like that. You feel me?" Ace replied with slight humor in his voice over his Babygirl's concern.

After Nikky did exactly what Ace said, he told her that he would be there after he makes a stop. Ace wouldn't explain anything that was going on to her, he simply instructed for her to call him as soon as she got in from work....

At 6:05 a.m. slumber finally took it's effect as Ace dosed off for a few minutes. He was dreaming that someone infiltrated his inner circle. The C-1 was attempting to set him up while the Feds waited outside for him to exit, so they could move in and placed Ace under arrest.

BOOOOOOOOOOOOOOOOOOMMMMMMMMMMM !!!!! Ace quickly jumped up out of his dream state, extremely perplexed in a sudden state of shock. "They here Boo! They here!" Ace yelled frantically as he shook Iesha to wake up.

"ATF! GET DOWN ON THE GROUND AND PUT YOUR HANDS BEHIND YOUR HEADS!"

Is all Ace heard continuously as the screaming agents stomped loudly throughout the entire downstairs section of the house. It sounded like the war in Iraq was going on inside his new fine home, because over 30 highly trained armed agents dressed in all black armored gear, from head to toe were now violently rummaging throughout the house.

The kids were in shock and disbelief as they witnessed their father look to be uncomfortable for the first time in their young lives. Ace was always calm, cool and collective, but at the moment he wasn't acting his normal self. Ace quickly yelled out to the agents through the door of the master bedroom, that there were women and children in the room with him who were very frightened. Ace assured the screaming agents that he had no weapons, and that he simply wanted to come out of the room incident free.

Ace was only concerned about his family's safety, and no one needed to get hurt. He knew the screaming agents were running off of pure adrenaline and fear. Ace was afraid one of the agents would shoot out of excitement; triggered off the adrenaline rush they were highly amped up on. Ace wasn't concerned about getting locked up at this point; he just didn't want Iesha or the kids to get hurt in the process.

The head agent made Ace surrender from out of the bedroom first, followed by the kids and then Iesha. Although subdued in zip-cuffs, Ace finally relaxed a bit after seeing that no one got hurt. One of the agents was black and allowed Ace to sit on the floor in one of the living rooms next to Iesha and the kids.

While the tactical team of federal agents searched through the entire house looking to gather any kind of drug dealing, or money laundering evidence, Ace politely asked the angry agents not to ransack his home because there was nothing there to find. The kids were tough and courageous like their father. They didn't cry or complain. Ace assured them that he was going to be alright, as he overheard the agent who initiated the search talking.

"Shit! There's got to be something here. He can't be completely clean so look again and KEEP LOOKING!" The team leader demanded sternly in an aggressive manner, as he slammed his hat on the kitchen counter top full of frustration and anger. Ace just listened and thought to himself, "*Yeah, yeah keep looking. But you won't find shit cause ain't a damn thing here to find.*' as he stared silently with a cold evil glare...

As the Feds continued their search, Ace was taken into custody. The Feds informed him that they adopted one of the gun charges he still had pending in state court...

*　　　　　　*　　　　　　*　　　　　　*

Iesha was driving on her way to take the kids home to Rain's house. Once the Feds had finished searching and confiscating all they wanted, they told her they would be back but she was free to go. Moments later, Iesha pulled into the gas station and turned on the cell phone to call her mother.

RING, RING, RING

"Iesha! Oh my God. I have been calling you all damn morning!" Mrs. Marissa replied with relief, happy to finally hear her daughter's voice.

"Mom, you won't believe what happened. The Feds just ransacked my damn house! They did all that just to lock Ace up for a simple gun charge he already had for like a year—"

"I know. They came here and tore my house apart too. Plus, it's all over the news. " Mrs. Marrisa replied, interrupting Iesha in the middle of her trying to fully explain what had happened. Due to her frustration Iesha wasn't too sure if she actually heard or understood her Mom's last comment correctly.

"What do you mean they came over there too?" Iesha questioned as she went to use her bank debit card to pay for the gas. The card declined, so she pulled out another debit card which also declined. Iesha carefully viewed both cards as she reached for one of her personal credit cards. *"Now wait a damn minute! Both these cards go to our joint accounts. I know there's plenty of money in both of those accounts. What the hell is going on?'* She thought strangely to herself…

As Ace rode in the back seat of the tinted out Ford Explorer, he realized he had seen that very same truck somewhere before. It was all too familiar to him. Ace was handcuffed with a pair of zip cuffs. There were two special agents assigned to transport him to the federal detention center in Philadelphia. Ace simply ignored the two agents attempted small talk as they were driving. One of the agents was trying to be extra Joe (too familiar) with Ace the whole ride from Jersey to Philly.

"So how long before I see the Judge about bail?" Ace asked nonchalantly, finally indicating that he could actually speak.

"Well, you will see a judge today. But there's a three-day holdover before you're granted a bail hearing." The agent in the passenger seat replied, happy to get some kind of conversation out of Ace after twenty minutes of driving.

"Three day hold over?" Ace responded disgustedly in a state of confusion.

"Yeah guy, three-days. But, there's always cooperation. You know?" The agent who was driving replied, with high hopes of Ace biting on the bait he just put on his invisible hook.

Ace just smiled arrogantly as he shook his head with disgust.

"Man, you got me twisted. Huh? I guess they ain't tell you that about me, when they told you everything else?" Ace asked sarcastically, knowing that he had way more problems with the Feds than just a gun charge.

"Who are they? And what is it that they should have told us Ace?"

"Well, let me see. Since yall base everything off of information. I figured that ya snitches shoud have told you that **MY TROUBLES ARE MY TROUBLES!** Never anyone elses' problems." Ace replied in a deep, cold, heartless manner, meaning exactly what he said. Ace always did business with that specific agreement amongst him and his associates...

CHAPTER 29
Bail or no bail? (It was all just a week ago)

August 13, 2005 while Ace was in the marshal's cage waiting to see a judge for his bail motion hearing, his lawyer Joe Morone came down to visit him. Joe is only one of Ace's criminal/entertainment lawyers, but all of his girls knew which lawyer to call when something was wrong.

"How are you holding up Ace?" Joe asked sincerely.

"I'm good. When am I getting outta here?" Ace asked eagerly.

"Well, we will see about that in just a few minutes. But, let me fill you in first on what's really going on. Apparently the ATF, FBI, DEA, and IRS put together a joint task force to raid 27 houses in connection to you. At some of the locations they obtained some drugs, a lot of guns, and a whole lot of cash!" Joe informed him.

"Fuck!!" Ace responded frustrated and angrily.

"Yeah. That's a good way to put it." Joe acknowledged, as he continued to inform him. "But, the good news is they didn't find any drugs in any of the houses that are directly connected to you. They did take your jewelry, furs, and some other items from each one of your girls' houses. I have all the documents of the listed items they confiscated from each of your properties. They also took a huge floor safe out of your house in New Jersey with Kim. Which, by the way, I need to know is there anything in there we should be concerned about?"

"Hell No!" Do I look crazy or stupid to you?" Ace retorted, as he went on saying. "My woman and kids live in that house. I'd never keep anything there. There is about $300,000 cash in the safe though, but I can vouch for it through the clubs."

"Alright. You're right; we can cover the cash. That's the least of your worries. As of right now, you are not indicted on any drug charges. So for now, we need to just focus on the bail hearing on the one gun charge. They do plan to pick up the other gun charge you have open in state court as well, but as of right now you are only federally indicted on the one gun charge. So lets just relax and go in here to try to get you a bail. One good thing in your favor is that you are actually already on bail for over a year now on this same charge, and you never missed any court procedures once you made bail. With that said, I think we should be able to get a federal bail today. I did call a friend of mines that I think you should hire as co-counsel alongside me. His name is Robert Simone. He's here and he's good. He's been around for a long time. He knows the judges and the prosecutors personally, and they respect him. Robby's good Ace – he actually represented himself on his own charge when the Feds indicted him for money laundering on Joey Merlino's case. Shit! He even won the case Ace." Joe replied matter factly as he stood to leave.

"Alright, tell him he hired. Just get me up out this joint, Real talk." Ace replied, not even caring about how much the lawyers were going to charge him at the time. He was highly frustrated behind the 3-day holdover, which ran over the weekend - only business days counted, so Ace hasn't seen or talked to anybody in a week.

"By the way Ace, you have too many women! I must have gotten over a hundred calls from Kim, Iesha and Nikky combined. Only God knows who else will be calling me and leaving messages on my voicemail asking about you. Each of them calls me four to five times a day since you have been locked up. How is he? When is he getting out? When can I go see him? And so forth." Joe said in a playful way mocking the girls' voices, as he quickly remembered.

"Oh Yeah, I got a check from Michelle for $15,000 too. She said she owed it to you, but she didn't want to give it to none of the girls. I will put it towards your legal fees, because Robby wants $25,000 for this one gun case alone. Oh, and one more thing - I should warn you that Iesha and Kim are both upstairs waiting in the courtroom, and both of them are prepared to put up the property to post your bail."

"I saved you a headache with Nikky coming here. She called me yesterday asking what time was your court hearing today. I told her she should just stay home and relax because you will be fine. She came by my office last week crying and explaining how they raided her place too. Kim is the feisty, aggressive one. You might want to wear your helmet when you see her. She is actually upset with me because she found out about your new place with Iesha, and told me that I was her lawyer too so why didn't I tell her." Joe replied with laughter, as Ace just sat there shaking his head listening.

"I had to tell her, listen Kim, I am Ace's attorney. Although I've represented you on a few real estate matters in the past, you are not my client. I did all those things for Ace, because he is my client. I did advise her that she needs to discuss her personal matters with you, not me, but right now we all need to just focus on getting you out of jail."

Ace was finally called upstairs to magistrate court in front of the Honorable Judge Faith Simmons. Once he entered the empty courtroom it quickly filled up 3 minutes later with about 50-75 people. Iesha and Kim were both in the courtroom, but neither of them knew exactly what the other looked like.

Co-Counsel Rob Simone had let the judge know that a rental property located at 116 S. 46th (5 unit apt. building) was free and clear from mortgage or liens. It was worth $300,000 and prepared to be posted as bond in Alton Coles's behalf. He also instructed the judge that the owner of the property Mrs. Kim Laphney was indeed Mr. Coles's woman and children's mother, who was present in the courtroom today, ready and willing to sign for his bail. Kim looked over at Ace and whispered *'I love you'*, Ace nodded his head in response. As he looked back to scan the room, he saw Iesha, and as soon as they made eye contact she blew him a kiss.

Judge Faith Simmons had reviewed all the circumstances in the case, and after hearing brief arguments from both the defense and prosecution; she proceeded to give her ruling as to the bail.

"Well, I will say this first. I do not agree with the government that Mr. Coles needs to be detained without bail because he is a **danger to society** or **a flight risk**. I do not think Mr. Coles is a danger to society. However, I see four other prior dismissed gun charges, which concerns me. I do believe that Mr. Coles carries his weapons to protect himself in the entertainment world he's heavily involved in. Unfortunately, Mr. Coles you are a convicted felon, which means, it is illegal for you to carry guns, so I am going to detain you because I believe that if I were to give you bail today, you would still carry a gun. I noticed that you were already on bail for one gun charge, before you actually got arrested 7 months later, yet again on a different gun charge. You have enough gun issues already. Therefore, my final ruling is no bail!" Judge Simmons replied as she slammed her gavel.

Rob Simone had told Ace not to worry because the judge actually looked for reasons to consider giving him bail. It even looked like she was actually going to grant the bail for a moment, so he wanted to put together another bail package for next week. Only this time Rob would apply for Ace to be on house arrest, instead of just going for straight bail. Home monitoring conditions should be more effective for Ace, because he wouldn't need to carry a firearm if he was confined to the house. Rob wanted to put together some extra amenities to enhance the bail motion. He figured the judge would most likely grant the new bail motion, if Ace hired some professional armed security from a license, bonded facility. Suddenly, Rob informed Ace about something peculiar that he noticed after the hearing today in court.

"Ace, did you notice the whole courtroom cleared out right after you got denied bail? I bet everybody with the exception of your family, was an FBI agent in that courtroom sitting back on those benches. Hang in there champ, we gonna try to get you out of there ASAP, but whatever you do, **DO NOT TALK ON THE PHONE** over at the detention center." Rob retorted in a low stern tone, as Ace stood up to be taken back into marshal custody....

Kim and Iesha suddenly glanced over at each other. They were both crying as they watched the marshals put Ace back into handcuffs escorting him away. They had both witnessed Ace get into trouble with the law before, only difference was each and every time prior to this, he actually made bail. It didn't matter if they gave him a **ransom** (spiteful high ass bail), Ace would always make bail, and he always won the case in a motion before trial. Therefore, this was a total new experience for them all. After Kim and Iesha glanced at each other, they both recognized each other's tears as Ace was put into cuffs. As Ace slowly disappeared through the side courtroom door, Iesha and Kim simultaneously wondered the same exact thing to themselves: *"Who the hell is she? Why is she here? And why is she crying?"*...

CHAPTER 30
Visit Day (The clean up)

Three weeks had passed since Ace had been locked up and held without bail. His lawyers Rob and Joe decided to push the **reconsideration of bail hearing** off for at least another week or two. The lawyers wanted to get official appraisals done on a few of his properties to have it properly prepared. Ace was lying in his bunk at **F.D.C.** in Philly, on his assigned unit (5 North, cell 507) when he was awakened by his celly.

"Yo Ace! They call you for a visit. I keep hearing the guard yell for Coles"…

Ace only put Iesha on his list, because at F.D.C Philly you could only have one friend approved on your visiting list at a time. Although he wanted all three of the girls to be on his list, it simply wasn't an option at this specific facility.

Iesha showed up to the visit at 6:30 a.m. sharp, standing in the brisk September rain waiting for the doors to open. F.D.C didn't start processing visitors until 7:30 a.m., but even at this time of morning, the line would be long each and every visiting day. It was first come, first served. **F.D.C was something like a refrigerator full of cooperators put on ice, but ready to heat up that stand once it's their turn to cook a nigga.**

If your visit came at the same time as your separations visit came, one of you were hit. Some inmates had separations on other inmate (if someone who was telling on him) or (sometimes they'd put sep's on co-defendants) within the same facility. Whoever family came last simply had to wait until the three hour visit was over with, hoping there was enough time left in order to see their loved one.

When Ace walked on the dance floor (visiting room), everybody recognized him. He was greeted with fake smiles and handshakes, and looked at like he was a gourmet steak dinner to the rats who were desperately hungry to jump on someone's case in hopes to get home faster. Ace noticed Iesha immediately and walked over to her to greet her with a warm, tight hug and kiss.

"I miss you Boo."Iesha replied, as she placed her face under his chin partially crying.

"Don't cry Boo. It's gone be alright." Ace replied, in a smoothing low tone, trying to comfort her.

They sat down and talked about so much that the 3 hour visit seemed like a 30 minute visit...

Ace had instructed Iesha to collect money from his uncle Hak, and more importantly he needed her to contact two very good, close personal friends of his named **Caution and Minute**. Iesha carefully listened to his entire request so that she wouldn't miss a beat. She was extremely depressed seeing her man with a bad haircut, dressed in a fresh jail green jumper (F.D.C inmate uniform). Iesha loved Ace so much he was still fresh to death to her, even in his unusual attire. Ace was her Boo and soon to be husband, and she was willing to do whatever he needed her to do to help him get out of jail.

"Visits are now over!" The guard replied loudly.

"Listen Boo, I will beat this case. Even if they supersede me for drugs on that secret sealed indictment, I'm a win! So if I have to ride it out in jail without bail until trial – **FUCK IT** – SO BE IT! Here's where the true test begins for **us**. Nothing else mattered until now cause **love is tested through adversity.** I've prepared you for this. I always told you this could happen one day. So do you **truly love** me?" Ace asked sincerely, as he stared through her eyes like he could read her soul waiting for her response. Iesha simply shook her head yes.

"Then we will get through this together? Or do you want me to sever our ties? You know I respect honesty and I can holla back when the smoke clears if you ain't built for this."

"YES BOO! Don't talk foolish; of course I'm riding with you. That's no issue. I'm just gone put this whole Nikky situation on the back burner for now. You need my support and now ain't the time for the bullshit. But, I do have feelings Ace. I know she wrapped up in this whole mess too, but I'm a leave it alone for now. I got a memory like a computer, so I will be bringing this back up once you get back home. I love you and I'm riding till the wheels fall off. I ain't gone nowhere, I'm just scared Boo. You gonna have to guide me through this, cause I never been subjected to nothing like this in my entire life. I just want you home! I need you. I don't care about a big ole wedding any more. I just want to get married soon as you get home. You need to be done with the drug game, so we can focus on us when all this is over." Iesha replied sincerely, as they stood there holding each other to say their goodbyes…

Due to the amount of envy and jealousy they already had for him, once Ace got locked up and held without bail people started hating on another level. He had been winning for so long, it seemed like everybody wanted to see him lose for once. Plus, Ace got so much media attention, it added more fuel to all the gossip.

One of Iesha's so-called girlfriends had told her the name of the pretty dark-skinned girl **Nikky**. They even informed Iesha that not only did Nikky get raided, but that Ace also lived with her as well. Nikky told the whole city she was riding with Ace no matter what, and Iesha briefly brought all that up on the visit.

Iesha was extremely upset after two agents came over her mother's house last week to hand deliver Iesha a subpoena. The subpoena was for her to come forth at a federal grand jury procedure for money laundering accusations against her and Ace. When the two agents were leaving her Mom's house, one of them showed Iesha a picture of an attractive dark-skinned woman driving a 4-door black Mercedes Benz. To add insult and injury the jackass agent asked Iesha if it was her in the picture just to be smart. Iesha snapped at their sarcasm because they knew damn well it wasn't her. They knew exactly who the woman in the picture was, because they took the photo from Nikky's house during the raid.

To actually see the picture of the woman she had been hearing all the rumors about, caused Iesha to have a constant mental visual of Nikky, which made her furious. Iesha and Nikky were both dark-skinned and very attractive. They may have favored each other a little, but they hardly looked *exactly* alike besides those descriptions. The Feds simply play a vicious game of divide and conquer. The agents were working hard at chipping away Ace's strength, causing distress and turmoil in his relationships with each girlfriend one at a time....

   *   *   *

After she left the visit Iesha pulled over to a pay phone and dialed the number to Uncle Hak. Hak is Ace's real uncle (his father's younger brother). Ace told her on the visit to get whatever money Hak had of his, which should cover her on the mortgage and bills until he got out of jail. The Feds had frozen seven of Ace's business accounts, his personal account, and even his joint account with Iesha.

The Feds intentions were to put a serious amount of financial stress on him and the girls' altogether. Neither Iesha nor Kim could use their personal accounts or credit cards. The government had frozen anything that had to do with Ace until the outcome of the case. Ace wasn't even indicted for drugs yet, but when the Feds come they apply extreme pressure. The Feds love to put that knee in your neck, making it difficult for you to live both emotionally and financially.

The government often used these deadly tactics so they would have a better chance at winning their cases. No alleged criminals could obtain a good enough lawyer, if he/she couldn't get to enough money. Freezing bank funds would help with that, and the frustration it could potentially cause to the women was an extra effort to hopefully use them against him as well...

After putting $3,000 on Ace's books, Iesha had arranged to meet up with Hak later to get whatever money he had for Ace. Iesha prepared to dial the other phone number she had repeated to herself over and over again, before she got in her car and jotted it down on a tissue after the visit 30 minutes ago...

Ace had instructed her to drive to a certain pay phone to make both calls, and they would know what they had to do once they got the message from that specific phone line. Ace had shit planned for years just in case something like this was to ever happen to him. *You can learn a lot from watching old gangsta movies, and reading true crime novels.*

Iesha repeated the number again as she dialed **2-6-7-6-9-9-6-6-0-1...RING, RING, RING**...

"Hello." The female caller answered nonchalantly.

"Yes, can I speak to Caution or Minute?"

"Depends on who calling." The female voice responded in a calm, intimidative tone.

"Uhh, it's **Fatboy's** fiancé." Iesha replied nervously, scared of saying any of Ace's nicknames over the phone, yet determined to come through for her man.

"This is Caution. Is my Fatboy alright?" Caution replied, now sounding concerned and less intimidating. She was fully alert now, and waiting for her instructions. Caution knew the routine and the phone number Iesha was calling from all too well, she also knew exactly who Iesha was, even though Iesha didn't know her at all.

"He's fine for now, but he said for yall to give away those gifts and vacuum." Iesha replied not fully understanding the message herself, but that's all she was told to say.

"Consider it done! Let him know we will start wrapping those gifts, and clean up **ASAP!**" Caution replied matter factly, quickly hanging up the phone without another word.

CHAPTER 31
"Drug Indictment" (Superseded)

IT HAS BEEN 7 MONTHS since Ace got arrested. He was back up for yet another bail hearing, after getting denied at a recent reconsideration bail hearing over 5 months ago. He had become accustomed to sleeping until late afternoon, due to his gambling the rest of the day away for commissary after waking up. That was Ace's way of bidding; simply to pass time for him. He even lost twenty pounds quickly, after he started working out regularly. Ace figured he'd turn a negative into a positive so he used all the free time he had in jail to get back into shape.

"The court is noting your request for bail, but due to the nature of your crime and the government's argument that you're a potential flight risk, I'm going to have to deny bail at this time." The judge said before banging the gavel, making Ace madder than a pimp with one hooker in is stable….

*   *   *

On March 6, 2006, Ace's celly woke him up suddenly.

"ACE! Get up Pimp! You all over the news and radio! They talking bout' you got caught with 1800 kilos of cocaine, crack and $25 million in cash!"

"WHAT! I didn't get caught with shit! I'm here on a nut ass gun charge! What the fuck is you talking about?" Ace snapped, anger evident in his tone. Ace was tired and irritable from being woke up so suddenly with the bullshit, he was ready to whip some ass.

"I don't know, I couldn't hear it. I didn't have my Walkman on. But I did see a picture of you, your house and your Bentley on the news. Them nut ass niggaz in the common area out there gossiping about what they say they heard. You know niggaz always exaggerating so we got to turn to KYW News on the radio to hear the shit for ourselves. Or you can just wait, it should come back on the 6:00 news." Shaft replied. Ace got up quickly. He went to the phone to call Iesha, to see if she heard or saw anything. He didn't get an answer on either one of her cell phones, which was strange to him.

229

The whole seven months he had been on lock down, Iesha always answered one of her phones no matter what time he called. Sometimes Ace would even call her at 6 a.m., as soon as the cell doors were unlocked and she would answer. Now Ace was puzzled as to what was going on with Iesha, or was she simply up to no good after seven months of no sex. Jail plays a vicious mind game on a nigga at times.

Oh, now she's trying to pay me back, huh? Bitch, where the fuck you at? Ace thought, and then hung up. He picked the phone back up, trying to call Kim.

He got no answer.

He tried to call Nikky on her house phone and cellphone.

Again, he got no answer.

For the first time in seven months after his arrest, Ace was really concerned now. He was frustrated and pissed off altogether. He was now nervous and upset because he didn't see the news reports. Ace had only heard exaggerated hearsay from niggaz who didn't even see the news themselves. Niggas always repeated gossip and added yeast to their versions about what was actually said.

Ace started stressing because he couldn't get in touch with any of his women.

What the fuck is going on? Where are my girls? And why the fuck haven't any of them answered their fucking phones yet? He thought before trying to make another call to Iesha.

"RECALL! RECALL! IT'S 3:45.TIME FOR LOCKDOWN FOR THE 4:00 COUNT!" The C.O. said over the intercom system at the F.D.C.

The C.O.'s voice irritated the hell out of Ace, but his anger was mainly due to the fact that he couldn't reach the girls all day. Ace sulked while heading to his cell for the 4:00 p.m. count.

The doors were unlocked at 5:00 p.m. After the count cleared, Correctional Officer Mrs. Stevens had allowed the inmates to leave the televisions on while they ate their chow. Mrs. Stevens is one of the coolest guards working at F.D.C. She's a young black female guard who stood 5'6", weighing 140 pounds with a natural attractive look to her. She's caramel brown with a pretty smile that always got Ace's attention.

When Ace looked at her, he thought to himself. *Damn! If it wasn't so many rats and nut ass niggaz in this jail, I'd go and holla at Sis. I don't even be cracking on Chics no more, but when I get outta' here, I'ma find her sexy ass. She's a nice look. I could do that.*

At 5:15 p.m. the news Ace waited to see, but dreaded to hear came on. Watching the broadcast, Ace was frozen still as he listened.

ATF Agents arrested 22 people, including the CEO of Takedown Records. In Philadelphia, Special Agents in charge of the Philadelphia Division of the Bureau of Alcohol, Tobacco, Firearms and Explosives (ATF), announced today the indictment of 22 people, including Takedown Records owner Alton "Ace Capone" Coles and 21 others arrested on firearms, drug trafficking, financial and wire fraud charges, as well as conducting a continuing criminal enterprise.

The 198-count indictment, returned by a Federal Grand Jury on March 5th, alleges that a drug distribution ring and continuing enterprise ran by Coles was responsible for the distribution of approximately 1200 kilograms of cocaine and 600 kilograms of crack cocaine in and around Southwest Philadelphia from 1998 to August 2005.

The Indictment also lists 35 firearms recovered by ATF, often from suspects in possession of, or dealing in, cocaine. ATF seized approximately $1.5 million in currency as well as 6 luxury vehicles, including a Bentley Arnage, 12 Philadelphia residences and 2 homes in New Jersey from Coles.

All the inmates turned and looked at Ace, who paid them no mind. Even Mrs. Stevens paused at what she was doing to listen in about the infamous inmate on her unit.

"The ATF had made combating violence in Southwest Philadelphia a priority." Agent Nikko stated. "We not only have targeted the shooters and the dealers on the streets, but also sought to seize their ill gotten assets and charge those that have assisted in illegally obtaining or hiding them."

The Anchorwoman returned, concluding the top story.

This violent gang is allegedly responsible for at least 37 shootings and 14 murders. Investigators say that Ace Capone put more than $2 billion worth of crack cocaine on the streets over the past seven years so that 1800-kilo indictment is modestly well preserved. The alleged ring leader Alton "Ace Capone" Coles has ties to some of the biggest names in the Hip-Hop Music Industry. Coles was frequently seen at the recent attempted murder trial of rap Star Beanie Sigel. When Coles was previously arrested last year on weapons charges, he was driving his Bentley that was confiscated in the seizures. Investigators say a Bentley registered by Hip-Hop Mogul Damon Dash. We'll follow this ongoing case as it continues....This is Nancy Peloski, ABC News.

        *   *   *
    *

THE FOLLOWING DAY, Ace was already up when the doors popped. He was devastated from the news he saw yesterday, and he still hadn't heard from any of his girls yet. Ace had been up stressing all night long, concerned about the fact that he hadn't heard from any of his women. Ace decided to take a shower after he got off the phone with Michelle *The Source* Brown.

"Ace you need to just calm down and relax because I'm hearing the stress in your voice. I heard about you on the news and I know it's all a bunch of exaggerated lies. You know they did the same thing to Beans. The media always do stuff like that to make the story look good."

"I know, but they making me out to be some kind of monster."

"I know baby. Just calm down and wait on your lawyers to get there. I'ma get on top of finding out what's going on with Iesha and see why she hasn't answered the phone."

"Thanks Michelle."

"Okay Baby, talk to you later." She said before ending the call.

Michelle actually never cared much for Kim. She didn't even know Nikky, but she would still find out what's going on with all of them to calm Ace down.

When Ace exited the shower, he noticed a new but familiar face on the unit. Jihad was assigned to the unit Ace was living on last night.

"Damn Pimp! What they get you for?" Ace asked Jihad as he walked towards him and shook his hand.

"Man, they raided me on the same day they ran up in your crib over Jersey. I'm cool though. All they got was a gun and some money." Jihad replied.

Ace and Jihad stepped off to Ace's cell to talk. He gave Jay some shower shoes, cosmetics and food to hold him over until store day. As Ace was on his way to the phone to call Michelle back, he noticed another familiar face on the unit...

After Ace hung up the telephone with Michelle, he felt absolutely sick to his stomach about the terrible news he had just received. Michelle informed Ace that she hadn't heard anything about Kim yet.

"Oh yeah?" Ace said, sounding sad.

"Yeah, but when I called her for you, I left several messages for her to call me back. I did talk to Iesha and her mother. Ace, she got indicted for money laundering. Her mother had to put up her house to bail that girl out of jail. That's why she hasn't been answering her phones. She was only in there for a day."

"That's crazy!" Ace gasped, he couldn't believe his ears.

"That's not all...Nikky got locked up too, and she's still in there...at F.D.C. where you at, waiting on a bail hearing for over three days ago."

"Listen Michelle, whatever you do make sure you get Babygirl out on bail, even if you have to put up your property to get her out. Get her outta' there. I'll cover it." Ace sincerely informed her.

"I'll try to take care of it Ace."

"Michelle, please get her out by any means necessary." He emphasized before ending the call with her.

Ace walked back to his cell after the phone call to be alone. The other new familiar face on the unit walked over to Ace just before he reached his cell.

"What's up Pimp?" Dee replied.

'Stress, that's what's up!" Ace said, shaking his head in frustration. "When they get chu'?" Ace asked in a highly frustrated and concerned tone.

"Man they raided the whole projects the same day they knocked you off. They even raided my girls' crib out in Chester. I only got caught with a half of brick of powder, but I had a gun in the crib too. I can eat the coke, but I need my Chic to eat that gun for me because gun and coke together equals too much time. The crazy part about it is they didn't even lock me up when they raided and found the shit. They finger printed me and took my picture, and then they just left and said they would be back. They come back hard on a nigga eight months later with a sealed indictment. That's what's scaring me pimp. It's some funny shit going on." Dee replied nervously.

"Pimp, I'ma ask you straight up cause I know it's some funny shit going on and I think shit about to get nasty. Real talk! With that being said, I know I'm one of the last of the Mohicans so I'ma GO HARD! What chu' gon do?" Ace said sternly with full concern waiting for his answer.

"Pimp, I aint even gon' front like I want to go hard. I don't want to play with these people. I don't think Latisha gone eat that gun charge for me. That Chic been on some funny shit every since her uncle died in that plane. I'm trying to plead out to something like 12 to 15 years and bow out gracefully. I ain't tryna' get life! I got a lawyer once they raided the crib and didn't lock me up. My lawyer says he can work a deal for me. Them people know I was on that plane when it crashed, and I can't figure out how the fuck they know that. But I know I don't trust my Chic, so if a decent deal goes through for me, I'm sitting down! One thing for sure, two things for certain Pimp, I ain't doing no tellin', so you good. " Dee said.

Truth be told, that's all Ace had hoped to hear. He couldn't afford to have Dee cooperating against him, because he'd be up Shit's Creek without a paddle for real…

~~~~~

THREE DAYS LATER, Dee and Jay went to court for their arraignment hearings. Ace couldn't figure out why Jay was coincidently raided on the same day he was arrested in New Jersey. Ace went to the phone, in hopes of contacting Iesha, who he still hadn't spoken to. Ace listened to the ringing phone, as someone picked up on the third ring.

"Hello?"

"You have a prepaid call from ACE! An inmate at a federal facility; you will not be charged for this call. To accept this call dial five ---*Beep!* came the sound of the automated operator being cut off.

"DAMN BOO! I've been worried sick about you, and literally going crazy! Are you alright?" Ace asked in a sincere and concerned voice. He was relieved to hear Iesha's voice; for the simple reason he hadn't talked to her in over a week.

Iesha began crying uncontrollably as she spoke, "Boo, my parents are involved now! I got locked up! I almost went to jail if my mom didn't put her house up to bail me out, and I'm facing 20 years Ace." She sobbed over the phone

"What chu' mean you facing 20 years? You can't talk to me?" Ace asked, frustrated and puzzled by her statement.

"Is that the reason you haven't been answering my calls?" he asked, anger evident in his tone.

"NO! I didn't have my phone cause they took them when they locked me up. You the one told me to stay with my mom, and she didn't want me talking to you. I tried to explain to her that I can't just abandon you like that, but she says if you love me you will understand." Iesha sniffled.

"What the fuck she mean she doesn't want you talking to me? She outta' pocket! REAL TALK!" Ace snapped. He was now extremely pissed off, as Iesha continued to cry.

"Why didn't you just come see me on my visiting day and tell me what it was? You could have even wrote me, so I wouldn't have been stressing like crazy all that fucking time!" Ace said.

"I can't Boo. I'm sorry, but I'm not allowed to visit you anymore. My mom said not to write you either. ACE GET ME OUT OF THIS MESS!" Iesha cried before lowering her voice to a whisper.

"Listen, I love you. My mom is coming upstairs now. I gotta' go. But I love you sooo much. You remember that." Iesha said as she quickly hung up on him.

Ace was now angry and frustrated. He slammed the phone, thinking *No you remember that! Mrs. Marrisa you on some funny shit, huh?*

Ace went to his cell, he stayed there stressed out and confused about a lot of issues. He wondered what was going to be the outcome of all of this. He also wondered when he would see Iesha again.

Ace knew his stress would soon be on another level, cause Dee and Jihad didn't even know each other and got raided on the same day. Once Dee and Jihad returned from court, they informed Ace that they were all Co-Defendants on an 1800 kilogram cocaine conspiracy.

They explained to Ace what had happened at court, the only news that made him feel better was finding out that Nikky had actually made bail. She was released on her own signature, so Dee, Gotti and other co-Defendants quickly assumed Nikky would probably end up cooperating against Ace.

Ace reluctantly ignored the thought. He knew the only people who could actually hurt him the most at trial, was the niggaz—not the women. The girls truly loved Ace. Niggaz on the other hand, only tolerated Ace because they had to fuck with him to eat.

Kim had also remained on bail. Kim and Iesha were only charged for money laundering. Everybody else was charged in the drug conspiracy. The Feds also arrested officer Mac McKenzie, and charged him as one of Ace's bodyguards who provided Ace with law enforcement assistance to obstruct justice. Iesha, Kim, Nikky and officer McKenzie were the only Co-Defendants who had actually gotten bail. The other 18 Co-Defendants were held without bail with the exception of Dante Tucker and Tyrek **Hammer** McGeth, who were both on the run.

Ace thought they were the two smartest niggaz out of the bunch, because all of them were supposed to go on the run and pay up when the Feds caught up. Ace was the only one who never had the opportunity to flee. He was detained since the first day of the raids on an unrelated gun charge. Everybody on the indictment knew damn well they'd most likely be going to a Federal prison for a very long time, especially the individuals who were caught dirty with cocaine, crack and guns.

Ace and his girls got raided and were absolutely clean. No drugs were found at any of his places. Only thing the Feds gathered, as evidence on Ace was the money out of the house he shared with Kim. They also got a gun he had at Nikky's house, which he already made up his mind to swallow himself. Ace's motto was: ***His Troubles Are His Troubles!*** Ace was too thorough to allow Nikky to go down for something that was his or even hers for that matter. Ace was a real nigga and a respectable man. He would die without the blink of an eye for the women he loved and his children before he allowed them to be harmed in anyway.

LATER THAT NIGHT, Ace called Nikky on her house phone, because her cell phone was still going to the voice mail, and she answered the house phone on the third ring, and accepted Ace's call without any delays. She knew the only person calling her from jail was her Ace.

"Hello?" She said.

"Babygirl, you okay?" Ace asked sincerely.

"Yesss." Nikky replied with a small crack in her voice as she whined softly.

"Don't cry Beauty, tell me what happened?" Ace replied sincerely.

"They talking bout' I served some damn body, and they found a gun in the dumpster outside this big ass apartment complex which anybody probably threw it in there. They had the whole block blocked off with fire engines and all. Anyone could of threw it in the damn trash, but they gon charge me for it. And for them to think I served somebody, I'm just so urked!" Nikky said, frustration apparent in her tone. Ace just listened as she continued talking.

"Why Iesha and Kim ain't get locked up?" She asked, wondering why she was the only girlfriend of his who stayed in jail for three days.

"They got locked up too." Ace told her.

"Well, I sure ain't see them. I was stuck in a cell in the SHU (the Hole) for 24 hours a day until I got out on bail. I couldn't even get a phone call to let my family know where I was at, and I just came home not too long ago. I must have soaked in the tub for at least three hours straight to get that stinky jail smell off me. That place is filthy dirty. I still keep itching just thinking about it."

"Well you out now Babygirl and you ain't going back to jail. That belongs to me, you understand? Ace replied harshly, trying to make it clear to her that she didn't' have to worry about the gun charge at all. He was going to swallow it to protect her.

Ace tried to be discreet as possible on the telephone, but it didn't' matter because he wanted her to be calm. Nikky knew she didn't' serve anybody so she wasn't worried about that. The Feds got shit twisted. Nikky's biggest fear was the gun she threw away that night for Ace.

Although Ace's lawyer advised him not to talk on the phone at all, he had to let Babygirl know he safeguarded her. Ace actually used another inmate's pin number to call her so nobody could trace the call back to him.

"Alright, this phone about to hang up Beauty. I love you and I will check on you later."

"I love you too Baby and I'm here for you no matter what happens." Nikky replied sincerely.

"I know Babygirl...I know." Ace said as the time lapsed and the line went dead.

"COLES TO THE LEIUTENANT'S OFFICE!" An African C.O, shouted in his funny accent.

Ace quickly hung up the telephone, and walked over to the officer's station.

"Lieutenant's offices for what?'' Ace asked the funny talking C.O.

Ace was puzzled as to why the Lt. wanted to see him.

"I do not know. Put on your bus shoes and go by thee door." The funny talking C.O. answered with a shrug of the shoulders.

When Ace got to the Lt's office, he was given an incident report for using another inmate's pin number for the telephone. The Lt. also informed Ace that he now had separations on every floor in the detention center.

"So what chu' saying?" Ace asked.

"I have to place you in the S.H.U until we can clear this up or your separations move out of here."

Ace was immediately sent to the S.H.U. (The Hole)He was placed on lock down 23 hours a day with 1 hour out of his cell for recreation. They even placed Ace on single rec-along status: meaning he could only go to recreation by himself. Now Ace was being treated like Hannibal Lector himself.

For the first eight months Ace just didn't get it. He gambled all day, playing cards or betting on sports. Ace had five different people pin numbers that he used each month outside of his normal 300 minutes. He had money put on different guys books to use their telephone and go to the store, so it was all fun and games for Ace until the big superseding indictment came. The drug conspiracy would be bearable for him if the girls weren't involved. Shit just got real, and being placed in the S.H.U helped him to realize just that.

Iesha had hired Ace a new lawyer named Dennis Conan. He's one of the best, if not the best lawyer Philly had to offer. Dennis Conan was on the top 50 of the nation's best lawyers list that was listed in the **Super Lawyers** Magazine. But even with the best lawyers, Ace still had to fight his case from jail. Being in the S.H.U only made it harder for him, because he only got one 10-minute phone call every month. On top of that, he couldn't get a visit from none of the women actually he needed to see most.

Ace had a friend name Saudia who now visited him every week. She stood 5'8" and weighed 170 pounds, with an ass like **Buffy the Body**. Saudia held Ace down, but he still wanted to see Iesha, Kim or Nikky. Point Blank! This particular cold rainy day, Ace left his visit with Saudia from behind the screen pissed after hearing about all the rumors concerning him and his girls. He was the talk of the town and the girls were too, simply because they were with Ace. Ace went back to his cell and simply lay down in the dark cold lonely room. Suddenly, he felt extreme pain in his chest. A knot quickly formed in his throat as tears began falling down his face. For the first time in over 20 years, the 32-year-old gangsta began to cry. All the pain and frustration he endured over the last few weeks mixed with the lies, rumors, and deceit had finally taken its toll on him.

Ace had been to plenty of funerals and never even cried for the dead homies he had love for. The last rage of cry he actually had been last year after his cousin Stink got killed by his so called homie and childhood friend Tab. That was the last time Ace had shed a tear to release a lot of anger and pain.

Back in January 2005, Stink was subject to murder inside his van in a gas station on Woodland Avenue in Southwest Philly. All Ace found out about the incident was that someone had tried to kidnap Stink by hog-tying him with plastic zip cuffs. Stink was a beast in the streets. He fought for his life, literally breaking the plastic cuffs, as he damaged his wrists severely to get to the gun that he had hidden in his van.

Shots were fired inside the moving vehicle as it crashed into the Getty gas station on 70th Street. People watched in awe as Tab jumped out of the van, running away, while bleeding like a hog.

Tab had called Rahim, who is Ace's cousin, trying to explain what had happened right after he got away. Once Tab heard Stink had died, he actually turned himself in the next day.

Tab knew he wasn't safe on the streets, and he didn't want to go to war with Ace. Ace had way too many goons who were already on Tab's top. Ace wanted Tab's head by all means necessary, and Tab knew just how dangerous Ace could be. Tab turned himself in with no intention on fighting his murder charge to win, and stayed in protective custody. Tab knew Ace was capable of getting a nigga from jail that had nothing to lose to kill him for a few thousand dollars.

Tab was actually added to the superseding drug indictment. They brought him over from the county to the Federal Detention Center, adding another separation on Ace, which kept him in the S.H.U longer than expected.

Tab was initially at C.F.C.F on State Road, charged with the homicide of Ace's cousin Stink, but now he was living in F.D.C charged as one of Ace's Co-Defendants...

Ace never witnessed this type of pain, and always been able to hold his composure. Today everything came crashing down on him, and he just needed to cry to release his frustrations. Ace finally realized he was still a human being and men can cry too.

Why do the girls have to be involved with my case? These Feds are some slimy, cruddy mothafuckers! Ace thought.

*Why are these folks tryna' take every single thing that I own and worked hard for? They know damn well most of my property and businesses have nothing to do with drugs! Why did Stink have to die? Why did Tab, of all people, have to kill him? I knew I couldn't trust somebody close to me. It was him all along that I been dreaming about... I'ma make alot of people pay for their betrayal in the worst way possible. I want mothafuckers to suffer, and they gonna feel my pain when it's all said and done. **I WILL WIN!** And since they want to treat me like a fucking animal, I'ma act like one!* Ace told himself before taking a step to his cell door. He looked out the small window to see down the tier at the others cells, glaring with an evil, cold stare....

CHAPTER 32
(Caution & Minute (Assassination)

It was 6:00 a.m. when the guard opened the slot for breakfast.

"Coles, you goin out to rec?" The officer asked.

"Nah. I need that phone early today. My 30 days is up, and I have to make an important phone call this morning." Ace replied tiredly.

Ace was a bit upset cause once again he had been disturbed in the middle of a wet dream. He was dreaming he was about to fuck the shit out of Golden Girl from Power 99 F.M. He had listened to her show last night, and the topic was *how do women prefer to be fucked?* Some like it **slow & steady,** others like it *hard, fast and rough.*

No matter what topic the Golden Girl decided to touch on, there was always controversy. Ace now regretted the fact that he had let her slip by when he was home on the streets. Listening to her radio show every night made him desire her sexually in every freaky way known to man. He visualized how he just had his dick inside of her wet, tight,landing stripped shaved pussy, when the slot opened for breakfast disturbingly broke his sleep - ruining his wet dream before he could nut.

Ace got up to get his tray and thought to himself, '*Damn, I gots to get some of that pussy when I get home. G.G. always talking all that freak shit, now I want to know what that pussy be like, I bet she got that good snapper pussy too!*

    *   *   *

At 9:30 a.m. Latisha was leaving the clinic from her 8:00 a.m. doctor's appointment. She didn't want to have Dee's baby, and been having difficulties since the abortion she had a few weeks back. Latisha oddly noticed the same two women she had seen at least 3-4 times earlier this week at the clinic today. As Latisha left the clinic, she walked towards her car and quickly realized she had a flat tire.

Latisha was already frustrated and angry, so she didn't refuse assistance when the familiar woman offered her help. Latisha had recognized the woman as one of the women in the clinic, and since they were headed in the same direction she gladly accepted the ride. Unfortunately, it was a ride she would regret for the rest of her short life. When Latisha got in the passenger seat of the all black tinted out Yukon, another individual who was already lying in the back seat put out her lights…

*   *   *

"That shit feels so good baby. Ummmmmm shhhhittt, slow down a bit daddy. Pphhhh yessss just like that. Damn, I love it when you fuck me slow Ace." Caution moaned softly, as she rolled her eyes in the back of her head with her tongue sexily sticking out of her mouth.

"I'm in control of this shit back here. SLAP!" Ace replied aggressively as he smacked her on her ass, while fucking her from behind. "Now arch your back some more and play with that pussy for me. Since you wanna talk so much, eat Minutes pussy for me, and you betta' make her come quick too! I want that pussy soaking wet before I fucks the shit out of her next." Ace demanded seductively.

"Oooooohhh shit – yes daddy!" Caution replied quickly turned on even more after hearing Ace's demand, as Minute switched position from licking Ace's nipples, while holding the shaft of his dick.

Ace was standing with his Timberlands on, slowly stroking the shit out of Caution's tight, wet pretty pussy, as she was on the edge of the bed **on her knees, ass in the air, face in total passion buried in the pillow.** Minute lay back while loving the view of Ace punishing Caution from the back. Minute began erotically playing with her own fat, completely bald eagle pussy, while lustfully waiting for Caution to place her warm, wet tongue into her love nest. She loved watching Caution's fuck face as Ace stuck hard dick to her, she bit on her bottom lip, eyes slammed shut, rolled to the back of her head preparing for climax…

"Caution! Answer your damn phone. It might be Ace calling! What the fuck was you thinking about?" Minute asked angrily, puzzled at her friend for lunching so hard.

"Oh-Shit! My bad!" Caution replied as she quickly snapped out of a daydream about a threesome they had before Ace got locked up, she reached her phone just in time. "Hello."

"This is a prepaid call from *'Ace'* – an inmate at a federal correctional facility. To accept the call press 5 now, if you want to block—**Beep!**"

"Hey Fatboy, what's good?" Caution replied excitedly. She was happy to hear his voice because she missed him so much."

"What's good is my dick is hard, what's not so good is the fact that I'm in jail so ya sexy ass can't even help me get off a nut. What's up though? Where's Minute? I called like three times, what took you so long to answer the phone?"

"That's my bad baby, I was lunching for a second. But, she right beside me. Matter fact, since you still in the **SHU** maybe we can help you get one off, unless you got a celly? " Caution replied seductively, as she reached over to open Minute's blouse.

"Nah, I aint got no celly. Aye, you take care of dat? Did yall drop off those gifts?"

"Yeah baby. Everything has been taken care of. We even cleaned up after the party. Minute put some more money on ya books yesterday too, so check your account."

"That's what's up. I see I can always count on my girls to hold me down, huh?"

"You already know! We will do anything for you Fatboy!" Caution replied proudly.

"Anything huh?" Ace asked, as he smiled devilishly to himself. He was still semi-hard from the wet dream about Golden Girl. The little privacy he had in the cell by himself, combined with Caution's sexy voice and freaky suggestions, caused him to ask. "Aye, you got one of yall toys handy?"

"Yesss. It's a strap on right here." Caution replied flirtaceously and matter factly.

"Alright, then let me hear you tear Minute's pussy up so I can get money and bust a nut to get rid of this hard dick." Ace demanded in a strong manner with a deep, low, soft tone of voice.

"Ummmm, I thought you'd never ask." Caution replied, as all three of them engaged in an erotic, freaky 10-minute phone sex session....

They had those names for good reason. **Caution** is a super-bad bitch at 5'7" weighing 139 pounds, caramel brown-skinned, slim and gorgeous. She was like one of those sexy specimens a nigga would cut out of a magazine to hang on his wall to admire. Her stylish, nice grade of shoulder length hair, and the captivating set of light brown eyes she possessed caught a man's attention every time she made eye contact with him, which is the very reason niggas knew to beware of Caution. Her sexy look fooled their ass every time. Just when a nigga thought he had him one, she would take his ass for everything he had.

      Minute was a total opposite of Caution. Minute stands about 5'10", which is quite tall for a woman. She is thick like a black version of **Co-Co** (Ice Tea's wife) in all the right places, with absolutely no stomach. Her weight was sexily proportioned with the rest of her body. Minute was crafty and had more heart than most niggas. It took her a second to spot her target, and a minute to take their ass out. Together Caution and Minute were unstoppable. That being only one of the many reasons Ace kept them on his team, cause he also had an ironic relationship with the both of them.

      Caution and Minute are two of Ace's best and most trustworthy companions. They were two women in a full fledge relationship with each other who really loved him. Ace was the only nigga hitting them off with the dick on his *or* their demand. When Ace needed them to put in work everything always went according to plan. Caution was the bait for the target, and Minute took their ass out – *mission accomplished!*

      Niggas should have known just because Ace was off the streets, didn't mean niggas couldn't be touched. Ace has a serious goon squad that consisted of bitches and all. The most dangerous thing about them both was they truly had love for Ace, so whoever crossed him would definitely pay sooner or later. Ace was now the subject of a major federal indictment that could possibly determine the next 20 years or more of his life. With that said, all *or* any potential rats they knew of would fall harder than dominos.

Ace's squad didn't fully trust Kim, Iesha or Nikky. Caution and Minute were females so that was to be expected of them, but Ace's male goons were skeptical about those women's loyalty as well. Ace warned Caution and Minute, and the rest of his goons not to lay a finger on any of his women. If someone were to so much as attempt to intimidate one of the three, they would be dealt with **demonically**.

Truth be told, although they were happy in a relationship with each other, Caution and Minute were kind of jealous when it came to Iesha, Kim and Nikky. They knew Ace put those three women before any other female in his life, including them. But, Caution and Minute questioned if those same three women would ride with him all the way to the end and if so, with as much **loyalty, faithfulness, dedication** and love as they had for him???

*   *   *

Kim was leaving a party at a small bar in West Philly, when a bald headed tall heavyset nigga walked up to greet her. Kim was on some secret pay back shit, because of all the women she found out about since Ace's arrest. She gave the nigga her phone number for future convo. She already been on plenty of dates since Ace's arrest, and had no conscious about it at all. Tone got in the car after locking Kim's number in his phone. He shook D-Rock's hand as they both smiled at each other.

"Now all you got to do is fuck the bitch and make her feel special. Her disrespectful, dumb ass might even invite you over his house." D-Rock replied with laughter.

"Yeah, the chic is all dumb drunk right now. I should have pressed up on her and tried to smash tonight, but I want to reel her in good so she thinks I'm feeling her. Then we gonna rob her ass blind."

"I know one thing though, his chic Iesha is way too scary. I don't think we gonna be able to get at her the same way we gonna get at Rain and Kim. They go for anything, but she ain't going for any ole thing. The chic Nikky play the bars real tough, so we just have to follow that bitch. My man tell me he knows where the chic lives at, so we gonna check on that address in a few days." D-Rock replied.

"Shouldn't be too hard. All we got to do is look for her car. I hear she drives a black buggy eye Benz. Anyhow, we 'bout to get at both of his nut ass babymoms. They should have some nice **paper** hiding around somewhere. I know that nigga got money stashed a bunch of places. Remember though, we can't hurt Rain! That's my girl's sister. Rain and the kids are good peeps, so we just gonna do a cat burglary when it comes to her. That way, she won't know who did it, and it doesn't shake her up too bad. Ya feel me? Now Kim is different. Once I get inside the house, we just gonna **take it** (tie her up/home invasion). If she don't act right, we will just kill that bitch. So she best come up off that safe, drunk ass, stinking bitch! Know what I'm talkin' 'bout." Tone replied with an evil glare in his eyes....

CHAPTER 33
"Mail call" (Real Love?)

The guard knocked on the door of cell 805 waking Ace up, as she slid several letters under his door.

"Coles, you got a lot of love as usual. Damn near the whole bag is yours." C.O. Wyhee replied, as she slipped the last couple pieces of mail under his door.

As Ace briefly scanned through the mail, he was surprised to see a letter from Iesha. It had been months since he's last heard from her via letter. There were two letters from Kim, 12-18 pages long, that he quickly tossed to the side. All Kim did in her letters was complain about past issues. Kim had a bad, drinking problem now, which she somehow blames Ace for as well. Every time she got drunk she would cry, sit and write him a deceitful letter.

Ace decided to open Iesha's letter first since he hasn't heard from her in a while. The letter seemed a bit disturbing as he read it:

Hi Boo,

I probably won't write as much anymore cause they use everything against us. I am stressed out and very scared. I spoke with your mom and she talked me into going to church. I needed that. I cried and cried all through the service, while praying to God repeatedly. But, I don't think God even hears me! (Sadface) Sometimes I just wish I was dead, cause then all the pain I'm experiencing would end. I'm so confused and frustrated. I don't know what to do. You were always there for those answers, but now things are different and more difficult. You say everything gone be alright, but I don't see it that way at all. I wrote this letter to address a few things about the rumors you say you been hearing. I ain't DOING SHIT!! NO CLUBS!!! NO NIGGAS!!! NO NOTHING!!! So stop listening to the dumb shit that some chic done probably report to you, who most likely want you herself because you fucked her, so she lies about me. She don't know me, or live my life so tell the bitch to mind her business cause she got me FUCKED UP!!! I'm mad as hell you even entertain the thought cause you know me. I love you so much it's gotten me into trouble, so come on now Ace. I just want this nightmare over with, and my family says you should understand that if you really love me. I will continue to pray for us, but God ain't hearing me so soon I may be coming there too. (Sadface) I'm ending this letter now, before I get myself into more trouble.

Love Always,

Iesha (your fiancé)

P.S. Maybe they will put us in the same cell? Which I doubt, but I may seriously kill myself if I actually have to go to jail. I still love you boy. Hold ya head up!

Ace sat there confused, angry and in lots of pain. He understood where Iesha parents were coming from because she was their daughter. But for them to want her to go on with her life and completely abandon Ace, it was if they counted him out altogether and he didn't respect that one bit. They didn't even give him a chance to see if he would win, or see if the time he got would be doable enough for her to bid with him.

Ace had explained to Iesha long before his arrest, some of the consequences and sacrifices she had to make being involved with him. He kept his end of the deal as far as their relationship was concerned, but now Iesha wasn't fully dealing with her responsibilities properly as his fiancé.

Iesha didn't fully abandon him at first. She just put great distance between them once she got indicted. One of her bail conditions stated that she could no longer visit Ace, because she was now a co-defendant on his indictment.

Ace felt betrayed by her because she stopped writing as much as she used to, and she stopped taking his calls. Things weren't the same between them anymore; she pretty much tried to move on with her life, thinking that it would give the Feds reason to leave her alone. Iesha still loved him so she respected Ace's feelings. She even hoped to be with him again if he actually beats the case, which is the reason she didn't want to tell him the rumors he heard were in fact true.

Iesha rode it out with Ace for twenty months before she actually started dating another man. The people who knew Ace well lost respect for Iesha altogether, because he was simply too good to her. After all he had done for her, it absolutely crushed him to see she wasn't worth shit. She abandoned the man she supposedly loved, at the hardest and lowest point of his life, which hurt him even more because he was actually fighting that much harder to get back home to her.

Ace looked at the remaining letter he hadn't read. Only three of them mattered to him now, and they were all from his babygirl Nikky. As he opened the letters he quickly viewed the photos she sent. He gazed at the beautiful smile she had in the photos, and then turned it around to the back, which read: „ *This girl still loves you no matter what! I'm riding till the wheels fall off'*

Ace smiled as tears slowly built up in his eyes and ran down his face. He had been down a little over two years waiting to fight his case. Ace also been in the SHU for the last eighteen months, simply because he had a high profile case. Nikky's support thus far had been non-stop throughout his whole bid. She pressed five no matter what time he called, and she wrote him a letter each and every week.

Truth be told, Ace grew to love Nikky more and more as time went on. He suddenly realized maybe she was worthy of his love. The Feds indicted her, her lawyer tried to influence her, her family had their concerns, but no one could convince her to keep away from Ace. His love for Nikky was now equivalent to the love he had for Iesha and Kim, because of her non-stop support and the love she had for him. Nikky was his friend, lover and supporter, who stood her ground firmly when things got extremely difficult. They didn't even have any kids together, and she was the last woman to come into his life. But, she would not abandon him under any circumstances, simply because she loved him.

Nikky was even content with her position as girlfriend number three. She got involved with him under those circumstances, so she didn't care what anyone else thought or had to say. As Ace continued to read her letters over and over again, he gazed into Nikky's pictures and thought to himself. *'Babygirl, I'm gonna show you a new life when all of this is over with. You just hang in there, and you'll see. You think you now me, but you have no idea what I'm really built like. I love you Beauty.'*

Ace finally picked up the two letters he tossed to the side from Kim. He had grown extreme hatred for Kim for a few different reasons. Kim had been on some sneaky conniving shit since he had been down. Although she tried hard to keep her actions discreet, she failed to realize one important fact. **A nigga of Ace's stature always heard everything.**

When you deal with a boss who deals with a lot of people, somebody always was gonna break their neck to tell any kind of news. She didn't even realize that most niggas that tried to talk to her, simply wanted to get one up on him. It's part of the game; it wasn't even about her. Don't any **real nigga** want a **playa's** babymom or ex-girlfriend as his main girlfriend or wife. Once a female deals with a man who is popular, it stains her like a permanent scar. Therefore, most niggas they date afterwards simply want to **smash**(get the pussy) when it's convenient then **keep it moving** (bounce).

Ace frowned his face when he started opening the letter he received from Kim, *'Man, what this funny-style ass bitch want?'* he quickly thought to himself.

251

Kim didn't realize that Ace had a point of no return. They had been through so much during the years, and because they shared kids she took for granted that he would really leave her. Ace could feel some kind of betrayal in his bones, not to mention the fact that he never fully trusted Kim.

Her non-stop complaining and nagging in her letters only pushed him farther away. Two of the things he hated most about Kim were her **ghetto frame of mind** and her **filthy trashcan mouth** (often used profanity).It seems like every letter she was writing said **'Fuck everybody else! It's time to choose me or them!'**

Ace was simply sick and tired of Kim altogether. He no longer had the same love for this woman. They did share two beautiful kids together so it was difficult for him to completely let go, he always tried hard to hang in there for the sake of the kids. Now he started to dislike things about his stepdaughter Shakeria, who he raised as his very own since he started a serious relationship with Kim. Kim's poor parenting skills and lack of respect for a man seemed to have turned Shakeria against the only man she knew as a father.

Ace began to see for himself who truly loved him, and who simply loved what he could do for them. He remembered back when his Nana told him *„to love and be with who love you, not just who you love.'* **Love is tested through adversity**. Ace sadly expected more out of Kim and Iesha. He had more time in with the both of them, but during his bid he actually got more love and support from Nikky.

The last letter he opened was marked legal mail, but it was already opened, which upset him every time. Disregarding the violation of his legal mail, Ace simply smiled as he quickly noticed the contents of the legal notice. Ace read the date he had been waiting on for over two years now. Ace finally held in his hand the confirmed date he would pick a jury to start trial….

CHAPTER 34
"Trial 1" (Biggest drug case in Philadelphia)

It was December 16, 2007 and Ace was scheduled today to pick a jury for trial. Ace, Gotti, Jay and three of the girls were listed together in the first trial (out of 4 separate trials in the case) as co-defendants. The trial is expected to last at least eight weeks on the violent drug trafficking conspiracy.

They had a good defense team, but when it came to conspiracy charges, lawyers become foolish and desperate for self, their own clients. Lawyers seldom strategize together properly to actually show effort in trying to win a conspiracy case. Instead, they seem to go in looking to point the finger at the guy the government gunned at the most. Ace's lawyer hadn't warned him of this point before-hand, but Ace would soon see that it wasn't just the U.S. -vs- Alton 'Ace Capone' Coles...

About a week ago, Ace had talked to Nikky on the phone, to have her go get his suits for trial. Ace had lost over 70 pounds since he was first arrested back in August 10, 2005. He now weighed 198 pounds, with an athletic muscular physique. For two years Ace had been working out daily and now sported a six-pack to accommodate his new improved look. He even cut his beard off for trial purposes, which made him look 10 years younger and less intimidating.

Ace looked like a young savvy businessman today, in his new blue, with light blue, white pin striped, **Calvin Klein** suit. Nikky had extremely good taste in high fashion, which is why Ace chose her to dress him for court. She went and purchased several suits from Neiman Marcus, from designer names like **Armani, Gucci and Christian Dior**. She also picked out something simple like **True Religion** or **Red Monkey** jeans, with nice fitted Polo sweaters and white button up shirt underneath, matched with a pair of **Prada** shoes on his dress down days. Ace simply couldn't fit any of his many custom made suits from Distante's anymore.

The jury was picked out of a 258-jury poll, which consisted of people from all over the outskirts of Pennsylvania. Out of the 258 potential jurors, 85 percent of them were white, while the remaining 15 percent included a mixture of Black, Hispanic and Asian nationalities. When the judge asked the jurors how many of them had heard about the high profile case; and at first only two people raised their hands. Exactly 60 seconds later at least 250 hands reluctantly and simultaneously raised their hands as well, acknowledging the fact that they all followed the media attention prior to being pulled for jury duty. *„ What the fuck? They were gonna actually remain silent and book us with prejudice.'* Ace thought to himself in awe.

Truth be told, the potential jurors were scared to even sit in on the jury of the alleged violent drug trafficking gang's trial. So once the actual jury was picked they would remain anonymous, and picked up from an undisclosed location each day for trial. Although the U.S. Marshals would escort them each day, all the media attention caused the members of the jury to be both intimidated and scared.

One potential jury consistently raised his hand in an attempt to get off the jury selections every chance he could with every question asked. He used every excuse from - having to care for his elderly mother (who was on her death bed) to who's going to feed the dog, all in an attempt to keep out of that box.

At the end of the 5-day jury poll process 20 jurors were finally selected to sit as jurors. There were 12 jurors with 8 alternates assigned to sit in the box, with a non-paying job to decide guilty or not guilty on the 8 -week long continuing criminal enterprise drug conspiracy trial....

Once the trial started, the prosecution presented its case. There were three prosecutors alongside a slew of government experts and agents to represent for the government. The young, ambitious, hungry, aggressive prosecutor, Mike Brunshek, took the stage first in presenting a theatrical opening for the government. It was similar to a well written stage play with "A" list actors, as the scene was set for the trial of **Capone's Cocaine Gang (C.C.G)** to start.

"Good morning ladies and gentlemen of the jury. You will see during this trial that the man sitting right here before you, Alton Coles, is the leader and organizer of a violent cocaine trafficking drug distribution gang. You will hear testimony from witnesses who lived with him, sold drugs for him, and who laundered millions of dollars in cash for him. The government will provide evidence that Alton Coles distributed at least 1200 kilos of cocaine and 600 kilos of crack (conservatively valued at no less than $25,200,000) between January 1998 – August 10, 2005." The young prosecutor barked loudly as he calmed down a bit to further explain.

"Coles obtained kilogram quantities of cocaine from various sources, primarily in Texas and Mexico. He then had it transported to the Delaware valley region, where it was distributed in cocaine powder and crack form. The drugs were distributed through various co-conspirators to various customers of the **C.C.G** in Philadelphia, Baltimore, New Jersey and elsewhere."

"The C.C.G used various locations to store and manufacture cocaine, as well as to store firearms, money and other paraphernalia. The government has conducted a series of raids and collected over 1.7 million dollars in cash. When agents searched, perhaps the largest drug storage facility, at 333 Essex Ave, Lansdowne, PA, they found 18 firearms, a 12-ton hydraulic drug press (used to repress/repackage kilograms of cocaine), 64 used wrappers used to wrap kilogram quantities of cocaine, digital scales, and a wide variety of different cutting agents and drug packaging paraphernalia."

"Coles laundered enormous amounts of cash through all of his girlfriends and others through a variety of transactions, including his purchase of a half-million dollar home in New Jersey, using structured funds and a fraudulent loan transaction with his fiancé Iesha Richards. Coles also purchased and paid for various automobiles by using various nominees.

The government will introduce a wide variety of evidence at trial concerning a number of episodes of C.C.G drug activities. This evidence will consist of Police arrests from 1998-2005. ATF investigative activity during 2004-2005, including surveillance, search warrants, telephone analysis, consensual recording with co-conspirators, cooperating witness testimony, the testimony of non-conspirator civilian witnesses, wire interceptions, and the result of extensive financial investigation by the IRS.

You will also hear about the violent activities of shootings, and murders such as an incident where members of the C.C.G and another gang rival traded a volley of gunfire. The battle took place just a few feet from a schoolyard, and a block away from a church. Six people were shot, one was left for dead, and police recovered 97 fired cartridge casings fired from at least 12 firearms.

Ladies and gentlemen of the jury, after you are introduced to all of the evidence in this trial, you will find that all of these defendants are responsible for their parts in this conspiracy. And you must come back with an incredibly undoubtful verdict of **GUILTY** as charged." Brenswick replied, as he convincingly prepared to prove his hour-long opening speech into action before the jury....

Ace had a strong defense, but with all the media attention it seemed impossible for him to get a fair trial; yet alone, actually win. When CS-1 took a seat on the stand to testify against Ace, it absolutely crushed his very heart and soul. CS- 1 was no other than Kim Laphney.

Ace finally realized why Kim had been acting so funny since his arrest. She was fighting her own demons by drinking and trying to make herself actually hate the man she really loved. It was revealed that back in 2002 Kim had already in fact, began cooperating with the ATF. *„Rotten Bitch! She always said she was gonna kill me. I guess this was her way of putting a bullet in my head. This bitch thinks she gone just hand me over to the Feds – so she can run off with some of my money, Huh? Well she got another thing coming! She got me fucked up!'* Ace thought to himself as a million sinister,thoughts crossed his mind.

Once Kim sat up on the stand and painted him as a drug dealer, it caused all the other dominos to fall. Her credibility enhanced the credibility of all the other **rats** (cooperators who ate that cheese) and actually lied through their teeth to get a **5k1** (departure motion). Little did Kim know her testimony alone allowed the over exaggerated lies of other cooperators to have foundation.

Ace didn't even personally deal with most of the niggas who cooperated against him. They only knew of him through second and third hand street gossip, which usually is not allowed in court. But when you're co-defendants in federal court, there is an exception to the hearsay rule. The unfortunate fact of the law is that it allowed the cooperators to **overkill** on non-existing bullshit.

When CS-5 took the stand explaining the plane crash that left Tyrone Jackson dead, it caused a devastating effect after the Feds revealed their number one **star witness**, Dezman Fakon, also known as Dee, to testify. Outside of being a really good rat (best of snitches to exist) Dee was deemed reliable for many reasons. There were hospital records and all to corroborate his presence at the plane wreck. Dee didn't even show any remorse over his deceased girlfriend, Latisha's death. All Dee worried about was the **50 years to life** he plead guilty to in hopes of the **5k1/3553/ Rule 35** (package deal he had). His only care was eating all the cheese he could to get from under that mandatory lengthy plea.

The late Latisha Jackson was in fact, CS-2. Unfortunately, she never got the chance to testify at trial. Her dead corps was found still burning wrapped up in an old carpet, inside of a flame broiled abandoned vehicle in Fairmont Park a few months earlier.

Somehow the Feds had figured Ace and his crew had everything to do with the vicious murder, but didn't possess the evidence to charge them for it. By having Ace locked up in SHU as a high profile inmate, everything he did was monitored and recorded. However, the Feds couldn't determine when or even if Ace ordered the hit. Latisha had disappeared before Ace even got his legal material with her statement, so the government was left clueless.

The Feds always had tactics to compromise with their investigation. Most times they would permeate the trial with all kinds of accusations just to get a lot of prejudicial information before the jury. Those tactics, along with Ace's **bad boy, gangsta** persona, and his lavish unaccounted for million dollar flashy lifestyle, made it easy for the government to convince the jury to a guilty verdict. The celebrity friends and major hip-hop promotions defense couldn't even help him at trial. Even with all that credibility, Ace couldn't explain the money he had in the bank, or the cash he possessed during the raids. No young, black, ghetto, hood rich nigga could legally account for that amount of cash and real estate properties he had accumulated over the years. All that and some is what caused him a big fat guilty verdict...

Caution and Minute went to support him in trial. For the first time since they had been involved with Ace, they disregarded his demands for them not to show up at trial. They wanted to support their man too. They both made a mental note to kill Kim once they saw her take the stand against Ace. During the trial, Ace often wondered to himself if he regretted the judgment he made by not allowing them to kill Kim in the beginning.

He strangely still had love for his kids' mother even after she took the stand. You can't hate a person as much as Ace hated Kim, unless you actually love that very same person. The more his kids crossed his mind, the more he knew he couldn't see their mom murdered. Ace shrugged it off trying to erase the murderous thoughts, hoping a car would just maybe hit the bitch one day soon and die. He definitely knew that she would never be involved in his life ever again. Truth be told, Ace still had a lot of love for Kim. Their whole relationship he did his best trying to love, sympathize and understand her, but the pain of her ultimate betrayal was too much for him to swallow....

It was 12 days of deliberations before the jury handed over their decision. Iesha and Nikky were the reasons it took so long to agree on the verdict. Ace hands were too clean so in order to find him guilty, the jury had to find the girls guilty too. All Ace could hear was '*GUILTY, GUILTY, GUILTY, GUILTY, GUILTY, GUILTY, GUILTY, GUILTY*' echoing repeatedly in his ears over and over again.

What hurt him most was when he saw Babygirl get off the Marshals elevator with a shiny pair of silver handcuffs on. Nikky's bail was immediately revoked, so she was on her way to be processed over to the female unit in FDC. Ace couldn't even look at her; he was in too much pain as he noticed the tears slowly welling up in her precious innocent eyes.

Nikky had been in a state of total shock every since the verdict was read. Her family was devastated and fell out in the middle of the courtroom floor. Nikky's funny (white version of Steve Orkel) looking lawyer had the audacity to snap out at the jury behind the conviction, even after his poor performance as a lawyer. He actually thought he had her charges beat once Ace took the stand accepting her gun charges as his own.

Ace took the stand in his defense trying to protect Nikky and Iesha, after his lawyer advised him that the only way to defuse the case was to lie in attempt to explain the wiretap. Ace owned up to the gun by telling the jury to find him guilty of that specific charge, and that Nikky was innocent of any wrongdoing.

As much as he could no longer stand the very sight of Iesha behind her discreet abandonment, Ace still lied to the jury telling them that although she had a joint account with him that he did all the transactions - Basically telling them if anybody was guilty of money laundering it should be him, not her.

Ace thought about the support Nikky's family showed him because of her. With the exception of a few, his own family didn't even come through to support him in trial. One day his cousins Lynda, Karen and Aunt Sissy came through to show him some love during trial. His brother Mitchell, cousin Lynn and Aunt Sheila from off his father's side of the family also came through a couple of days as well.

Only two of his artist from his label **Takedown Records,** Bugsy and Philly Swain showed up to support him. Friends were a no show. Niggas from the streets didn't even show their presence in the courtroom to make it a little harder and embarrassing for the cooperator's to snitch on him. Dee, Charlton Fuckus, also known as GunHo, Anwaar, Zoon and a slew of others ate that cheese, lying, getting off with ease and enjoyment in hopes of extremely lighter sentences.

As Ace sat in his cell, his vision seemed blurry. He thought about all the false accusations the media had made about him during the 8 week long trial. They really struck a nerve, assassinating his character, when they falsely accused him with having part in the death of **Joe Smith**. The extremely prejudicial newspaper article read:

Terree 'Tab' Walker was a known associate to Alton "Ace" Coles and awaiting trial in connection to a double homicide outside the Philadelphia Zoo. Investigators believe Joe 'Stink' Smith's death was a result of a botched attempt by Coles to hold him for ransom. The trunking theory gained support as the homicide investigation unfolded, Walker is a suspected enforcer for the organization which authorities said was becoming more violent as it expanded it's operation beyond Southwest Philly.

The case became even stronger when Tab's DNA matched a trail of blood leading from the vehicle that contained Stink's body in the backseat. Joe 'Stink' Smith was tied up, shot 20 times, and left in the back of his SUV. Before he died, he identified the shooter as Teree Walker, who was a known associate of Coles'. ATF and police files depict Ace Capone as calling the shots for an organization that abducted and ambushed rivals, killed competitors, and moved large quantities of cocaine and crack.

Ace balled his face up full of hidden rage and anger, as all the pain of events he had been through during the course of this indictment heavily crashed in on him. The indictment itself literally sabotaged his whole life. Now his kids would definitely suffer behind it. His financial legal abilities were disturbingly affected. Now his kids would surely be affected because Ace faced a potential **20 years to life sentence on the 848-kingpin statue** alone.

All the love Ace had for the streets just turned into hate, as he thought to himself. *'What the fuck did I do to me?'...*

Ace came to realize that it wasn't anyone else's fault except his for all that had occurred. Amazingly, he didn't even blame the rats anymore. He felt like he was the one who allowed them to be a part of his empire, so he blamed himself for the bad decisions. Ace had gotten careless and comfortable, which caused him to fall victim to the street life.

Ace decided to call on the one who handled his affairs - the only one capable of completely fixing everything at this point. The one he should have depended on in the beginning, but he had too much faith in his money and lawyers. All the pain, agony and frustration he encountered throughout his hardship, caused Ace to call on the best of all planners. Ace called on Allah (God). He finally submitted himself mentally to put his trust and faith in God. As he prostrated during his last rakat he made a dua (personal supplication) to the Almighty God:

'Oh Allah. I seek your forgiveness and your mercy. I recognize my faults, and my poor choices. I realize that I bought forth my own destruction with my own hands, and I beg for your mercy. I humbly submit to you. I've recently learned that you always answer the prayer of the one who is in distress. I'm in so much distress right now it hurts. I come to you full of humility, in extreme pain, and I ask for your relief. Take away my pain and protect me.' Ameen!

     *   *

     *

Ace had a cold dark glare in his eyes while staring out the window of his cell. He could see people walking freely in downtown Center City as he thought to himself: *„I will be back out there. Shit, I been winning all my life! All the fuck I know how to do is win! Ya Dig? Yall know, yall heard of us!'*

TO BE CONTINUED...

GO HARDER

CAPONE'S COCAINE GANG
THE SEQUEL

Still loaded with more suspense and drama, Go Harder (Go Hard pt. 2) continues the must read novel. It's another page-turner that will fill in the desperately wanted to see blanks – tying up very loose ends to some of your favorite characters. Enjoy this brief sneak preview into part two as Ace Capone takes you on another journey – to one of the illest, realest street stories ever brought to life on paper. This book has not been rated yet…Ace again proving a famous quote – the hottest street deejay in the game '**DJ Kahlid**' says: *"All I do is win-win-win-win-win, No matter what!" "It's a movie babyyy!"*

CHAPTER 1
'Revenge or Acceptance'

July 9, 2008 Ace was scheduled to be sentenced. When he got to court his sentencing was cancelled, and his lawyer informed him of a new problem. After Ace was found guilty at trial, the feds didn't stop there. The government was still interestingly prying for information as to Alton 'Ace Capone' Coles.

The **ATF,FBI, and IRS** had somehow found out about a safe deposit box Ace had under an alias. Ace had a few other safe deposit boxes, but only four people actually knew about that specific box. The new potential indictment could possibly lead to a tax evasion or money laundering count.

Ace didn't care about the charges; he was upset about taking yet another loss. The feds executed a search warrant for the safe deposit box, and found over 700,000 dollars in cash. There were also blue prints and deeds to other real estate properties they knew nothing about prior to the breach in the box as well.

The government wasn't surprised that even after three years of incarceration and a guilty verdict, Ace still had access to large amounts of money. They were sure that he had more somewhere else as they planned to launch an investigation in hopes to retrieve it all….

*   *   *

Rain was at FDC to visit her kid's father. Ace walked out on the dance floor (visiting room) looking angrier than usual. Since trial was over, he had grown his beard back, which made him look even more intimidating when he was mad about something.

"Damn Rain! Why you let them greedy fuckers find that fucking money?" Ace said, with frustration.

"Al, I kept calling your Aunt and she wouldn't go get it. I don't know why you made it where as only you and your aunt could go in that box? She scary as hell, I even told her that I would go there and act like I was her to get it myself. She just kept bullshitting."

Truth be told, Ace's Aunt Luba didn't want none of his women to get any of his money. Luba thought it was a bad idea. She figured the girls would most likely get themselves robbed or killed, by becoming spendthrifts after her nephew's conviction, drawing all kinds of unwanted attention and putting themselves directly in harm's way.

After seeing all that media coverage people gossipped even more from knowing what the feds already had taken from Ace. The feds had seized over 6 million dollars in property, 1 million dollars in cars, and over 1.7 million dollars in cash. That's not even including the disclosed amount of funds that were still frozen in his bank account, or the new wealth they acquired from the breach of the safe deposit box.

"Luba is a certified asshole for letting them get that fucking money. They got them deeds to that property too. Those buildings alone are worth a lot of money, and I had plans to sale that property. Luba fucked me over big time. I got a muthafuckin headache!" Ace said, full of frustration and resentment, as he leaned back grabbing his face with both hands putting his head in his lap.

"So what now Al?" Rain replied sorrowfully, as tears began to slowly form in her eyes. Rain never called him Ace. She always called him 'Al', which is short for Alton. She didn't like to see him frustrated; it was way out of his character. Ace always handled things smoothly, always having a laid back, calm demeanor at all times. Today was different. The pain and anxiety he had been under lately took effect, allowing his frustration and rage to show outwardly.

Ace couldn't even answer her question: „**What to do next?'** He had already told her to get that money from the box with instructions to do a few different things with it. **First:** She was supposed to take 150,000 dollars to go pay for Nikky and Iesha's appeal lawyers. **Second:** She was supposed to split the remainder of the money between herself, Keisha and Nikky.

"Do you still want me and the kids to move wherever they send you once you get sentenced?" Rain asked in a low concerned tone, finally breaking their silence.

"Fuck!" Ace quickly spat out of disgust, before he went on to explain: "I don't even know yet. I just need a little time to think shit over right now. I do know this – I CANNOT AFFORD ANY MORE LOSSES! REAL TALK!" he said loud and stern so that he was clear.

Ace sat there in a cold, dark trance as he was in deep thought. *'Okay! Think Ace. They only found one box. It's between four people who crossed me by giving up that information. That means I got two more boxes tucked away safely. Those banks are not too far, but then again the feds never find what's right under their noses. Not without help! Only Unc and me knew about those two, but we both locked the fuck up. Damn! I should have trusted Rain or Keisha a lot more with access to my money. I need Hak to get out of jail a.s.a.p.'*

Rain just sat there looking at Ace concerningly, sensing that his frustration was building back up.

"Calm down Al. Just relax so you can concentrate better. You always come out on top. I got to give you credit for that. When it's all said and done, I know you gone make out. My son is taking this extremely hard, but he will be alright. All your kids love you more than anything, so just focus on getting back to them. We all need you." Rain said, convincingly as she forced a smile on her face, desperately trying to encourage him.

"Yeah, I do always seem to have made it out on top in the past, huh? I mean I already knew I'd come to the feds one day, that's why I always prepared you for this, ya dig? I always thought I'd only face 10 to15 years tops. And with the type of lawyers I'd hire, I figured I'd end up with at worst 5 to 8 years one day. My overall mentality figured it would have been worth it because I'd still be young and rich. I honestly never expected to face a fucking life sentence for shit. Real Talk! Shit, all the time these cocksuckas trying to give me I should have just robbed banks or Brinks trucks with intent to kill anybody who got in the way. My fucking P.S.I came back recommending that I get life plus 155 years. Now how the fuck I'm a do that? What? I supposed to die in jail, and then come back to life to do another 155 years?" Ace retorted.

"Now that they postponed it, when do you get sentenced? I don't even see how you lost trial, because they didn't prove their cases at all. Does it look good for you to win on appeal?" Rain asked nervously.

After hearing the **P.S.I** recommendation, she was scared. Nobody actually thought Ace would get life. Everybody knew the feds gave out **football numbers** (double digits). Dudes didn't try their hand by taking them to trial knowing they were facing **letters** (Life). Niggas usually either **plead out**(copped a bad deal) or **snitched**(told/copped a good deal), , in which both deals give the feds a **98 percent conviction rate**.

"I don't know when they gonna sentence me now. The trial got split into four separate trials because it was too many of us. I'm thinking after all the trials are over with, then they will sentence me. My lawyers say my appeal looks good, but it's gonna take anywhere from twelve to twenty-four months after I'm sentenced to get back in court on appeal." Ace replied.

After the visits were over, Ace went back to his unit to get on the telephone. After the disturbing call, Ace headed to his cell in pain with a lot of regrets. Everything was weighing down on him extremely heavy. Babygirls' conviction and the fact that she was in custody now was the straw that broke the camel's back.

Ace called Nikky's sister, Manda, and she explained how hard Babygirl was adjusting to her incarceration. Nikky had been in the SHU on the female side of eight South in F.D.C. She was immediately administered to the SHU the day she lost trial. Nikky had even made suicidal threats behind the thought of doing a 10 to 15 year prison term. It was simply too much for any woman to digest. Nikky had never been to jail in her entire life. So, being placed on 23 hours a day lock down in the hole made it even worst. Nikky had to be placed on medicine because she was going insane. The only reason she'd been placed in the S.H.U was because she's Ace's girlfriend.

Ace made the news on a daily basis because he was being labeled the biggest drug Kingpin that came out of Philly since **Aaron Jones** and the **J.B.M era**. Truth be told, Ace had done it even bigger than Aaron had a chance to. Ace established a lot of legal wealth from his businesses and in this date and time success was far greater.

Once in his cell, Ace thought about the call that sent him to his cell upset and frustrated.

"Ace is my sister really going to have to do all that time?" Manda cried out with tears, in extreme pain. Ace felt her pain through the phone. So it caused him to cry as well.

"I do have one last trick up my sleeve. I don't want to do it, but I gotta use my Ace card on this one. I am Ace Capone remember!" Ace said rhetorically, while tears slowly fell from his eyes.

Niggas had officially changed all the love Ace had in the streets into pure hatred. All niggas did was gossip like a bunch of kitchen bitches. Some people hated on Ace so bad it was simply pathetic. In reality, they actually wanted to see him lose. The same streets Ace repped so hard his entire life, backbit and slandered him in every way imaginable.

Niggas had thought and said everything bad about him before they would even attempt to think or say one good thing about him.

When Ace first got knocked, they thought he would snitch simply because the Feds got him. When Ace went to trial, they called him crazy, and thought he was stupid, thinking he could never win against the Federal government. They based their assumptions on the Feds history of convicting everyone they wanted to take down. Niggas anticipated that Ace would get his face blown clean off at trial, but even if Ace had pleaded out, niggas would have still hated on him.

They would have probably said, **"If he was really Gansta he would have went to trial!"** It don't matter what you do just like 2-Pac said, "NIGGAs GON' HATE YOU FOR WHATEVER YOU DO!"

A certain crew of hating rat ass niggaz on five North in F.D.C had the audacity to clap when they saw the verdict on the news that Ace had lost!

Ace finally figured out now: **You damned if you do and damned if you don't! The streets don't love ya; they just want to kill ya!**

Ace now hated the streets and all the snakes that walked through them. Nikky's conviction caused Ace to have a lot of regrets. Truth be told, Ace could stand it a lot better if he would have lost and she would have chosen differently prior to trial. Ace thought back to the visit he had with Rain.

Prior to trial, Ace had told Rain on a visit to call Babygirl and tell her, "If the Feds are willing to offer her a deal for no jail time, then tell her to go ahead and cooperate against me."

"I'll do that soon as I leave here baby." Rain told him.

When Rain delivered Ace's message to Nikky, Nikky ignored Ace's message and went to trial. Nikky had no interest in helping the government take Ace down. She wouldn't play any part in seeing the Feds give Ace 20 to Life in federal prison. Not to mention that fact that Nikky's lawyer told her that the Feds wouldn't even agree to those terms. They wanted her to do some kind of time no matter what, because they knew they had Ace by the balls.

They wouldn't promise Nikky what kind of time she'd actually have to do so Nikky would be a casualty of war. The case was never about her; it was about her boyfriend, Ace Capone.

Rain loved Ace too, so she made sure to deliver the message half ass. She didn't want anyone to ruin the chances of her kid's father regaining his freedom. Rain had caught a state case with Ace back in 1996. She stood tall without telling. She figured the other girls should do the same. Even though her criminal experiences were not federal, Rain was pregnant with Ace's son, Na'ail at the time. Rain only got arrested because she wouldn't allow the cops to lock Ace up for a simple drug possession charge, so they locked her ass up and charged her for the same drugs too.

Ace was full of regrets. He wished that he had made Babygirl take the cooperation deal to testify against him for less time. Ace realized that the pain he experienced now behind her conviction is too painful altogether...

The news Manda had given Ace on the telephone about Nikky caused him to go and pray. He needed to seek some comfort from a higher power. Ace wanted to talk with no one other than Allah.

In the name of Allah, the Most Gracious, The Most Merciful...Oh Allah, I ask you to comfort Nikky and take away our pain...Please open a door for me...Please create a situation that will allow me to get my freedom back...Whatever door you do open I will walk through it fully focused, Ameen!

CHAPTER 2
"'Sentencing" (Flashbacks of Betrayal)

On April 24, 2009 Special agent Mike Nikko had noticed two familiar faces outside the federal courthouse on 6th and Arch. The young kid had grown up quite a bit over the last four years, but he still looked just like his father. His mother accompanied the familiar looking teenage boy as they walked into the courthouse. Sensing that the woman seemed to be lost in need of direction, Agent Nikko walked over to assist her and her son.

"Can I help you?" Agent Nikko asked politely.

"Yes, Hi, I'm looking for Judge Carter's courtroom for Alton Coles' sentencing."

"Courtroom 808 is Judge Carter's. It's right over there. Sentencing doesn't start until 10:30 a.m., so you have quite some time. It's only 7:30 a.m. right now." Agent Nikko replied matter factly after looking at his watch.

Keisha had come early because she wasn't sure the exact time of Ace's sentencing hearing.

Agent Nikko and a team of other agents were there with gun sniffing dogs to make sure the entire perimeter was secure. The government had gotten recent information that a team of street thugs could possible attempt to break Ace out of court.

Whether it was the look of concern on Keisha's face, or the innocent look in Lil Alton's eyes, Agent Nikko suddenly no longer believed that the last minute breakout information had any truth to it. He somehow felt compelled to have a conversation with both Keisha and Lil Alton.

"Listen Keisha, I know who you are. My name is Special Agent Mike Nikko. I'm the head agent on Ace's case. I would like to try and explain some things to his son if you don't mind?"

"There's nothing to explain. You guys know what you've done to him. I'm sorry, but y'all just don't play fair at all. His trial was rigged up by the media, and yall have the audacity to go after a life sentence." Keisha replied angrily in disbelief.

"Well, all I can say is that the law is the law. Everyone has to abide by the law." Agent Nikko replied.

"I hear all that, but this is his first incarceration. What ever happened to giving people a second chance? Why are yall pushing so hard to give him a life sentence?" Keisha replied sincerely, as her demeanor and Lil Alton's quietness caused Agent Nikkos' heart to soften up a bit. He continued conversing with her about Ace for several more minutes...

Truth be told, Agent Nikko didn't' seem to actually hate Ace. He just did his job as a federal agent by investigating him. He felt like the potential life sentence was extreme himself, but he was sworn to uphold law enforcement so he stood by his fellow teammates...

Ace sat in the holding cell awaiting to hear his fate, when he saw the marshal's walk Gun-ho and Moe past his cell. Even after trial, the two government cooperators were simply not finished. There was no reasonable conclusion as to why either of them would be at court today, other than to testify about prior violent acts Ace did, to ensure he could get an **elbow** (life sentence).

After seeing both of them, Ace became furious as he began to have flashbacks of all the betrayal he encountered. He thought about the abandonment he received from Iesha and Kim, which often hurts his hearts when he thinks about it. Ace always expected niggas to shit on him, which angered him but it didn't hurt him. It only hurts badly when someone you truly love shits on you.

Ace was really trying hard to build his faith. He knew that if Allah can forgive him, then who was he for not forgiving anybody else for what they had done. Although this made sense to him, he was still human. Ace still had his shortcomings, so he constantly battled back and forth with his own demons. His anger and frustration boiled over to the thoughts of all the snitches and fake friends who fucked him over during his bid. All Ace could think about was some serious get back on all of those who crossed him during his hardship. He even thought about those who actually caused the hardship, including the government.

Ace contemplated revenge on everyone who played a part in his downfall. *" Muthafuckas got me counted out, huh? Never count me out! I will be back. When it's all said and done. I want all yall to remember my cocky ass smile. Bitches ain't shit, but hoes and tricks, and niggas don't love ya they just wanna kill ya! They hate me because they ain't me! Fuck em! You rotten muthfuckas! It's all business now. Real Talk!'* Ace thought to himself as he stared blankly with an evil look in his eyes.

"Coles!" The middle aged black marshal yelled loudly for the fourth time, finally snapping Ace out of his cynical day dream state. "You alright Coles?" He asked sounding slightly concerned.

"For sure. I'm good." Ace replied, unconvincingly.

"Alright then. Lets cuff you up big guy. It's your turn, they're ready for you."

"Then let's get to it." Ace replied nonchalantly, as he turned around to allow the marshal to cuff him…

As Ace walked into the empty courtroom, he immediately noticed his son, and forced a smile on his face so that Keisha and his boy wouldn't worry too much. Keisha could not force herself to smile back; she was very concerned for him. Even Lil Alton felt extremely uncomfortable, but the younger version of Ace held his composure strong for his Mom and Dad.

The clerk came out of the Judge's chambers and told both the Prosecution and Defense that Judge Carter was ready to start the hearing. In less than a half a minute the whole courtroom was bombarded with spectators, and a slew of news and media reporters. It seemed as though all of them must have been in the hallway, waiting for the highly anticipated hearing to start. The courtroom looked as if the government professionally organized it.

The newspaper writers and television reporters took up the first three rows. Rain and Ace's two kids, **Na'ail and Nyrah** had finally walked in, along with his two stepdaughters, **Sharaina & Toya** to support him. The courtroom was fully packed wall-to-wall with more media spectators than anyone else.

"All rise, the Honorable Judge Carter presides." The judge's clerk said, loudly, as everyone except Ace, stood acknowledging the Judge as if he was a king or God himself.

Once the judge began to speak Ace's mind went blank. At that moment all he could do was look at the faces of his three beautiful, young, innocent children. All three of them stared in a state of confusion, wondering what was going to happen to their Dad next. Ace has been locked up for over four years now, and the kids just wanted their Dad to come home.

Ace knew in his heart that sentencing was going to be bad for him today. A knot formed in his throat after he had seen the look in the Judge's eyes. When the judge fixed his mouth to say *'Life plus 55 years'* Ace didn't' even hear him. Ace's hearing went numb as he simply read the Judge's lips. He knew he was about to receive a big fat life sentence.

The plus whatever didn't even matter to Ace because he figured they did it for TV. The look on his kid's faces caused him to get teary eyed in public. His anger started boiling over as he made a promise to himself. Ace vowed to get his life back **by any means necessary!** It was all business to him now. He made good business on the streets so he planned to continue with his trade, which was always doing good business.

Ace had blocked out the actual court procedure. His body was there, but his mind was elsewhere as he thought to himself. *'I'm the King and niggas are pawns. My knights, rooks, bishops, and even the strongest piece; My Queen, is gone and have to be willing to play their positions to the fullest in this game. It's all about loyalty and sacrifices. Kings are to be protected with your life! Point Blank!'...*

Maria sat home crying as she watched the 12:00 p.m. Channel 6 news, covering a ten minute breaking news segment on the rap mogul, drug kingpin sentencing results of Alton 'Ace Capone' Coles. Maria wanted to come to the trial to be supportive to Ace, but her uncle Roberto, told her it was too risky for her to attend. Roberto knew Ace was a very intelligent and crafty man, and advised Maria that when the smoke clears, Ace would be fine. He didn't' believe for one second that Ace would lay down to that type of time or allow the government to win. Roberto knew from doing good business with Ace that one day soon he would get out...

     *   *   *

Three days later, Ace was in his cell on five south when mail call was called. He went to retrieve his mail and quickly noticed more supportive cards from different people from all over just showing love. Alot of people followed the case and didn't agree with the life plus 55 years sentence he received for drugs. One particular card caught his attention before he read it. Ace looked at the return address from a Tea from Detroit, Michigan. For some strange reason this one piece of mail stood out to him. He didn't understand why, but he felt some kind of spiritual connection as he read the card:

*Alton… I am a firm believer that **"everything happens for a reason."** I read your story, and I am a thousand miles away from you. My heart aches every time I hear of someone being sentenced under the harsh drug laws. My brother was also a victim. At the tender age of 21, he was incarcerated and sentenced to life…he is 39 now.*

*But the most important thing is…. **He hasn't given up hope**. And if you don't get anything out of my letter – please understand this…I pray that you don't give up either. Right now, I know that it seems like a storm that will never pass over…but it will. Continue to have **Faith** and Pray. Whatever your religion may be –it all boils down to faith and prayer. I pray that you have a support system,. And I pray that whomever it consists of, they **ride** with you, until you become **free**.*

*No man deserves to be sentenced to Life behind bars for **"conspiracy"** or any other affiliation with drugs – Period – It's not "us" that is bringing it over here, but "they" don't want you to do or be better than ,,them" –so they have figured out a way to lock "us" all up.'*

Hold you head!
Tea

The letter was inside of a nice, small thinking of you card that had two bears on it, which read Thinking of you with all my love. Ace had been getting a lot of fan mail since the case began, especially when it started making mainstream media (CNN). Usually he would just read the letters and pray to Allah that they be rewarded for their kind thoughts and support at such a troublesome time for him. But something was different about this particular card and letter. Ace felt the need to respond to this mysteriously interesting **'Tea'** person. Due to all the hardship, Ace fully confided in Allah (God) now. Ace focused in on all his signs, warnings, and something spiritually occurred, which made him, sit down that night to write the mysterious 'Tea' from Detroit back.

As -Salaam-Alaikum (May Peace and Blessings be unto you)
Tea,
*How are you? I wanted to write you back and thank you for the card and words of encouragement. Also I can see your bother has a good supporter cause his sister (**Tea**) seems to be a sweetheart (smile). I will keep you and your bother in my dua's (special prayers). My religion is **Islam** and my faith is strong. I trust in **Allah** (God) and I believe in my heart that he will allow me to have my life back. **Insha-Allah** (God willing)…*

The next two years gonna say a lot for me. If I get this new trial or at least re-sentenced to some doable time, when I get out I plan on doing things a lot differently now. I have been down for over four years now, and I've really realized and learned a lot. May Allah (God) reward you for your good deed (writing me a letter of encouragement), you take care of yourself. I don't know who you are, but I like your style! Real talk!

Holla Back,
Ace

Capone
P.S. – By the way everyone calls me 'Ace' or 'Pone'. Some of my closest friends call me Na'ail. You can call me what you choose to (smile)…But nobody calls me Alton. My own mother calls me Ace. LOL. (Smile). I'm in the process of making some serious noise, so listen out for me sometime in the near future. I always seem to be heard (smile) Al-humdi-illah (All praise to God). Please keep me in your prayers as you will continue to be in mine, and feel free to stay in touch! (Thanks for the card/letter).
As-Salaam-Alaikum

GO HARD PR. 2 TO BE CONTINUED...

Since ya telling on me...tell the world about me...Ask ya girl about me...She'll probably tell ya how I put it down – put it down. You know how I put it down. Put it down....
Every time
I come around!
(Drake/Bun B)

No one ma should have all that power...The clock tickin I just count the hour...'''
At the end of the day got damn it I'm killin dis shit...
I know damn well yall feeling dis shit...
I don't need ya pussy bitch – on my own dick!
(Kanye West)
What's it like on appeal for a dope-boy
(Ricky Ross da Boss)

"Ace's Sincere advice to the streets"

If you one of them young niggas dropping 4 ½ ounces (of coke) in a pyrex pot of boiling water, filled with 63 grams of baking soda to cook-up crack. Next: dropping ice in the boiling water to cool it off quickly, while spinning the gooey cocaine (in its purest form) so that it locks onto the butter knife/ taking out of the pyrex pot. Then stretching (adding B-12/cut) or whipped raw until it's hard.

You need to now to go learn about the federal status on these charges, **846** conspiracy (faces 10-Life); **924c** (using or carrying a firearm during a drug trafficking crime) is 5 years **additional** (ran consecutive) and if you have **more than 1 (924c) it's 25 years** more for each/every one after the first one; **851** (if you have prior arrest history they can enhance your time – which automatically doubles your mandatory minimum **(example: 10 - Life = 20 – Life). (2 priors = mandatory life)**

Learn the real consequences to the game if you in it, cause at the end of the day – them numbers don't add up (it ain't worth it)…Insha-Allah you will see it this way – how you gonna win in a game where everybody is against you? **1. Cops/Feds…2. Rats** (snitches)…3. Stick up boys …4. Scandalous Bitches…5. Hating ass gossipping niggas…

Take it from me: it's like shooting craps (a game of chance) and you bound to lose…I humbly encourage you to **Quit** while you're ahead! **Real Talk/Point Blank/Flat Out!**

Reality Check
(a gansta speaks)

I want to take the time out to give yall a reality check on a few issues that burn me up when I overhear it.

1. I'm sick of hearing people (specifically men) argue/debate over which celebrity has more $$$ than the other. They both way richer than you, so "put the gun down and step away from the car please!" You make no sense arguing about the next man's $$$ - especially when you barely have any money yourself. Point Blank! SMH

2. I hate to hear a nigga talk bad about a random actress (movie, video, reality show etc.) Saying she ugly, she alright – all she got is a body, etc or simply comparing her to the next chic. That's the same nigga who probably don't even have a chic of his own, don't go on visits – or if he does go on a visit he got a gorilla visiting him. **Gorilla:** meaning a female that's out of shape, tore up, hair never done (or wears a cheap wig/glued in tracks), she's unattractive to most men. True some woman may look better than others (which depends on ones preferences), but the reality of it is simple – **all women are beautiful**. Point Blank!

3. When dudes foolishly shout the saying "M.O.B" (Money over bitches) with intent to put $$$ before any woman. Reality check playa – a smart man hopes to have a faithful, honest women as a wifey, plus the truth is clear – a woman is Allah's (God's) best gift to man. (Way better than $$$, jewelry, cars, etc.) Real talk!

Hate Detector

If you always point out something negative every time someone tells you their good news – then you's hater!
Example 1: "My lawyer thinks I should get some rhythm on my appeal…" **A hater's response:** Don't too many people win on appeal – the feds designed this system for everybody to lose. I seen (such and such) get back on appeal, and when he got back in court the judge gave him more time than he had the first time around."

Vicious Hater:
Example: "Did you hear about the next 18-1 ratio) under the crack law? A vicious hater's response: "I don't care about stuff that doesn't pertain to me – I got locked up for a gun. That's crazy! They didn't come with any new laws for me. I did 15 years for a gun and had to do all my time." You's a **vicious hater!** SMH

Example 2: When a dude knows dirt on another dude (who has a nice looking woman), and the vicious hater uses that dirt as ammo to go holla at (the other dude's female) as soon as his man gets locked up/killed…or when the female is vulnerable (just broke up with her man) simply because the hater has no swag/game – to get pussy respectfully on his own accord. **You's a nut/creep/vicious hater!** SMH
(To read/share a slew other hate detections on various issues go to **http://newmediasourze.info/AceCapone/acecapone.html** and/or go to my facebook fan page: *GO HARD A.T. Capone*

Barbershop Debates
(a gansta speaks)

I don't do this, but for the sake of debate – I'm going to take time out to reveal some of my opinions on these classic barbershop topics. Here's my top 10 list on certain debatable issues (note: my list is not in exact order) of course a lot of folks gonna agree/disagree with **my** list. Keep in mind that it's "**my list**" – which is coming from a true hood nigga/hustler/gangsta's perspective, but feel free to go to this website: **http://newmediasourze.info/AceCapone/acecapone.html** to share your list/comments and/or go to my facebook fan page *GO HARD – A.T. Capone* to share your lists/comments as well.

Top 10 Hardest/Hottest rappers: (2005-2011)
(1) Jay-Z   (2) Lil Wayne   (3) Rick Ross   (4) Kanye West   (5) Young Jeezy (6) Jadakiss   (7) Drake   (8) 50 Cent   (9) Beanie Sigel   (10) Meek Mills

Top 10 Hardest/Hottest Hood Novels
(1) True to the Game (2) Dutch   (3) Block Party (4) BMore Careful (5) Imagine This   (6) Let that be the Reason (7) Coldest Winter Ever (8) Deadly Reigns (9) Larceny (10) Go Hard The Takedown of Ace Capone

Top 6 Sexiest female rappers:
(1) Nikki Minaj   (2) Diamond (3) Trina   (4) Foxy Brown (5) Eve (6) Lil Kim

Hardest/Hottest rap crews: (2002 – 2011)
(1) Rocafella/State Property (2) Dip Set   (3) G-Unit (4) Cash Money/Young Money (5) Maybach Muzic

Best Rapper Alive/Ever:
JayZ (this is undisputed….to pay homage) "Head shotz….nigga fuck ya vest"

Top 5 Philly's Most Known Hustlers:
(1) Aaron Jones (2) Daryl Shuler (3) Ace Capone (4)
Giovanni   (5) DumpTruck

Top 5 Hardest/Street DJs: (2005 – 2011):
(1) DJ Khalid   (2) Green Lantern (3) Drama (4) Kay Slay
(5) Funk Flex

Under-estimated artist who GO Hard (grind/hustle) I
recognize/respect most:
(1) Jim Jones (2) Fabulous (3) 2 Chainz (4) Maino
 (5) Future (6) SouljaBoy (7) Waka Flocka (8) Wale (9)
Tone Trump (10) Yo Gotti

Key to Life Publishing
P. O. Box 266
Warren, Michigan 48090

INMATE ORDER FORM   DATE: ___/___/___

Inmate Name: _____
ID#_____
Facility Name: _____
Housing# _____
Facility Address: _____ City: _____ State: _____ Zip: _____

****
PURCHASER'SINFORMATION*****************
Purchaser's Info: (if different from inmate)
_____
Address: _____
City: _____ State: _____ Zip: _____
Telephone # _____ (NO PERSONAL CHECKS
ACCEPTED)

Please make money order payable to **Key to Life Publishing**

Payment Method: ☐Facility check ☐ Money Order/Cashier's Check

FAMILY MEMBERS CAN ORDER ONLINE VIA PAYPAL USING E-MAIL: KNOWLEDGEISTHEKEY@ROCKETMAIL.COM

ITEMS ORDERED
1. GO HARD – The Takedown of Ace Capone Qty: __1__ Price: $17.99
2._____   ____ _____
3._____   ____ _____

Subtotal $_____ Add: Standard Shipping **$5.50** = **Total $**

THE TAKEDOWN OF ACE CAPONE

A must read novel! You ain't read nothing until you read this action-packed filled with suspense novel.

Inspired by a true story: This is a dramatic/exceptional story of love, sex, passion, murder, betrayal, drugs and politics…..

This novel will take you on a bizarre twist as Ace Capone, leader of a $25 million dollar violent drug trafficking organization is subject to a federal investigation. This classic novel is a very suspenseful page turner that will constantly keep you on the edge of your seat, anxiously wondering what's going to happen next. You will see the game for what it's worth from all angles, and feel this unique story from different character's point of views.

Discover the life of what it's like as the boss's wife, and the consequences of simply choosing to be the girlfriend on the side. Witness how the investigation starts…from the government agents, prosecutors, and the snitches that all conspire to takedown Ace Capone and his entire organization.

The street game is like a big game of chess, your next move is your best move! Learn the game by reading this sure to be one of the realest best sellers thus far. Strategize or experience the consequences of the streets in full view if you're in the game, and were fortunate enough to escape self-destruction thus far.

Life in prison?...Death before dishonor?...Who will die?...Who will live?...Who really wins?...Who really loses?...Who will 'GO HARD.?

Order Form

Name:_____

Address:_____

City, State, Zip_____

GO HARD - The Takedown of Ace Capone----------------------------------$17.99

QTY---

Total--

Shipping and Handling $5.50 first book $1.00 each additional book.

Make check or money order payable to:

KEY TO LIFE PUBLISHING, P.O BOX 266, WARREN, MICHIGAN 48090

@1ACECAPONE   GO HARD A.T. CAPONE   Purchase at **amazon**.com

Acecaponegohard@hotmail.com   Keytolifepub@hotmail.com